no SHELTER for GUILT

no SHELTER for GUILT

A NOVEL BY
Carl E. Linke

₣

Philip-Forrest Publishing

℗ Philip-Forrest Publishing

This book is a work of fiction. Names, characters, businesses, organizations, places, events and incidents either are products of the author's imagination or are used fictitiously. Any resemblance to actual persons—living or dead—and events is entirely coincidental.

Copyright © 2020 by Carl E. Linke
All rights reserved.
Published in the United States by Philip-Forrest Publishing
Visit at: www.carllinke.com

Cover Design by Carl E. Linke
Interior Art by Sedki Alimam
Author Photograph by Tina Lee

ISBN-13: 978-0-9827421-1-2
Library of Congress Control Number: 2020916821

PRINTED IN THE UNITED STATES OF AMERICA
First Edition: (October 2020)
1 2 3 4 20 19 18 17

This book is dedicated to those in need of a hand up

and to those who offer the same.

Your stay here will be like "rests" in music—where no notes are played but the silence is necessary for the composition. A time to appreciate the unspoken and less obvious qualities of life.

—Nat Burkhardt

Chapter 1

I had killed a guy. It was eating me. There's always death on the streets. Holes that have to be filled. This one was deeper than most.

People never bother to talk to panhandlers like me. For most, I'm invisible or, at best, repulsive street art. For the few who bother to look, I'm a homeless man, though I prefer houseless or property-challenged. Regardless, I am a roamer or free ranger ... on a spiral staircase to hell.

My old man was a preacher. He preached Bible, booze, and beatings. Not hard to guess in which order. I chose his two favorites.

This life of mine started when I killed my best friend. A guy named Ben Keller. He begged me—well, nearly begged—not to do it. I had to. I didn't listen. (Nobody ever listens to a panhandler, either.) Now I needed to find his wife.

I'd sidestepped the law, bondsmen, and bounty hunters for over three years. I was always looking over my shoulder because of the voices. Yeah, the voices. In my head. They were always there. I call them the Vigilantes, capital V and plural. Nastier than tracking dogs, they stayed on my tail, toying with me, playing with my mind. I mean now ... right now, this very minute ... they're telling me not to talk about this. They say some strangers I shouldn't trust.

My name? Call me Chili. More habanero than the slushie. Sure, out here, I have other names, several really, but Chili works best. Target on my back. Voices in my head. Judge and jury, I have none. I met loneliness out here. For me, it wasn't an "eye for an eye" existence. It was all about motion, where "every action has an equal and opposite reaction." I took a life, so I had to give life back ... to the less fortunate. Loneliness dictated my penance which was to write letters for the other lonely souls, letters to return them home while I just kept on moving on.

At the ticket window in Jacksonville the pudgy agent with the Oliver Hardy moustache said the next bus out of town was headed to Myrtle Beach. I was on it.

Chapter 2

I arrived in Myrtle Beach one afternoon in late October, 1987. well after the lunchtime crowds had straggled back to their workaday worlds for the post-munch drowsiness. I drifted inside the bus terminal in my usual fashion, reading posters and signs, getting a feel for the area. The most interesting find was a bulletin board which listed items—lost and found—which included people, as well as animals and other items of value that people longed to bring back into their lives. After reconnoitering the place, I tapped one of the bus chaperones on the shoulder.

"Hey, pal. Can you tell me where I might find the local homeless shelter?"

When he turned to answer me, he jerked back and hesitated. "Now why in the Sam Hill would I have any idea where a shelter is, bubba?" he said, shifting his weight from left foot to right and back again before he went back to cleaning the windshield on a bus parked at the terminal departure dock. It didn't surprise me. Usually all I get is the stare, the sneer, and the silent cold shoulder. The fact he said anything was a bit surprising since I am not what you might call an Ivy League poster child. An oil-stained Steelers baseball cap shaded my face. The faded-green flannel shirt and frayed knee-less jeans showed signs of three years on the road with infrequent washing in sinks and streams. Beyond that my earthly wardrobe consisted of a denim shirt, a gray sweatshirt, and a tattered pair of chinos crammed into the weathered canvas backpack I picked up in trade for a flashlight. There is a name, Filippo Rustici, inked on the inside flap of the pack. Beneath that, less legible, I could read "Isonzo, 1915."

My last shower with soap was in Biloxi, two weeks and three cities earlier. The world had begun to smell like ammonia all the time. I hadn't realized it was me.

Signs and displays reminded me that it was Halloween. Over the prior week a lingering Indian summer had appropriately spray-painted foliage yellow, orange, and red, then whisked the leaves from the trees to blank dew-doused grasses along the highways.

Outside at the rear of the station a guy bundled in an old army field jacket with Jackson Pollock stains down the front sat on the sidewalk with his back against the brick building. With his head drooped, chin against his chest, it was no stretch on my part to imagine this fellow was in a similar boat as me.

I nudged his foot with my toe. "Hey, brother, is there a shelter around here?" When he didn't move, I tapped him with my shoe a second time.

He hesitated but rolled his head back. His face was an expected complement to his worn clothes. Plum-colored circles painted the loose skin below his eyes. Gray stubble-shaded cheeks with a week's worth of five o'clock shadow. Thinning gray hair clung to his forehead. He strained to look up through partially opened eyes.

"What?"

"A homeless shelter. A place to bed down for the night."

"It's full, man," he said before his chin rolled back to his chest.

"Full? Tonight? Already?"

"It was full last night, that's why I'm sitting here. They kicked me out of the station."

"You waiting on a bus?"

"No, man. Just sitting. I ain't goin' nowheres." His voice was weak, tired, unwilling to wake up.

"Make you a deal. You show me where the shelter is and I'll buy us some grub."

"Ain't got no money," he said. He swatted at a fly circling his head.

I bent forward, closer to his ear, and slowly and deliberately repeated, "I said I'll buy the food. Just show me where the shelter is."

He remained seated. "It's full."

The joker was either deaf or too tired to listen. "I'll take my chances on that. It's still early. They probably haven't even opened the door yet. Food. Come on, man. I'll get you some food."

He looked up and blinked a few times in the midday light, then agreed with a nod.

In the upside-down world of the homeless, food stands on top of the pyramid, followed by a bed, then sex or alcohol, depending on the mood. He rolled to his right, grabbed two plastic bags bulging with whatever, and using his shoulder against the wall to steady himself, managed to stand. I followed his slow lead.

Myrtle Beach is mainly a beach resort town. Cutesy souvenirs and colorful beach attire filled the windows of shops clustered alongside bike rental kiosks, surfboard outlets, and ice cream parlors. Gulls soared overhead in a breeze filled with the salty reminder that the Atlantic was only a few blocks away.

For the most part, when I'm not battling voices in my head, I'm a fairly decent conversationalist, but my guide and walking companion was a total mute. The guy didn't utter a peep as he shuffled past chinchy arcades, gaudy tattoo parlors, tacky no-tell motels, a non-denominational house of praise, and "authentic local cuisine" greasy spoon restaurants.

Six blocks later he broke his silence. "That's it." He pointed at a windowless brick building. A former warehouse, now shelter, typical of what I had grown accustomed to over the years. Above a set of double steel doors was a four-by-eight sheet of plywood, painted white with black hand-painted letters. The Ebenezer House of Rest was a landmark at the corner of two prominent highways. Outside the doors, men of all ages milled around. Some sat, backs against the wall, staring at cars as they passed. Some leaned against shopping carts loaded with bags of cans and assorted metal items. Others trolled the sidewalk while they puffed on cigarettes.

"It don't open till five," my escort said, "and your ass better be in line then, or you ain't going to get a damn cot." I nodded in agreement. The time was just shy of three-thirty. "Hey, thought you was going to get us something to eat?"

"Yeah. Sure. Let's walk on down a bit and see what we find."

We walked maybe two blocks before my newest silent partner started chirping. "There. Pancakes. There. That'll do. In there."

The sign next to the door flashed with laser brightness as we entered. *Hot stacks served 24 hours a day.*

"So, my name's Chili. What's yours," I asked as we sat down. My companion was already deep in thought eyeballing the menu and didn't respond.

"Say, what's your name?"

"BJ."

"Just BJ, no names beyond the initials?"

He looked up long enough to say, "Bobby John Bennett."

"But BJ?"

"Yes," he added. "Just BJ," and went back to studying the menu until the waitress took our orders.

"Well BJ, pleased to meet you," I answered looking down at a couple in a distant booth. "You live around here?"

"Nope, just visit often. I'm a drifter. You know, one of them nomads. I hail from down the road in Plantersville, but hang out in big cities usually. Charleston, mainly."

"What brings you here?"

"Beach. Like the beach," he said wiping condensation off his water glass. "Myrtle Beach is the best 'cause tourists with a vacation attitude come here with the yen for fun times always and they always have extra loose change."

I nodded. "Makes sense. You spend a lot of time in shelters?"

"When I can. Don't like them much. What 'bout you?"

"I travel a lot, all over. Usually hit the shelter when there's room. Just like talking to the guys. You meet all kinds out here," I said.

BJ chuckled and shook his head. "Yep, all kinds."

That was the last I heard from BJ for quite a while. The waitress brought the first round of pancakes and BJ was ready for seconds before I was half-way through my stack. Although it was mid-afternoon, the pancakes were hot indeed. Served with a choice of syrup—maple, blueberry, or strawberry—plus a stack of foil-wrapped pats of butter, we rounded out our order with enough bacon to feed a Little League baseball team. I hadn't eaten since before boarding the bus out of Jacksonville the day prior. The "All You Can Eat Breakfast - Anytime" cured the hunger in both of us. In the end, BJ knocked down eleven pancakes before he had all he could eat.

With my backpack and his bags in tow, we lumbered out of the restaurant satiated and ready for a siesta. We headed back toward the shelter. I listened while BJ rattled on and on with the typical hot air to prop up his street cred. Then, two cops, probably driving their usual beat along the Strip, as BJ called it, pulled up alongside us and slowed.

Casual discussions with local police had not been on my to-do list for three years. I looked away to scout a quick exit if I needed to lose the cops quickly. There was a good chance they'd seen my face on a "Wanted" poster back at police HQ. When I looked over my shoulder, the cop closest to the sidewalk slid his sunglasses down the bridge of his nose and squinted. The voices in my head were loving his cue. We continued to walk; BJ drifted closer to the curb.

"You know what I hate more than a cop?" BJ said, turning toward me. Then, turning to look back in the direction where we'd been, he continued in a loud voice, "A dick-head nosy cop."

"Watch yourself, buster," the cop said. "You don't want to go there." The car continued to inch along the pavement. Looking at the side-view mirror, I spotted the officer riding shotgun watching us.

BJ upped the ante. "You ready to run?" he asked me in a soft voice. He must have read my mind. Before I had a chance to respond, he added, "Watch this." He turned his back toward the police car, grabbed his waistband, bent forward, and mooned the cops. By the time BJ had his pants back up and grabbed his load of bags, the flashers on the patrol car were on. We retraced our steps back down the street, this time at a full sprint. The siren came on while the cruiser waited for traffic to clear for its U-turn. I followed

BJ. We cut through a parking lot, slipped down a side street, and crouched behind a dumpster in an alley. Our Keystone Cops whizzed past with lights and sirens, lost in pursuit.

Panic pumped the adrenaline which sucked my chest to a vacuum. Blood raced through my veins. Pupils dilated to near blindness. It was a sensation I had experienced far too often in recent years. "What the hell are you doing, man?" I said to BJ next to the dumpster. "I don't need any cops." I'd been on the run long enough to realize I couldn't risk being near the police. I wasn't sure where my face might have appeared on a poster and what cop was anxious to claim the reward. My worries were short lived, however. The Vigilantes kibitzed faster than corn in a popper and prodded me into a fresh game of cops and robbers. "However ..."

I grabbed the thought before it left my head. "Why don't we change the rules a bit?" I looked around. "Here's the deal. You ever been in a race? A car chase?"

BJ shook his head. Sirens circled closer.

I grabbed him by the collar and pulled him further into the alley, talking as we moved. "I drove a Porsche in the '82 Le Mans. Sweet ride. Eight hundred and fifty horses. Ran at 7,900 rpm. Blistered the track at 183 miles per hour. Called it Moby Dick. It was a whale. Weighed almost a ton," I added as I dragged BJ behind me. "Let's give those bastards a little fun." We crouched down near another dumpster. A Harley with a sissy bar stood on a kickstand twenty feet away. "Come on."

By the looks of it, I figured the bike was probably ten or fifteen years old. Nothing to brag about and not a big loss for the owner. I climbed the side of the dumpster, found a stack of papers with a paperclip on them. I bent the clip into a U-shape. BJ kept an eye out for our cops while I slipped over to the bike, reached under the gas tank cowling, and yanked the wire harness down where I could see it. I hot-wired the starter with the paperclip. A simple flick of the starter button and the exhaust pipes belched. I cranked the throttle a few times then let the beast idle with its distinctive, mystical Harley pop-pop … pop-pop … pop-pop as I tip-toed the bike closer to BJ.

"Okay, brother. Let's find those dogs. We'll hop this rabbit out in front of them for a bit of a chase." I motioned with my head. "Hook your bags over the sissy bar and hold on. We're headed for the danger zone."

"I ain't getting on that thing with you. You're crazy, man!"

I reached out and grabbed the flap of his field jacket and pulled him up close. His leg was against the hot muffler.

"Ow!"

"Get your moony-ass on the bike. You started this shit." I stared a painful stare with my dilated pupils. "You wanted a little fun, well, I'm going to give your ass exactly what you bargained for, only one better." I lowered my voice and pulled him closer; he was stiff-as-a-board scared. "Get on the bike. Let's go," I snarled, then shoved him back a step, ripped the bags out of his hands, and draped them over the seatback. When I reached out to grab BJ, he voluntarily moved to straddle the seat.

Rocking the bike to get a feel for the balance, I revved the motor and dropped the bike into gear. We jerked forward. I backed off my grip on the throttle and dragged my feet as we eased into a slow, wobbly glide out to the mouth of the alley where it joined the street. Cruiser lights flashed a short block away.

I hollered, "Five, four, three, two, one," then sliced across the lane, missing the front bumper of the cop car by less than six feet. The cruiser tires screeched for a few seconds, which allowed me to widen the gap before the cops continued in chase.

"Hang on, BJ. I'm going to try something."

The old bike was more responsive than a match in a gas can. I cranked the throttle a full ninety degrees and the front wheel kangarooed off the pavement into a near-vertical wheelie. BJ grabbed my neck to hold on. I leaned forward and took him with me, bouncing back onto two wheels. I kicked in the afterburners. When we hit fifty miles per hour, I checked the mirror. No sign of the cops, just BJ with a death-grip on me, panting tongue-out like a dog with his eyes popped out in front of his nose. I laughed my ass off.

BJ hollered in my ear, the skin on his face flapping with the speed. "You ever drive one of these before?"

"Nope, but what's the big deal?" I released the handlebar and gave him a double-thumbs up after the speedometer backed down through forty-five. The vibration of the bike between my legs tickled into a hard-on. My pupils were still dilated. I couldn't focus. Buildings, signs, and streetlights faded to grey. The Harley floated. The throaty sass of the muffler broadened my smile with each tick of the needle as the speedometer raced to the right of fifty. The faster we went the more eerie the feeling became. It felt good. I felt good. I felt right. Faster still, as the rush grew warm and comforting. It was back. The naughty schoolboy feeling. I rocked the bike left and right. I pushed for more. We were flying.

The road was a slalom peppered with cars, pedestrians, and stray dogs in our path. In the rearview mirror all I could see of the police car was a dot with tiny flashing lights.

"Yee-ha! This is great shit, eh, BJ?" I yelled, letting the wind carry my words back to him. "Man was meant to fly.

You ever fly, BJ? So cool. So fast. Go ahead. Let go. Stick your arms out and fly, BJ."

He didn't move.

I wiggled the bike to shake things up a bit. "I said ... put your arms out and fly. If you don't do it, I'll crank up this hog until you see this pig fly off the pavement and into the wild blue yonder. Airborne. Now stick out your damn arms!"

BJ uncurled his fingers from around my waist and lifted his arms ever so slowly until they were at about a forty-five-degree angle, a perfect swept-wing for flying.

"Atta boy. I knew you could do it. See, we can fly." I lifted my arms out straight. "We're flying, BJ. Look at us." With the bike between my legs I steered with my knees, slight pressure this way and that. Without my hand on the throttle, even as the bike slowed, I checked the mirror and caught BJ with his eyes closed, his hair streaming straight back along with his tears.

We roared above sixty before sets of flashing lights appeared dead ahead less than a quarter of a mile. Cars stacked up behind the roadblock. Another police cruiser, this one heading at us. I squeezed the handbrakes and the bike screeched in a sideways skid. BJ groped to hold on and yanked me off my seat. The rear wheel slid past me. To avoid dropping the bike on the deck, I put my right foot on the ground and, instinctively, went to full throttle. The Harley popped upright, now pointed ninety degrees to the right, with a crowded four lane up ahead. With strip malls on either side of us, we zoomed through a gas station lot, bounded through tall weeds and trash in an empty side yard, passed three kids flying kites on the edge of a field, then rumbled underneath a billboard that read "Surf, Sand, and Sounds of the Sixties WBCH 103.1 The Tide." We came out in a strip mall parking lot, swerving around a few overjoyed shoppers who stepped back and tossed their bags into the air. I then nosed onto a perpendicular street, putting even more distance between us and our followers in blue. Cars all around us swerved out of our way as we shot past them amid a hail of horns and gestures.

I backed off the throttle as I looked behind us. One cop car made the turn to follow, with no sign of the second car. In my peripheral vision, BJ sat white-knuckled, his forehead pulled into a washboard of wrinkles above his eyes, fused shut. Specks of pancakes were plastered to his chin.

At full throttle it took no time at all to outrun that cruiser and hit Highway 17, with the speedometer reading seventy. I didn't bother to check on our followers. At the first crossroads, I made the turn, slowed the bike to local speed, and cruised street after street until we managed to end up back at the pancake house. It was simply convenient at this point to park our ride by the dumpster where we found it. While BJ sat and composed himself—still a bit green around the gills—I stomped around in the alley, slapping at the walls, kicking cans. "That was some shit! Oh baby. Brought back memories. On the track. We need to get us a car. Shoot, let's go get their car. Dress up like cops. Ride around. Pick up chicks. Shoot, no. The beach. Surf's up!" My motor mouth rambled faster than sparks from a sparkler. "Come on, we still have time to make it to the line at the shelter. Need that cot for the night." By the time we reached the shelter, there was no sign of the cops.

Our little chase had lasted less than fifteen minutes. I sputtered on about our adventure for over an hour, boasting about how we out-foxed the entire police force. "Shoot, there must have been a dozen cars after us. Roadblocks on every street, around every exit. Trapped like rats, but we escaped." And the tale grew as it went on. I worked the shelter line, front to rear, blabbering, pounding my chest with my fist, flailing my arms, nose-to-nose and changing the topic with each face. I cornered one guy and argued why the moon landing was a total hoax. With the next guy I summarized the principles of supersonic flight. Topics rolled off my lips: the migration of butterflies, risk of skin cancer, why we need sleep, where's Jimmy Hoffa, Stonehenge, the truth about Elvis and Kennedy, the Bermuda Triangle, angels on pinheads. My usual serving of wisdom received with the usual response: bug eyes, furrowed brows, and middle fingers.

Toward the end of the line, a guy leaning against the wall casually told me to shut the fuck up. I didn't much care for his tone or his insensitive comment, so I did the natural thing—I stepped up nice and close and went off about proper listening techniques. After a little pushing and shoving and my short monologue, I moved on. Then the Vigilantes spoke up, louder.

"Which one is after me?"

There. He's there.

Call the ball. Call the goddamn ball!

You said … you said …! Bolters. Can't. It's hot. Too hot.

Shut up.

"Don't tell me to shut up. You shut up!"

The voices had travelled with me, hounded me, since my friend died. He wasn't haunting me; none of the voices were his. They were strange voices, many voices. Gruff. Whiny. Arguing and pushing ideas that weren't me but controlled me, nonetheless. Weird things. Unsafe things. Illegal things. Distracting things. But the voices hadn't told me to kill him; the voices came after he died. They played against my heart.

I blathered on in private conversation with the voices, trooping the line. Nervous hands fiddled with my cap. From time to time I would drill a deep stare into the eyes watching me. I was a highly energized, walking, talking Van der Graaf generator, repelling everyone that came near. My pulse outpaced my ability to breathe. Suddenly, out of the corner of my eye, a shadow appeared in the second-floor window of the building across the street.

I stopped talking mid-sentence. My jaw tightened. I walked to the curb and sat, my eyes fixed on the window. The eyes of all the guys in the line stabbed my back. A guy the size of Gibraltar toward the end of the line hollered, "What the hell are you doing, man? What are you looking at? Get back in line. Move up."

"That guy. Up there. In the window. He's got binocs around his neck. And a gun."

"What guy? What are you talking about, man? There ain't nobody up in no building."

"Yeah. There. See?"

The longer I stared, the longer the guy in the window stood there, unmoving, sniggering.

Chapter 3

The shelter doors banged open. A husky man the size of a lumberjack and a similarly broad woman sauntered out. Babe tied the doors open while Paul Bunyan barked at the men in line. "Form a line, single file. No pushing, just get into a single line. Keep your things with you."

I hopped up from the pavement and took a spot in line behind BJ. People complained about me cutting in. The crush of bodies behind me pushed forward. My eyes never left the window.

Inside, the shelter was one large room. Concrete floor. Empty storage racks crammed willy-nilly against the walls, towering over us. Remnant sections of conveyer corralled into a heap of metal dotted the corners. Rope barricades with signs that read "Danger: Keep Out" warned against entry. Toward the back were two restrooms. One door read "WOMEN" but the "W" and "O" were crossed out with a wide, black marker similar to the one that had been used to draw a large penis and balls beneath the lettering. Next to the other door marked "MEN," a heap of cardboard boxes sat in a pool of water that seeped from under the baseboards of the restroom wall. The ventilation system recirculated air left over from the Truman administration and gave the place a distinctively rotten smell, a fragrance to which I'd grown accustomed through my three years on the streets. The shelters were no Ritz-Carlton and most rated a notch above health code standards. Though it was Halloween, the smell was neither a trick nor treat.

The staff, each dressed in uplifting Halloween costumes, assigned cot numbers and allowed us to stow our belongings. I wasn't about to hand over my backpack—too much risk if I'd need a quick exit. Cots were arranged in rows of ten, five across in two sections separated by graffiti-covered plywood partitions on wheels. As folks settled, a staff member blasted an airhorn.

From a mic on a platform at the end of the hall, a guy dressed in a toga with a plastic olive wreath crown read the shelter rules: no booze, drugs, or loud music, no leaving the building, no walking around after lights-out, and a few others that didn't amount to much. Then, joined by a gal dressed as Little Orphan Annie, he invited us to dinner.

The dining area was tucked in the corner opposite the restrooms. Faded orange and green tablecloths covered long folding tables, decorated with jack-o'-lanterns, witches' pots, and open plastic skulls all filled with candy. Paper cut-outs of spiders and ghosts were scattered across the tables. At one end of the chow line stood a mannequin of Frankenstein's monster, arms outstretched in a zombie-walk. At the other end was a coffin someone had crafted out of cardboard painted black. Inside, a small skeleton lay with a toothbrush in one hand and a bar of soap in the other. The female volunteer servers for the night were Snow White, Cinderella, and a harem dancer, belly exposed; an unfortunate choice of costume given her bear-like shape. One of the male servers was a Zorro—mask, cape, boots, sombrero cordobés, the whole nine yards—and the other had a sheet draped over his head with eye holes. The meal was mostly casserole and salad with pop-tube biscuits, baked but only semi-hot. At another table, a stormtrooper was ladling punch into paper cups. Each of the servers wished everybody a "Happy Halloween," such as it was. For me, there was nothing happy about anything.

The invigorating high of the chase had evaporated. The excitement, the adrenaline, all the energy that revved me for the previous hours dissolved into doom. I tussled with the Vigilantes' barrage of doubt and desperation.

Punch splashed from the paper cup in my hand as I skirted the tables and took a seat in the corner behind a wooden crate the size of a large boulder. My fork separated noodles from peas and pushed chunks of tuna to the side; none of it appealed to me. As I stared at the plate, the same shadow I saw earlier in the window faded in and out. Moments later, a nightmarish image of the police cuffing me on the motorcycle sent me into an ice-cold panic. Wide-eyed, I imagined how that scene would play out. Stealing the Harley and leading the cops on a wild goose chase would amount to peanuts once they connected me to the guy I'd killed. Years of eluding the law, done. A trial. No defense.

A ghost from the serving line broke my trance.

"There are plenty of seats at the table. Go ahead. Pick one." This character was straight out of Dickens's *Carol*, a friend of Jacob Marley. He slowly raised his arm and pointed toward the others chowing down across the room. His words barely registered.

My uninvited visitor pulled off his sheet and took a knee in front of me. When I lifted my chin, I realized the face beneath the cover was far from ghostly. His flushed, red cheeks featured stubble longer than mine. He could have passed as one of the nightly guests. His plaid shirt and pressed chinos, both freshly washed and lightly starched, told me otherwise.

"You're welcome to sit with the others. Come on. I'll join you. We can shoot the breeze a bit, if you'd like."

I squinted at his blurry face. His congenial smile melted into bewilderment. He blinked a few times before I dropped my chin and rolled my head away. That drove my message across. He grabbed his sheet and walked off.

While others ate, I slipped back to my cot. Along the way, I started to cry. No reason. It wasn't the voices; they'd grown silent. It was the emptiness, loneliness. The haunting aloneness that had shrouded my thinking since before the first bus ride. I was adrift. No direction. Nothing made sense. I wanted things to be the way they were. I wept like a baby, even questioned the need to breathe. Life had become suddenly unimportant. Behind the tears, I thought about my friend's wife. I had to fix things. I had to find her.

When the harem dancer from the food line appeared, she bent down, noticed my tears, and left. Minutes later she returned with Snow White. They sat on either side of me on the cot, the three of us in a cloud of silence. After a while, a soft and cautious voice asked, "What's wrong?"

I continued to cry, leaning forward with my elbows on my knees.

"Can we help?"

"It's fucked up. Everything is so fucked up." I picked at a torn fingernail. "They know I'm in here. I can't let them nab me."

"Who?"

"Them. The guy. The shadow in the window." I reached behind Snow White for the pillow to cover my head. "He has a gun. I saw it. He always has a gun. They sent him after me, to take me back," I mumbled, muffled by the pillow.

"Who?" one said.

"A gun?" the other said.

"Take you where?"

"Why?" they asked back-and-forth.

"He follows me. I see him. Everywhere. Waiting." I pulled the pillow tighter around my ears. "I know he's there."

The women said nothing, obviously confused. They sat with me, my head helmeted by a pillow that had comforted countless heads before mine.

At a loss of what to say or do, one of the women finally said, "Hey, trick or treat. This will make you feel better." She thrust a fun-size candy bar in front of my nose. When I didn't move, she lined it up next to my foot, then the volunteers left.

This shelter was louder than others. Even with my head muffled by a pillow, the whispers of the Vigilantes continued. I slipped from my seat to the floor and slid under the cot, my head wrapped by my pillow. The voices, several voices, continued:

You are a dumbass.

Why'd you come in here?

You know they'll get you.

They're bound to catch you sooner or later.

When they do, it will mess with your mind.

Make it easy. Stop all this bullshit running. Kill yourself.

Let's get this over with now and be done with it.

I scrunched the pillow tighter. It helped with noise, but it couldn't keep me from crying. I didn't hurt. I was lost and nothing seemed right.

Later I slid out, hunched over, to take a leak. As I approached the closest restroom, the one with "W" and "O" crossed out, my legs weakened. Everything turned white. I took a knee until my head cleared then stepped inside the restroom. All the stall doors had been removed. I could see there was nobody else in the room, but all the commodes were full. A stream of murky brown water flowed through a dip in the floor and out the doorway. I made my way to the other men's room. With my forehead against the wall of the urinal, I peed. When I flushed it was as if all the troubles of the day went down the drain. Maybe it was just pressure off my bladder, but I was relieved nonetheless. My shoulders relaxed. My back loosened. I wasn't giddy or crazy-happy, but I felt good. Exhausted and upright, I headed back toward my cot.

Around the room, groups were playing cards; a couple guys were playing chess. A number of men were already sacked out on their cots with covers pulled over their heads. I chatted briefly with the guy on the cot beside mine. With my energy restored, I wandered, joining in conversations up and down the rows of cots, swapping the typical shallow crap about how our days had gone and how we'd been cheated.

On the other side of the room, a guy was holding court, some sort of pow-wow with a group of guys standing around his cot. At one point he poked one dude in the chest several times before the guy slapped his hand away. Curious, I crossed the room. As I approached, the black guy on the cot was fumbling with a Rubik's cube. He looked up and waved the others off. Each rolled their heads in my direction as they passed. None appeared happy.

"You ever figure that out?" I asked to open conversation.

"Shit no," he said, bent over, a veil of dreadlocks shrouding his face. His long, thin fingers continued to spin the cube with little apparent interest in aligning the colored squares.

I stood next to his knee with my arms folded across my chest. I interrupted his concentration—well, at least his efforts. "You know those things have a basic formula for figuring them out." I cocked my chin for emphasis.

He tilted his head and pushed his dreadlocks away from his eyes. He had too much nose and a too big mouth for his face. His lower lip curled in. He squinted as he looked up, pointing his scruffy, goateed-chin toward me. "Listen, brother. I don't need no help," he said with the sneer of a prizefighter. His lazy-tongue drawl carried his "don't bother me" attitude. He slapped the cube onto his cot. "Like … you can do this shit, right?"

"I can do it. I'll show you." Uninvited, I sat down.

He slid away and flipped the cube to me with a cocksure stare. I locked eyes with him for a moment then examined his work with the cube. A couple of rows were complete, but the sides were a random matrix of the six colors. No side with more than one row. I twirled the cube a few times to scope out colors and positions on each of the sides. After a few twists, a white cross appeared along one face of the cube. A few more twists and the cross grew into a solid white layer. I flipped the cube over and, in less than a minute, tossed it back, solid colors on all sides.

"Solved, brother."

"How the …" He looked at the cube on the cot but wouldn't grab it.

"It's all in how you hold your head."

"What the …?" He turned the cube to inspect each of the sides.

"How long have you been working on that?" I said with a chuckle slight enough not to embarrass the guy.

"Shit. I don't know. Dozen years." He tossed the cube back onto the cot, unimpressed. "No biggie."

I'd been in dozens of shelters over the past three years. I knew most homeless guys didn't usually volunteer much about themselves, their personal sides. I adopted the same practice, for the same reasons. If asked, I rarely got my details right. So, when this guy volunteered his name as Emmett Pharren, I told him my name was Chili.

"Cute, man. That ain't no name. What you go by really? What's your real name?"

"Chili. Everybody calls me Chili. That's what it is, brother."

He gave me a smug look and nodded. "That's cool. That's cool, man. Say, show me how you do that shit."

"Do what shit?"

"Get them damn colors all together like it s'pose to be."

The lights in the shelter flickered.

"Lights-out in five," Frankenstein's monster said, walking between the cots. Other costumed volunteers walked between other rows to spread the same message.

I walked to the front counter and asked the overnight volunteer, no longer wearing his Zorro mask but still in his cape, if Emmett and I could sit at a table in the dining area, away from the sleeper cots, and talk, quietly. The volunteer said, "Sorry, there are rules. On your cots at lights-out." A man of about fifty, he seemed to be intent on maintaining the rules. He had no authority to change the rules and no reason to make an exception for us, but I was still curious about what Emmett and his boys were up to. Now that my troubles had passed, I was awake, not ready to sleep.

I bent forward and whispered to the volunteer, "Look, pal, we're not going to disturb anyone. Just let me talk to this guy. We'll be quiet as church-mice, promise. If we get loud, you can break up our session and tuck us in for the night."

"Sorry. Can't let you."

"Come on, man." I stepped back, popped up my chest, tall and erect. "That guy, over there, needs to talk to someone. He's in bad shape," I added, doing my best to appear sincere and professional, albeit louder than before. "Catch my drift?"

"You think so?" he said, leaning back in his chair. "And what makes you think you're the one? You some sort of Sigmund Freud or something?"

The guy was pissing me off. I leaned across the counter to get as close as I could to his face, waiting for the Vigilantes to chastise me for using them in my ploy. "See, I have these voices in my head. They tell me I need to listen."

"Nope." He reached to his right to adjust a coat-hanger antenna he had wired to a mini-television hidden below the countertop.

"Would you accept a bribe?" I said, stretching my neck toward him.

He laughed and hoisted himself more erect in the chair. "From you?"

I took a step backward as frustration silently boiled my face to a steamy red. After a few heavy breaths, I calmed myself.

"Listen up, Kemosabe. You put everybody to beddy-bye. As of this minute, it's just the three of us, you, me and my friend over there." I drummed my fingers on the counter as I looked out over the space filled with cots. "Now, chances are, let's say, if something started here, say, a disturbance, all hell would break loose. I mean, in a shelter full of homeless men, down on their luck? That would be a terrible thing." I turned back to point at Emmett sitting on his cot fiddling with the Rubik's cube. "That guy needs help. Bad. Bending a simple rule this one time wouldn't hurt a soul and I promise I won't tell anybody. Scout's honor. But you see, having a riot break out under your watch? And you sitting all nice and pretty and all. That wouldn't look good for you, now would it? And for me? I would disappear faster than cotton candy at a church bazaar. Nobody would be any the wiser." I leaned my elbows on the counter, cupped my chin in my hands and smiled a Cheshire cat's toothy grin. "So, be a sport. Let me and him sit over there and talk. Nice and quiet like and nothing's going to happen. Okay?" I stepped back and rocked on my heels, my hands shoved deep in my pockets.

The volunteer rolled his eyes, looked side to side, anywhere but at me. He checked the dining area and pointed with his chin. In a monotone he added, "Sit in that far table in the corner. Keep the noise down. I hear as much as a peep out of either of you and you're in your cots or out the door."

I smiled. As I walked away, I looked back, winked, and offered the guy two thumbs up as I headed to my cot to retrieve my rucksack.

Chapter 4

Emmett—if that was really his name—followed me to the eating area. The dark corner hid us from the others in the hall, but offered ample light. Emmett smacked the Rubik's cube down on the table, yanked out a chair, and plopped into it. The volunteer at the desk flashed a finger as his warning for quiet.

"Okay, brother, show me how you did that shit. This little baby's gonna make me some scratch."

"Whoa! Hold up," I said.

He scoffed.

As I reached for the cube, he snatched it into his gut and looked dead into my eyes.

"You're dipping into my game here," I told him, drumming my empty fingers on the table. "Before I give you my big secret, what are you offering?" I watched the smile build on his face. "Why don't you tell me your big secret. What's going down here? You and the brothers have a major pow-wow over there?"

"Why, that ain't be none of your business. Just family talk is all. You know, black-on-black." His dreads dangled to block his eyes.

I answered his smile with a grin and upped the ante with a chuckle. "Sure enough. Something this white boy needs to know?"

"No, no, no. Why you need to know? You some sorta dick cop or narc or something?" He held the cube in front of his chest and looked away. "Just family talk's all. You know, talking 'bout what's going on and all."

"Okay then. Share some of that with me. I'd like to hear." I nodded and waited

He lowered the cube to the table and looked back toward me. I could see the white of his smile behind his veil of dreads. "Don't be no preacher man now, neither. I ain't got time for no preaching."

He tossed the cube from one hand to the other. Dollar signs grew in his eyes as he watched the arc, back and forth, panning deep into the darkness over my head. His head never moved. Only his eyes. Between throws, he stared in a catatonic absence. When he managed to breathe, he would toss the cube again. And, again he watched it fall and stared. Unexpectedly, he banged the cube on the table.

"You want to know? You want to know about me?" He leaned in. "Shit, I'll give you the whole damn story, but you gotta show me your shit. And …" he paused, "you don't say nothin' to them brothers I was with tonight, understand?"

"About the cube?"

"About me," he insisted. "Me or the cube shit."

"You go first," I offered. I pushed back, crossed my legs and arms, and waited.

His head rolled back as his lips puckered to hold in a response or build a lie. Balancing his chair on its two back legs, he dropped his chin and began. "Homeless just like you, and like all them dicks on them cots. I been homeless a long fucking time. Grew up in Georgia, in a place so small you could hear somebody fart clear on the other side of town."

I muffled a laugh and watched him spin the cube.

"There weren't no jobs in town. I worked at a McDonald's for a while, then for a lawn company. That's when Uncle Sam had the draft board send me my personal invitation letter. I ended up in Nam as a gun bunny. You know what that is?"

I shook my head. "Machine guns?"

"Nah, man. Big guns. Artillery. Pumped big bullets at Charlie for ten months. Those shells weigh about forty pounds. You do that for days, especially in a firefight, and you almost die without nobody shooting at you. That was my day job."

"Day job?"

His smile broadened. He looked away but kept talking. "By night I was the doctor. I did what helped nearly every sorry dude in the bush. I was their pharmacy, their drug store. I could get my hands on just about anything. Mostly they wanted weed, hash, and heroin. Kids in the villages would hook me up. I'd trade for C-rations and candy. Them kids knew better than to give them drugs to anybody but me. They knew I'd shoot their sorry slant-eyed asses if they did." He chuckled. "I made beaucoup bucks dealing. After ten months in the bush they sent me back to the rear to begin processing out. Month later I got caught. Busted me two ranks back down to private, took a couple months' pay, and shipped me back stateside to Fort Benning, Georgia."

I moved up, leaned over the table, elbows down, chin cradled in my hands. Most guys in shelters won't say much about themselves. His openness made me wonder how much of Emmett's story was true. I couldn't tell by his eyes; his hair wouldn't allow it. His story flowed, not like he was making it up on the fly. Still I wondered if it was really his story. He seemed too willing to reveal himself.

"It didn't take long to set up shop in the States. I had my homies back in Nam send me shit. Nobody ever bothered to check inside body bags coming in, least not for drugs. I was making a killing."

Emmett pulled a toothpick from his pocket and poked at his teeth as he continued, slowly. "Then, that shit changed. First, a damn MP caught me weaving down some dirt road at Benning. He found a few bags of weed in the passenger seat, enough to get me slammed. The Army court-martialed me again. Busted me to an E-nothing, took away all my pay, and sent me on my way with a Bad Conduct Discharge. Packed up my shit, lit up a joint, and headed to Bama for business. Same day, some honky State Highway Patrol pig pulled me over for speeding. When he pulled me over, he said he smelled marijuana, or so he thought—like he was some drug-sniffing dog. Said he had probable cause to search my vehicle. Bastard ripped open my backseat cushion and found my stash, a kilo of weed, three bricks of hash, and what was left from a kilo of heroin I shaved off for myself earlier. In court, I went brain dead. I was my own attorney. Judge hammered me."

It was graveyard-quiet over in the cots. Occasionally I looked over at the front desk. The volunteer, with his feet up, reading a magazine, hadn't paid us any attention. Emmett's story seemed clear to this point. Not much room for questions other than, "How long?"

"Spent six fucking years in the Valdosta State Prison. Went in as a twenty-year-old punk kid with a bad attitude. The brothers there fixed that most ricky tick. They let me know right away that I wasn't in Kansas anymore. Wasn't in charge, neither. At twenty I was one of the young'uns, cute enough to be their boy-toy." Emmett cocked his head to the side and closed his eyes. "Sick. That's sick shit." He stopped talking and stared at the table.

"What was prison like? Did it do anything for you? Change you?"

"It took two years till I earned some credibility with the brothers," he said, lifting his head, his upper lip curled. "That's when I did a damn-damn on this new guy called Droop, sent him to the infirmary. That was my cred. Shit cost me. I laid low from that point on, hoping I could snag a break from the parole board. Never happened." He folded his hands on the table. "I did my time. After that they gave me some old clothes, a bus ticket, and a pat on the ass and said sayonara, mofo. I went to my kid sister's place in Savannah."

"When was this? When did you get out?"

"Nineteen eighty."

He grew still. When his head dipped, I thought he'd drifted off to sleep until he cleared his throat. "Nobody wanted to hire a guy straight out of prison, especially a dealer." His face offered a look of questionable sincerity. "I can still smell the nasty breaths of them that poked me from behind. I have nightmares of the cocks I sucked to survive. That's what keeps me straight. I ain't goin' back to no Valdosta."

Emmett pulled at his ear and looked around, careful not to look at me. "Without no job, no money ... My sister's husband didn't want no drug dealer living with them. Said I needed to pay part of the bills or else leave. I booked. Hit the streets. Been here since. Seven years."

"So, now ... have you been working? You have any kind of job to keep you busy, out of trouble?" By his earlier actions and expressions, I could guess his answer, but I waited for him to talk it all out. He didn't add any more.

Stories like his take up residence in shelters all over. I did my best to give Emmett the better part of my doubt. I waited then asked if his sister was his only family.

"None around. Had three older brothers. The eldest shot the youngest brother when they was fighting over some bullshit thing over my old man's car. Killed him. They locked him away for murder. Doing life in Reidsville. The other brother, Darnell, disappeared. Nobody ain't seen or heard from him since my other brother died. Don't need those assholes, no how."

He pushed back from the table, stood up, and played with his dreads, pulling them to the back while he looked over my head into the rafters. I figured we were done. I didn't want to stare at the guy, didn't want to make him feel self-conscious. I looked out over the dark sleeping area, conscious of the smell of tuna noodle casserole, cardboard, and oil remnants from the warehouse, all the overwhelming B.O. of the place.

Emmett surprised me when he spoke again. "My sister, she told me she'd give me another chance if I was clean and straight and had a job to pay bills," he said, sliding back into the chair. "I been in and out of jobs. Bosses don't like my attitude, don't want to deal with me. Nobody willing to take a chance on me. Got a part-time job now. Work in a warehouse, but don't make shit. Ain't got enough to get my own place. Barely have enough to eat. I hang in this place when I can get in. Won't let me in all the time, say it's not a permanent place, so they kick my ass out for a few days, then I come back." He slid his hands across the table pushing the cube in my direction. He leaned his elbows on the table, flipped his head back to get the dreads out of his face. His expression became gloomy, serious. His tone changed; it became strangely apologetic.

"What I really need to do is go back to my old man's farm. Back to Lily, Georgia." Emmett stopped. He looked me in the eye and said, matter-of-factly, "That's my story. That's all that's happening. See ... my brothers and me, we just be talking about what's goin on. Not about me, and you best not be sharing this with them. Now your turn, Mr. Chili man." His voice became lighter and direct. "Tell me your damn secret."

I was okay with most of his story until the last comment. Still at a loss, weighing his words, I debated whether I should go tit-for-tat with some BS story or oblige him. I paused to think it over.

Chapter 5

I had heard versions of similar stories during my three years of running. I'd listened to confessions by countless others. Guys trying to come across as macho when, in fact, they were suckers. Some bragged a bit more than their activities warranted. Emmett's broken-record version had a few scratches where things skipped a bit. The stories, though, seemed to share a common thread. Behind the accents, drawls, and lisps through missing teeth, I surmised there was a core message. People want to have meaning, a purpose for their lives, for what they do or want to do. They want to make a difference. They want acceptance. They believe in hope. Emmett was probably no different.

I leaned across the table. "Farm? You want to go back to your old man's farm?"

"Yeah, away from the bullshit city stuff. Away from the temptation to deal again," he said, though I detected a lack of sincerity.

"Farming's a lot of work. Hard work. Physical work." I knew I wasn't telling him anything he didn't already know.

Emmett cocked his head to his shoulder, half dazed or asleep, and talked out of the side of his mouth. He explained how Titus—his father—worked himself to the point of exhaustion every day, then would drag himself back to the house, grab a jug of moonshine, and collapse soon after. Emmett and his brothers would put him in bed. The next day, the same. And the next and the next. Each day the old man would work Emmett and his brothers that much harder.

"So why would you want to ..."

Emmett jumped in, this time with a bit of artificial frog in his voice, a sympathy plea. Rolling his head, he said, "See, man, on Sundays, he'd drag us all to church. We'd all sit there, listen and sing. Not a one of us dared to move. My old man weren't big, but we respected him. See what I'm sayin'? And after every service, we would go back to the house and my old man would preach to us some more. He'd sit us down at the kitchen table while Mama and my sister, they fixed dinner while the old man preached about love and shit. Reading from the Bible and all. My brothers and me, we was all kids. We all thought he was full of shit, sitting there still sweating out the 'shine from the night before. I understand how ..."

He stopped mid-sentence and looked away. While his fingers fumbled with the Rubik's cube, his eyes looked for answers in the rafters.

"You said you have a job. Why leave that and ..."

"I told you," he chimed, occasionally looking in my direction. "Damn, man, they told me my appearance was too sloppy and I was late too many times or I refused to follow instructions. All just bullshit." Emmett glanced toward me with a pouting-puppy face. His voice carried further than intended. The volunteer at the desk looked up and shook his head. He raised his finger with a warning. I cautioned Emmett to keep his voice down.

His sincerity—as well as his story—seemed questionable. The farm was a safe place. Off the streets. Convenient for him. No rules. No regulations. His own boss. He continued to fidget with the cube, studying the color of each side, one by one.

I caught myself locked deep in thought with an unfocused stare at the cube. I looked away, saying, "You really think you want to go home? You think your old man would have you back? Thought you said your father kicked you out, told you never to step foot in his house again."

"Yeah, that's what I said. That's what he said ..." he said, placing the cube down, "but I've changed, brother." His voice shifted again, from contrite to cocky. "I mean, my old man's getting old, man. Someone got to take over that farm. Say, you going to show me about this cube or not, man?"

"Your sister," I said. "Can she help? Talk to your old man?"

"Hell no. Tried that. She don't want to get into no pissing contest about me with the old man. Besides, her asshole husband won't let her do nothing for me. Afraid she going to get wrapped up in some drug shit or something. I ain't talked to her but once since I left her place, been six years almost. Come on, man. Show me your shit."

"Tell you what. I'll write a letter for you. To your sister or your old man. Whoever."

He pushed back from the table and crossed his arms, his face fixed with disgust, then added a laugh. "A letter for what? Just show me the cube shit."

Now it was my turn to mess with his mind, but with the intent of helping, if he needed it. "I mean a letter. I've written letters, lots of letters. Wrote them for guys who had it worse than you, guys in shelters. Guys who had tough lives on the streets and learned a lesson or needed a hand to lift themselves out of the shelter and off the streets. I've written letters to employers and banks, judges, wives, families. I've written to them all. Tell me who. Your sister? Your old man? I would tell them I know you and you want another chance. All you want is the chance to prove yourself."

"Man, you crazy."

"Look, you've got nothing to lose. I write the letter, mail it, and the worst thing that happens is nothing, so you're no worse off, and maybe, best case, it gets you back where you want to be, off the street."

Emmett sat there, arms crossed, disinterested. I waited. Finally, he chuckled, lifted his head, pulled himself back to the table, pushed his hair behind his ears, and flashed a big grin.

"Shit, man. You go right ahead and write your damn letter." Then his face soured. "But first, you going to show me how you do that shit with this cube."

I spent a solid thirty minutes sitting there. I tried my damnedest to "Dick and Jane" this character through a beginner's method for the puzzle. The slower I went, the more his eyeballs spun. It wasn't long before his heavy eyelids got the best of him.

"Look man, I had enough. I ain't going to get this shit. Go write your damn letter. I'm going to bed," he said, standing.

"Can do. I'll show it to you in the morning."

After he walked off, the night security volunteer approached my table. "Okay, hit the sack. You're up way past bedtime curfew. You got your guy all squared away, now go," the guy said with his redeemed air of authority.

I couldn't help myself. I had to speak up. "Pardon me. I believe I failed to share with you the fact that I am a state-certified, undercover psychiatrist, recently assigned to assist the growing population of homeless people in Myrtle

Beach. Actually, it's kind of a casual sting operation, you know, to catch abuse by volunteers in the shelters. Hmm. Guess we don't want to go there."

"Yeah, and I'm the tooth fairy. Get to bed, pal."

"That guy, the guy I was talking to, he needs help. I promised I would write a letter to give him a hand. You know, a good Samaritan sorta thing. Give me an hour or so to whip out the letter. I won't make any noise. I'll just sit here, quietly by my lonesome, and create the magic of mind-bending. Deal?"

"No deal. Get in bed."

"Let's not go through this again. For all you know, I'm just one of them homeless dudes. But, then again, I might really be on that sting I was telling you about."

"Ya know what? I've been working this shelter for three years and I've never had anyone get under my skin as much as you have in the last three hours. Guess I'll take my chances. Get in bed."

"Wait. I can't sleep. I have insomnia." I raised my eyebrows to expose wide eyes.

"What a crock. Then go sit on your cot or just lie there and watch the ceiling."

"Come on, man. Have a heart. Where's that good old Ebenezer-Haven-of-Rest Christian spirit? I'm not asking for anything for myself. It's for that guy. I'll be quieter than cotton."

He turned and walked back toward his table without answering. I wriggled my fingers in the air to bid him farewell then dug into my rucksack for a pen and sheet of paper. I was never without a stash of paper and government pens. I cracked my knuckles and put my fingers to work, assuming a nom de plume with a clerical identity to legitimize my intentions.

October 31, 1987

Dear Mr. and Mrs. Titus Pharren,

I am a servant of the Lord and Savior Jesus Christ! Praise and glory to His name. Hallelujah! Hallelujah!

My mission is ever-present to the lost souls on the streets, wanderers in the woods, seekers of shelters, the downtrodden, the socially rejected, the homeless. With them I make my home. For them I knock on the doors to the Kingdom of God.

With my right hand on the holiest of books, our inspiration and living word, the works of God Almighty himself, the Bible for mankind, I swear to you that your son, Emmett, is a changed man. He has heard the word of God and repents. His sins they are forgiven in the eyes of the Lord and he wishes the same from you.

The words of 1 Timothy 5:8 tell us, "If anyone does not provide for his own, and especially for those of his household, he has denied the faith and is worse than an unbeliever." Let the gospel reign. Hallelujah!

Open your hearts. Rid yourself of all bitterness and anger, for it is not what I ask of you—it is what our Lord and Savior expects of you and what your lost son

no SHELTER for GUILT

Emmett begs of you. Be kind and compassionate, for he is your own son. Believe in the goodness of the Lord, our God, who is merciful and forgiving. As you forgive your son, so will God forgive you. Cleanse your heart. Trust in the Lord. Hallelujah!

The Lord is thy light and He showeth the way. Thou shalt follow Him. Prepare thee the way of the Lord. Take your son back into your life.

Praise Jesus! Amen.

As a humble servant and messenger, thus be it done in the name of the Almighty and eternal God of Moses.

Truly and respectfully yours,
Reverend Bob White
Baptist Missionary
Messenger of His Sacred Word

Chapter 6

The next morning, the volunteer staff brightened the day with a flick of the light switch, long before the sun would cast its weak rays on the street. We were told to strip our cots, drop sheets at the end of each row, and move on to the dining area. I filled my tray with the kitchen's finest in cereals, juice, and coffee, then stood on the edge of the room waiting to catch Emmett to discuss the letter. I found him seated, surrounded by the guys he'd entertained the night before. I walked to the table, politely nodded to the others, took out the letter and an envelope from my stash in my thick vinyl folder and slid it under Emmett's tray. He looked up but said nothing.

At 6:45 I walked out onto the sidewalk and froze. There were two police squad cars parked across the street. They had apprehended two of the guys who I saw with Emmett. I overheard one cop say to them, "... on suspicion of drug possession and distribution." Down at the corner, another cop loaded BJ, my Harley-riding buddy, into the back seat of a squad car.

The Vigilantes piped up. *We told you not to talk.*

I grabbed the strap of my backpack and beat feet with long strides, my hat pulled low on my head. The flashing lights and presence of police stirred up others leaving the shelter. There was a disturbing buzz with an occasional threat launched by dozens of onlookers clustered on the sidewalk. The chaos blocked my getaway. As I broke

no SHELTER for GUILT

through the crowd, a guy shouldered me from behind. Shoving hard, he ran past me down the street. The dreadlocks left no doubt; it was Emmett. Without breaking stride, he chucked something in a trashcan and sped off.

Weaving my way through the crowd, when I reached the trash, I felt compelled to take a look. Scattered among bottles, newspapers, plastic bags, and tall soft drink cups were two halves of the envelope I had given him and the confetti scraps of the letter in my handwriting. With all the activity around me, my smirk grew to a self-satisfying grin knowing my intuition about Emmett and his story had served me correctly. Still, I sensed in my heart that I had done the right thing. Efforts to help Emmett or any of the others for whom I had written letters were justified. I considered the letters a part of my repentance for killing my friend. I would like to think they were all good, that the letters were all successful. They all united the homeless, the letters were the hand up they needed. To the best of my knowledge, Emmett's was the first letter ever dismissed outright. It never even made it to the post office. The rejection begged the question, had Emmett lied about his need or was he actually afraid to send the letter for some deeper, more personal reason?

With the comments by the police echoing in my head. I ducked down a narrow, dirt path between two clapboard buildings. Bags of trash lined the walls and broken glass paved the ground. The strip was a graveyard for discarded car parts, empty food containers, and deflated beach toys. One ample bikini top added paisley color to the fan of a sun-starved dwarf palmetto tree halfway down the path. I paused long enough to hold it in front of me for a quick hoochie-coochie dance, then kept walking, twirling the skimpy top as I daydreamed. Preoccupied with images of the tits filling the bikini top, I didn't see the snake until I had already stepped on it. I fell backward and caught myself with my hands, landing in a bed of broken glass. Blood oozed from my hand, now a pin-cushion of broken beer bottle fragments. The shock of seeing a snake offset the pain in my hand. When I hopped up, the snake had slithered off. I plucked shards of glass out of my left hand as I walked. The cuts, though small, continued to bleed. I wrapped the bikini top around my hand and continued through a maze of alleys. I wandered, peering around buildings for signs of police until a Greyhound bus passed by. I followed its exhaust, which led back to the station.

The agent at the ticket window was right out of a Coppertone ad minus a surfboard. Shoulder-length blond hair, oily and straight. Body bronzed beyond ethnic recognition. Remnants of zinc oxide caked to his nose. He had an obvious liberal interpretation of the company dress code. He wore an unbuttoned blue-gray short-sleeved shirt bearing a Greyhound logo. He draped the Greyhound shirt over a pineapple-printed Hawaiian shirt in a puke-peach color. It soon became obvious his forte was not customer service.

I coughed a couple times to pull him off his stool, away from his liter bottle of Mountain Dew and copy of the *National Enquirer*, items in his life-support system. "I'd like a ticket on the next bus out of here."

"Whoa, dude! Tough night with the babes?" he said, admiring my hand wrapped in the bikini top. "Musta been great fun. You scored a souvenir, at least."

I shook my head and looked away to see if others had noticed my hand. I turned back to repeat my request. "I'd like a ticket on the next bus," I said in a measured tone, soft and slow.

"Where do you want to go?" he mumbled, slowly, his eyes drooping in a hung-over style.

"I don't really care," I insisted. "I just want to get out of here."

He chuckled. "The night couldn't have been all that bad," he said with a nod toward my hand. "What's your rush there, dude? Surf's up!"

Undeniably, even aside from my hand wrapped in the bikini, my appearance wasn't the best. I'd been without a shower for weeks, and my moustache had merged with a thicket of facial stubble. If the bars on the cage at the front of his window had been an inch wider apart, I would have grabbed this kid by his throat. He was maybe twenty, maybe not. Old enough to vote, drive, and drink, but I wasn't sure if his brain had fully developed quite yet. As it was, I needed a ticket.

"Look, dude," I said with colloquial emphasis, "I just want to get on the road to anywhere. When does your next bus leave?"

"Bus to Charleston leaves at 9:47. About an hour."

He took his eyes off me and looked over my shoulder. I turned to see what had distracted him and saw two young girls in Daisy Dukes and loose halter tops looking back at the window, smiling. My surfer friend returned their smiles, then looked back to me.

"It's a local. Going down the road is all. Short ride. Won't take you far from here."

"Are there any seats available?"

He nodded. "Eight bucks."

"Okay, give me a ticket on that one." With my good hand, I pushed the bills under the barred ticket window.

The kid-agent slid the ticket under the bars. "Have a nice day," he added with a smirk. I shook my head and walked to the front of the terminal.

If the police appeared, I had a plan. Until then I paced in the sun in front of the molded plastic bench by the window, alert for any signs of the law.

Settled and less concerned about the police nabbing me, I thought about Emmett and the things he had said about his father. I could relate to many of them: The alcoholism. The bullying and abuse. The preaching. And deep in all of that, I could relate to what appeared to be love he had for his old man. The concern that he felt, his need to help his aging father—even if he had been bullshitting me. I once had those thoughts. My father wouldn't have me back, either. So I never went back then it was too late.

I stayed close to a corner exit in the station while I waited for the bus. Despite prompts by the voices, thoughts of people and letters I'd written tumbled through my head.

When I boarded that 9:47 bus to Charleston, I threw a letter in the trash, one I'd written long ago. It was to Mary Kay Keller; I had nowhere else to send it.

Chapter 7

On the road ...
bus-bound on highways to byways, for twenty-six days, I roamed. Letters penned in cities along the way—Charleston, Lexington, Louisville, Raleigh, Cincy, and Chattanooga. Letters for suffering people, past mistakes their millstones. Letters for souls suffering for no damn reason at all.

Those in the shelters.
Disappointment clouded their eyes, never hate.
Worthlessness that metastasized in lonely cells.
A loneliness. The pain.
More than pain. Existence within the pain.
The nightmare of waking the next morning.
Or
The peace in not waking anymore.
In it all, a freedom of will and spirit and conviction.

Mine was a life outside that bubble.
I was not suffering.
I was running.
I was running to or from the one-person focus of my existence.
Questions, never answered.

Chapter 8

For weeks I crossed state lines, from South Carolina to Kentucky to North Carolina to Ohio. Over the miles I thought about Emmett. I never really decided whether or not he was telling the truth in his story, and quite honestly, I didn't really care. I wasn't interested in his past; I wanted to set him straight for the future. If he lied, he was probably not the first and, most likely not the last. Regardless, I was going to keep writing those letters.

I ended up in Chattanooga mid-morning on Thanksgiving Day. After the brittle-gray cold of Cincinnati, the hospitable warmth of the Tennessee holiday sun was a welcome change, one for which I was truly thankful.

A matronly traveler—wrapped in a long, heavy, fire engine-red coat and sitting solo on a plastic bench, bags at her feet—was kind enough to give me directions to the nearest shelter. "It's a good five-mile walk," she'd warned, but with time on my hands I took advantage of the sun and fresh air, neither of which are regularly found on a bus. Holiday window-shoppers and families walking off turkey and dressing crowded the sidewalks. I greeted all with a smile and a tip of my cap, to no response. When I reached the shelter, my smile faded. The kind lady had not bothered to mention that the homeless shelter was for seniors with mental issues. Despite theatric appeals worthy of a Tony Award, I was denied a stay. The staff there quickly assessed my need and graciously offered a ride on their shuttle after

no SHELTER for GUILT

it completed its daily circuit, taking guests to holiday events around town, scheduled to return around 3:30 or so. The men's shelter, Humanity Mission, was closer to mid-town and another seven-mile trek, but waiting three and a half hours didn't appeal to me. Given it was a holiday, the need to be in line early dictated my decision to walk. With the aid of a crude map the staff penciled out for me, I hit the pavement.

The route meandered via busy highways and into residential neighborhoods. The tease of browned turkey and spiced pies filled the air and memories of family feasts warmed my heart. My mother in her cranberry-stained apron and dad carving the bird assisted by a three-finger pour of his favorite Wild Turkey. I'd keep my distance, eyes affixed on the annual TV football classic between the Packers and the Lions, my quiet time, a relative calm before the storm I knew would follow. But after a few miles, my route took me to my usual surroundings: manufacturing slums, rundown warehouses, pawn shops and fast food places.

Outside a corner burger joint, I spied two figures milling around a dumpster. As I watched, one guy climbed onto the back of another guy and, leaning in, pulled out two large black trash bags. I watched as they ripped open the bags and rummaged through the contents. I couldn't tell what they found, but both of them started shoving things in their mouths. Hell of a way to spend Thanksgiving, I thought.

Shortly thereafter, the splash of a blue-and-white light strobed across the restaurant wall, surrounding trees and the two shadows by the dumpster. The flashes triggered something inside me, then I made a terrible decision. But, before I could react, a voice rang out.

"Hold it right there. Drop what you're doing and put your noses in the dirt, flat out." The male voice came over a loudspeaker from a police car. "Now! Move!" the cop ordered.

Dressed in his navy-blue uniform with a three-inch black belt tucked neatly below a protruding waistline, the cop scrambled around the front of the cruiser, slowed, and sauntered toward the boys, one hand on his weapon and the other adjusting his belt buckle.

By the time I was close enough to be a part of the party, the cop had the two—both probably teens—standing, hands against the dumpster, legs spread-eagle.

"Whoa! Whoa! Hold on there!" I hollered as I jogged a little closer. "What seems to be the problem here, officer?"

Startled, the cop turned toward me, and as he did, he placed his hand back on the grip of his service pistol.

"I come in peace." I raised my hands so he could tell I wasn't toting a weapon. I spun my baseball cap to the side so he could see my eyes. "What did my boys do this time?" I asked, walking slowly toward the group. "I mean, these guys ... I keep telling them to knock off the bullshit and they're still out here pranking around. Just last week I had to drag them down off some telephone pole over on the other side of town."

I looked across and shook my head at the teens with parental disdain, but kept talking. "Daredevils ..." I said with my chest pumped up and arms akimbo, well within the officer's personal space. "Damn, when I was a kid, I did crazy shit, too. How about you, sir? You look like the type who might have been in just as much trouble back then." The cop wasn't amused.

I stepped back and nudged a finger into the cop's chest, well protected under his bullet-proof vest.

no SHELTER for GUILT

"Careful, sir. Step back. Assaulting an officer is an offense," he warned. His thick neck grew thicker as he leaned toward the radio microphone on his shoulder. "Code 8, 10-20 is Cyprus and Yardtown." He pointed at me with his chin, "Are these boys yours?"

"How long have you been on the force? I mean you can't be but, what ... thirty? Shoot, when I was—"

"Sir, I asked if either of these boys belong to you. Are you the father of either of them?"

I shook my head.

"Sir, I caution you that you are interfering with an officer of the law in the execution of his duties," the cop said, head cocked to the side. He looked away, toward the teens, and motioned with his arm. "You boys come over here. Sit on your hands. One right there." He pointed. "And you, right over there." He pointed toward a spot thirty feet away. "Face away from each other and be quiet. Don't move or make a sound unless I tell you." The boys, visibly shaken, stumbled over each other as they fumbled about to follow the cop's demand.

"Oh, pardon me for not introducing myself," I said moving opposite the boys. "Folks call me Chili. Just kinda goes with me wherever I go, so I call myself Chili." I gestured a bit with my hands flat out, sort of rolling them around each other, a little abracadabra trying to make something disappear.

"Sir, please back off. Let me continue."

I leaned back, wide-eyed, with my hands blocking my face. "Ya know, those flashing lights present a real danger to my health. They're disturbing my peace. What do you say you turn those damn things off?"

The teens chuckled; the officer didn't. He stuck out his neck and glared at the boys while he closed the distance

49

between the two of us. "Sir, I have no idea who you are, Mr. Chili, but these boys are trespassing and stealing, and—"

"Trespassing?" I dropped my hands. "I don't see any signs that say, 'Keep out.'" I stretched my arms to either side, ready to be nailed to a cross. "Hell, I'll bet those guys inside that restaurant couldn't care less what goes on outside those doors. Now, I grant you, they may want the boys to come inside and buy their food rather than dumpster dive for leftovers out here."

"Sir. They're diving, they're stealing. It's against the law. So, I suggest you mind your own business. Walk off and I'll do what I'm paid to do."

With the sight of most cops I made myself scarce, vanished. But this guy seemed wet behind his ears, a rookie stuck with holiday duty nailing two kids for his solo arrest, so I persisted.

"Could I maybe talk to you man-to-man like … just for a minute?" I started to walk away, curling my finger in the air motioning for him to follow. He didn't take my lead so I stepped back toward the guy. I sensed from the squint in his eyes that he was not pleased with either my presence or my comments. I mirrored his squint and his stare while the Vigilantes whispered in stereo, as in good cop, bad cop.

Tell him to kiss your ass.

You need to get as far away from this guy as soon as you can, like pronto.

He's going to arrest your ass and send you up the river.

Don't give him any reason to haul you in. Beat it. Now!

The cop's full of shit.

They've been looking for you.

Grab his gun and blow his brains out.

No! Your brains.

I rubbed the back of my hand across my mouth to cork an outburst. Without another word, I backpedaled the distance to his squad car, never taking my eyes off him. With my foot on the rear bumper, I continued.

"Say, hey, when was the last time you had something to eat?"

The cop stopped pestering the kids and looked my way.

"Donuts?" I asked. "Two, maybe four, early this morning? Maybe another while you were driving around?" I cupped my hands around the sides of my mouth to project my voice. "Probably had a sub or Philly cheesesteak or a smothered hotdog or something for lunch? Or, are you a tuna guy? Tuna's good for you, ya know. But gotta watch that mayo. Nasty stuff."

The cop gave me his full attention. He shuffled his feet, adjusting his wide uniform belt with a gunslinger's quick-draw holster that now hung lower on his hip. His bulk blocked my view of the boys. I stepped around to the side of the car and sat on the trunk lid just above the rear wheel.

"Anyway, see ... these boys are on the streets. They don't get much food. They don't have money to buy food. You ever been hungry? I mean, hungry-hungry? I mean, haven't had a meal or anything to eat for, let's say, days?" I peeked inside the cruiser and saw a nameplate on a clipboard. "Seriously, Officer Gilbert, you ever been hungry? Doesn't look like it."

"Okay, sir, this is your last warning." He snorted.

"And ... didn't I tell you to turn off the damn lights? They're making me sick. Are you going to do it or do you want me to?" I walked around the back of the car to the driver's open window and leaned in.

"Sir, get away from that car." He took a few steps in my direction, stopped, and looked back at the boys.

I moved back to the rear, pulled my hat back to the front but lifted the bill so he could still see my eyes. I lost my smile when I asked, "You ever sleep on a park bench? You ever sleep under the stars? I mean other than say, Boy Scout camp?"

I dropped the tone of my voice an octave and slowed my delivery for effect. "In Nam we slept in rice paddies. When I was a Navy Seal, we didn't sleep for days. We humped scuba gear in rucks and got in the water, swam five miles or so, and slapped satchel charges on the bottoms of tankers in Hai Phong. Great stuff. Ever blow up anything? Cool as shit." I laced my fingers, cracked my knuckles, and crossed my arms in front of my chest as I leaned against the car. "I'm sure you're just a pretty boy. Young. Strait-laced and all. Gotta keep that image up, right? How long did you say you'd been on the force?"

"Sir ... I'll say this again ... I'm in the middle of an arrest here and—"

"Maybe you aren't listening to me, Officer Gilbert," I challenged, taking a few steps toward him. "These boys don't need arresting. They need food."

"Another outburst and I'll arrest you for interfering with an arrest."

I chopped my argument into bite-sized thoughts so my friend in blue could swallow them. "Goddamn it, the food or whatever's in that dumpster is going to the dump. It's waste. It's discard. It belongs to Mother Nature. Mother herself told me she doesn't give a shit. In fact, if you'll walk inside with me, I'll pay the management for whatever it was these boys ate."

I pointed toward the dumpster. "Come to think of it, by them taking food out of the dumpster, they're decreasing the operating cost for the restaurant. Maybe we should go in and demand the manager pay these boys for minimizing his dump fees." I turned back and pounded my fist on the trunk lid, pointed at the officer, and pounded the car again. "Don't you know, Americans send almost two hundred metric tons of trash to landfills every year?" I walked over and snatched a couple of smashed drink cups with the restaurant logo off the pavement and hurled them frisbee-style toward the cop.

"Sir, I'm warning you ..." he said, heading toward me looking back to keep an eye on the boys.

"Trash increases four percent per year. Four and a half pounds per person per day. In twenty years, it will be seven pounds per day. We live in trash. It's all trash, everywhere." I rummaged around the lot for more evidence to sling at Gilbert. His walk was slowed by his sagging pistol belt, worn like the rookie he was. This Town Clown didn't give a tinker's damn about the teens or their plight. All he wanted was to make an impression on someone, his boss. Hauling in two kids on a holiday. That's dedication above and beyond for a new guy trying to make a name for himself. The more I agitated him, the more flustered he became. And the last thing I needed to be doing was to be playing games with a cop, but ...

"For Chrissake, man, it's Thanksgiving. Have a heart." I whaled on his car with the bottom of my shoe, first his tire, then the bumper. "Damnit, put yourself in their shoes. It's not," kick, "fun. It's not," kick, "easy, ... and you're just adding to their pain." As he approached the cruiser from one end, I rotated around to keep him on the opposite side of the car. "Give them a warning and let them go." Round and round we went in our version of musical chairs. I stomped, jumped up and down, and flailed my arms furiously. "I'll buy them a fucking meal, a little Thanksgiving something. You know, pilgrims and Indians, turkey and pumpkin pie, dressing and sweet potatoes, all of that. You should be goddamn thankful for what you have, and let these boys be thankful for what they find, little as it might be. Come on. For this one day. This one meal." I joined my hands in a pitifully pious altar-boy appeal.

Officer Gilbert was tired of the game. His face puffed up, fatter than his original fat face. He was set to haul in the kids. My Thanksgiving thoughts didn't seem to have any impact on the matter. He walked back toward the boys, told them to stand, and marched them over to his cruiser. I watched and listened, but kept my distance. He put the boys in the back seat of the squad car and looked back toward me.

I took a step toward him and he said, "Stay where you are." I kept walking toward him. He moved to draw his weapon. "I said stay where you are. You take one more step toward this vehicle and I'll put you in the back seat with them."

I stopped. The cop got in the car but didn't drive off. He turned to the back seat and talked to the teens. I couldn't hear what he said or how the boys responded. Gilbert rattled on for quite a while before the boys opened the car door and walked over to me.

"He told us you should take us inside and buy us that meal you promised." I looked back toward the cop. He was watching. I nodded with a tip of my cap.

The boys and I turned to go into the restaurant. Before I stepped away, I took another look at the cop and yelled, "Happy Thanksgiving, Pilgrim!"

I saw the cop reach for his radio mic. The squawk in the speaker came through loud, followed by Gilbert's voice, equally loud. "I gotta 5150 here. See what you can find on a guy that calls himself Chili." He turned off his flashers and drove away.

With the chance that the dispatcher would find my name somewhere, I worried Gilbert would be back. I hustled through a bag of burgers and fries with the boys—not exactly the turkey dinner Mom would have served them at home. They finished and left. I ordered a strawberry shake and headed out the door at the exact time Officer Gilbert reappeared.

"Hey, you. Chili. Stop," he yelled, crawling out of the cruiser door.

With his words, I was off to the races. I tossed my shake into a bush by the door and sprinted in the opposite direction, away from the cop. The more he hollered for me to stop, the faster I moved. I headed away from the restaurant toward a line of trees that never seemed to get closer despite how hard I ran. Gilbert pursued, alternating between yelling at me and talking into his hand-held walkie-talkie. By the time I hit the woods, Gilbert's belly got the best of him. He reversed course and headed back to his car. The tires screeched as the car bolted away from the curb. I slowed to listen for the siren; it faded. It seemed he was headed away from me, but there remained the chance he would stumble across me later. I checked my map and headed for the Humanity Mission to join the line outside the doors before they opened.

Turned out, the shelter was a converted distillery and smelled like one, even outside. Across the street, a graying man in an open, olive-drab field jacket leaned his chest against the handle of a grocery cart filled with trash—possibly, his personal possessions—as he nudged it along the gutter of the pavement. His hair was nothing short of a bush, uncovered, atop his head. He wore thin jungle fatigue pants with cargo pockets bulging on his thighs, exposing his butt cheek through a hole the size of an apple. With fingerless gloves he tugged the cart over the curb and parked it up against the building. Without the cart to support him he shuffled forward using the wall of "Brewski's Liquors and Such" for support. When he couldn't open the door, he shook on the cage that covered the glass. He poked his nose between the bars on the windows. He went back to the door, rattled the bars several times before kicking it, and went back to his cart.

Conscious that Officer Gilbert might reappear, I paced in and out of line, but made a point not to lose my place. Sudden movement inside a window on the second floor above the liquor store caught my eye. I saw a face behind that barred window. *Maybe the store owner, or a tenant? Or a cop, one of Gilbert's buddies. And what if it's a sniper?*

I wasn't taking any chances. I slipped behind the guy ahead of me to hide my face and shield myself from a direct line of sight. How many times had this happened? And nobody ever believed me. Someone. Someone was always watching. Someone with their beady little eyeballs on me. It was only a matter of time.

A sick feeling came over me. I plopped down with my back against the shelter wall, out of the sunset winds, careful to remain hidden behind the legs milling around in front of me. The others around looked my way and teased me up and down the line. I scanned the sidewalk, then buried my head in my hands. One of them, somebody in that line, was definitely after me. Someone—undercover—would pop up and arrest me. Slap me behind bars. I could never survive jail. It was like Emmett had said. Constantly waiting for abuse. The threats. The fear. Mentally, there was no way I could handle it. The voices. The Vigilantes told me. *End it,*

no SHELTER for GUILT

somehow. A knife? A noose with bed sheets? "I am so fucked. My life is fucked," I said to myself. "I should be out there soaring. Up there with the birds, soaring, but I'm not. I'm here, in this god-forsaken line for the umpteenth-time. Same bunch of guys. Different faces. Different places. All down on their luck. They're all down and out but they're all better off than me. Worthless. I'm worthless. Fucking worthless," I muttered to myself. "Can't even hide worth a shit. I need to hide. I can't hide."

When the shelter doors opened, I didn't move. I sat there, on the pavement, totally oblivious to all the movement around me. Neck-deep in a quicksand of dread, my mind raced.

"I shouldn't have done it. I should have listened to him. I should have bolted," I thought, oblivious to the movement around me. "I should have just listened. If I had, I wouldn't have killed him. He wouldn't be dead. I wouldn't need to run. If I weren't running, I wouldn't be in this line. But I can't stop. I need to keep moving."

The guy behind me kicked me square in the knee with the toe of his cowboy boot. "Move up, man. Come on." I couldn't get up. My head remained buried between my knees. When others started yelling at him, he shook his head and passed on by. As the line passed, a shelter worker physically lifted me and tucked me in at the tail-end of the line.

Inside, the residue of charred oak barrels and the caramel drip of whiskey, familiar as it was, no longer excited me. Waiting to sign in, I noticed a bulletin board covered with business cards offering day jobs. A small sign in the middle caught my eye: IF YOU ARE GROUCHY, IRRITABLE OR JUST PLAIN MEAN, THERE WILL BE A $10 CHARGE FOR PUTTING UP WITH YOU. I was definitely out ten bucks.

"Chili?" the guy at the desk asked after I put my name on the guest list. "Sir, I need your full name."

"That's it," I said with scant strength to open my eyes and none to raise the corners of my mouth. "What you see is what you get."

"Hmm ... Chili. Yeah. Okay. Yeah, I heard someone talking about you earlier. May be looking for you."

I'd never been here before. Didn't know anyone in the place. Certainly wasn't accustomed to hearing that someone was looking for me. Definitely not words I wanted to hear.

"If I remember who it was, I'll let them know you're here," he said with a smile. "Have a good night." I thought about Officer Gilbert.

Paper cutouts of cornucopia flowing with corn, pumpkins and colorful leaves positioned on the tables did little to hoist my spirits. The giant room had the makings of a medieval banquet hall plunked in the middle of a grand chemistry lab with stainless steel tubing, copper pipes, and polished tanks ranging in size from breadbox to ginormous. Long tables ran end-to-end down the center, draped with white plastic tablecloths. In the back, a serving line offered a traditional feast with all the trimmings. In one corner a group of early arrivals clustered around a black-and-white television to watch the football game. Others milled around as groups and singles. I went straight to my assigned cot. The guy next to me threw his bag onto his. It bounced and fell on the floor with a thud.

"Hey," I cautioned with a dreary look at the guy.

"Shut up," he fired back. He proceeded to throw things randomly around the floor to annoy me further.

When the volunteers hollered that it was chow time, I stayed flat on my cot. Food or the chit-chat at the table didn't interest me in the least. Who needed to eat? Just going to get hungry again, then eat again anyhow. Maybe. And the bullshit chatter of who won the jackpot for the day or the best spot to hang your sign. Such bullshit. It was all bullshit. Sitting around talking about puny shit, about nothing. I didn't need it. Besides, my brain was fogged with thoughts of ending all of this—the running, the hiding, the existing.

"Aren't you going to eat?" a female voice said. "We have a special Thanksgiving dinner over there. Plenty of food." My forearm covered my eyes, blocking the bluish-white light of the old vapor lamps high in the rafters. I pulled my arm away. The face behind the voice looked down on me with a smile. She was a babe, maybe early thirties, a little younger than me. Her expression and interest sparked a flicker of excitement that faded just as quickly.

"No, thanks. I'm not hungry."

"Not hungry? It's Thanksgiving!"

I put my arm back over my eyes without saying another word. She left. I stayed on the cot for quite a while, not sure how long; it could have been days, for all I know. A crackling thunk from a speaker at the far end of the hall jolted me out of my daze.

"Test. Test. Test one. Test. Sound check. Test. Test. Sally sells seashells ..." Next, a few chords on a bass guitar and rhythmic, tinny clangs of a cymbal added to the noise. I rolled to my side, leaned on an elbow, and pushed myself into a sitting position on the edge of the cot. Upright, I massaged my brow with my fingertips and explored the source of the racket through narrowed eyelids.

Two guys stood next to a third behind a microphone stand on a platform at the end of the hall. Each had a guitar strapped around his neck. A fourth sat behind a drum set. The guitars started with a reverberating, heavy, deep background behind the electrifying twang of the third guitar.

Then, with a roll-up from the animated drummer, one loudmouth behind the mic screamed something totally unintelligible into the mic in a miserably fake British accent. What followed was an apocalyptic din that exploded in the hall. The amped voice of the angry screamer tortured the microphone with noise that rattled the stained concrete floor. It was difficult at first to name the tune through the feedback-squeal of the speakers. Words sunk in over time. The group sang—or attempted to sing— "Sgt. Pepper's Lonely Hearts Club Band." My hands plastered over my ears reduced the volume but did little to harmonize the voices, and nothing to stop the squeal. The longer they sang, the more the lyrics slurred to an angry thrum.

Seated, I rocked on my cot. Eyes closed. Ears firmly clenched between my hands. Two words echoed—lonely hearts. Louder and faster, repeated, over and over. My brain boiled. The urge to run up on stage, rip the plugs out of the amps, and punch my foot through the drums—but the total sum of my energy was only enough to flip my stomach. I needed quiet. I needed to get away.

The Vigilantes voices swelled, louder than the band. *Crawl out of here now, you wimp. Oh no. Oh no. It's too far for wittle Chili. Heck, the staff would stop you. They would sit down and cuddle up to you with their soft voices and try to reason with you. Besides, the doors to this place are locked. Nobody leaves the shelter once you are in. Rules.*

The bubbling in my head was ready to burst. Behind closed eyes I saw my heart floating outside my body. It was a gory mass, a blob. Pulsing and pounding, getting bigger by the minute. The amps squeal seemed to say, "Dive, dive, dive." Between the squeals, my heart pounded in my ears. I rolled onto the floor and hid face-down under my cot, my head buried beneath my arms. When the song ended, the squeal disappeared. The foursome, without a word, launched into their next song softly, quieter. I remained on the floor, slowly recapturing the rhythm of my breath, now exhausted and numb.

The cute shelter woman from earlier returned. She sat there, above me, silently. She waited a good while. When I didn't emerge, she left without a word. The band played on.

Chapter 9

I remained under my cot, safe, through the night. After lights-out, I listened to the clunk of the second hand of a wall clock the size of a semi-truck tire tick through every tock of every minute of every hour. My brain seethed with bits of squandered actions and haunting inactions and unfulfilled dreams of my life. Flashbacks of Officer Gilbert running toward me in a *Chariots of Fire* slo-mo replay, his service pistol flopping at his side. He came closer and closer, while I seemingly ran in place, all narrated by the Vigilantes.

He's got you, you dumb bastard. You're screwed, you fool. Hear those sirens. Outside. Cops coming. No, wait, they wouldn't have the sirens on, would they? They'd sneak in, quietly. Snatch your ass up. But what if it's more than one car? They might surround the place. Block all the exits. Shit. Trapped. Wait. No, there's no way they know you're here. Or is there? No. But the guy at the desk—he said somebody was looking for you, looking for Chili. Someone inside? He said he would let them know you were here. They know.

I had to get away.

The morning staff volunteer making her rounds was taken aback to find me on the floor. Without as much as a greeting, a smile, or a nod of thanks I crawled out from under the cot, grabbed my backpack, and bolted to the door only to find it was chained and secured with a padlock. I pounded on it, first with my flat hand then with my fist. Finally, I kicked at it, hard.

An elderly gentleman in chinos and an oversized argyle sweater approached. "What's the problem here?" he said calmly.

"I need to go!" I huffed. Frustration forced my eyes to bulge and nostrils to flare.

"I'm sorry, sir," he said, his tone straightforward, "we don't open the doors until seven. You'll need to wait."

"I'm having a panic attack. I need to get out of here. I need to go. I need to go now!" I heaved.

"But, sir, maybe someone here can help with—"

"You don't understand. Nobody understands," I screamed. "I need to go, now! Please, please, please, please, please," I begged, "please open the door. Now! Please!" I squeezed my head. Suddenly, something came over me. I grabbed the guy tightly by his shoulders and shook him. "Open the goddamn door!" I bared my teeth. With a sigh, I let the guy go, and I wiped my hand over my face and began to hyperventilate.

Keeping his eyes fixed on me, his face iced over in terror. He reached into his pocket and pulled out a ring of keys. His nervous hands dropped them. He rushed to pick them up, then fumbled for the right key. When he unlocked the door, I burst through. The chains slammed hard against the door as it rebounded off the outside wall. I was free.

The pre-dawn blackness was cold, dry, undisturbed, and void of any police presence. The stillness resolved my state of mind and silenced the chaos of the previous night. Though I could breathe again without pain, the urge to hide under a park bench or burrow a safe place in a thicket remained. Time, and only time, would settle the torment in my head. The feeling wasn't new; I'd been in this dark place for a long time. My relief would come in one of two ways— being rid of the incessant chatter in my head which, by experience, I knew might take days, and leaving this place. Eyes half-shut fighting the lingering pain, I retraced my steps to the bus station where the next bus out of town was bound for Birmingham.

Holiday travelers heading home monopolized the cracked-vinyl seats on the bus. Usually I could find a spot away from others and be alone, an occurrence that carried a high correlation to the fact that my time between showers was measured more often in weeks rather than days. On this trip, with only two seats open—one alongside a would-be sumo wrestler and the other next to a pencil-thin guy—I opted for the latter. Before the bus hit the highway, before even the briefest of introductions, my seatmate—Jimmy Pickett, a proud, talkative native of Turkey Knob, West "By God" Virginia—launched into his life story and sermonized about Thanksgiving.

He said he was twenty-nine but he looked ten years older, maybe more. By appearance, he was a meatless guy who had lost the tooth lottery. The teeth he did have were overlapped and decayed which gave him a smile that resembled a pile of Scrabble tiles staggered on end. His eyebrows looked like wooly caterpillars marching across his forehead. Unshaven, he sported an additional tuft of chin hair that bore a striking similarity to rusted steel wool. He never seemed to care that I maintained a distant stare. I didn't need conversation. I had plenty overlapping in my head.

"All these damn people on the bus. I'll bet they is all going home. Had their fill of turkey and gravy and going back home, stuffed. Where's home for you?" he asked in a voice coated with nicotine and an accent nurtured by mountain life.

"Don't have one," I replied in a quiet monotone.

no SHELTER for GUILT

"Don't have one? What ya mean you ain't got no home?"

"I'm homeless."

"Yeah, me too ... and glad of it. Been that way for five years. Folks kicked me out when I was nineteen. I was working in the mines with my old man, but they found out I was smokin' weed and lost my job. Old man said I weren't living in his place no more if I was smoking dope. See, Franklin, my old man, were a miner, but got injured and never really recovered. Has that black lung stuff, too. Sickest bastard you ever saw, but still goes down in the hole. There wasn't much around there 'cept the mine. I couldn't find a job. Then ... then knocked up this little tease. She told me she was eighteen when she weren't but fifteen. Her old man told me I had to marry her. I wasn't buyin' it, so he told the sheriff. Ended up in prison for rape. Spent four years and two months in the Huttonsville Correction Center back home."

"Tough," I said. I then made the biggest two-word mistake of the day. "Why Birmingham?"

"Oh, I ain't going to Birmingham. I'm getting off in Gadsden. Hookin' up with another buddy I know from the Center. He's got an auto body shop there. Says he can show me some things so I can work for him."

I nodded as I turned my head to avoid his cloud of ashtray-breath. He was quiet for a short minute, a comforting reprieve.

"You believe in God?" he asked, seemingly unwilling to enjoy the silence.

Stunned by the topic, I sighed, "Yeah," my brief reply with hope for more silence.

"Not me. And all this Thanksgiving crap. I thought about all that kinda shit in the Center. I mean, why do people have to be thankful? I ain't got nothing to be thankful for. Not then. Not now. I mean, life sucks if you think about it. Really. I ain't got two cents to my name. Spent just about all I got from pawning my old man's tiller to get the ticket for this bus. You ain't never seen life like there is in a mining town, has ya?"

I ignored the question. He refused to let it rest.

"It ain't good. And ya can't leave. Where ya going to go? Hell, being in jail was my best time. Ate good. They taught me some things. I still ain't got a diploma, but I can take that GED test sometime. And ya know what? If there is a God, all this is His fault. I ain't seen Him never help me. Not in school. Not in the mine. Not with that judge. And certainly not with that little bitch. I mean, why she has to tell me that she was old enough? Then, why she has to get pregnant? She coulda done something to get rid of that baby, too. See, God just screwin' with me. I ain't never get no break."

"But you're getting a job, so that should—"

"That ain't God. That was me. God supposed to drop things on you. Just give you them things. I had to go find me that job myself."

It pained me to reply. I turned in my seat to face the guy. "Well, did you consider the fact that once you were in prison, God was actually taking care of you? He gave you a means for food. For training. For friends. You didn't get those for yourself. Well, maybe the friends, but God just dropped all the rest of that on you, as you say."

Not that anything I said was enlightening or anything, but Jimmy didn't respond. I think he had to untangle the concept. And for fifteen blissful minutes, he was quiet. For another hour after that, I was not so lucky. Fortunately, his sermon ended in Gadsden.

no SHELTER for GUILT

After too many stops along the route, we arrived in Birmingham at sundown. I made no attempt to find a shelter. I had no need for company and writing letters was the furthest thing from my mind. I wandered the streets until I found an abandoned building. I used a brick to bust out a window, crawled through and spent the night. Ripped-up carpeting and foam pads laying around provided a nest for sleeping and cover for warmth. Nevertheless, my every exhale formed a frosty cloud.

In my waking moments, I wrestled with how to track down Mary Kay Keller, if that was still her name. Where to look? Who to call? Leads? All without leaving a trace for the law to track. My concentration fogged by the Vigilantes.

Rarely, but when I could, I slept, exhausted from the battle within. I was either too weak to stand or found no need to. I didn't leave that nest. Curled in a ball, I didn't go outside that building for days. In those hours I could hear things, everything. The hum of the wings of flies. Clicking sounds of parking meters. Trees talking amongst themselves, talking about me. My only comfort was a restroom but no utilities. At times, I was too weak and disturbed to get up. The mere thought of moving, walking, became a process of hours, trying to remember the basic mechanics of putting one foot in front of the other knowing full well that the energy it would take would rob from my strength to open my eyes. I relieved myself in my nest while I stared, unfocused, plucking splinters from cracks in the rotten wood floor. Holding a thought was like gripping smoke. From a rumble to a roar, the battle for dominance in my head continued. In my hideaway, I argued aloud.

"I'm not crazy. I'm not crazy."

Oh, but you are.

"Bullshit. I'm not crazy! It's the sickness. I need ... I just need—"

You are crazy. Don't fool yourself, man. You killed him. It's that simple.

"I just need to find her. Once I find her, I can end this and—"

Ah, another victim? She'll be mad.

"I'll tell her ..."

Tell her what? That you killed him?

"Shut up. Damn it. Just shut up. Leave me alone. She'll ... she'll—"

Ah, so wrong. Did you ever consider that he's not dead? It's Chili that's dead.

"Bullshit. No. Shut up. That doesn't make sense. I'm here. He's dead. I killed him."

She'll tell you. She says Chili is dead.

"No. No. Leave me alone."

You don't have the guts. You're too weak. A pussy just like your old man. How did you handle him, huh? You're a pussy and she'll—

"Leave me alone. Just ... just shut the fuck up and leave ... me ... alone."

I yelled. I screamed. I cried. Yet the voices drilled deeper, reaming my brain, no stopping them. All I knew was there was no life with or in the voices. They were just that, voices. Endless voices. I bawled myself to sleep, time and time again.

After three days, maybe it was four, pangs of hunger chanted for food, but the thought of facing people held me in the nest. Two days later, late in the evening, I slipped out. At a deli counter in a grocery a few blocks away, I grabbed a handful of ketchup and relish packets. They appeased my growling hunger, if only for an hour. By the seventh day, the Vigilantes had won their victory. They told me. *Leave.* No destination. No closer to finding her, I left only to satisfy the voices.

The next bus out took me to Mobile, but not far enough to outrun the cloud of melancholy. The voices locked me away with no visitation. People were a threat, talking to them or smelling them, even seeing them. For several days I hunkered down near the cruise line terminals in a shed filled with sandwich-board signs for destinations like Jamaica and Cozumel.

Eating was not a necessity. On days when thoughts of food teased my imprisoned appetite, I swatted flies as I rummaged through the trash from cruise liners, then dined with rats that shared my private isolation and darkness. One rat in particular—one I named Attila—would eat from the palm of my hand and sleep by my feet. Having slept only three times in the previous two weeks, when the rabble in my brain quieted, I crashed for twenty straight hours and returned to the bus station.

Chapter 10

I arrived in Charlotte late on December 13. In my planning, I'd had no hope of finding Mary Kay Keller there, but it was the next bus and I'd been there before. I knew the shelter—the "Little Room in the Inn Motel," a reclaimed five-and-dime store—where I had once spent a few nights. It was relatively close, a couple miles at best. Time was my biggest concern. My shoes were in no shape for jogging, and for that matter, I wasn't either. I made good time but as I approached, I ran into a motley group headed away from the shelter.

"Ain't no room in the Inn, if that's what you're thinking," one yelled.

"Where's everybody headed?" I asked as I changed course to follow them, remaining on the opposite side of the street.

"The woods. Another starry, starry night. Be colder than a witch's tit, too," came the response from a guy whose drawl matched the Confederate flag on his cap.

The gaggle traveled with the usual banter of the streets, nomads headed nowhere. One lugged a worn-and-torn military duffle bag over his shoulder. The number two man carried four trashcan-sized plastic bags, most likely his life's possessions. The mouthy guy across the road had a backpack with a large plastic bottle of pop sticking out of a pouch.

no SHELTER for GUILT

Not long after I ran into them, the road curved to parallel a rail yard. Tracks packed with flatcars, boxcars, and assorted tankers ran a dozen rails wide on the other side of a rusted, ten-foot chain link fence breached by rolled-back sections of wire. The night wind swept a reminder of diesel fuel over our heads. As we walked, the woods on our left thickened to jungle-like. Absent streetlamps, we relied on the memory of a guy up front. Eventually he left the side of the road and walked into the woods. I crossed over and joined the rest.

We stumbled down a beaten path with the aid of moonbeams cast between fractured clouds. Deep within the thicket of shrubs blanketed by kudzu vines, we could hear voices and pounding metal-on-metal. In time, flickers of light pinpointed a number of campsites.

The first sighting was a guy pitching a tent near a semi-permanent shelter constructed out of wooden pallets and tarps. The place had a door framed with wood. The door itself was a collection of campaign signs, the type posted on lawns or near busy intersections. Candidate names and photos with their catchy election slogans— "Burn Crime: Firestone for Sheriff" or "The Buck Stops Here. Vote for Elaine Doe" and others. On one side of the hooch a propane tank fed a hose to the interior. The place had a roped-off side yard with lawn chairs near a well-used firepit.

Deeper into the woods, campfires cast splotchy phantoms of city lights. Shadows, of mostly men, popped in and out. The few women we passed were obviously attached in some way or for some reason to the men they were near.

By inspection, this was a semi-permanent encampment where discarded materials—as well as people—provided shelter, but offered very little more. Communal shelters with tarps tied into adjacent tarps. Corrugated sheets of metal roofing latched to trees with wire or twine formed rough sheds, some covered with tarps, others with thatched roofs of branches woven with plastic.

Despite the ramshackle appearance of things, the area was clean. Trash and excess hung in bags from trees. The cloud of diesel that had hovered overhead earlier released our senses to the smoky campfires and stew pots. As the wind shifted, it also carried the unmistakable stench of urine.

Campers and tent dwellers exchanged greetings with familiar faces in our group. The duffle-bag man dropped out of line and joined a burly, bearded guy in a heavy down parka nestled near a campfire. I continued with two others, but not much farther.

We passed a small site where a waif of a girl argued and kicked at the shins of a Neanderthal-looking older man, fighting to free herself from his grip. My travelling companions remained silent and continued on. I stopped, sensing this was more than a one-sided lovers' quarrel.

"Hey, what's the problem here?" I said as I strolled closer. They were standing outside a lean-to where a small fire smoldered. They turned to watch me approach, the girl tugging to free herself. "Do we need some help here?" I said.

"Yeah, bright eyes, could you shove that big, fat nose of yours up your ass and walk on down the path there?" the guy said. He let the girl loose, took a step in my direction, and stopped short.

I held up my palms toward the guy. "Just trying to help out here, fella. Don't mean any harm. Just thought I'd offer."

no SHELTER for GUILT

"Ain't nothing wrong, pal." He squinted against the campfire smoke.

"And your lady friend here? She okay?" I looked beyond the girl's male spokesman. She shook her head, but didn't speak.

"She's just fine. Now, git along little doggie." He turned his head to look at the girl.

"But—" I started.

The big guy caught me with a sucker punch just below my temple on the left side. I reeled backward, stumbled over a pile of firewood, and landed flat on my ass. Cartoon birds flew circles over my head. A gong sounded through my ears as I sucked in a deep, startled breath. I rolled to an elbow, shaking my head. My vision cleared and I could make out the torn leather boots of the guy who had decked me as he moved closer. I crawled backward a short distance then shook my head a second time. When I did, I heard a clap of thunder in both ears. It didn't come from the weather, it moved me into an entirely different world.

The ape's boots vanished. My peripheral vision was gone as were my other senses. There were no more campfires. No more stoves. No moonglow. Even the people were gone, all except one—the oaf that'd hit me. I could feel it. Him and me, mano a mano. Gladiators in the Colosseum. I shook my head once more. This time the gong disappeared. I heard a bell and an old-time familiar jingle. *Friday Night Fights are on the air!*

I stood and took a step backward. He lunged to grab me. My quick left jab surprised his nose with a crack and a fountain of blood. The guy bled like a pig. He grabbed his face then dropped his hands. I took the opening to slam a second punch to his gut. He folded over at the waist and took my knee square to his chin. He wobbled and fell flat on his back. Three moves, two seconds, one knockout. The fool never saw a one of them.

Before he moved, I stepped up and kicked him square on the side of his ribs. "You mess with Chili, you get the heat, asshole." I pumped my fists in the air, hopping up and down around his head. He moaned and rolled to his side. "You want a piece of this?" I pounded my chest with my right fist then kicked dirt in his blood-smeared face. I crouched down on a knee, close enough to blow in his ear, where I could smell the stink of his blood.

When he rolled to his back, I stood with my toes just shy of his skull. His eyes were askew, half-opened, enough to see me standing over him. Before he could refocus, I hopped into the air and came down hard with both knees skimming his scalp as they crashed to the ground. He choked and I laughed.

"Get up, mutha," I said, backing away. "I ought to bury your ass right here. Get up, you pussy. Come on. Make my day."

I looked over at the girl. I couldn't tell if she was about to cry or laugh or scream or, maybe, join in the fight.

A crowd grew. "What the fuck you think you're doing, man?" said a voice from beyond the smoke of the smoldering fire. Another: "Get up and punch his lights out, Ben." There were rumblings of many more voices. A guy pushed his way to the front of the crowd and stepped toward me. I turned, shrugged my shoulders a couple times, tilted my chin up, and, staring at him, shook my head ever so slowly while I opened and clenched my hands into fists several times. He stepped back.

Before anyone else got involved, I grabbed the girl around the waist and pointed her down the path I had taken into the camp. She reached for a rust-red wagon by her leg.

I pushed her hand away then grabbed the wagon, full of bags, bottles, and a filthy pillow. We stumbled off into the dark, trees now swallowing the scant moonlight. Behind us we heard cussing and yelling from the camp, but nobody followed.

When we got to the road, I picked up the pace, strutting like the cock of the walk. By then the skies had cleared. We raced down the street under the moonlight. I rambled on and on about kicking ass while I pointed out constellations above. The girl struggled to keep up. Finally, I turned, dropped the handle to the wagon, and waited.

Her hiking sandals, more duct tape than anything else, failed the test of speed walking. In the dim light, her gaunt cheeks were rosy-red, a price paid for keeping up under the burden of her layered look—a T-shirt, hoodie, and an oversized down jacket that looked like it had survived a serious knife fight. Best I could tell, the girl was a scrawny kid prematurely aged by the street. Knobby knees, simply bones wrapped in chapped skin, poked through holes in her jeans. Her dirty blonde hair, matted and tangled, swung down around her face like vines in a jungle.

"Holy shit. Did you see how I whaled on that sucker?" I grinned and slapped the side of my leg as she approached. "Wham! Bam! Thank you, ma'am. Your buddy there didn't have a clue what hit him." I bent backward at the waist, looked heavenward, and with arms outstretched, I let the world know, "I am Chili! I am the greatest. Bring it on. Come one, come all."

The girl stood there, her eyebrows squished together, shaking her head with doubt. A familiar electricity energized me. I shuffled circles around her, shadowboxing the spirits of the street.

"I'll take all comers. One at a time. Hell, I'll do two at a time, I don't care. Ha! Let's get it on." Adrenaline is such a beautiful thing; it had me soaring. "Come and get it, you punks! All you punks, come and get it," I hollered, looking back toward the woods. I kissed my knuckles on both hands. I ran to the middle of a trash-covered empty lot near where we had stopped. Hopping up and down I said, "Let's set up a huge tent. Yeah, a circus tent. Here. Right here. Yeah, a tent with a ring. And ... put a sign out. Charge people to come and try their luck—you know, go a round with me. Come take a bite out of Chili. I am the greatest!" I spun with my fists high in the air, stopping momentarily to take a bow to the imaginary crowds on each side of the lot.

She gawked in disbelief as I continued to shadowbox in the glow of a streetlamp. My arms were pistons, snapping out and back fast enough to snatch the moths nearby. I juked left then right, light on my toes, ducking with one-two combinations, then slid back, bobbing side-to-side. Pop. Pop. Pop. Movements all blurs. When she didn't move, I strutted back and shadowboxed circles around her, grunting animal sounds.

"Watch it!" she screamed, covering her face with her hands. I stopped with the punches and switched to jumping jacks, hopping sideways in a circle around her. She peeked through her fingers, turning slowly to keep me in her sights. In time, she lowered her hands, breaking into a qualified smile.

From the middle of the field I darted about, waving my arms and flipping my hands, handcrafting my colossal charade. "We can set up shop ... here. Have our own little fight club, I mean." I dashed across and made an X in the dirt near her feet. "We can challenge guys, take bets at the gate, here." I raced back to the middle of the lot, jabbing at air, making mincemeat of the night. "I can bust some heads. We'll make a bundle," I yelled. "Beats making cookies for a bake sale, doesn't it? How's that sound, huh?" I grunted. "Need some cash? I could use some cash." She shook her head, sporting a face of amused bewilderment. I laughed.

After a while we moved on. We walked several miles, away from the woods. No place to go. I didn't care. I yammered on and on; the conversation was all mine. Every once in a while, I would look over and notice she was a few steps back, half bent-over, struggling to keep up. A wooden bench with a precarious slant provided a rest spot. Metal plates, plastered across the back, promoted local businesses with sun-washed advertisements—Charlene's Hair Stylists, Thimble Tires and Auto Repair, and The Donut Hole. I stopped blabbering and looked over as she approached.

"Hey, I haven't even asked your name. I'm Chili, but I guess you kinda figured that out by now."

She grabbed the back of the bench, flopped down leaning forward and, without looking, replied, "Debra. Debra Trixton. Everybody calls me Trixie." She hesitated. "Is that really your name? Chili, I mean." She chuckled with a grin, still catching her breath.

"Well, my nickname, it's my handle. My callsign, you know like 'Rubber-ducky' or something."

"So, what's your real name?"

"Robert White. Bob White. Like the bird. Chili's much better."

"Yeah, I agree," she said with a smile. She leaned over, with her elbows on her knees, searching for air.

After a brief silence, I looked toward her. "Are you all right?"

She nodded. Her eyes, cupped by the sockets of her bony cheeks, bulged as she inhaled, deep and often.

"I'm sorry about all that," I said.

She bobbed her head in agreement.

The brisk walk and marathon monologue had mellowed me. My heart rate settled. I was tired, thinking clearer now. "Punching your friend, I mean—"

"He wasn't my friend."

"Oh ... well ... okay. And all my talking there. I do that sometimes. It's just ... I don't know. Something comes over me and ..." I stopped explaining and lifted my head to look around. I noticed a low-slung two-bit motel across the street. Eight units with door access to a dimly-lit gravel parking area lined with weeds.

"You up for spending the night in that place?" I pointed toward the "vacancy" sign that flickered on the marquee across the way.

She hesitated. Her expression flattened, her eyes set further back but her cheeks slack and relaxed.

"No, I'm not suggesting ... Separate rooms, sure. I have a little cash. Government disability check, you know."

She stared at me, then at the motel and back at me with no expression on her face.

"Sure."

In all honesty, we hadn't seen a single car drive by since we left the camp and started our journey down the road. Nor had we seen any people. It was as if mankind had been wiped out and we were the only two humans left. I wondered if there would be anyone at the desk to check us in. With only two cars in the lot, there had to be vacancies.

A gust blew trash tumbleweed-style across the parking lot as we entered the motel. With a tap on the call bell at the front check-in window, a night clerk appeared from behind a partition. He was short on words. "One room or two?" he asked as he eyeballed us with a hollow *Twilight Zone* stare, shifting his gaze between the two of us without moving his head.

"One," the girl replied quickly with authority. I flinched and looked at her. She nodded. I echoed the nod to the clerk.

"Pay up-front. Room's $39.95 a night. Cash. Card costs you five bucks extra, service fee. No TV. One with a TV costs ten bucks more." He stepped back from the barred window; undoubtedly, he'd detected neither of us had bathed in quite some time.

"No TV," she answered.

She wasn't shy. Maybe tired, but not shy. Not the least bit timid, either. She looked over to me. I reached for the cash I carried in a holster around my ankle, gave the clerk two twenties and he passed me the key. In the true nature of the motel, the key was attached to a large, yellow diamond-shaped plastic tag marked with a worn, circled number seven embossed in the middle.

Access to the room was from the parking lot, with no interior hall. The inside was more of a pit than the exterior of the building. When I sat on the edge of the bed it sagged so much that I nearly slipped off; nonetheless, a bed was a luxury, much improved over a cot or a bench or the woods. Motel nights over the past three years had been few and far between. In my weakened state, tonight I needed one. It was obvious, as Trixie slipped off her coat and melted into an overstuffed armchair in the corner, that she needed one too.

"I could use something to eat. How about you?" I offered.

"Sure," she replied. Her voice was softer than when she had talked to the clerk. Breathy. Weary. Exhausted. She didn't lift her head from the back of the chair; she just stared at the ceiling.

"Food. How about pizza? Let them deliver. We don't need to go out."

"Sure. With pepperoni."

"Your choice. Right about now I'd eat the box, too," I said.

The small chest of drawers had a three-ringed binder of brochures and menus from local restaurants. When I grabbed it, I noticed it was tethered to the harvest-gold princess phone on the chest. I picked the first pizza menu and picked up the phone to dial the number.

"Front desk," was the response rather than a dial tone.

"Sorry. Trying to order a pizza."

"You need to dial eight first to get an outside line ... just like the card by the phone says," the clerk replied in a condescending tone. "Local calls only. No long distance."

As I dialed again, Trixie walked back to the door where I'd left her wagon. "I can help pay for the pizza." She grabbed an oversized canvas handbag and dumped the contents on the bed. The pile of assorted items included a tiny plastic doll; a fake rose; a keychain with three keys; bobby pins; a small notebook; a penlight; and tampons. With the exception of the tampons, everything she touched caused her to pause, emotion reshaping her expression. "Here, here's some money for the food. It's not much," she said, extending her hand with a wad of bills.

"No. Dinner's on me. You can buy next time, how's that?"

Visibly relieved, she returned the bills to the pile, grabbed a rubber band, and tied her hair in a lump behind her head. She started to place her personal trinkets back into her bag.

"Memories?" I asked as she picked up the doll from the bed and fell back into the large chair. The frosted globe ceiling light created very dim conditions throughout the room, yet ample enough light to notice the tears in her eyes when she rested the doll on her knee. With thumb and forefinger, she held each of the doll's hands in a playful dance, adrift in a world of her own. I had grown accustomed to spending time and hearing stories of the homeless men, but never a woman. It appeared life on the street was different.

"Something special?" I asked. I pulled out the wobbly desk chair, spun it around and took a seat with my chin resting on my arms across the back of the chair.

Trixie played with the doll, staring at it as if she were the doll's partner, the two of them enjoying a brief happy moment.

"This doll is the one thing I have that's real," she said. "It was my baby's."

She put the doll in her lap facing out, without releasing its tiny hands. She sat there briefly before she eased herself back into the chair, clutching the doll to her chest and closing her eyes. Gently, she rolled her head from side to side across the back of the chair, as if she were rocking herself, or her baby, to sleep. When she stopped, she opened her eyes in a distant stare toward a spot on the wall over my head.

"I'm a failure," she confessed in a matter-of-fact tone, then added, "I've failed at everything." She let the doll drop onto her lap, covering it with her hands. "I tried a career. Failed. Tried marriage. Failed." With a note of desperation in her voice, she added, "I tried motherhood." She stopped for a long, poignant communion with the doll. "Failed." She rolled the doll face-down next to her in the chair, hidden from her eyes and voice. "I've even failed at suicide ... three times. My entire life's been screwed up. And now ... this is it."

Her eyes wandered to find the corner where the ceiling met the walls and talked, uninhibited. "I wasn't a bad kid, but after my dad ran off with some chick, my mom remarried a guy named Frank Ballard ... an A-number-1 premium jerk. That bastard had it out for me from day one. He abused me in every way possible. He was in my head and all over my body, inside and out. He'd come home from the bottling plant where he worked and, if Mom wasn't home—she was a nurse and worked crazy hours—he was on top of me. If I refused, he'd smack me and threaten that if I told mom, he would kill both of us. My only safeguard was dance. I'd go to the studio and work on my ballet for hours to avoid the creep. I was safe there. I loved it."

Trixie, who had only met me hours earlier, was offloading her innermost thoughts and fears. Private things. Maybe she didn't care what people knew, or maybe she really wanted someone—me, for some reason—to know. I was willing to listen. She closed her eyes and kept them closed when she continued.

"I was good, good enough to be asked to join a dance company when I graduated from high school. That was my ticket away from Frank Ballard and his bullshit abuse. I moved in with a guy I met, Dillon Rawls. Shit, eight months later out popped little baby Lila. To this day, I am not sure who the father really was, Dillon or that asshole Frank."

"Dancing? Before the baby? After? That doesn't seem like it—"

"Well, our little happy family lived on. While Dillon watched Lila, I danced. In the company they were super strict about body shapes. They told me I needed to lose weight if I wanted to be in the corps de ballet on stage." She stopped and looked down at the doll. "So, after the baby I went on a crash diet. I stopped nursing because I stopped eating. If I ate anything at all, I purged it. Fasting, laxatives, diuretics, even enemas. Yes, I lost weight."

Her movements were slow and graceful, her ballerina heart in motion. Cuddling the doll, she rolled it over, hiding it at her side. She stroked its hair. Over and over she repositioned the doll as she talked.

"Trouble was, I lost too much. The head of the company said I was too thin. Now I was afraid to eat, afraid I would gain too much and they would drop me. And they did. That's when I started drinking."

The mention of it, the drinking, was a seismic crack in my own story. My father, then me.

"That became my next screwball mistake," she continued. Her eyes wandered from her hands, to the door, to the ceiling, but never toward me. "I drank sunup to sundown some days. Day after day, I drank to forget. The more I drank, the less I remembered. I couldn't take care of Lila because I was drunk all the time. Dillon went to court to gain full custody. He won and kicked me out. I wasn't able to do anything on my own and sure as hell was not going back home. So, stupid me, I joined a cult."

"A cult? What? How? I mean, surely there was someone, anyone, a friend to go to for help. Why—"

She smirked. "One of the guys I drank with regularly handed me a flier about Heaven's Gate. Ever heard of it?"

I shook my head.

"They were preaching a new salvation, a new place not on Earth but a new, higher level of existence, a kind of alien life. La-di-dah." She rolled her head. "It got me thinking. I had to get away from the existence I was in, so I joined. We traveled in vans to recruitment rallies around the country. I gave up everything—family, friends, what possessions I had. Plus, by doctrine, I had to give up my sexuality, my entire individuality. So, I did. I was a rag. I stopped drinking. I lived their lifestyle for over two years. Gradually I realized that they would never follow through on any of their promises, so I returned to this reality, to life back in Atlanta."

She pulled the rubber band off her hair and ran her fingers across her scalp, pulling at the nest of tangles and wiry clumps. Finally, she looked at me. Not a casual glance, but a fixed stare, wide-eyed and cold. "I was scared. Scared that the cult would come after me. In my dreams, I heard them chanting. Their special words. I heard them praying. It was all so real. I could feel them. It was almost as if they were there. All of that fucked with my head. I was scared, real scared. I had no place to go."

She kept rubbing her hands and looked down again. She squinted to fight back tears. "I couldn't go home," she said, her voice choked with emotion. "I tried to contact Dillon to ask to see Lila but he never responded. I did learn he had given my little girl to my grandparents. Then ..." her face wrinkled. She chuckled, then leaned back and looked at the ceiling again. "I tried cutting myself." She continued to chuckle and wept. "I cut my wrists, but not deep enough. I bled a lot, but not enough. I cried for days. Still a loser, another failure. I tried a second time and failed again. Tonight, when I saw the blood on that dude's face, I freaked out. I remembered there was this cult ritual, this crazy ritual where people cut themselves and then smeared blood all over their bodies. We always did it standing naked in a field."

She rolled her head against the back of the chair again, seeming to quietly fight her need to cry with her will to laugh. I waited. And, as I waited, so much of my own life jogged through my head. How I admired my father for what he was but hated what he did. How I left home and never returned. How my cult-life was so different yet similar to hers. And the haunting dreams that recalled so much. And the message the Vigilantes constantly delivered. *Kill yourself.* Nothing I could say at this point would matter. She needed to let it out.

"There's nothing I can do. Nothing will fix this," she said. She curled her arms over her head as tears dampened her cheeks. "I've been robbed. I've been raped. I can't trust anyone, especially on the streets. The cult is still out there and if they find me ..." She clenched the arms of the chair, inhaled, and forced the next words in a steady stream. "I have no job experience, so I peddle sex." She exhaled deeply. "I turn tricks. Yeah, that guy ... that guy you decked in the woods; he was a one-timer. I sold sex to a bunch of guys, some in that camp, others around town. Started with a sleezy pimp. He caught me cheating on him. He beat me, really beat me. Kept me out of work for weeks. I couldn't go back to him. I found a few johns, enough to get food. But I had to get out of Atlanta so I worked my way here. That's it. I gave some poetry I wrote to some chick. Said she could get it published and would send me money, somehow. Haven't seen a penny."

"Poetry? What kind of poetry? Can I see some?"

"No. I haven't written any since then."

"But you write? About what? Your life? Conditions? What?"

"I wrote about the two things I know. Dance and dreams of a little girl."

Trixie pulled her knees up to her chest and wrapped her arms around her legs. Tears lingered on her cheeks. I watched her and listened to the hum of the heater by the window, white noise to drown my thoughts.

In time, she sighed and ran her arm across her face. "Sorry, I don't mean to cry, but it never ends. Huh, real life sucks!" She massaged her forehead with her fingertips. "All I want ... all I want is to see my baby." Amid sniffles, she added, "I want to hold her. Play with her. She's going on four now and I haven't seen her since she was just about to turn one." She rubbed her hand over her nose. "She was trying to walk."

She managed a grin, though tears continued to dribble down both cheeks. "She's probably running up a storm by now. I want to see her smile. I want to hear her laugh. I want to take her to see Santa to see if she cries or pulls his beard or what. I want a chance for a real life. Not this ..." She trailed off and wiped away the tears. Finally, she looked down and smiled a bit. "But thank you," she managed, "for bringing me here. I didn't mean to drag you into all of this, but you asked about those things in my purse. They're all I have. All I can trust."

A knock on the door startled her. "Delivery."

Chapter 11

The pizza delivery kid had probably lied to get his driver's license. A beanpole who was over six-three, popping bubblegum, ball cap turned backwards, he stood there with music cranking out Guns N' Roses from earphones connected to what looked like a box of crayons dangling from his belt; actually, it was a Walkman. He handed me the pizza box and I handed him the cash. Before he turned to leave, he stuck his nose in the door and peered around the room. With the flat of my hand, I shoved him out and closed the door in his face. I placed the pizza on the bed.

Trixie avoided looking in my direction after her story. To respect her privacy, I looked away—though, out of the corner of my eye, I could see her in the mirror. Still in the chair, sniffling with her head bowed, she held her doll, stroking its hair slowly. What I saw wasn't an addict or cult member. I saw a mother, a daughter, a victim. She was human. I thought of my own mother and how much she had cared for me when I was young. I thought of the torture she endured as a wife. I thought about how much I missed her. Trixie wanted what life had stolen from her. She wanted to be with her daughter.

"Quite a story," I said rubbing the back of my neck, not yet comfortable enough to risk a look at her. "You're a brave gal."

She hung her head low. She put the doll aside and fiddled with loose threads on the strap of her handbag. Her head shook ever so slightly in disagreement.

"Maybe I can help," I offered, still looking away.

It took her a while to say anything, and without looking up she said, "How?"

"I write letters. I write some poetry, too, but letters are sorta what I do as I travel." I waited for a reply. When none came, I continued, "Suppose ... suppose I write a letter, a letter you can sign. It would be a letter from you to, say, your mom, to explain how you've grown. To ask her if you can come home."

"No."

I was prepared for some pushback. I'd experienced it from the others before, but her response was bold and loud.

"It can't hurt," I said. "In my mind you've nothing to lose. I write it, I mail it, she gets it and says yes, great. If she says no, or doesn't respond, so be it. You're not out anything but a signature. I'll provide the stamp."

"No," she replied, louder than before. She paused a long pause as I turned to face her. She pulled her bag to her chest, raised her chin, and slowly turned toward me with a set jaw and furrowed brow. "Not my mom. Send it to Mimi and Papa. Send it to my grandparents." She looked away.

I took a comforting breath and nodded to show I understood. "I'll send it to whomever you like."

"My mom would drag me back to that bastard Frank," she said. "My grandparents will understand. I've been too screwed up in the head to explain anything in my life to them."

"Let me try to explain for you. Worth a try."

She turned and looked at me as rivulets of tears lined her face. She didn't smile, but the tension in her face was gone. She pressed her palms to her eyes as she sniffled.

To avoid any further meltdown, I opened the box on the bed. "Ready for some pizza? Dive in. I'll see if I can find a vending machine for some pop."

I wasn't away long, but by the time I returned to the room, a third of the pizza was gone. I handed her a can and pulled out a slice for myself. She guzzled her drink and eyed the pizza.

There are only a few select activities, better than eating pizza, that can happen in a motel room.

"Go ahead, have another slice," I said.

When she reached for the box, she belched and sat back quickly.

"Oh. Excuse me," she said with an embarrassed grin. We both laughed.

"Mind if I take a shower and soak for a while?" Her cracked lips finally offered traces of a smile.

I smiled in return. "Be my guest. Soak as long as you'd like. We have the tub all night."

She closed her eyes, took a deep breath, and struggled to work her way out of the sagging chair.

"While you do that, I'll start on that letter for you. Take your time. Relax. I'm a slow writer. Actually, a slow thinker."

She grabbed her handbag, another bag from her wagon, then another slice of pizza before she closed the door to the bathroom. The lock clicked.

I heard the shower for probably five minutes and listened to the tub fill for minutes more. Over the next twenty minutes, only the occasional sound of an unfamiliar tune in a relaxed hum broke the silence from the bath. There may have been other notes or noise, but I was immersed in letter writing, the sound of my pen competing against the heater chugging in the background.

A good while later, Trixie appeared wrapped in a bath towel, escorted by the fragrances of floral shampoo and bath soap. "Sorry. I didn't have any clean clothes," she said, the towel neatly tucked high on her chest, flapping loosely on her thighs.

Though no longer anorexic, she carried no extra weight on her twiggy ballerina frame. Her legs were sticks, halved by bony knees. Her blonde hair, previously matted and snarled, lay damp on her shoulders. She sat on the far side of the bed with her legs crossed, her knees protruding outside the edge of the towel. My attention was piqued more by the scars on her wrists than by her legs.

"Mind if I have some more pizza?" she asked.

"No. Go right ahead. Help yourself. I think I'll get cleaned up." I stood and grabbed my backpack. "Here. While I shower up, why don't you take a look at this and tell me what you think." When I reached forward to hand her the letter, I snuck a deep breath of her freshness. At the bathroom door, urged by two thoughts—whether she would read the letter, and her scent—I looked back. "No holds barred. I can change any of it that you don't like."

"Why do you do this?" she said as I closed the bathroom door.

I stepped back out "What?"

"Why do you write letters? I mean, why write letters for strangers?"

I took a step back, dropped my pack, and leaned against the wall facing her. I placed my hands behind my head and smiled, enjoying her perfume and thinking how to answer. She kept her eyes on me.

"I guess ... I guess it goes back to when I was a kid. I took a lot of shit from my old man. He was a preacher, but also a closet alcoholic. I was his punching bag. Most times he didn't know what he was doing. To protect myself I learned to box. I'd take shots at my dad, but I never wanted to hit him. I respected him too much. I mean, he was the guy who taught me to catch a pass and shag a fly ball. He showed me how to tie my shoes and shave. Besides, he didn't know what the hell he was doing. Most of the time he was too drunk. But one time, I saw him punch my mom. That's when I hit him. The only time."

"When it was time for college, I needed references. Teachers wouldn't step up. My grades sucked and I'd been a bit of a wild-child—family life, ya know. So, I approached my old boxing coach, Grady O'Sullivan, a real corker; that was his term. Irish Catholic. Tough as nails. He said he saw a lot of himself in me. I needed three letters for admission. I could only get the one. His letter was so good, it got me into college in Louisiana."

"So, you went to college? The boxing coach got you in?" Trixie asked as she twisted strands of her damp hair.

I nodded. "Grady checked out to the Great Beyond the year after I started school. I write letters because I owe it to Grady. He ... his letter ... changed my life, such as it was. I want to do the same for others. My payback to him."

"Have you always written letters? For strangers?"

I nodded. "Well, not always. For three years now."

"Just wondered." She picked up the letter I'd given her and started to read. I lingered a bit, looking, then stepped into the bathroom.

The shower was a heavenly respite. How something as simple as water rolling off of my head could rejuvenate me totally—body, mind, and spirit—amazed me. The flow. The tactile sensations. Drops individually launching from my eyelids. The pulse of water on my face. The soothing warmth on my neck. Endless hot water, the panacea for pain, inside as well as out.

Out of the shower, the scratchy bath towel proved barely long enough to tuck in on my hip but draped just low enough to cover my dangling parts. I walked back to the bed. Trixie's towel had relaxed quite a bit at the top.

"Sorry. I guess the bath made me hungrier?" She smiled with a sheepish squint. "I left you the last piece, though."

"That's all right." I chuckled. "Gotta keep my youthful figure out here on the road, you know." When I patted my stomach, my towel popped loose, but I caught it and tucked in the end. "Comments on the letter?"

She was all smiles. "I like it. Mimi and Papa will be impressed if they really think I wrote it. I did make some changes. I tried to make it sound more like me, personal, you know."

She handed me the letter. We discussed her changes, back and forth, as we hammered out her intent. Her edits made great sense. She was right, they added a more personal tone. When we had agreed on everything, she grabbed the pizza box and dumped it over by the small trashcan in the corner. She came back to the bed, dropped her towel, and climbed in under the covers.

I coughed. "Uh, I think I'll work on these changes and clean this up before I sack out. I'll sleep in the chair, don't worry."

"No, no. Sleep here. In the bed. You paid for it," she urged. "I won't bite."

I raised my eyebrows and smiled. "Let me fix this first." I turned off the bedside lamp and returned to the bathroom.

I lost track of time while I reworked my first attempt. When I finished, I crept back to the sleeping area as quietly as possible. After placing the letter on the small dresser at the foot of the bed, I wrapped myself in an extra blanket from a shelf near the bathroom and settled into the cushioned chair in the corner.

"Come on. Get in the bed," she said in a forget-about-it voice.

I hesitated, but knew it might be a long, long time before I would test the luxury of a mattress. A slice of streetlight slipped through the curtains. I dropped my towel on the chair and slid into bed, holding my own on the edge of the flimsy mattress.

I nestled onto my right shoulder, lost in thought. Arms tucked under the pillow, I stared into the bar of white at the curtain. Minutes later, the bed tilted deeper to my side. Trixie gently squeezed my shoulder and eased herself closer until her skin fused with mine. She was still. Quiet. Warm.

My thoughts—of her earlier words, her life story—all confused me.

"Aren't you lonely?" Trixie asked.

"Sometimes ..." I paused. "Isn't everyone?" It wasn't a question I needed answered. I thought of Ben Keller. I thought of Ben and me. Then, I thought of his wife, Mary Kay.

Trixie fell silent for a few minutes, then asked, "Life. You said life as it was. What was it? What was your life?" she whispered, her breath against my back.

Her touch electrified my body, but her words shocked me even more. "It's not important."

"Why? I told you my story. Why won't you tell me about you? I mean, we are in bed together."

It wasn't what she said that moved me, but how I heard it. A soft voice laced with the sugary-comfort tinge of Atlanta southern belle. I didn't want to talk about me, about anything. For that moment, and though it may have been the lingering effects of the shower, nothing, nothing in the world could have been better than being this close to a woman. I hadn't asked for it. I hadn't asked for anything, least not a friendly ear to confess my past, but the words still slipped out.

"I killed a guy."

I felt her body tighten, but she didn't move.

"He was my best friend."

A cloud of silence hovered over us until her words broke through. "Is there more to your story?" she said hesitantly. "There must be."

The perfume of the shampoo, the warmth of her skin, her gentle touch, all of it—for whatever reason, I told her my story, the whole story, the story I'd never shared. How I met my friend in college. How we did everything together. How I admired, even idolized the guy. Enjoyed his family. His wife and kid. And the end, how he begged me not to do it. I told her how I wanted to make things right with his wife. I wanted to simply show her how sorry I was. When I finished, the silence drifted into the room once again.

Trixie didn't talk for the longest time, understandably so. Finally, she spoke. "You've got to find her," she said, with no further explanation.

I rolled to face her, cautious to maintain a space, still aroused. "What?"

"I said ... you've got to find her, face her."

"His wife?"

"Yeah. All of this, the voices, the faces in windows, everything. They're all you. Your guilt. None of that's going away until you look her in the eyes."

"Wait. What? Is that the typical cult response? The grab-the-world-by-the-balls universal cure sorta thing?" I cringed; my words suddenly didn't seem fair.

She tucked her chin, but let her eyes drift up toward mine. "Yeah. Sorta. Look, the voices feed you their bullshit propaganda, they isolate you with their threats. They control you. Those dreams? Those are the voices. It's their mystical manipulations. All of them seeded by the voices to keep you off balance, to make you think what they want you to think." She locked eyes with me. "If I learned anything from being in that cult, it was that running away with them wasn't the answer. Running away from them was. It was facing my mistakes. You need to end this, this running. You need to end it with her, find her. That way you'll break free, free of the voices. Seeing her will be your forgiveness. Face her. Tell her what you feel. You are the victim, not her. Like you just said, her forgiveness is all you want. To hell with everything else. I realized I need forgiveness from Mimi and Papa. Your letter. That's why I said yes to your letter." She broke into a smile. "Your letter is something I could never have written on my own. It's beautiful. Thank you."

"Wait. I can't. I told you, I killed ..."

"You need to face her," she insisted. Don't run from her—run toward her. Don't let her hide from you. Find her and face her. Deep down inside you know that's what you want—what you need to do. Do what you have to do and sort out the consequences later."

I rolled onto my back. It sounded crazy, but she was right and I knew it.

She reached an arm around my waist and snuggled closer without any more conversation. Her hand slowly worked its way up my arm, her chin nestling against my shoulder. Long fingers stroked my chest, building a heat recalled from years ago. I turned away. Her numbered breaths whispered slowly from behind. I shrugged off thoughts of my story, the years on the road, the voices that taunted me. All of that disappeared with the magic of her touch, inching pleasurably lower. I placed my hand on hers, held it gently, then moved it to the side of her leg. She rolled back slightly, enough for me to slide my fingers up the inside of her thigh before I pulled away. Once again, I lay still and listened to the hum of the heater, the only sound.

"I just wanted to thank you," she whispered, running her hand across my hip.

I took a deep breath to examine my feelings before I responded. "It's been an interesting night. I think you should get some sleep, here ... where you're safe and warm. We should both get some sleep."

She caressed my neck with an affectionate kiss, then rolled back through the dip in the mattress and slept through the night. I, on the other hand, lay awake, restless for hours.

When I finally fell asleep, I was haunted by the nightmare that followed me, seeds of the voices. I was in another world. Another time. Dead and looking down at myself, out of my body. Around me again ... flashing lights. Sirens. Images. The scene repeated itself, over and over. It wasn't a hallucination. I was asleep or thought I was asleep, but it was so real. So vivid. So familiar. I awoke in a sweat, my pulse racing. Sleep never returned that night.

The next morning, we walked to a nearby diner for breakfast. Neither of us talked much, sharing neither the

no SHELTER for GUILT

stories nor the heat of the previous night. Instead, we talked about the letter.

1987 Tallyho Drive
Grisham Park, GA

My dear Mimi and Papa,

    I made a huge mistake. I abandoned my baby, the child I love more than anything on this Earth. I saddled you with raising her. Please believe me when I say I am sorry.
    I was lost on a dark and lonely path. I have done unspeakable things to survive. I walked back from suicide three times, unwilling to make my misery yours.
    Overwhelmed and brainwashed by a man and his cult, I cried for God, yet all I heard was the echo of voices in my head. It was the loudest voice—your voice of kindness and caring, your love—that gave me courage to walk away from a life that would have forever taken Lila from me. I have overcome my fears of the past knowing of your love.
    Each day I was away I lost twenty-four hours of her young life. Her first steps. Her first words. Her first cry for Momma.
    I don't know that I can ever repay the time, but I will repay every penny you spent to make a home and a life for Lila,

my sweetness. I want to be her mommy, to raise her as my little girl. My bond with her will be stronger than the tide to the moon. I'll do everything I can to prove myself to you. I'll find a job. I will set the best example to raise her to be strong and healthy and happy.

    I will provide for her completely if you will take me back. Let me come home. I will listen to you. I'll accept your guidance and requests if you will share your heart and let me return. I will never let temptation and weakness pull me out of your lives and Lila's life again.

All my love forever more,

Debra

Trixie approved the final version, thanked me, and left.

Chapter 12

As thoughts of the previous night lingered, it dawned on me, among other things, that I'd failed to ask the true names of Trixie's grandparents; all I had were Mimi and Papa.

After wandering streets all morning, I found a comfy step outside a fashionable boutique where I could fly my sign with prospects of picking up needed cash in my cap. As hours ticked by, the foot traffic increased. The steady stream of people all gave me the usual—a stare, some with a comment, or, for most, a glance and a quick snap of their head, refusing to look anywhere but straight ahead. In the distance, maybe a few blocks over, I heard the faint sounds of a marching band against the thump-thump of bass drums. Curious, I jammed my sign into my backpack, retrieved the change from my hat on the sidewalk in front of me, shoved the money in my pocket, and fell in with the walkers, who quickly gave me space, extra space. Everybody was headed toward the beat of the drums.

As we moved, I watched a guy wearing an open peacoat over a pair of bib overalls and a flannel shirt come out of a burger joint up ahead. He was holding something wrapped in his hand. He peeled back a corner of the wrapping and took a bite. While he chewed, he rewrapped what he held in his hand and, after looking to see if anyone was watching, he gently placed it in a street-side trash can. He walked back to the building and took a seat on the sidewalk, resting against the wall, watching passersby. A moment later, as a crowd of older people approached, he returned to the trash can. He rummaged around inside the trash for a moment then, pulled out what he had deposited earlier. To watch him devour what he held was like watching an animal ripping its prey. The approaching group slowed and watched in amazement. A distinguished looking man in a long, heavy woolen coat and scarf, stepped away from the others and went up to the guy. They exchanged words, cordially, while the others watched. The older man escorted the ratty-looking guy back into the restaurant. A few minutes later, the two of them emerged and shook hands; the older man rejoined the group and walked off. The disheveled dude, who had placed and retrieved the food from the trash, now had a large meal bag in his hand, an obvious, sympathetic gift of the gentleman in the long coat. He carried the large white bag back to his spot against the building, pulled out a napkin, unfolded it, placed it on the ground, and proceeded to lay out three pieces of fried chicken, a huge burger, a very large sleeve of fries, and a tall drink. I didn't know whether to laugh or go slap the chiseler.

Like lemmings, the crowd on the sidewalk moved deeper into center city. My curiosity caused me to follow. As I walked, the march music I heard earlier transitioned to familiar seasonal tunes. of the Charlotte Christmas parade. I found a vantage point between heads and kids on shoulders in time to watch block after block of high school bands separated by floats from an unimaginable number of civic organizations, churches, and businesses until the guest of honor arrived. Dozens of little people dressed as elves danced and scurried side-to-side handing out red-and-white striped candy canes to the bug-eyed kids who lined the curbs. Atop an enormous float, buried in mounds of fake snow and littered with faux-gingerbread men, Rudolph led eight reindeer poised to bound from rooftop to rooftop, pulling a humongous red sleigh trimmed in ornate-golden snowflakes. On the back, toys and wrapped packages bulged from a red-velvet pack large enough to hide an elephant. Waving and laughing from the seat was jolly old Saint Nick himself, his coat front shaking like a bowl full of jelly. When the police car at the tail of the float appeared, I melted into the crowd and slipped away with the others, sharing the spirit of the yuletide and singing "Rudolph the Red-Nosed Reindeer."

I was several blocks from the shelter, with plenty of time to be in line for a cot, when the rain started. A strong wind out of the north swept in and cut through my weathered field jack stenciled on the front with "EGA" and "USMC." I'm not a Vietnam vet, but I can honestly say this one piece of apparel would never be considered surplus.

I remembered I still needed to mail the letter for Trixie. As I made my way closer to the shelter, I looked for a mailbox. Fortunately, I saw one in front of a drug store down a side street. The drizzle of rain increased and slapped the ground in a steady downpour. I jogged to the drug store and stood under the entrance way, out of the weather. I pulled out the letter and looked it over one last time. In my uncertainty, I had simply addressed the letter to Mimi and Papa. The letter echoed inside the mailbox when I dropped it through the slot. The hollow emptiness sparked something inside me: thoughts of Trixie and what she had said the night before. I had to face Mary Kay. I knew Trixie was right.

I took refuge from the angry rain in a nearby phone booth. Drops the size of marbles pelted one side of the booth; the other side was a rushing waterfall. The contrast was a visual depiction of an impulse growing inside my head.

I dropped a quarter in the slot and dialed one of the few phone numbers I could recall. It was the number I had dialed almost daily years ago. Before it rang, I hung up. I leaned my head against the payphone, the receiver still in my hand. Flashbacks of hundreds of calls just like this one, and the voice over the phone saying, "Hey, Chili. What's going on?" My best friend, Ben Keller. My stomach and heart locked my lips. I knew that voice wouldn't answer, but I wasn't sure what to say when his wife did, if she did. I had to know she was there.

I slid the coin from the return bin and deposited it a second time. After a deep breath, I dialed. "Please deposit forty-five cents," a message instructed in a calm, polite voice. I rummaged through the junk in my pockets to find the change. The phone chimed with each coin I deposited. Seconds later I heard the three-toned signal then the familiar voice recording: "We're sorry, you have reached a number that has been disconnected or is no longer in service. If you feel you have reached this recording in error, please check the number and try your call again." I let the recording play out then hung up. I was ready for the second call.

I grabbed the change from the return bin and dialed the operator for assistance. Searching my brain, I remembered the name of their neighbor and asked the operator to connect me. "That will be seventy cents, please." I dropped the same coins in the slot and waited. After three rings a voice said, "Chambers residence. This is Jeanna."

"Oh hi, Jeanna. This is Bob White. We may have met a few years back. I'm a friend of the Kellers. I just tried to call them. It seems that the phone has been disconnected."

"Oh, yes they no longer live there. You said your name was Bob White? When was the last time you talked to them? You heard about Ben, right? That was so terrible."

"Yes, Bob. Yes, it's been a while. I recently learned he died. Tragic. That's why I wanted to get in touch with Mary Kay. So, do you know where she might have gone? Where does she live now?"

"Well, I think, I heard Atlanta, maybe, or maybe Macon, but I'm not sure. I don't have any phone number or anything. It was kind of a sudden move and all. I'm sorry I can't be much help. So, I take it you must be a—"

I hung up before she finished her sentence. I was confused. My brain went haywire, again. A million thoughts raced through my head. Crazy things. Dribs and drabs of nonsense. How should I get there? Should I pop in or call her? Did the neighbor—what was her name— recognize my voice? What's the weather? Should I buy new shoes? What if she calls the cops? I need a car. What's so important about life? How should I do it? One thought stepping on the next, never finishing. Energy swelled inside me. It was Jeanna. No, Trixie. Her touch. The perfume. I had to move, now. I couldn't sit still. There was this fire in me. Growing. Burning. It was happening again. It was time, time to travel.

Chapter 13

Trixie had lit my pilot light. I disregarded her words and went for the heat. I dialed up that flame and went crazy-wild, on fire, living in the moment. Too hyped to sit around for a bus. I hitchhiked out of town. Picked up by a babe with yellow-brown eyes like a creature from the wild, I shagged her for days in the empty horse trailer she was hauling from Camden. Banged a maid a handful of times in a no-tell motel outside of Columbia and, on the eighth day, did a kinky red-head who picked me up driving a big rig to Augusta. I was living on sex and saltines.

A while back the docs at the clinic tagged me with what they called bipolar disorder. Said I wasn't nuts, just happened to get crazy-wild for a spell, then dead-depressed for an extended period. Kicker was not knowing. The episodes could be sparked by most anything, pop up most anytime. Up one minute, down the next. Up an hour or a day, down for days or weeks. It was always random. They had a long, involved diagnosis and a simple solution—medicate with lithium. Easy for them to say. The drugs made my hands shake, blurred my vision, gave me an itchy-rash on my legs, a constant upset stomach, and squirts of diarrhea. Sucked. My decision, years ago, to stop taking the pills was the best decision I had ever made. Off the drugs, I was anywhere from an unbridled stallion to a desiccated slug. I took my chances with the lows and highs.

Chapter 14

My face—cracked and wind-blown from walking against a freak Arctic cold snap—forced me to curtail my hitchhiking. I had to focus. I reverted back to the oft-travelled luxurious accommodations aboard the Greyhound fleet, although the ticket agent in Augusta nearly caused me to keep on trekking. Fortunately, the fire inside me which had burned so brightly the previous days had fizzled. My focus was back on finding Mary Kay Keller.

The agent, an older woman maybe in her sixties—probably too stubborn to retire or caught up in her power-position at the ticket window—gave me the third degree when I asked for the ticket to Atlanta.

"How fast do you need to be there?" she replied, pushing horn-rimmed glasses back up her nose.

I did a double take. "Makes no difference to me, just need a ticket."

"What in tarnation do ya mean 'makes no difference.' There's a direct bus, an express, and several other locals. They all cost different."

"Right. I get that, just the next bus headed out."

"Really? Sky's the limit, and time to get there's no factor? Must be nice." She looked at me skeptically over the top of those glasses.

I stepped back. All I needed was a simple one-way, one-seat bus ticket. "I really don't care. Could you please just sell me a ticket for the next bus?"

"Well, all right then." She pulled her glasses down a tad and looked me over for a second time, then pushed her specs back up and looked at the schedule tacked inside the window, then at the clock above the chart. "Next bus, headed to Atlanta, hmm, twenty-three minutes. Ticket's going to run you seventeen dollars and sixty-eight cents."

"Okay, I'll take—"

"But since you don't care when you get there," she started with bitchy sarcasm, "you can wait an extra seven minutes and catch the ten forty-nine local. Makes six stops. Cost you six bucks less. Only eleven something."

"No, I'll—"

She interrupted again. "Or, if you're willing to wait and hang around until half-past noon, there's a bus headed that way. Only three stops and will cost you a dollar less than the other local. Gets you in fifteen minutes after that other local, too. Great bargain for—"

Then it was my turn to interrupt. "Pardon me, ma'am. I just want to be on the next bus, thank you." I tipped my head toward her, looked all around, and whispered, "So ... imagine I just killed a guy and I'm running from the cops and I need to get the hell out of dodge, like pronto." I looked around again and leaned closer. "Mum's the word, okay? Let's keep this between the two of us." I winked. She pushed her glasses farther up her nose. "So ... please may I have that ticket on that next bus to Atlanta? That would be just fine."

She hemmed and hawed under her breath. I couldn't tell if she was chewing gum or had some nervous tic that caused her jaw to wiggle side-to-side. She kept looking back at me while she worked. Behind her she had a honeycomb panel with assorted colored tickets in various slots. "That'll be seventeen sixty-eight." She pulled a yellow ticket, then stamped it. Turning back toward me, after I placed two ten-dollar bills in the till, and she slid the ticket along with change under the metal cage at the front of the window.

I walked away. "Bus will be out that door," she hollered, pointing to the left. "And if you don't mind my saying so, take a shower," she added, a little softer but still loud enough to catch my ear.

My ride-of-the-day, the silver and blue bus with the Greyhound logo racing down the side, had seen better days. Like so many other drivers, my guy collecting tickets outside the bus door looked like he was the original, the one and only person to ever sit behind the wheel. His pants were long and baggy. In a fashion statement left over from decades prior, he puckered and cinched them around his waist with a too-long belt the tip of which hung a good foot below his buckle. His uniform—the typical short blue jacket, wide tie loose around his neck, and white shirt—may have fit him when he started, but had long since become oversized in his senior years.

I climbed the three short steps. Inside, a glittery bell ornament with a sprig of Christmas-tree fir hanging from his rearview mirror offered a welcoming yuletide bouquet though, halfway down the aisle, the seasonal scent of pine gave way to the smell of mothballs from the naphthalene deodorizer in the restroom.

The interior of the bus shared the same aged look of the exterior. Most seats were worn and cracked. I elected to sit closer than usual to the front. As soon as I sat down, I jumped up. The seat cushion was littered with cracked vinyl as sharp as punji sticks. I plucked out a half dozen or so and pressed the others flat.

The ride from Augusta to Atlanta, on a somewhat circuitous route—not quite as direct as the friendly ticket agent had suggested—was slowed further by an unexpected, freak snowfall. With only two days left before Christmas, the bus was packed with people and packages. A soldier with two stripes and a smile from ear to ear was headed off, probably on leave for the holidays. A young mother held a baby with Louis Armstrong lungs who cried at every stop. A crotchety old man with an ascot and scarf sitting in the back passed around a bottle in a brown paper sack with his "ho-ho-hiccup-ho" liquid cheer.

My seatmate was a grandmother from Detroit. Her daughter, a stewardess, had invited her for the entire holiday week. Grandma Schneider was loaded with what she called "the perfect present" for each of her three darling grans. Hot video games of the day: *Super Mario Brothers, The Legend of Zelda,* and *Ghostbusters.* After she waltzed me through her life story, I politely put my head against the window and dozed.

As I slept, I evaded the inner voices and dreamed about Christmas past, as a kid. The happy days when my grandmother visited and brought presents. The days—few as they were—when my father was sober enough to put on his red flannel suit and act like Santa. How he would drive to the hospital up the road in Portsmouth, visiting the kids in the hospital. I went along, playing the game, dressed as the elfish Santa's Little Helper. Seeing the kids smile when my pop went into their room was probably the best part of Christmas for me, because I knew my old man would be deep into the eggnog soon after, and that wasn't a merry sight.

The snow continued to fall after we arrived in Atlanta. The ride, despite interruptions from grandma in my ear, was a chance to relax and warm up a bit before standing in line for a cot. As it turned out, the Salvation Army ran the

no SHELTER for GUILT

Healing Shepherd Mission not all that far from the bus terminal. Nightly they converted their gym into a dorm and served a meal from a small concession booth-sized kitchen in back. With temperatures dropping fast, they opened the doors early, but still well after my toes had grown numb. My holey, holy Air Jordans were no match for the snow. Inside, the hot soup and pot roast supper with soft, overcooked vegetables, mushy potatoes, and thick gravy was just what the doctor ordered, sort of.

The following day, I considered hitting the mall to catch generous last-minute shoppers at a weak moment, a panhandler's Christmas wish. The enclosed space would also serve as a daytime shelter from the cold. Instead, I opted to hang out in the metro library. I didn't feel much like talking, and definitely felt no holiday spirit. Besides, I needed the time to focus on my search.

The reference desk was my first stop. There I requested a copy of the Atlanta phone directory. It didn't take but a minute, standing and scanning the names until I found a listing for Mary Kay Keller. Address and phone. *Merry Christmas.* I copied her numbers on a scrap of paper.

The usual and customary blessing of a library at this time in the year was the warmth. I moved to an overstuffed chair where I tried to catch up on Hitchcock, Sherlock Holmes, and *Sports Illustrated.* The Vigilantes would have nothing of it. They drowned out the classics and shaded the sports. A hazy image of Mary Kay Keller appeared and disappeared, page after page. I stopped reading and returned to plotting. I found a city map, the MARTA bus schedule, and the number for a taxi company.

By appearance, conditions outside had worsened and no doubt the temperature had dropped below freezing. Under stone-gray clouds, I left the library early to ensure a spot at the front of the shelter line. Snow, falling in blankets, brought back memories of snow days as a kid, free from school. The good old days when snow forts and snowball fights could last all day. Though the thoughts warmed my heart, they did nothing to warm the chill in my body. To beat the burn of the cold, I humored myself, scraping flakes into strange looking snowmen. Some had nubby arms; others had long noses. A few had large clown feet. I left them in front of unsuspecting businesses.

Blocks short of the Mission, I passed a gym. I hadn't been inside one for years. I walked back and stepped through the door, where a welcome air of analgesic and sweat quickly melted my frozen spirits and more. The place was one large steam room. Humid, noisy, and with the unforgettable lure of canvas. It was a boxing gym, the kind of place where I'd spent so many hours years ago. Heavy bags. Light bags. Speed bags. And, in the middle of the space, a full-sized ring—ropes, turnbuckles, canvas, corner stools, the whole shebang. Nearby, a sinewy guy with a shaved head squirmed to position his protector with his hands wrapped and taped. This is Christmas, I thought.

"Hey, can I get in a round or two?" I said, approaching the guy still fixing his gear.

"You ever been in a ring?" He looked me over with a scowl.

"Plenty of fights."

"No, not fights." He walked closer. "You been in the ring?" the guy asked again with a deliberate, deeper scowl. He was Latino or Filipino or something, about my size, though he had me by ten pounds or so.

"I've boxed some," I said, not pushing my previous skills or admitting I had been out of the gloves for over fifteen years.

"You got any gear?"

"No. Maybe borrow some gloves? You need a partner?" I asked.

"Yeah. I'm up next. My buddy's home with his kids. Grab stuff out of that first locker on the right over there."

I weaved around guys shadowboxing and others slapping punch mitts the coaches held to get to the wall of dented, green wall lockers. I dropped my backpack and field jacket and sorted through sets of protectors and head gear until I found ones that sort of fit. I took off my shirt. My shoes were soft soled, so I left them and my jeans on. All the gloves were fourteen ouncers, which worked fine. I heard the bell. The pair of boxers in a halo of a floodlight over the center of the ring had finished.

"Three rounds. Light with footwork. Chester, there in my corner, he'll work the bell. Two minutes, okay?" said my new opponent.

"I'm good." In my boxing days—active boxing days—three-minute rounds were the norm. I wasn't about to press my luck with any additional clock time. I was enjoying the warmth and thrill of doing something that had brought me so much joy so long ago. How did Santa know?

After the two guys in the ring crawled out, I split the ropes and climbed in. I went to the corner opposite Chester. I limbered up briefly with a few weak jabs, a few sloppy and slow upper-cuts, did a couple deep knee bends and turned toward the center of the canvas. I nodded to my unnamed opponent. Shortly after that, the bell rang.

The cocky guy opposite me strutted to center-ring. I strolled out to meet him, pounding my gloves against each other to make sure they were tight. I didn't have time to wrap my hands and nobody had bothered to tie the gloves. When we met, we touched gloves customarily, then stepped back. Chester jumped in the ring, pushed his guy back, and walked up to me. He grabbed my right hand and tied the glove; then he did the same with the other glove. While he worked, I watched his guy prancing around on his toes, sizing me up. Chester crawled back through the robes and rang the bell again.

My opponent opened with a few jabs. I returned a few. We were both right-handers, which was good; that meant we both circled in the same direction, usually to our left. He was light on his feet, a sign he had spent a lot of time in the ring. He slipped left, then shuffled a few steps right. His movement was smooth whereas I plodded flat-footed, following his lead.

He wasted no time before he hammered me with a one-two combination to the head. I retreated clumsily, beyond his reach, and shook my head to reset my blurred vision. He stepped in, ducked down, and landed a solid blow to my gut. On my empty stomach it felt like his fist came out my back. I bent forward, put my gloves on his shoulders and pushed him back. He skipped forward and exploded with a couple jabs and another punch that missed my chin. I rolled to my left and threw a glove that caught him in the ribs to move him back. After a pathetic volley of shots to his head and body, my arms began to burn. The light gloves now weighed a ton. Fortunately, Chester called the round with the bell.

Two minutes in the ring and I was sucking wind faster than a Hoover, but remarkably, there was no blood. In my corner, I collapsed on a stool I pulled in from the apron outside the ropes. I had no water or anyone for coaching or words of encouragement. With my legs outstretched and my arms—limp as over-cooked spaghetti—draped over the ropes, I struggled for air.

"Hey, chump, next round let's pick it up, can ya?" Chester hollered from across the ring. "I need my boy here to get a workout. He ain't even breathing hard. Give him some shots. You know, his head, a few to the belly. Try to get inside on him, if you can."

Oh, how I wanted to comply, but my focus at this point was solely on breathing. Simple survival. Surely, closing my eyes will allow more air to enter my lungs, I thought. And with luck maybe, just maybe, enough left over to pump up my legs so I could answer the bell for the next round.

Slow, long breaths. Exhale. A satisfying rhythm. Exhale. Recovering with my head bowed, chin against my sternum, it was clear my decision to celebrate Christmas in the ring was a bad one. I snuck a peek at my opponent. He was on his feet, dancing back and forth on his toes, pounding his gloves together before I heard the bell ring to start the second round. I hopped up.

My opponent made the first move. He tucked his chin deep, turned his shoulder, and tagged me with a lightning-fast jab. He backpedaled two steps. When I stepped in to meet him, he caught me with a right hook that nearly took off my head.

"Hey, chump," Chester yelled. "Do something. We ain't got all day." I assumed he was talking to me, not his boy.

With my gloves guarding my face, I sidestepped to my right before he caught me with two seismic shots to my stomach. I dropped my elbows to block my mid-section. Then the dude stepped in and slapped my face with his gloves. Not punches, just slaps. One on the left cheek, then a couple on the right. As the guy stepped back, the world around me turned black. A Milky Way of tiny dust particles flickered. It was a sensation reminiscent of my youth, a familiar scene.

I lifted my chin and looked across at the other boxer. Voices in the building buzzed in my ears. My vision blurred. I blinked and, in that millisecond, the guy I was fighting, changed. I saw the face of my old man. I remembered how he would punch me, then slap me around, taunting me, encouraging me to step up and "fight like a man." I stood and stared, my arms at my sides.

With his boy bouncing on his toes in front of me, I heard a voice—not Chester's—hollering, "Come on. Box! Do something." It was my old man, grinning, mocking me with a wink. Yelling at me. Then his face appeared behind the voice. This was my chance to give him exactly what he asked for.

I slipped my head to the right, crouched down, and countered with a solid right cross to my opponent's chin. Perspiration sprayed into his eyes; he wiped them with the back of his glove.

On my toes now, I ducked to the left and smacked him with a straight left hand that spun his head the other direction. His eyeballs rolled back; only the whites showed. His mouthguard popped halfway out. Dazed, he tottered, flat-footed. "This more of what you wanted, old man?" I shouted. Then I stepped inside and hammered his body with a volley of punches. Stepped back. Landed another right to his nose. Danced backward a step then back in with a straight punch to his midsection that doubled him over before he dropped to a knee. I backpedaled and hopped into a jig.

"You want a bite of Chili?" I felt thorns and needles flowing in my veins. Waving my gloves, I motioned him to come at me, then lunged toward him and stuck out my tongue. "Come and get it, old man." As he struggled to get up, I stashed my gloves behind my head and did a belly dance, thrusting my loins in his direction, swaying my hips hula-style, with a little Elvis shake of my knees. I didn't wait for him. I took one step and stood him up with an uppercut to the chin. Close enough to be a dance partner, I pounded six rapid-fire punches to his gut, stepped back and laced him with another right to his cheek that left a gash just below his eye.

In the background, I saw people moving toward the ring and heard—or thought I heard—Chester yelling something. What he said didn't register.

My next jab brought more blood, which brought out the bull in me. "Come on, punk," I yelled, loud enough for the entire gym to hear, and they did. I backpedaled then started to moonwalk away from my challenger. Now everybody in the gym hustled ringside. I did a lazy boxer shuffle forward and landed another rapid-fire number on the guy's stomach, then shuffled back.

"Give up yet, ace?" I held my gloves at my side and motioned with my chin.

When he stumbled toward me, I peppered him with a right, then another rock-hard right, and a third. That's when the towel flew past my face and landed in the center of the ring. The crowd yelled. I couldn't tell what they were saying. My old man staggered toward me one more time, blood dripping off his chin; he had a dazed, demonic look in his eyes. In a nanosecond, everything in me landed on him.

Left and right. And another left. Up and across. Head to gut. "Take this, motherfucker. And, this. Your cheap-shot shit. I owe you."

Someone grabbed me in a bear hug from behind. My opponent wobbled, then planted his nose on the canvas. I wrestled with the body on my back but managed to straddle the prone man in front of me.

"Come on. You want a Chili? Come and take a Chili. Big bites. Try. Get your ass up and fight like a man. Get up. Get up," I kept yelling.

"Shut the fuck up. Get back, asshole," Chester yelled in my ear. Another guy, a smaller Latino guy in sweats, came in to help Chester drag me off his boy. They shoved me into the corner and pushed me down on the stool.

I jumped up, arms outstretched above my head. "I am the greatest," I yelled. "I am the greatest. Ali! Chili! Ali! Chili!" I chanted. When Chester left my corner to check on his fighter, I pushed the little Latino guy aside, hopped up on the ropes, and sang out, "Bada boom, bada bing, I am the king. I need a crown! Where's the crown?" I patted my head with my glove. "No ... no, no, no ... what I need is a dog, ooga, a big dog for a boxing tour around the world. No, no, get me a wolf ... yeah, I need a wolf, or a wolf-dog. Howl-l-l-l. Woof, woof, woof. Howl-l-l-l-l. Howling to the moon. Howl-l-l-l to the moon. Books ... books, books, books, books. I need books, classics, great reads, lots of them, the world will pay attention then. Great, great, great, great, great. That's great, just great." I did a backflip off the ropes onto the canvas.

"Shut up, man," the little Latino guy said. He came up from behind me and slapped a towel in my face. I pushed it aside.

"Nobody takes Chili. I'm hot as fire and cold as ice. Nothing can take me."

The Latino guy stepped in front of me, spun me around, and shoved me back onto the stool. I pushed him aside and took a swipe at him. He ducked, grabbed my shoulders, and draped my arms around the ropes. "Shut up, man." He kneed my chest back against the turnbuckle and held me there.

Chester and a trainer from ringside helped my opponent to his feet and dragged his lifeless body to the corner opposite mine. He didn't look like my old man anymore; he was just another boxer. When they plopped him down, he showed no more strength than a slinky. A spectator from outside the ring hopped onto the canvas to check the guy's vision, then his reflexes, and finally his nose. Both eyes had already swelled closed with shades of black and blue pooling around them. Chester shoved a wad of cotton up each of the boxer's nostrils and wiped the blood off his face with a wet towel before he draped it over his boy's head.

I hadn't noticed, but a heavy-set black man, the size of a sperm whale with feet, wearing silky, pajama-like sweats, stood outside the ring next to my stool. As he bent over the ropes his Afro scraped against my cheek. He had too much nose and too big mouth for his oval shaped face. He tapped me on the shoulder. "Listen! You get your ass out of my gym and don't you ever step foot in here again. You understand me?" Anger hissed out of him like a pressure cooker. "If I ever see you around here again, I'll call the cops." His cigar breath caused me to gag. Obviously, the guy was not the least bit impressed by what I had just done.

"S'okay, Richie. S'okay," the Latino guy said. "I get him out. Dos minutos."

"Listen, you little faggot," the large man with the Afro said, waving his arm, pointing toward the entrance. "Get his ass out of here and both of you stay out!"

The Latino guy cowered, turned, and spread the ropes for me to climb through.

My chatter started up again. "Not very cute, you fat ass. I'll go where I please, do what I want. I am the greatest!"

The Latino pushed me along and motioned for me to take off the gloves.

"Yeah, yeah, sure. I don't need gloves." I jogged over to the equipment locker just like Rocky did in his movie. Slapping out air-punches, towel around my neck, big grin on my face. Eyes in the gym bounced between two subjects: me and the guy they were hauling out of the ring. I threw the gloves into the locker, peeled off my protector cup, grabbed my shirt, and karate-kicked the locker door shut.

"What're you fools looking at?" I wrestled to pull my shirt over my sweaty body. "You boys want to see a show? Take a look at this." I flipped the bird on both hands and pumped them up and down in the air, then grabbed my nuts, and let loose with a hee-haw laugh.

The little Latino escort returned. He stood there, looking at the reactions from the crowd in the gym. Satisfied, nobody was pleased with my gestures, he snatched my coat sleeve and started to tug on my arm.

"Hey, hey, hey! Ease up there, amigo. Watch the merchandise. Got this from Napoleon. Love antiques. New one coming soon to a theater near you. Maybe yellow, no, gold, like a cape. Champions wear capes and crowns, you know. Like kings. Time to walk. Do that penguin walk, that winter wonderland waddle thing." I put my arms stiff along my sides and demonstrated. "Yellow snow outside. Time to see sweet, sweet Mother Nature. Come on. Whistle while you work."

I kicked open the front door that had obviously been kicked several times before and ran outside, dove head-first into a landing as pretty as any on a carrier deck, dropping onto the snow-packed sidewalk. I rolled over and lay there, looking up, laughing, tracking individual flakes, little Space Invaders, floating directly into my eyes, onto my face, attacking my entire body. My only defense was laughter. I lay there in the cold, wet snow and laughed. After I'd laughed a good bit, my father's face materialized out of the frosty air. I laughed to tears.

Chapter 15

My escort had followed me out. In the cold, he shook his head and immediately pulled a pint of liquor out of his duffle bag for a three-second belt, then offered me the bottle. I was comfortable on the ground, in the snow, laughing at my old man, and the only thing that could change that was a bottle. I sprang up and chug-a-lugged on the bottle before handing it back, the burn setting my insides on fire.

The on-again, off-again light snows built quickly into a mini-blizzard, with blasts of full whiteouts. I laughed. I felt like I was a kid again. I ran around trying to catch flakes in my mouth, slipping and sliding, spinning like a top.

When the world around me grew dizzy, I stopped; that's when the flakes started talking to me. Cute, friendly phrases. I fumbled about trying to catch them for conversation. My tongue—fresh off my friend's bottle—fluttered far too fast to form words. Sentences started, then a different sentence came out. At times, nonsensical rhymes. "Snow be damned when modern man removes it day by day. 'Tis sun that shines to make it fine and soon it melts away. But oh, pray tell when all is well, do we do what we do to you. Get up and send thy spirit in, for it is snowy, too." Chasing the snow, with the effects of the bottle and the aftermath of the ring, the surroundings grew a bit tipsy before I found myself face-down in the street.

"Where you go now?" my companion asked, doing his best to work the broken zipper on his jacket.

Back on my feet, I looked in his direction but couldn't make out if there were three of him or just one that gave me the bottle. Unsteady, I rocked to regain my balance. As flakes landed on my sleeve, I analyzed each one while my body fought to stop weaving.

"Did you know every snowflake ever made is unique? I said, pointing to the most recent one to drop. "They come in thirty-five basic shapes. All have six sides and they are made of hexagons. The largest snowflake may have been over a foot wide and the largest single day snowfall was over six feet deep."

My nose was less than an inch from my sleeve when a clear thought emerged. "Ho, ho ... holy shit. Tomorrow's Christmas Eve," I screamed. It wasn't the charge from the bottle; it was the sickness. I grabbed the guy's fur collar. "We need to buy toys for the good little girls and good little boys. Lots of toys. Yeah! Heck yeah! We need to get them to kids on Christmas." I released him and pounded the sides of my head, harder and harder, parading around in circles, in a drum major style. "Go house to house playing Santa. Giving toys. And to hospitals. Toys and puppies. Toys and puppies. Come on, man." I grabbed hold of his sleeve "We need to buy toys and puppies. It's late. I'll buy you something, too. What do you want?" I squinted. "You're looking a bit peaked, my friend. I could buy you ... buy you some ... Where'd you say you were going?"

"You crazy, man," the guy said with a hurt look on his face.

I tapped down on his shoulders then started to shadowbox, circling him. He pulled out his bottle and took another healthy swig.

"What's your name, man?" I continued to dance, duck, and dip, throwing punches at my imaginary opponent. "My name's Chili."

"Sal."

"Say what? Sal? Sal what? What's your name?"

"Diago Saldana Paquanto," he said. "Sal."

"Where you from, Sal?"

"Puerto Rico."

"Well, pleased to meet you, Sal from Puerto Rico. Come on. What d'ya say we go find us a pair of holiday wenches under some mistletoe and give them a poke of yuletide cheer? Not much time left to be naughty or nice. What's one more naughty thing for the year, right?" I stopped throwing punches and trudged back to drape my arm over Sal's shoulder.

He pushed me away. "Nah, man. Get off me. I need to get to the shelter."

"What'd you say?"

He spoke fast and slurred with an accent too thick to understand. "The shelter, man. The shelter," he repeated, more deliberately.

"What? Me, too. 'Tis the season, I guess. Fa-la-la-la-la-la-la-la," I sang as I danced a jig in front of Sal. "We're all homeless. Everyone's fucking homeless. We're all here on borrowed time." I spun around to get shoulder-to-shoulder with my new buddy. He was shorter than me with darker skin. In the streetlight, he had the wide nose of a boxer and sores and blisters all around his mouth. His lips were all busted up. "How long?"

"What?" He started to walk. I stayed with him.

"How long have you been on the streets?"

"Siete ... seven years."

"Whoa! No lie?" I said. "So, you're headed to the shelter? Me, too. I need a cot." A sudden flash of nausea chilled me and made me woozy as the last little pump of adrenaline faded. I bent forward with my hands on my knees to let the moment pass.

"Come."

The Mission wasn't too far. By the time we arrived, the line was already dozens long. The snow had stopped, but those in line were covered. Apparently, they'd been there through the worst of it.

We had probably been in line forty-five minutes when a shelter volunteer popped out the door. Dressed in a down ski jacket with a yellow toboggan hat, he passed out cards with numbers on them and announced they had added cots for Christmas, upping the total to sixty-seven. I leaned against the building and stared at the card he gave me. On any other day I would end up sleeping on a bench or in an alcove entrance to a business, up and out of the wind. But the star of Bethlehem was upon me. My number was fifty-nine; I lucked out. By the time we entered, my cold sweats had stopped along with my energized chatter.

I spent two nights at the Healing Shepherd Mission. The first night a church choir of men and women decked out in top hats, long coats, and dresses straight out of the 19th century serenaded us with carols. The second night, Christmas Eve, the mission served a holiday banquet with all the trimmings: three meats—turkey, ham, and roast beef—with mashed potatoes, green beans, Jell-O, salad, and pumpkin pie. Two ministers popped in with their Christmas blessings of peace on Earth and goodwill toward men; both were overfilled with figgy pudding. I blew them off.

Initially, I didn't see much of Sal after we entered the Mission. He had mentioned spending several nights in the shelter. When I saw him, he was always walking, stoop-shouldered with another man, never the same one and usually away from the sleeping or recreation areas. I hopscotched about in my usual fashion, listening to remarkable stories of survival and disheartening tales of despair. On my second night, after the meal, there was a noticeable tryptophan-lull in the room. A few hard-core types played cards in the corner. A number dozed while watching the final minutes of a football game. I found Sal, alone, on his cot.

"Merry Christmas, Sal," I said as I sat down.

He looked at me, his face drawn.

I said, "What's wrong there, amigo? It's Christmas Eve."

"No merry," was his short, dejected reply.

It might have been a combination of many things—the banquet dinner, the holiday, loneliness, fatigue, the weather, phase of the moon—but I had a difficult time talking to him. We sat side-by-side on the cot, looking at the floor most of the time. When my eyes wandered, I noticed several copies of the *Daily Racing Form* on his duffle bag. Circled names highlighted three tracks: Aqueduct, Hialeah, and Gulfstream Park. I thought that might be a point of departure to spark conversation.

"You like horse racing?" I asked.

"Sí."

"You ever bet on the horses? I see those papers there." I pointed.

"Sí. Yeah."

"You win? Your horse, I mean."

"Sometime." He never bothered to look up. He sat bent over with his elbows on his knees and his head in his hands.

"Did you win today?" I asked, figuring the outcome may be the source of his glum.

Sal lifted his head and cocked it to the side away from me. "No."

"Eh, tough luck. Maybe another day," I offered as encouragement. "You bet a lot, I mean, often?"

"Sí. Every day," he said, turning back toward me.

I was taken aback. "You must win often if you make enough to play every day."

"No. I had job. Mechanic."

"Had ... a job? That's why you're here?"

"I have trouble."

"Hell, we all have trouble. What? What kind of trouble?"

Sal hesitated. He reached across and flipped over the racing forms. "I owe. I owe the bookie mucho. I guess I'm, how they say ... addicted."

"To gambling?"

"Horses. Only horses. Racing." He reached back across in front of me and grabbed the racing forms to study them.

"Ever tried to stop?"

"Try. No can do. Still owe bookie."

"You tried to get help? Friends? Family?"

"No. Mi familia, I cannot go see. They find out ..."

"Find out what? That you gamble? That you can't pay, or what?"

He dropped the papers and cradled his head in his hands again. "I lie to them. I not tell them truth."

"Truth? About how much you gamble? But you tried to stop, so ..."

"I come here, to this shelter. These men they pay me for ..." He stopped there and looked over, then turned away. Others passed by looking at Sal, nodding. Clearing their throats.

With his accent and broken English, it was a little difficult to understand. The fact that I had seen him with several different men throughout the night explained his comment, and maybe the sores around his lips. After his pause, he continued.

"I get HIV. I need the money or bookie, he kill me, he say. I can't stop. He kill me." He turned to look at me again. Tears welled up in the corners of his eyes. It was my turn to look away.

Sal was not the first person I had met on the street suffering from HIV. Others had been more open about their condition, the why and the how behind it. Sal was more reserved.

I had to pry. Sal wouldn't talk freely, and when he did, I struggled to make sense of what he said. It was a reluctant game of twenty questions, me guessing answers and Sal responding with cryptic responses. One constant in everything he said seemed to be his sincerity, the truth in his replies. Either that, or he was one hell of an actor. Fear was his great motivator.

From what he shared, his concern was less about his own life and more an issue of family. His parents immigrated to Williamsburg in Brooklyn in 1958 when Sal was eight. They struggled to make ends meet. His father, Ricardo, labored in the Brooklyn Navy Yard while his mother, Alanna, worked in a laundry facility. On their income they managed to raise Sal and his two younger sisters, but had no opportunities for rainy-day savings.

"I dropped out of school early to help with money at home. I was a mechanic. Then a guy took me to the track, to Belmont Park. I spent more time at the track and less time on the job, calling in sick or using other excuses to miss work.

"Yeah, that's how it usually begins. Little here, little there, then—"

"Si." He shook his head. "I owe more ... and more. I borrow money from friends. I steal from family and pawn to pay what friends I could. Then, I just stealed all over. Never could pay my debts, ran away to avoid the bookie."

"So, have you been on the road a long time, running?" I drew the parallel to myself.

"I get jobs. Mechanic. On and off. Still gambling. Not working now. I get debt and skip town to new place. Find new bookie. When no bookies, I find men. Two years I find them." He looked down at the floor. "I know I liked men many years, but only two years for money. I get HIV. I only find men in shelters."

When the volunteers dimmed the lights, we realized our time was up.

I offered a slight smile of encouragement, hoping to brighten his spirits. "Sal, it's Christmas Eve. What do you want for Christmas?"

"I want to be home. I want to be with my family. I am sick and I want to get better. I want to live," he confessed. His tears were gone. His face was sincere and honest.

"Sure. I understand." I nodded. I thought for a minute and added, "I can help. Talk to you in the morning."

I patted him on the knee, smiled, and walked back to my cot where I immediately grabbed my writing gear and slipped off to the restroom. I sat on the toilet seat to ink out a letter that would get beyond his parents' beating hearts and touch their souls. The drip, drip, drip of a leaky faucet provided a rhythmic white noise to help me concentrate.

Mr. and Mrs. Ricardo Paquanto

    I am sorry for what I have done. I am sorry for disgracing the family. I am sorry for my lack of respect. I tried, I really tried. I wanted to do my best for you, to help you. You have given me the greatest gift a person could ever want, the chance to build a lifetime in the greatest country in the world, the land of endless opportunity. I allowed myself to take a different path. I have paid the price. I have missed you.
    I am a broken man. I am very sick with HIV. Every day on the streets makes me sicker. I am weak. I fear for my life, but with the days of life I have left in me, I want to be with you to work, to provide for you the way I should have years ago. I was selfish. I was wrong. I am sorry. I want to come home. I want to feel the warmth of your embrace, a simple hug.
    I need to be with you. I need to be home. I will abide by the consequences if you will take me back.

With loving respect, your son,

Diago Saldana Paquanto

    "Merry Christmas," I said, shaking Sal to wake him early. "I have a present for you."
    Sal rubbed his eyes and sat up. Before he took the letter from my hand he said, "Wait, el baño," he said, still half

asleep and grabbing his crotch. He scooped up his duffle bag, walked off, and returned a few minutes later. "Okay," he said placing his bag under his cot, the smell of alcohol on his breath.

"I've written a letter I think you should send to your parents." Sal didn't react. I wasn't sure if he had understood my suggestion. "There's more to it than that. If you're willing to let me mail this letter after you sign it, I'll rob a bank or something to pay off your bookies. Just give me their names and amounts you owe."

"Qué? You pay them? For me?"

"Merry Christmas. Can you read? Can you read this letter?" I handed him the sheet of paper. He stared long and hard, longer than it should have taken to read the few words. I noticed his lips moving as he looked on.

"I sign and you pay the bookies?" he asked, his eyebrows knitted together.

"Deal?"

"Deal!" Sal allowed a smile to brighten his face.

While we ate breakfast, he provided the street address for his parents and the information about his debts and debtors. I explained he should return to the shelter regularly to ask if any mail arrived for him. Sal never questioned the letter or the payments. I was certain I would see Sal again.

Writing letters had been a cleansing, a confession of sorts. The simple physical movement of a pen on paper was a catalyst for sharing the emotions, feelings, longings I had had building inside me. Acknowledging the imperfections of personality and soul. Justifying underlying causes of shortcomings. A look at the person and a look at the letter opened so many seams of my fractured past. Relationships I'd had with family and friends. Opportunities lost. And, through it all, they always had seemed to end with thoughts of Mary Kay Keller. I had pulled out the slip of paper where I wrote down her address. Soon after, the spell was broken when the day shift volunteers herded us all out the door.

Chapter 16

Christmas morning. Expecting a lump of coal, Santa offered a little something different—polar winds and floating flakes churned to a frenzied froth, rare weather for Atlanta. Walking the streets was nothing short of a personal trek to the North Pole. The city was a ghost town; everything was closed. The library. The post office. Coffee shops. The usual shelters to spend time, stay warm and catch some sleep. Closed. Even the traffic lights were left in a blinking mode. I walked, street after empty street, eager to find a public space to spend time out of the elements. Museums. Art galleries. Shopping arcades. Nothing. The bus station booted me out. The guards at the train station sent me on my way with a *bah* and a *humbug* farewell. I returned to the beloved white Christmas.

Every few blocks I'd duck into a storefront entrance nook to rub my hands and warm my ears. I'd use the time out of the storm to wipe melted snow from my face with a dirty sock out of my backpack. Despite the lack of humankind, I was not lonely; I wrestled with the voices reminding me that I wasn't supposed to be in Atlanta. It was my will that put me here to find the wife of my friend. She was in Atlanta, maybe, according to Jeanna; plus, the phonebook confirmed it. The fact that it was Christmas made my visit questionable.

It was around noontime, where I was tucked close to the front of a pizza joint, that I recalled the letter I'd mailed to Atlanta a few weeks earlier. Trixie, the girl I'd met in Charlotte, had me send her letter to an address in a suburb of Atlanta. I had choices. I could walk in the snow all day, pay that visit to my friend's wife, or drop in on Trixie's family. I decided to take the easy way out first and visit Trixie's grandparents, then close the day in proper order by facing Mary Kay Keller.

Curled up and out of the wind, several feet back from the curb, I waited. Never saw a cab or a bus or a single car. The only movement I noticed was the traffic light that constantly blinked red. It was Christmas, and it was true: nothing was stirring, not even the proverbial mouse. I rummaged through my pockets and pack for change and the phone number for the cab company. My hands were too cold to search for long; I never found the note with the number. I did find some coins.

The first telephone booth I found was the apparent site of earlier merrymaking. A shattered eggnog bottle and an empty pint of bourbon on the floor filled the frozen air with a sour, nauseating stench. At the end of a twisted wire cable hung an empty hard plastic shell for a directory. Back to the sidewalk I went.

I passed several pay phones on the sides of buildings, but none had phonebooks. A few blocks farther—somewhere between frostnip and frostbite—I came across another telephone booth that did have a book, such as it was. A good number of pages were missing, ripped out for worthy causes, no doubt. Fortunately, the T-section of the yellow pages was intact. I called a taxi, and twenty minutes later it appeared. When I stepped out to open the backseat door, the cabby leaned across, saw me, and sped off. "Merry Christmas to you, too, pal," I hollered. I returned to the telephone booth and emptied my backpack hoping to find enough coins to place a second call for a cab. My luck held. Not only did I scrounge enough change, but I found the note with the taxi company which also listed Mary Kay Keller's address. I placed it in my shirt pocket. The second cab appeared in less than ten minutes.

The cabby, an older man wearing a black yarmulke woven with a pale green edge, had a Styrofoam carton with Chinese food in the passenger seat. The smell has definitely more appealing to that of the first phone booth, but not one that I was accustomed to on Christmas. A typical cabby, he took the liberty to talk most of the way, a running commentary on Atlanta. He peppered me with questions and shared a CliffsNotes version of his life. Apparently, according to my cabby, it was traditional for Jews like himself, to eat Chinese on Christmas, since neither actually celebrated the holiday in the traditional Christian way.

Despite the chatter from the front seat, the cab was a Christmas miracle, a gift from the Magi indeed. First, it was a heated shelter from the cold. And second, I was headed to Grisham Park, just inside the perimeter road—a long ten-mile walk under any weather conditions.

When the cab pulled up in front of the address I'd given, I was undecided. I asked the driver to wait while I reexamined my commitment. What if I had the address wrong? What were the names of the people? Mimi and Papa wouldn't go very far. What was I going to say to them? I remembered the street number because it was the same as the year, 1987. And Tallyho Drive was as easy to remember as "righty-oh, old chap." That much I recalled. This had to be the place.

Strands of big-bulbed Christmas lights hung from the eaves of the roof alongside ominous silvery icicles that dipped and dripped a pattern in the snow. Drifts piled against wooden snowman figures on the lawn. The front door, wrapped in foil with a giant bow, was an oversized gift box. I told the cab driver to wait and stepped out of the taxi. With the snow cover I couldn't find a walkway, so I trudged a path directly to the steps of a small porch. I cupped my hands to warm them one last time and, with a few anxious exhales, rang the doorbell and waited.

Carols played in the background as the door opened. "Merry Christ ... mas," a voice said with a greeting that lost its cheeriness somewhere between the eight maids a-milking and the seven swans a-swimming. In the doorway stood an elderly lady with Santa's girth. She eyed me once and closed the door.

"Hi. Excuse me," I said with the door in my face, "may I talk to you a moment?"

"It's Christmas. Go away."

"Uh, yeah ... Merry Christmas," I replied. "My name is Bob White. I just need one minute of your time, please."

"What is it?"

"Well ... I am an acquaintance of Trixie, or rather Debra, Debra Trixton, and I—"

The door opened a crack. I took a small step backward and held the strap of my backpack with my left hand, unsure where I would go from there.

"She's not here," the woman said through the slight opening, her eyebrows dipping with a concerned look. Then the door closed again.

I stood there, my blurred reflection looking back at me in the gift-wrapped door. I turned and stepped off the porch, headed for the cab. A gust of wind blew up. Trixie's words returned to my ears. *You have to face the woman.* This wasn't that woman I was seeking, but this was the time. I knocked on the door.

"Please, if you'll give me one—"

Once again, the door opened, wider than before. The woman stood in front of me, her feet spread and arms crossed. Dressed in a rather large, but tight fitting, lime-green velour sweatsuit with yellow trim and a racing stripe of the same color down her legs, she filled the door with a defiant lean to the rear. "Look, if you're from that cult group, you can just leave right now."

"No, ma'am, I'm not. I happened to meet her, Debra, just a few weeks ago. She needed help."

"Where? Where is she now? What's that girl done this time?" Her tone was filled with more chagrin than curiosity.

"I saw her, well, met her, in a homeless camp in the woods in Charlotte."

"In the woods?" She gasped. "The girl is living in the woods? Glory be."

"Well, ma'am, that particular night she was—"

"Lordy, that girl isn't ever going to learn. Never going to grow up. She's done lost her marbles, that girl. Ain't nothing you can do for us here, Mr. White," she said in a tone that had deeper meaning. "Why don't you just head on back to the woods or wherever you just came from?" She closed the door.

My head rocked back in frustration. *Face the woman.* "She wants to come home," I said, loud enough for her to hear through the door.

The door cracked open. "How do I know you're for real?" Her eyes rolled through another once-over, top to bottom.

The question caught me off guard. I had no proof, no background. The only story I could share was our night, the discussions in the motel. "I … I … don't know what to say other than she wants to come home. That's what she told me."

"She can go home anytime she feels like it. Her mamma's been wondering where she is."

"No, she doesn't want to see her mother. She's afraid her stepfather might pick up where he left off."

"Guess that's for them to figure out, now isn't it?" The door began to close again when I heard a young voice inside say, "Mimi, Mimi, come quick, I want to show you something."

"She wants to see her daughter," I said, shifting my pack to my other shoulder. "She wants to be a mother."

"Baby, I'll be right there after I talk to this man," the woman said, looking away from the door. She turned back to me. "How do you know that? How did you know she has a daughter?"

"I know just weeks ago she sent a letter to you about her daughter," I said. The door opened a hair more, barely enough for me to get a peek inside. Through the opening I saw a little girl, probably Lila, clutching her Mimi's leg.

The expression on the woman's face shifted to a simple, curious Mona Lisa smile. She rubbed her forehead and looked down at the little girl beside her. I was an unkempt, unexpected, unfamiliar visitor on Christmas morning, but she invited me in.

"Thank you."

The cabby honked twice and waved.

"Excuse me one moment, please. I need …" I ran back to the cab, paid the driver, told him to take off, then backtracked through the snow and accepted her invitation.

Mimi introduced herself, then Papa, as Annette and Roger Maxwell. We talked, regularly distracted by Lila with her new toys from under the tree. Annette asked all the usual and expected questions: where is she? what is she doing? when did you see her? how is she? Her questions about me were similar. I felt guilty lying to her, but as a fugitive, there were no good, honest answers. When she mentioned the letter, I explained I had written the letter with emotion provided by Trixie—her tears, her confessions, her contrition, and the feeling of loss and abandonment she carried in her own heart. How she was prepared to go to court to prove she was a loving, concerned, and capable mother.

Mimi was overjoyed to hear that her granddaughter had changed and was finally ready to accept the responsibilities of her choices. Mimi's concern was how to tell Trixie—she called her Debra—that she was welcome to come home, to Mimi's house, anytime. I said she could send a letter to the shelter, but Trixie might not ever go there. I told her I would try to find her and pass on the message, but my travels were unscheduled. Annette understood.

We talked and snacked on honey-baked ham sandwiches with chips and pop. I felt guilty stealing the family Christmas. As the hour grew late, I asked if I could call a cab. Annette insisted that Roger would take me wherever I needed to go next. I thanked her but reminded her it was Christmas, a time when families should enjoy the spirit of the day together. Besides, driving in snow is not a familiar experience for people in the South. She agreed and allowed me to call a cab. I returned to midtown shortly before 5 p.m.

The ride back into town, undisturbed by a quiet cabby, with the radio tuned to an Atlanta Hawks basketball game, offered quiet time to reflect on some of the things Annette Maxwell had said. Her words, even phrases, sounded very similar to the things my parents had said to me as a kid growing up. The yearly warning to go to bed early and sleep tight or Santa wouldn't come. And how I would always sneak out to watch my dad put presents under the tree, yet I still played the game and rushed out Christmas morning, screaming with joy. And how I laid low by the end of the morning when my old man crawled into a bottle or bowl of eggnog because I knew what to expect. By four each Christmas day, the coast would be clear. On Christmas night, I always said the same prayer. *Baby Jesus, heal my dad's heart and save his soul, before it is too late.* A prayer never answered.

The taxi driver confessed up-front he didn't know where the Mission was, and I had no address. One more frustration of the day. Fortunately, I was comforted by my time with Mimi and Papa Maxwell. I asked the cabby to just take me back to the heart of the city, then sat back and enjoyed the slow ride over the snow-covered icy roads. At a traffic light on a deserted street, a bar's neon sign caught my eye. Maybe the only place open and, at the moment, my sole escape from the weather. I dumped the cab and went inside for a few selfish sips of seasonal cheer.

The place was a scene out of an old-time movie. Darker than a cave. Cozy church-pew seating in wooden booths. Chalkboard specials on the wall. Two couples hovered kissy-faced over tables in the dim corners. Carols played softly over hidden speakers. A lone bartender wore a bowtie with tiny lights that lit up while he dried glasses in front of a wall of taps. Above him, a dropped ceiling with a surreal version of da Vinci's *Last Supper* ran the length of the bar. I grabbed a stool at the far end where, over time, I formed and reformed a phalanx of empties under a thin, soft light. With both hands wrapped around a longneck, my head drooped lower. The clock above the rack of wines ticked away the quiet time, violated by my three-word mantra: "Give me another."

The quietude took me to another place, my own *Christmas Carol*. Foggy or cloudy, I wasn't sure. I was on a cot, in a cage, no, a jail cell. The jingling sounds weren't Jacob Marley's chains. A jailer jangled a ring of keys as he approached, singing his off-key rendition of "Jingle Bells."

I struggled to lift my head. "Hey, Mac, where am I?" I asked, my words garbled and hoarse.

"Ho, ho, ho. You, my dear sir, are on death row," he replied, rocking back and forth on his heels. His thumb was tucked into a wide, brown belt which served only as decoration. His gut stretched the waistband of his pants worn well above his navel and high-water above his ankles.

I rolled my head to the side. "Where ... where in the hell am I?"

"Son, you done dipped one too many times into that bowl of grog. You can't remember were you are? Now, ain't that a damn shame." He laughed a ghoulish laugh as he rattled the cell door. "Why, this is murderer's row and you, my dear fellow, are in the dance hall about to walk through the 'valley of the shadow of death.'"

As soon as he said the words, a cacophony ricocheted from ear to ear. First, a Klaxon horn pulsed, loud—on, off, on, off. Then a bell. Not a soothing tinkle or simple chime. Not a church bell, but rather a shrill school bell, the one on the wall above the door that announced those late for class. Or, maybe, a fire alarm. Then a siren. I struggled for air. I strained to scream. nothing came out. What difference would it make? There was no one around, nobody, nothing. Just the noise that drummed louder. Something was wrong. There was danger, but nobody to do anything. No panic. No movement. No people, only me.

The horn, the bell, and the siren rose louder. Back and forth. Then, as if the noise in my head collided, bursting into flames, I was inside a tremendous fireball. Flames—orange, yellow and white—roiled around me, but there was no heat—only this stench, a caustic, acrid, and pungent odor of burning plastic and fuel. All the sounds were louder, the flames grew angrier, and with them a distant voice said, "Gas. Gas. Gas man." Then another voice, a different voice, not one of the persistent hecklers in my head. A familiar but different voice. I heard it. I felt it. *Chili. Don't. Pull* ... And again, *Chili. Don't. Pull* ...

Was there someone there? Could anyone else hear me? Someone who knew my name? I tried to scream. The flames, the fire. All around me. No heat. Then, the face of the woman, Mary Kay Keller, appeared. I saw her face. In the flames.

"Hey, bud. Hey. Wake up, man."

When I dared to open my eyes, the light was much dimmer than the fireball. I squinted several times as I fought to focus. I smelled beer.

"You checked out on me there for a minute, pal," the bartender said as he dropped two of my empties into a bin, his holiday tie flashing in my eyes. "Tough Christmas? You alone? Problems? Woman?"

I couldn't remember. I thought I was with somebody but couldn't remember. I wanted to explain what had just happened, but couldn't. I tried to piece things together, but all that remained was the face and the smell of beer.

"I'll have another," I said, slipping out of my brain fog.

"Really, pal, I think maybe you should call it a day, lay off. You've had enough. I don't—"

"Give me another damn beer, asshole," I snorted, my eyes crossed.

"Stop right there. I don't want to hear it." He held up both hands in front of my face. "Not a good idea, buddy."

I pushed my stool back and stood, wobbled a bit, then leaned across the bar. My stomach lurched toward my throat in sudden protest. "Give me another goddamn beer or I'll turn this place into Armageddon." The lovers in the back booth looked over.

"Hold on," he yelled. He walked up to the edge of the bar, spinning a glass in a towel. He put the glass down, wiped his hands on his apron, leaned over, and put his nose a whisker's distance from mine. "Look, my friend. It's Christmas Day. And I'm all for being jolly and merry," he said slowly and deliberately. "I'll give you another beer. Last one. But not until you sit your ass down and keep quiet. Just sit there. Relax. Catch your breath. And when you finish that beer, you settle up, walk on out that door and head on home or go wherever the hell you want, but out of here. Any questions?" He scowled, backed off, and reached into the cooler under the bar. "It's Christmas. Think about Christmas past, maybe happier times. Just sit there and relax, pal." He slammed the bottle on the bar; foam gushed out of the top.

I laid my forehead on the bar, crippled by the rise of a headache that was taking no prisoners.

Shortly after, I heard the bartender say, "Here. Try this."

Through narrow slits in my eyes, two fuzzy-looking figures appeared in the background along with two coffee mugs in front of my nose. Gradually, the two mugs merged into one filled with black coffee.

"No dice."

"It's on the house."

I moaned, rolled my head toward the bartender, and slurred, "I want a beer. No, make it a shot, bourbon, a double." I rose up, holding tight to the edge of the bar. "Nah, make it a beer. A draft." The bartender turned to face me. "No, a bottle." Hiccup. "No, a glass." With my head squeezed firmly between my hands, I choked out, "Check that. How about a Bloody Mary?"

"I told you before, ace. I gave you your last beer. That's it. Time for you to pack up." He cracked his knuckles and walked off.

I slumped over on my stool and dropped my forehead on the beer-drenched surface of the bar. I swear I saw Elvis walk through the door. And, behind him, the ghost of Christmas past.

"I killed my best friend," I said, words destined for no particular ears, except maybe my own. Drool oozed from one corner of my mouth, working its mumbled, nightmarish monologue. A voice crackled over the intercom, 'Don't do this, Chili. It's not right. Don't do this. Back off, man."

"No. No. I got this, Gas Man. Going down!"

My lazy tongue stumbled on the words, but droned on. "Fucking circus. Voices. Talking on top of each other ... bam, bam, bam!" I paused before I followed with, "My best friend. Hot seat." His name hung over me. Then, I remembered reading words as they scrolled upward on the inside of my eyelids.

"Too low. Power! Power!"

"Easy with it."

"Easy with it."

"Nose up. Max throttle."

"Muscle-memory. It was just muscle memory," I confessed quietly to myself. "Belly-smacked the sonofabitch. Lost the front wheel. Slammed into the island at full power. A fireball. I was alive. He was dead." Emotion gagged me. "I never said goodbye. I never said I was sorry. I need to find her. She needs to know. I need to hear her say ..." I couldn't finish the thought. I lifted my head.

"Whattimeisit?" my four words slurred into one accented with a closing hiccup. I rolled my eyelids open.

The bartender was leaning on the bar directly over me. "Four-ten," he replied, his blurry expression nothing short of a fleshy question mark.

"Uck-fay e-may, I gottago." I raised my left hand and shouted, "Bartender, check please." I rocked upright on my stool when he slid the tab under my bottle.

I squinted to read the bill while I wiped my teeth with a bar napkin. I leaned forward until my nose touched the bar tab, then leaned back, holding the soaked slip at arm's length for a long-range view. At that distance, the numbers didn't even appear. I had no idea how long I had been on the stool and not even a guess as to how many drinks he'd served. Rather than talk to the butt-head bartender, I reached into my sock, threw two twenties on the bar and pushed back. I grabbed my backpack and, with the aid of the empty bar stools, felt my way to the door, listing to the right. The patrons in the back chuckled.

"Keep ...," hiccup, "... the change," I said as I pushed the door open. "Bah! Humbug, Frosty."

Chapter 17

The moon hung peek-a-boo, lost behind the uptown buildings. Evening shadows had long since sucked the warmth out of surfaces warmed throughout the day. The cold air sobered me, barely, not enough to manage a straight path down the icy sidewalk. The streets, still empty. No walkers, no cars, no pigeons, only me.

I staggered a few blocks with the aid of building fronts and street signs. As I passed a café, a strobe flashed in the display windows on either side of me. A flash, then another and another without the expected crack of thunder. It was rhythmic, psychedelic, not a dream. From behind, I heard a car crunching through the crusty slush along the curb. I lost my balance and nearly slipped when I wheeled around to look. It was a police car with its flasher bar on, creeping up the street without its siren. I wanted to melt into the building when I heard, "Hey there, sir, come over here." To my ears, it wasn't a pleasant kind of 'howdy-do'; to me it sounded more like you're under arrest. I pretended not to hear. I slid up to the nearest storefront to admire the display, watching the cop car in the reflection.

"Hey, you, buddy, come over here," the cop riding shotgun in the cruiser insisted.

Being picked up wasn't an option, and certainly not on Christmas Day. For a second, I considered making a run for it, but when my foot slipped on the first effort, I knew I wouldn't get far with them pursuing in a car. I tucked in my collar to cover my face, slowly turned, pulled my cap as low as I could, and did my best to walk a straight line toward the curb.

The cop was total business. Stern face, cap tilted back on his head. As I approached the car, he broke into a broad smile. "Merry Christmas," he said. He reached out and handed me a red-striped candy cane. "Need a ride somewhere? Tough to be out in this kinda weather. Hell of a way to spend Christmas, isn't it? Why do people sing about white Christmas, anyhow?"

With my frozen fingers it took a while to unsnap my field jacket's pocket to tuck away the candy. The bigger treat was the heat flowing out of the open car window. The last place I needed to hang out was in the backseat of a squad car. Not on Christmas or any other day for that matter. I didn't care how nasty the weather was.

"Merry Christmas to you, too, officers. Uh, thanks, but no thanks. I'll walk," I said, clearing my throat.

"Where you headed? Come on, we can give a lift if it's around here somewhere. We're just driving around, keeping the peace. Doing a damn good job so far. Not a peep." He stuck his head out the window and looked up and down the street.

"No, just headed over to my sister's place around the corner there. Not far. Holiday dinner thing. Family, you know." I tipped my cap, hunched my shoulders, and pulled my collar higher on my neck, then turned and walked back toward the window display.

"Really should get out of this cold, pal. Christmas is no day to be miserable, except us lucky bastards who get to work." His voice faded as the car continued down the street.

I remained by the storefront window until the cruiser turned several blocks down. About that time, a car that was probably a sixties-something battleship Oldsmobile slid around the corner a hundred feet away. The driver over-corrected on the skid, banged hard into the curb, and stopped. The passenger door flew open and a body rolled out. Someone inside the car hollered something I couldn't understand. About that time, a gym bag came flying out. As soon as the bag cleared the door, the car engine revved, the tires kicked up a rooster tail of slush, and the car crept its way into a slippery getaway. From the sidewalk the victim sat up and flipped off the driver. "Yeah, well, Mamma always did like you better, asshole," he said, then turned in my direction. I stared back, stumbled, and then headed around the corner and down the street to avoid interaction.

In my state of mind, there was no telling how long I had walked nor how far. There was no guarantee I hadn't walked in a circle, maybe more than once. What I did know was that it was late. I was getting colder. And it was a toss-up on which was going to burst first—my head or my bladder. There would be no Mission shelter, no cot, no nothing tonight. Stuck in a concrete jungle with no trees, bushes, or shrubs, I relieved myself in a Big Gulp cup I pulled from the slush along the curb; I filled it nearly full and placed it next to a sheltered MARTA bus stop. On the back wall of the glass enclosure there was a route map superimposed over major streets and roads of the city. From my shirt pocket, I pulled out the scrap of paper with Mary Kay Keller's address. Squinting, still shivering from the cold, I studied the address and eventually found her street on the MARTA map. It was only a few blocks over, but I was unsure in which direction.

Hugging building walls and storefronts, I made my way to Glenwood Avenue. The direction I needed to go forced me into the wind for several blocks. As expected, the street

no SHELTER for GUILT

address turned out to be a high-rise, and I had no clue of the apartment number. I could call, but wasn't sure how I could get her to reveal her number. I decided to wait it out, to watch for her if she appeared. Time was on my side. I started to sober up and waited out the ache in my head.

Without a bench, my sanctuary for the night was an alcove in front of a small haberdashery. I placed my pack on the ground, pulled my collar over my ears, assumed a fetal position, and put a T-shirt over my face while a pair of horny elephants stampeded through my head. With alcohol as antifreeze, I had doubts about surviving the night in the cold. Neither my doubts nor the headache kept me awake. My vigil across the street from the high-rise lasted only minutes. I passed out in a toxic fog.

The day after Christmas, my wake-up call came well before the sun. A rare snowplow crunched its way down the street, shooting ice and snow that landed just short of my feet. My surveillance renewed, I crouched in a tight ball against the bricks with weary eyeballs glued on the building across the street. I rehearsed my plan to intercept Mary Kay Keller.

Fortunately, the sun punched through the morning clouds; unfortunately, it brought snowmelt. Sitting on the sidewalk became uncomfortable. I scavenged a discarded plastic bin labeled "United States Postal Service" and used it as a stool, a little something to get off the wet pavement. I didn't bother to put out my cardboard sign, just my cap. Writing came first, so I grabbed a notebook from my pack.

The morning air was cold, but sitting in the beaming sunlight made all the difference in the world. Though my stomach argued, the lack of food didn't bother me. The absence of foot traffic didn't bother me, either. My pen wrote on its own with one eye on the apartment building and the other on my pad. Page after page, I wrote. Original poems. Lyrics of Christmas carols. Church hymns. Odes by Tate, Keats, Wordsworth, and others. I nearly filled the notebook I had. The words, nothing short of scribbles on paper.

To my surprise, the few walkers who passed almost all dropped change into my cap. Many even bothered to look and say, "Merry Christmas," or, "Happy New Year." Across the way, only a few bodies came through the doors of the apartment building. After a while, I wondered if there might be a back entrance, but I remained unwilling to leave my post on the plastic tub.

At mid-morning, I saw her, or at least I saw who I thought was her. It had to be her. She really hadn't changed much in three years. I rustled up my cap and coins, tossed my notepads in the backpack, and tailed her from my side of the street. Her long stride made it difficult at times. With few people out and about, if she bothered to notice, it probably looked like I was following her. If she looked my way, I'd pause and check out a window or tie my shoe.

After four blocks, she entered a drug store. I turned to admire the trays of goodies in the window of the German bakery on my side of the street, focusing more on the reflection in the window. I fidgeted around, clapping my hands to the beat of the oompah music playing through the glass. Minutes later, she emerged from the store and headed back the way she came. I did the same. When she turned to go into the apartment building, I dashed across the street, arriving in time to see her board the elevator in the lobby. Through the glass door entrance, I noted that it stopped on the fourth floor. I stood around waiting for another resident to leave. When an elderly guy came out, bundled like a polar bear, I dashed inside and pushed the elevator button for her floor.

When I stepped out on the fourth floor, there was no sign of her. All eight apartment doors were closed. Three had newspapers waiting in the hall. I chose the apartment without a paper, closest to the elevator.

"May I help you?" asked the short, balding man who answered my knock. He wore a sleeveless, white wife-beater T-shirt and pajama bottoms. He took a furtive glance at me without moving his head, but said no more.

"Sorry to bother you, sir," I said, quickly. "I was told Mary Kay Keller lived here. I guess I was—"

"Mary? She lives at that end of the hall, number forty-four." He abruptly closed the door. I had what I needed. I adjusted the shoulder strap on my backpack and walked to the end.

There was a peephole in her door. After I knocked, I stepped aside.

"Yes?" the voice came from behind the closed door.

"Uh, hi, Mary. May I talk to you?"

The door opened slowly, the security chain still attached. A short woman with gray hair appeared through the space, definitely not the woman I had followed. "Yes, dear? What do you want?"

"I was looking for Mary Kay Keller. I was told she lives here."

"Well, I am Mary Keller."

The mixed messages scrambled in my brain. "But ... but—"

"Yes. But what?"

"But I was looking for Mary Kay Keller. She ... well I thought ... no offense, but I think she is much younger than you."

"Well, I am Mary Keller. Mary Jane Keller."
"Do you know Mary Kay?"
"Who?"
"Mary Kay Keller? She was married to Ben Keller."
"No."
"Is there another woman that lives here? Young. Tall. Dark hair."
"No."

Don't let her fool you. You've come this far. Look inside, you idiot. She's lying to you. Go inside and look for yourself.

"Let me come in and look around." I stepped closer.

"Young man—" When she started to close the door, I squeezed my foot in. "No. You may not come in."

"I know she's in there," I insisted. "Open the door. I'll only be a minute. I need to see her. I need to talk to her." I pushed on the door with no luck.

"I told you, no. Leave me alone. Leave now or I'll call the police."

I had leaned back to ram the door with my shoulder, but the mention of police was kryptonite. When I backed off, she slammed the door. I heard the deadbolt engage. On her threat alone, I took the elevator down and left the building.

Chances were that the old man had steered me correctly to Mary Keller, the only one on the fourth floor. And since the woman I followed went to the fourth floor, chances are her name was not Mary Keller. Nor was it likely there was another Mary Keller, my Mary Kay Keller, in the building. Atlanta was a bust. My plan was a bust. The whole fucking plan was a bust.

Chapter 18

Following my dead end in Atlanta, days were nights and nights, days. I pried open a metal door to a maintenance cubby under a bridge and sat there with my knees to my chest, crouched in a solitude both cherished and despised. My only companions were the rats who allowed me there. I spent days sitting motionless in the darkness without blinking, listening to the faint sound of my breath. I ventured out only in darkness, walking in a trance, feeling nothing. When I stopped, I huddled in bushes or snuggled with a dumpster in a dark alley. I wallowed in fear, unwilling to make eye contact with anyone. I cried. Once I started, I couldn't stop, the flood gates were open. I obsessed over buried memories, my victim, police, and the absurdity of life. Nothing mattered. I cried, too weak to simply think. The voices pummeled me with their threats, excuses, and convincing arguments on how to end it all. I listened. I wanted to be rid of me, to lose the fog. Suicide. Unattainable. Me against the fog—and the Vigilantes.

Chapter 19

It wasn't until a pre-dawn ride from Atlanta to Macon over a week later that my head and my heart allowed me to breathe in public. On that ride, the seat next to me was the last seat—the only seat—available for a gangly twenty-something guy. He was dressed in a green seersucker suit—in January—with a yellow shirt and a cute, red bowtie that would have made Pee-wee Herman proud.

"Mind if I join you, sir?" he asked. He had this genteel way about him, his mannerisms as well as his manners. He oozed Southern. His choice of clothes. His choice of colors. His choice of words. I nodded and gathered the things I had spread across the seat cushion to defend my turf.

"My name's Daren Nielson," he said. "Yours?"

"Chili," I replied, placing my pack by my feet.

"Pleased to meet you, Mr. Chili." My seatmate, straight off of Tara and wearing a smile that divided his face in two, extended his hand. I turned and reached across to shake. A gleam of light caught my eye when it flashed off a thin, silver cross that dangled from a chain outside his shirt. I looked away and watched the driver cram the last of the baggage into the bin under the bus.

A scratchy voice on the overhead speakers announced our departure. As we pulled out of the terminal, the driver picked up his microphone and requested that we leave our overhead lamps off for safety. The dark cabin was comforting. However, the tranquility was quickly broken.

"What's your destination, Mr. Chili, if I may ask?"

His voice was simply fingernails on a chalkboard. I had not engaged in conversation with a body other than a ticket agent for weeks; I wasn't sure I remembered how. My stomach encouraged brevity. "Macon."

"I'm headed to Saint Leo's Abbey in Florida." His voice was mellow and slow, to some maybe a good ol' boy.

"Visit?"

"No, sir. I'm going to join," he said in a way that made me think of a kid running off to join the circus over the French Foreign Legion. "I've been called."

"What?"

"My life is in the hands of the Lord. Going to be a Benedictine monk," he proclaimed. In the dark, out of the corner of my eye, I could see the smile on his face and the slight nod of his head.

Needless to say, this was not the topic of conversation I had considered as my breakout from silence, but his commitment intrigued me. "Why? Don't you have to live the rest of your life in that place? In the monastery? Christ, isn't that like being in prison, a life sentence?" I said, then realized I was talking to a truly religious type.

"Oh no, sir. It's a Garden of Eden where everything I need is there, all provided. I will own very few possessions and everything I do, all of my works, I will offer to the glory of God."

I didn't respond. I thought about what he said. *Everything I need is there.*

"And I can pray several times a day with other monks or on my own."

Strange, I had done the same thing for weeks myself, except for the praying part. I had been alone. I gave up all my possessions, by choice, able to reverse the decision anytime I felt. I needed nothing. I survived. "But why? Don't you like sports or music? Girls? Anything?"

"Mr. Chili, the world needs prayer. The world is in terrible shape. People no longer listen to reason. There is so much more to life than earthly things."

No need to tell me that; I had nothing. Here we go, I thought.

"You know, Saint Paul tells us, 'There are three things that last: faith, hope, and love, and the greatest of these is love.' People need to love others. We need to feel the hearts and the love of others. We need to be connected to others. Prayer can do that. I have seen it. I know the true power of prayer. Do you pray?"

"No."

"Truly? You don't pray?"

"I did, but I don't."

"Sad."

"My father was a minister," I began. "Well, he worked in a steel mill but he was the minister for our little church."

"Where was that?"

"Southern Ohio."

He made a pouty-puppy expression in the dark. "And you don't pray now? Why not?"

I hesitated. I wasn't sure if I didn't want to answer or if I really couldn't explain why. I just knew I'd stopped years ago and never gave it another thought. So, I gave him the simplest answer which stopped most conversations. "I killed a guy."

Daren didn't say another word. I couldn't sense if he were thinking about my sin or praying for my soul. I stared out the window and dozed until I grabbed my pack to get off the bus in Macon.

no SHELTER for GUILT

"Have a blessed day, Mr. Chili," he said as I crawled past him to leave.

"Good luck to ya, man. Hope things work out for you." I wasn't sure about things for myself.

The bus was early into the station. A church bell banged out six solid bongs as I exited the bus along with three groggy passengers. Two people boarded.

A feather bed of gray clouds, low in the sky, threatened wet weather. Inside the station, I approached a short, smiley guy with a mop taller than he was to ask if he knew where the nearest shelter might be.

"I think there's one a few blocks down, but I'm not sure it's open. They open and close that place all the time. Union Gospel Mission it's called. In an old five-and-dime store at Poplar and Second Street," he said, his smile growing with pleasure.

Since rambling sermons by Brother-to-be Daren had kept me from a nap, my body screamed for a jolt of java. The coffee shop across the street didn't open until seven. I walked down a block. With no luck finding coffee, I propped my cardboard sign against the wall and placed my baseball cap on the sidewalk by my feet, an easy target for early-riser passersby. The sign read, "I'm a human being just like you. Bet my life sucks more. Wanna trade for a day?" While I sat, I doodled poetry on my pad. I admit, many of the words were lingering sparks of Brother Daren. I wrestled to reconcile with the concept of prayer. I questioned voluntary celibacy and contrasted the monastic life with the vagabond experiences of homelessness. I weighed his mention of faith, hope, and love against "Thou shalt not kill." When the coffee shop opened, I took a break.

Coffee on a cold and cloudy morning can be more soothing than a hot towel after a shave or scalp massage with shampoo. It was pure cupped lightning. A melt-in-your-mouth experience that sluices warmth from lips to belly button and beyond. A single whiff can be as satisfying as chocolate chip cookies straight out of the oven. I blew ripples across the top, half to cool it and half to soothe my body while I sat hunched over on a stool, clenching the Styrofoam cup as if it were the Holy Grail, at the beverage bar along the window, close to the door. I savored every last caffeinated drop, conscious of the pedestrians' eyes that watched me as they passed. Men in business suits with spit-shined shoes. Women bundled in heavy coats with floppy, turtleneck collars sticking out at the top. A doctor in scrubs with a plaid scarf around his neck. A construction worker with hard hat and mud-caked canvas pants. I watched another guy, much like me—grungy and weather-beaten—take off a backpack and a long overcoat, place them next to a tree in the median of the boulevard, and walk through the front door of the coffee shop. When a city cop wandered in behind him, I slipped out.

The directions to the shelter were simple. With all day to make the trek, there was time to find a spot with steady pedestrian traffic where my sign might pay dividends. There is a certain psychological balance between art and skill in finding the exact right spot. I knew one when I saw one. Some days were better than others. Let the search begin!

The earlier clouds lightened, but the skies remained overcast. I passed a barber shop and noticed a sign in the window. "Guaranteed you will look better after you visit." And in small print it added, "Unless you are ugly!" The morning air was still, a great day to let the coffee do its thing, to enjoy the chirps and songs of the birds. As I walked, I came upon the faint sound of a pipe organ, the notes stair-stepping louder from deep resonance to high-pitched horns. The source of the music was across the street, a church in the shadows. The hymn or arrangement reminded me of Sundays at my father's mill-town church. I changed course, crossed over, and climbed the ten worn concrete steps.

Two tall wooden doors that would have made Saint Peter proud opened to a light-starved windowless narthex where the music reverberated off walls of cold granite. A pencil-thin light cracked the darkness. I peeked through smaller wooden doors inlaid with silver lambs into an empty nave. The door creaked as I entered.

Inside, incense perfumed the air. Though veins of crumbled mortar and runaway ivy crept in and around the stone exterior, the inner chambers were pristine white, framed in splendor. Tall, white Roman columns with gold-leafed tops. Stained-glass windows, both tall and round, brightened every wall. Steps led up through the chancel to a sanctuary with three altars, each clothed in white. Behind the main altar was a reredos of white stone with carved images of the crucifixion of Christ. A tabernacle topped with a simple golden cross held majesty in front. As an unwashed body in tattered clothes, two weeks from my last shower, my presence was a sacrilege.

I stepped slowly up the center aisle, turned, and looked into the loft above the narthex. An organist sat erect, gracefully playing a piece. My musical ear was primitive, uneducated to most church music. The melody was a mystery.

Stairs near the side wall led up to the organ loft. I climbed the steps and emerged from behind a wall of pipes. "Bravo," I said as I applauded after he ended. "What was that you played?"

Startled, the organist flinched when he heard my voice. He slid left then right on the bench, contorting his body and looking around the organ until he saw me. His raised eyebrows and dropped chin assured me that I didn't appear to be anyone he had expected.

"One of the hymns for the weekend," he said with a worried look of uncertainty, seemingly unsure when the flight or fight response would take over.

"Well played. Excellent work on the organ. Haven't heard one played that well in a long, long time." I walked closer.

He scooted back. "Thank you." He blinked rapidly as I approached. "I've been at it a number of years," he said with a tremor in a diminutive voice.

The organist was thin with greased-down hair and a small moustache. He reminded me a lot of Inspector Clouseau in his brown sweater-vest over a plaid shirt atop corduroy pants.

"My father was a preacher in a small town in Ohio," I said. "When I was a kid, I played our church organ on Sundays ... you know, short, familiar hymns. I pecked out tunes to drown out the voices in the pews. They weren't much for singing. It was tough to do with that old pump organ. We called it Calliope Jane. It was ancient. Pedals wheezed and whistled. Had two keyboards. Six or seven stops across the front. I only learned to use two of them for certain pieces I could play."

He slid forward on his bench. "This organ has been in the church since it was built in 1928. Oldest one in Macon. Three manuals. Forty-eight stops. Not sure exactly how many pipes we have now. A couple have gone sour over the years and need some attention."

no SHELTER for GUILT

I moseyed around, wiping dust off stacks of unused hymnals and looking out over the church. The guy behind the console kept his eyes on me as I wandered.

"Any chance I could peck at the keys, play a few notes? You know, satisfy an itch," I said wiggling my fingers in front of my face.

His eyebrows rose above big, round eyes. He nervously rearranged his sheet music. Without looking at me, he eventually replied, "Well ... I don't know."

"Just a few notes. I mean it's been ages since I played anything. Press a few keys is all. Who knows?"

He placed the papers in a pouch on his lap, then turned toward me. "Okay, sure. I was about to wrap up. If you want to sit here while I gather some things, go right ahead."

He grabbed a device off the music stand and slid off the bench. The frown on his face suggested his concern. Considering my appearance, his concerns were justified. I came around from the other side and dropped my backpack on the floor as I hopped on the bench, still warm. I ripped off my field jacket, tossed it on my backpack, then wiggled my fingers above the keys in a faux glissando, up and down the scales. It felt good. Better than good.

My warm-up was quick, the old Liberace trick—lace the fingers, roll the wrists inward, and push the arms as far forward as possible, far enough to hear knuckles crack. Worked like a charm. While the organist opened and closed some dusty wooden file cabinets toward the rear of the loft, I nudged the keys. One finger pressed; a deep tone emerged. I broadened my smile and pulled back to study the console. The memory of one particular piece of music channeled through my body. The hair on my arms and legs stood on end. I placed my hands on my knees and took a few slow breaths, imagining flipping my hair over my ears the way

Bach might have done. My hair, too dirty to flip, was still tucked tight under my baseball cap.

Sitting erect with my chest popped out, my eyes in a straight-ahead stare, I entered a completely different existence. My arms inched forward and locked. As gentle as fog on water, my hands approached the keyboard. I took a breath of hesitant excitement. Then fingers on both hands simultaneously tapped notes an octave apart. Three at first. A breath. Another six notes. One hand mirrored the other. A two-second pause and a repeat of the previous notes, an octave lower. Again, a pause. Then, each hand added five pipes, one at a time, one on top of the next in an ghostly discordant harmonic resolved by a single, long soothing tone eventually shattered by an extended tap on a foot pedal that created earthquake qualities too deep to hear yet strong enough to rattle the gothic pendant lights above the pews.

The music was rolling thunder pumped by adrenaline now boiling through my veins. My fingers on both hands chased each other up the lower manual like crabs on a beach, then raced along the upper manual in similar fashion, before returning to the lower keyboard, pounding in melodic anger. Possessed, my body swayed—side to side, in and out, head rolling shoulder to shoulder—while fingers on two hands tip-toed through lighter notes to choreograph a dramatic sunrise over the darkest reaches of the altars below. Again, raising my nose defiantly in the air, the spirits inside me charged the keyboard, virtually grabbing the keys off the lower manual. Then, after each assault, my arms drifted away, feather-light.

Strangely, suddenly, the music evaporated. My fingers failed to move; they had nowhere to go. No memory to push them. A wave of nervousness washed over me. I looked up, away from the keys. The towering wall of

no SHELTER for GUILT

brushed-metal pipes in front of me and the space around me—the room, the loft—began to spin, slowly at first, then faster, in a carousel of splotched images and smeared colors. Slowly, from the blur, frozen bystanders appeared dressed in bright red and orange clothes, drifting in and out, backwards and forwards, looking at me, watching me as I circled, round and round. The only sound was the lub-dub of my heart loud in my ears.

Subconsciously, my lonesome fingers began to peck at the keyboard. Single notes and false starts that soon found a memory of a melody, another classic organ piece, the solo from "In-A-Gadda-Da-Vida." At the point in the solo where the right hand played a secondary melody of the Christmas carol, I shouted, irreverently, "God rest ye merry gentlemen," followed by an equally irreverent and boisterous laugh, before my hands trickled off the macabre melody and launched into a lighter ditty. Fiddling with the organ stops, the sound from the throaty pipes shrank to the windy-whistles of a calliope tooting out Joplin's "The Entertainer." I stood, hooted, hollered, laughed, and played before my hands left the keys to applaud their own work.

The organist looked deep in thought when he poked his head around the side of the console. He didn't smile. "Bach, Toccata and Fugue in D minor?"

"And assorted others." I laughed.

From below the loft came the slow, rhythmic clap of one unannounced listener. The organist leaned over the rail.

"'In-the-Garden-of-Eden,' I believe. Well done. Encore, por favor. Encore."

"Oh ... good morning Father," the organist said with a wave. "Didn't notice you come in."

"Bravo! Well done, Gerald. Can't say I expected to hear that here this morning but ... entertaining. And Bach, as well, I believe?"

"Exactly. But, sad to say, it wasn't me, Father. That was a visiting mystery artist. And I'm ... not sure of his name."

"Chili," I hollered, titillating the pedals with my toes.

The organist cocked his head back a bit and squinted. "Uh, our mystery guest is Mister Chili."

"Well then, Mr. Chili, excellent job. Maybe Gerald can have you join him this weekend for an extra special treat for our parishioners."

"Okay, I need to lock up things," the organist said and motioned for me to get up. "That was quite a performance. I don't think I've ever seen anything like it. Most impressive."

I nodded.

"And you say ... you played a little in your father's church is all?"

"Yeah, just hymns. That Bach thing I memorized on my own. When I was a kid, I saw *20,000 Leagues Under the Sea*, the movie. Ever see it? Captain Nemo played that inside the sub. You know, kinda spooky and dramatic. Everybody thought it was so cool. I wanted to play it, so my mom found a record of the soundtrack. I was obsessed. I listened to it over and over, until I memorized it. Guess it's like riding a bike, eh?"

As we walked down to the ground floor, the organist grabbed my hat and handed it to me. "We don't wear hats inside."

Based on the starched collar and black cassock, the surprise listener had to be a resident priest or minister of some sort. He was sitting in one of the pews well to the rear of the church. His wavy, white hair had long since lost the

no SHELTER for GUILT

battle with his forehead, which left the middle of his scalp a wasteland of scaly skin. Gerald gave a polite wave and departed. The priest asked me to join him. I took a seat in the pew behind him, dreading what might follow.

Chapter 20

"Welcome, Mr. Chili. I'm Father Holtzapfel. What brings you to us?" he asked.

I sat hunched forward. My fingers drummed on the bench seat while my foot still tapped the tempo of "In-A-Gadda-Da-Vida."

"Just passing by, heard Gerald there on your organ and stuck my head in is all." I kept looking around, avoiding the priest's eyes and, with luck, his intentions.

"Ever been here before?"

"Nope. Never." I stared at a peculiar image of a white bird in a round, stained-glass window.

"Are you from around here?"

"Nope."

"Where's home?"

I leaned back and stretched my arms wide with a grip on the back of the pew. "Everywhere. I'm a man of the world, so to speak, though others would call it homeless. I'm simply houseless," I said with a yawn. "Say, what kind of bird is that there?" I pointed toward the window.

He looked up at it. "A dove, a symbol of the Holy Spirit. Are you Catholic, by chance?"

It took all the self-control I had not to laugh. "Nope. Can't say I am any religion anymore."

"Anymore?"

"I was a Christian growing up. Dad was a minister in a small church. Let's just say I don't have that calling these days." I slouched a bit and crossed my arms, sensing a mounting interrogation about my churchgoing background.

"A calling? To be a Christian?"

"To follow any religion. I just can't believe in the God concept." I slouched lower.

No doubt, wheels were turning in his head. Outside, a cloud darkened the color of the stained-glass window above the altar. "Really?" he said more as a statement than a question. "An atheist?"

"Kinda bold assumption, I must say. Nope."

"Well then ... with all the wonders of the world before your eyes, all the incredible things that happen all the time, all the wonderous, almost miraculous normal functions within your day—breathing, moving, seeing, smelling, touching, loving ..."

I stopped him there and eased forward. I could feel a little something was about to happen. I was anxious to let her rip. "Oh, seriously," I rolled my eyes, "The God thing. Three persons ... just one God? Sounds like three gods to me. Explain that one."

He smiled and folded his hands in his lap. "The Trinity is a sacred truth. We are told in the Bible—"

"Sure, sure. Okay, okay. I know the Bible might say that, but come on." I lit up a broad smile and leaned back against the pew, ready to fire at will. "Some guys, some old codgers wrote that stuff. Probably sitting around in caves, hiding or maybe just looking for something to do, so the bastards ... oops ... started writing and the best they could do was to write about another guy, so one guy wrote his story and another guy read the story and said I can do better than that so he wrote the same story but added a few cool details the first guy had left out and then a third guy did the same and then a fourth and voila—there you have three gospels." I gave him my Jack Nicholson smirk. "Ya know, it's kinda like that game of telephone we played at birthday parties as kids. Whisper something into the ear of the person next to you, then he whispers it to the next person, and then the next around the circle and by the time it goes all the way around, the message is rather different. Maybe better. Maybe worse. Possibly unbelievable, maybe."

I came back to the specifics and sped up my delivery. "And that doesn't even touch on all that stuff about floods and arks and plagues and parting waters and walking days and months across the desert and then climbing a mountain and coming down with these heavy-ass stone tablets etched with rules that everybody is required to follow. Really? All of these, every last one of them, inspired by some spirit they can't see or explain?" I ran my hand through my greasy, hatless hair and ramped up my delivery speed even more. "Oh, and what about the bread and wine thing where it is really body and blood? Really? Now who can believe that shit, sorry, that stuff? Hmm? If it looks like a wafer and smells like a wafer and feels like a wafer, then it is a wafer, and there is nothing scientific or otherwise that can change that. Body? You believe that's really someone's body?"

"The transubstantiation is a tenet of the Catholic faith by which we believe—"

"See, I believe nature has a way of combining existing forces to cause events which create things," I said. Thoughts raced through my head. I could barely consider one before another appeared. I stumbled through sentences, faster still, leaning toward the old man. "And all that beauty and love you talk about, those wondrous miracles of daily life you speak of. I mean, religion is merely a product of our imagination straining to connect everyday life with the transcendent," I said as my smile faded, leaving the stain of

no SHELTER for GUILT

a scowl. I slapped the back of the pew. "I challenge you to walk with me for a day or, as they say in those church books, walk a mile in my shoes and tell me how much of your day was truly wonderful."

"Certainly, we all have our trials, our obstacles. But, despite your hardships, you are alive, aren't you? Have you ever been in India or Africa? Have you ever experienced poverty—I mean poverty as in starvation?" he asked.

"No I haven't, padre, but I've seen a lot of this country. And things aren't rosy for a whole lot of folks. But, see, you just made my point." I leaned in, my hands inches in front of his face, ready to axe off his ears. The priest had faith and didn't move. "If there is a God and He—or is He a She?—is good ... all-good and loving ... all-loving, why are your people in India and Africa starving? Why are all the people I see all around our country homeless? Where's the love?" I withdrew my hands.

He eased back, seemingly unsettled. He folded his hands like he was about to pray, then began to tap them against his lips and sighed. "To live is to share pain as well as laughter. God gives each of us, each of his children, challenges, crosses to bear. It's not by our clock but by God's divine timeline that life exists. A tragedy for one is God's way of sending a message to others, a more lasting and deliberate word that could change other lives."

"Seriously?" I began to stand to leave but decided to roll on. I leaned back in the pew, ran both hands through my hair, and grabbed my head. "And the little girl who has cancer? Or the one who is dying of heart failure?" My hands squeezed my cheeks and slid down in a stranglehold on my neck. "What about that plane crash that killed over a hundred people? Bang! All gone!" I scooted closer to the priest, then rattled off case after case, in breathless, rapid-fire succession. "And every war there ever was and all those guys in trenches or shot storming a beach and killed by the punji sticks in 'Nam? And the old lady run over by a car and the poor schmuck who hit her? Going to jail, for life? And if we're supposed to be temples of God, when in the hell—pardon me, why in the world would God put cancer in his own temple? And why would so many people be so obese if they were the temples of God? They some sort of circus tent for the Holy Spirit?" I pointed toward the window. "So why did God create crooks and cheats and bullies and felons? And what about endangered animals, the poachers, the dying forests, bleached ocean coral, our whole planet?" I took a breath and waited. The priest didn't say a word. And what could he say? I was right. I knew I was right and he knew it to, maybe. But I wasn't finished with him, or me.

"And, why did God put me here in the States and not in some backward, hole-in-the-wall country living under a tarp in the middle of nowhere? And why doesn't the stock market just go up and not down, so people don't lose money, their homes, their lives? And why do some people pay hundreds of bucks to sit in a box at a football game and rake in the dough on Wall Street so they can blow it on chicks while other guys, the schmucks, work in plants full of chemicals that are killing them? Yeah, and then, for the love of a loving God, they go to church and they get nothing for it? Squat, nothing but slapped in the face." I turned and pointed to the crucifix above the altar. "And why is it that you have to believe in Jesus and not Buddha or Abraham or Moses as the one, true savior of mankind?"

The priest summed things up neatly. "We each have our own crosses to bear." He folded his hands in his lap and gently settled back against his pew.

I came out of my seat and leaned over him. In one breath I laid it out: "Crosses? What cross do you have?" I spread my arms wide and looked all around. "You have this big church, this building, clean, dry, ornate. Pretty cushy place. Folks are on the streets. I walk with them. They're not in a desert looking for a promised land. They're just hoping for a promised house, yet they never see anything, nothing, not even close. They're invisible." I sat and turned toward the priest, ready to roll again. "What about the girl that got raped on the streets in Topeka last night, or the one in Brooklyn, and the high school girl abused by her stepfather who lives on the street, and all the other battered women? And the little boy whose father I killed?" I slowed. "The kid will never see his dad again. Why is it fair for a loving God to give them crosses that—"

"You killed someone?" Holtzapfel straightened and crossed his arms, reaching for his more serious, priestly look.

"Yeah. Yeah. There's no doubt, that boy and the boy's mother have suffered every day since. How much love do they get, huh?" Behind the words, a translucent image of Ben Keller's wife appeared in the window where I'd noticed the dove earlier. I closed my eyes, but the image remained.

"Have you paid for your crime?" he asked, then repeated to awaken me, "Mr. Chili, have you confessed? Have you paid for your crime? Have you confessed your sin?" He persisted and tapped his lips again with folded hands. I was sure he was praying.

"Sin? What sin? I sin all the time. Who can't sin? What's sin? Let him throw the first stone, isn't that what the Good Book says? I told you, I don't believe in religion. I don't believe God has anything to do with what I do or did, so what's to confess? Or, probably as you see it, since God is all-knowing, He knows what I did, I mean you could say God made me do it. God doesn't say, 'Okay, what's my man Chili going to do this time?' And then roll the dice. God knows in advance what I'm going to do. Right? He knows everything that ever happened or will happen, all that predestination crap."

"Free will, my son. God has given each of us a free will to make decisions. It was your decision to—"

"Not exactly a decision. Well, maybe it was ... maybe it was my mistake. Whatever. I killed him."

"And now?"

"And now, I run. Every single day. A fugitive. Running from the law. Living on the street. That's not living." I crossed my arms in front of my chest and leaned back. "Simple as that. I run from the cops. I run from that boy. I run from the kid's mother. I run." I turned and stared at a statue of a bearded man in a brown robe.

"You can't run forever. You know that, Mr. Chili."

"Oh, come on." I looked around the church at the other statues, all of them looking directly at me. "You don't need to tell me. I move around a lot. And it's not Mr. Chili, okay? It's Bob White. On the street they call me Chili, just Chili, not Mr. Chili."

"Then, Mr. White, I pray you find it in your heart to make amends. You are a temple of one soul. Go there. Spend time inside, inside yourself. Face your sin or guilt or whatever you intend to call it."

"Not sure I can do that," I said, looking him straight in the eyes, still thinking about the earlier image of the woman's face.

"I pray you turn yourself in, Mr. White," the priest whispered. "Accept God. Your judgement here on Earth is small compared to that which the Lord will make. 'Ask, and it will be given you ...' The priest slipped on a stoic face, the type used for fire and brimstone sermons, and continued, "His Divine Kingdom is His reward. Admit your sin. Killing is a sin. Seek His forgiveness. If you fail to accept the redeeming grace of God and fail to heed His word, His commandment—Thou shalt not kill—there will be consequences. Your penance of being homeless is not penance enough." He smiled slightly and added, "You can't sneak past sin. There's nowhere that far away, Mr. White." He sat back. When I bent forward to talk, he raised his hand. "Have faith, Mr. White. That God you don't believe in is a good God. And despite what evil and pain and suffering you see and feel in the world, he is a loving God, a forgiving God."

I laughed. "Oh yeah?" I flicked my finger right past his nose and opened my arms as wide as they'd go. "You want to give me this church and see what happens? You want m-m-m-me to come and play the organ this week and pr-pr-preach and see what happens? I know. I know." When I stuttered, I grabbed the back of the pew. My turn to smile—actually, my turn to laugh. "I was just p-p-p-pulling your leg, Father. I come in off the streets and hit church every Sunday. Sometimes make it to B-B-Bible studies during the week, too. Always looking for a place to get out of the weather, you know, occasionally find some c-c-cookies and p-p-punch somewhere along the line." My smile was a creation of the devil himself. I reached out and patted the old clergyman on his shoulder.

The priest studied his watch, pursed his lips, and tilted his head as he ran his finger around the inside of his starched white collar. He managed a wry smile. "Well then ... make yourself at home here, Mr. White. You're welcome to stay, sit, stand, kneel, sing, and pray or just quietly reflect with the

Lord for as long as you'd like. Allow the Lord to pass through you, to touch your heart," he said as he rose. He turned to walk off, but over his shoulder, he added, "And if you are available on Sunday, masses are at 8:30 and 10:30. I'm sure the congregation would appreciate your music." With a sigh, he added, "Bless you." With his right hand he gestured to form an air-cross—up, down, left, and right—in front of me then continued up the center aisle toward the altar.

"Oh hey, Father," I hollered, boosted by a muffled echo, "that little bit about me killing the guy? That's between you and me, you know, the old confessional rule. Sacred bond of silence between sinner and priest. What's said in the confessional, stays in the confessional sorta thing." He simply nodded, turned, and passed through a side door.

Lying to a man of the cloth in his own church. That's sure grounds for eternal damnation. The church was empty. No midday interlopers. It was all mine. The solitude awakened my inner voices. They crippled me with a heap of thoughts that stacked up in my head.

Play the organ.
Steal the gold vessels.
Dress up in those church vestments.
Coins from candle stands.
Eat the wafers.
Wine, somewhere. Find the wine.
Gold candlesticks. Steal them.
Sit in the small cubbyhole and listen to sinners confess.
Fire. Light this place up with a bit of sacrificial flame.

I checked side altars and alcoves, sanctuary and sacristy, the vestibule, side entrance porticos, and closets. I gathered all the candles out of the hurricane glass holders. I stashed one in my rucksack and bunched the others tightly together to form a wax mosaic at the edge of the altar rail. Then I grabbed the tall candles from the altar and wedged them into the middle. There were more than sixty candles, a potential pool of wax. Using a taper from the votive stand, I lit all of them.

"Come Holy Spirit. Enkindle in us the power of ... love," I yelled at the top of my lungs, stretching the last word in a deep slur. "Come on down," I hollered.

I turned to walk out and noticed two elderly women standing together just inside the massive doors. Their jaws sagged in disbelief.

"What are you looking at?" I said as I meandered down the center aisle toward them. "The Spirit of God is here. Light up, ladies." I waved my arms wildly. As I passed, I tipped the bill of my cap with a nod in their direction and walked off. I could have shared a boatload of sins with that priest. But I didn't believe in sin, so why bother?

The sun had melted the clouds. The day was now colored with blue skies marked by fortune cookie white clouds of hope dappled with others in shades of gray. I slipped into a five and dime to buy a box of multicolored chalk. As the earlier adrenaline rush of playing the organ eased, for block after block I colored the sidewalk with pithy, pertinent quotes for all to read. I admit, there were a few drawings, nothing racy or anything, but weird to say the least, a little something to allow my breathing to slow. The mishmash of thoughts cleared. I walked, lost in thought. Eventually I returned to a spot near the coffee shop to take advantage of the sidewalk traffic along with the warmth of the sun. I spread my field jacket on the concrete and watched as the man whom I'd seen earlier retrieved his pack and coat, undisturbed, from under the tree. How interesting that he felt he could leave what were quite possibly all his earthly possessions under a tree and expect nobody would run off with them. Where did he get that kind of faith in mankind?

As I thought about that man and his faith, the words of the priest kept coming back. His comments about how the simple things in life—breathing, seeing, hearing, smelling—are blessings in themselves. I considered his other comments, namely about confessing my sin. Was my act a sin, truly a sin? And confess to whom? A priest, the police? Neither would, nor could, offer the forgiveness I needed.

I recalled how Trixie had said that I had to face the woman, the wife of the guy I had killed. I knew it. I needed to reset my search. I needed to find Mary Kay. I owed her. And she owed me.

Chapter 21

Thank God—if there was a God that day—for the sunshine. Or was that Mother Nature? No matter how one looked at it, sitting on the sidewalk in the bright sunshine on a winter's day was a blessing. I people-watched. After three years I could spot personalities: businessman, doctor, lawyer, housewife. Those were the easy ones. I could also classify people as well. That one is a junkie. He's a mugger. She's a nymphomaniac. Those three are apostles. He's obviously a pimp. When I tired of people, I closed my eyes, fascinated by the smell of gasoline and oil, remnants of sunlight trapped in the Earth during the days when the T-Rex and Stegosaurus roamed.

The warming sun also brought out the best in folks, their coins, which brought out the best in me. I sang. I recited poetry. I recited classic soliloquies of the stage. The full brilliance of a street entertainer.

"Were those quotes from *The Prophet*?" The question came from a tall woman without the usual tinting of make-up. Her face was a pale white with streaks of dirt and eyes searching for sleep. Her hair was mussed. She wore a flannel shirt over jeans, very much the costume of a typical passerby with the exception of the shopping cart she pushed. Her load included plastic bags with clothing, a pillow, a boxy portable radio in a leather case, a few framed photographs, a small stuffed panda toy, and a coffee-stained ceramic mug. She stood in front of me.

"Yes it was," I replied, staring up.

She offered a warm smile. "I remember those lines from college, years ago."

"Then ... welcome to the Arts Corner, fair visitor. Visit often. I have dozens of those. Classics by Rumi, Bradstreet, Poe, Pound, Shakespeare, Frost, Sandburg, Gorski, Dylan, the Beatles, and the list goes on and on. And of course, my own, classics in the rough."

"So refreshing. What's your name? I haven't seen you here before."

"Chili. I'm new in town."

"Chili?"

"My parents hated me," I said with a laugh. She gave me an uncertain look, then laughed too. "What's your name?"

"Sheila."

"Welcome, Sheila. Care to join me?"

Her face lit up at the invitation. "Well, I was—"

"Please have a seat. I could use the company." I patted the sidewalk next to me, slid my field jacket over as a cushion for her use.

Sheila parallel-parked her shopping cart alongside the building and joined me. As people approached, I spouted off more poetry or monologue or sang a few bars of a showtune or classic oldie, anything to rouse the attention of the walkers.

"So, from college. Let me guess. English major?"

She nodded.

"Where?"

"Out west. Northern Arizona University."

I looked over at the collection of things in her cart. My smile escaped as I faced her. "And the cart? Those don't look like groceries. How long have you been pushing that baby around?"

"Three months, I guess." She chewed on a fingernail.

"You getting by okay?" I asked.

"Yes." She sniffled, keeping her eyes low and picking at her nails.

"Have a job?"

"Part-time is all. Had a second one, part-time, but it dried up a couple weeks ago. I haven't found a new one yet. I work about twenty hours a week, enough to buy food. I probably won't starve but could use a regular roof over my head or a good bed. What about you?"

"Three years out here, give or take a few. So, did you study Gibran?"

"Yeah."

"Just poetry? Any of his art? His religious stuff or politics?"

"Mainly poetry. He wasn't my favorite."

"Really? Who's your hero?"

Sheila settled back against the façade of the building and rambled on. At one point she commented about how nice it was to just sit and talk to someone with similar interests, in her words, "someone with a brain." As she talked, I cut her off frequently to perform my sidewalk shtick when people of interest came our way. We shared smiles, tag-teamed reciting poems and singing classic tunes. We both enjoyed the sunshine and the company, until I stepped into her other past.

"Did you find a good use for all your study, your arts? Are you, or rather, were you a teacher?"

"No." She lost her smile. "Jeff and I were the proverbial flower-children. Got married in the desert while we were in school. He was deferred from the draft, then drew a high number in the lottery. He found a good job out of school, there in Flagstaff. I stayed around the house. I never felt that teaching was my thing." Sheila bent forward and continued to talk while she adjusted the field-jacket cushion. "I couldn't have kids and my degree didn't qualify for much else, so I found out. I wasn't really great at writing. Besides, companies wanted journalism majors for that." She sat down again, legs crossed, Indian-style. "Jeff's company closed his plant in Flagstaff. They said if he was willing to move, they had a slot here in Macon. I didn't have family. My folks died a few years back in a car accident." She closed her eyes and turned away. Her head shook ever so slightly side-to-side while she chewed on her fingernail again.

"Sorry to hear that," I said, breaking the extended lull.

She faced me with a deep sigh. Her pace slowed; her voice quavered. "Right after we moved here, Jeff had some health issues which were eventually diagnosed as stage IV pancreatic cancer. He was a smoker. We spent what money we had on medical bills. God, the bills. They never stopped. Week after week, more bills. We took out a second mortgage on our house but ..." She rubbed her forehead and allowed her words to taper off.

Although people continued to walk by, my attention was on Sheila. After a pause, her voice forced its way around a lump in her throat as tears dripped in her eyes.

"All of that borrowing wasn't enough. Jeff died last year. I tried to find a job. Had no money to go anywhere. I took two lousy part-time jobs but didn't make enough to cover the mortgages plus utilities and food and medical bills and other stuff. The bank repossessed the house, and now this, this is who I am." She looked up with a wan smile and tears on her cheeks, her eyebrows wrinkled.

"It's tough," I said.

"No, it's not tough. It's crazy," she cried, flushed with anger. "My life was never supposed to be like this. I was doing things the way everybody said. Stay in school. Go to college. Get married. Raise a family. Contribute. And I get this? Why?" Tears were her only answer. "Why?"

"I'd say that Jeff's death definitely threw a wrinkle in the works. I'd—"

"What the hell? What do you know about death? The death of someone you loved. Someone who cared for you. Someone you cared for you more than anything or anyone else in the world. He was my world. Jeff was so sweet. So loving. So kind. He would have done anything for anybody." She pulled her legs into her chest and wrapped her arms around them with her head on her knees. She cried.

I let her cry. What else could I do? What could I say? I could have said I knew about death. I knew firsthand. I was a partner with death. But, as her words faded, the memories of my best friend crept in, riding piggy-back on what she had shared. Someone you loved. Someone who loved you. Someone who would do anything for anybody. That was Ben.

"I ... I can imagine how you feel. I ..."

She raised her head. Her lips curled and her eyes burned through me when she leaned across to slap me. I grabbed her wrist. She yanked her arm free. With a wide-eyed, demonic stare she reared back for second swat, then hesitated, cupped her face in her hands, and crumpled, releasing her head back down onto her knees. When she reappeared, her face was ripped with pain.

"You can't even begin to imagine," she bawled. "My world is gone. Gone!" She looked down and added, "I've lost my one love. I've lost my world. I've lost everything, even hope. Especially hope, the hope that any of this will change or could change." She tucked her head again.

I looked away. A small crowd had formed a few feet down the sidewalk. I held open my hands to them. "It's okay. She's okay," I said softly to wave the people along.

Sheila heard the caution. She raised her chin. "It's not okay," she cried, "nothing's okay." With arms still wrapped around her legs, she squeezed tighter and put her head back on her knees. The people on the street followed a wide path around us with their heads turned back toward Sheila.

"Sheila, I'll agree, I can't know how you feel. And there's nothing I can do about the past." I spoke slowly and softly, hoping to calm her. "But I might be able to help with the future." She didn't acknowledge me. "I think I know where you can find a job, if not directly, most certainly indirectly as a resource or word-of-mouth reference."

Sheila sniffled as she lifted her chin to look at me.

"Over a few blocks that way," I pointed, "is a Catholic church. Not much to look at from the outside, kinda covered in vines and all. Anyway, go there and ask to see the priest. His name is Father Holtzapfel. When you meet him, just say, 'Chili sent me to meet your loving God.' That's all you need to say, those words. He'll understand, guaranteed. I'm sure after you have a chance to share your story, he'll have a job for you. At the very least, he will introduce you to someone who will have a job, a good job, something that will finally use that college degree of yours."

Her eyes were quieter now, bewildered. She didn't talk, just stared off into the distance.

"Seriously," I continued with assurance, "go see him. The guy is amazing. Saintly sort. Works miracles. I saw him just a few hours ago. Great man." If that old priest was worth his salt, Sheila was an ideal candidate to prove his "loving God" theory.

People passed. I didn't bother to entertain them and nobody bothered to drop any coins.

"I'm not a Catholic," were the first words out of her mouth. "I haven't been in a church much since we moved here, I mean with Jeffrey and the medical problems and all. I mean ... you really think? And you said if I mentioned your name, he would know you?"

"Oh, he'll remember me. You can bet he'll remember me."

"If he's so good, why are you out here? Why don't you have him give you a job?" She wiped her cheeks with her sleeve.

"I have a job. I just do this for entertainment." She gave me another bewildered look. "I'm on a hunt. A bounty hunter, of sorts. I'm traveling incognito. I'm trailing someone, but I can't tell you any more or I'd have to kill you and I've only had to do that once, so ..." I said with a laugh. She understood the reference.

She fought back tears—hopefully, now, tears of joy—and patted me on my knee before she stood. She pulled her cart away from the wall. "Thanks. Sorry about all that." With a cherubic smile, she added, "'Doubt is a pain too lonely to know that faith is his twin brother.' Gibran said that. I should be a better listener. Good luck, Chili," she said as she walked off.

I slumped against the brick façade and closed my eyes. "Good luck to you too, Sheila," I echoed, softly. That priest would tell me—well, he would claim—that man has free will. And what had that free will done for Sheila?

And, for that matter, what had it done for Ben Keller? His life was cut short. And his wife? Her free will? She hadn't had weeks or months to say goodbye, to prepare. Did her feelings bother me? It was her husband who was dead, not me. I was alive. All of that bothered me, and why not? I once had it all. Education. House. Steady job. Travel. Career. I was flying high, moving fast. And now? I scooted up on the wall behind me with different thoughts in mind.

Sheila and I could not have been more different. I reveled in the peacefulness of homelessness. No phone calls to make, even fewer to return. No suspense dates. No meetings. No presentations. No reports. No evaluations. Just a sign, a cap, a sidewalk, and an imagination which, in my case, was often controlled by the voices.

Foot traffic decreased considerably throughout the day. I filled my time catching up on the news. The local newspaper I plucked from the trash fluttered like a jib while I read the blah-blah headlines and frontpage stories. Tucked deep on page three, a story entitled "Bloody Sunday" caught my eye. On this day, twenty-two years earlier, civil rights leaders and demonstrators marched across the Edmund Pettus Bridge out of Selma, Alabama. Yet, after all those years, the story carried a definite slant which begrudged African-Americans' rights under law. The reading went to my gut; it triggered something in me.

I grew restless, but I was weak, too weak, too troubled to stand. Thoughts boiled. I didn't have strength enough to lift my head. My waning energy wrestled with the words in the article. In my head I convinced myself that I had been there. I was there on that Sunday on that bridge in Selma. That I was the problem. I could feel it. I could sense it. It gnawed at me. I had caused the trouble on that bridge. I was the one responsible for the attacks, the beatings, the bloodshed. I felt the pain. The pain was my fault. I thought about the cops on the bridge, the cops now hunting me, chasing me. I closed my eyes to fight visions. Images splattered in my mind. The familiar sounds and sights. A siren. An explosion. The flash of blinding-white strobes. A distant line of green lights jiggled into red squares. A starburst of spectral color. I ran toward the lights. Then, the blackness followed.

When I opened my eyes, nothing on the street had changed. The guy across the street was still washing the windows. The dog peeing on the tree still had his leg up. The traffic light was still red. People in the crosswalk, still crossing. The entire episode—the images, all of it—had taken no time. Mind games, again.

My head fog cleared instantly when a police cruiser drifted beside the curb next to me. I looked down and away, hiding my face. The car came to a stop. One of the cops got out and walked toward me. I nonchalantly gathered my things.

"Excuse me, sir, may I have a word with you?"

I didn't look up. I threw the last of my notebooks in my backpack and sprang off the sidewalk.

"Sir. Hold it. Come back," the cop said as he followed in pursuit.

I darted down an alley and cut back to the next street. When I looked back the cop had made the turn behind me. The squad car pulled up next to him and he hopped in. I doubled back and returned to the alley, then made another cut into a second alley—a dead-end—climbed a wooden partition, and landed in a small, corralled trash bin enclosure. I squeezed in between two bins and didn't move. I waited. No sirens. No cops. Nobody in pursuit.

As I caught my breath, I talked myself through any of the many reasons the cop wanted to talk. It had to be the priest. He had called the cops. I told him I had killed a guy.

I guess because I wasn't in that little confessional booth, the priest-sinner relationship deal didn't apply; he didn't have to consider my sins as confidential. He talked to his God and did what he was told to do. The old "Thou shalt not kill," number seven on the "Ten Commandments" hit parade. I'd violated most of those deals over time, except number six: "Honor thy father and thy mother." My old man had made sure that I never broke that one.

When all was quiet, I ventured out; that was when the cops stepped in.

Chapter 22

I spent the night in the comfort of the county jail, in a private cell with a bench/bed-for-one made of formed sheet metal. As accommodations go, it wasn't half bad. Even the evening meal looked good, but I didn't eat. My stomach wasn't buying the idea of food. My head was still preoccupied with the question of who had tipped them off this time.

When I asked why I was there, the response was always, "Vandalism, public nuisance, and vagrant conduct." When I asked who presented the charges, I was told to wait.

"How long do I have to wait?"

"Until your hearing in front of the judge. Tomorrow, maybe the next day," the jailer replied.

I considered requesting a writ of habeas corpus, but that would require a lawyer or, at the very least, a form and swearing-in. In my situation, it would probably not take long for the system to determine my true identity and marry it up with bulletins and existing searches for felons and other criminals. I elected to lay low and quiet and hope this sleepy, southern burg could expedite an appearance before a magistrate of some sort. Standing before a magistrate would certainly entail a story, one I set out to create.

I didn't sleep much that night. Despite cautions from the deputy on night duty, I paced a good bit, battling the Vigilantes, wide awake, enjoying the excitement of incarceration. *We told you. You let your mouth run and, wham!*

You end up here. Killing your friend. Running. Crossing state lines. Next stop: Sing Sing.

A deputy sheriff led me into a courtroom the following morning. It was a small, stark room with a gallery section of fewer than a dozen chairs behind a railing. A podium stood on the other side of the railing at the foot of a dais with a large wooden desk. There were two people already seated in the gallery. I was placed on the opposite side from where they sat. I watched while another deputy brought a fourth person into the room. The three law officers then lined the back wall.

When the judge entered, someone off to the side said, "All rise. The court is now in session. The Honorable Richard T. Wanstead presiding." An officer behind me nudged me to stand.

"Please be seated."

I sat through two appearances that didn't go well before the judge called my name to approach the bench.

"State your name."

"Robert White," I said, looking around with a pasted-on smile. My fingers and toes began to tingle.

"Mr. White, I want to advise you that you are charged with vandalism of a place of worship, acts of public nuisance, and vagrant conduct. Do you understand the nature of the charges?"

"Yes."

The judge then rattled off the standard legal rights: the right to an attorney, the right to a trial, the right to remain silent, anything I said could be used against me and the other blah, blah cookie-cutter legal mumbo jumbo.

"Do you have a counsel present, Mr. White?"

I looked around the room. It was obvious that I had nobody present, but he had asked, nonetheless. I smiled. "No."

"Do you wish to have an attorney?"

"No."

"Court date for hearing this case is set for January 18." The judge took a long look at me then jotted something down. "Bail for these charges as presented is set at $2,500. Do you understand the bail?"

"I do, but—"

Looking at me a second time, the judge added, "If you cannot pay the bail, you will remain in the custody of the sheriff until such time that your arraignment hearing takes place. Is that understood?"

"Yes, but—"

"Do you wish to add something? Bail bond can be arranged with the aid of family or an attorney."

The bail was ridiculous. The candles in that church, if I'd pulled every last one of them and melted them to the end of their wicks, it would have cost a couple hundred bucks, at most. What was this guy trying to do? Why the high bail? Did he suspect ... "Judge, look," I said, "if it pleases the court, I don't have that kind of cash and I have no family to—"

"Then, Mr. White, I suggest an attorney. If you cannot afford an attorney, the state will provide one for you."

All well and good. The state would give me a legal beagle. So be it. My more immediate concern was sitting in a cell. First, my safety and second, my time. Time for the state and Feds to do a little background work to find me on a "wanted" list.

"Your honor, sir. I was just passing through town—"

"Mr. White, we will address the charges further at your next appearance, your arraignment on January 18. There is nothing further to—"

"Look, Judge, I don't have time to be sitting around in a cell. I'm on a secret mission here. I need to get back on the road. I'm trailing someone, see. I—"

The judge pounded his gavel once. "Will the deputy please remove Mr. White from the courtroom?" The judge motioned for the deputy to come forward. "Mr. White, you were advised of your rights. At your arraignment hearing you will have an opportunity to submit your plea. If at that time you or your counsel wish to make a statement, the court will hear it then. Until that time, you are dismissed and remanded under the custody of Bibb County."

The deputy walked up and stood next to me by the podium. When I didn't move, he reached for my elbow before I yanked it away. I followed him back to the jail.

I was placed in an intake cell with the two guys who had appeared before me in the courtroom. They were a Mutt and Jeff pair of good ol' boys. Within an hour, the authorities moved each of them, separately, into their own permanent cells. I set in my cell for several hours. When I was alone, the voices got the best of me. When they had booked me, they took all my belongings and inventoried them, and they gave me the classic orange jumpsuit to wear. The inventory would undoubtedly give them cause to search my name against other lists. It wouldn't take long. They would be hauling me back into the courtroom to read additional charges, serious charges. My mind went into a tailspin with crazy ideas. How could I escape? What story could I use? What defense could I raise? Then, I paused to think, how could I get to Mary Kay Keller? How could I find her? What other leads could I find? That was when it dawned on me.

"Mr. White," the deputy said as he approached the cell door, "you are a free man." He unlocked the cell. "Follow me to sign for your belongings."

"Wait! What's going on?"

"You're free. Charges dropped."

"Dropped?"

"Yes. Judge sent word. The prosecutor dropped the charges. Something about evidence."

I didn't ask any more questions. My need to know existed only as far as the front door. I quickly changed back into my street clothes. As I walked through the lobby, I noticed Sheila with the old priest talking to a man in a suit. The goings-on in my head were far more important than details. What I needed was to hightail it out of Macon, leaving no tracks behind, before whomever changed their mind.

Chapter 23

Following my release I thumbed a ride to Savannah, Georgia. Given my recent incarceration with the legal system and tormented by the Vigilantes' harassment, I was super sensitive to every sign or reference to law enforcement. Police headquarters, Savannah Law School, assorted law offices, the state bar exam building—all of them caused another detour.

My paranoia carried over to people in general. Reluctant to talk, I approached a panhandler near the bus station and learned there was a shelter, the Union Gospel Mission, on the far side of town. At the Mission, I joined the line late, but others wandered in after me, most stopping to bum cigarettes or finagle a hit from a bottle. Without looking, I shooed them away with a wave or a finger. Still quite conscious of my close encounter, I avoided everything and everybody. I stayed in my own little world in the shadows, eyes closed and head back against the building.

It took forever for the doors to open. When they did, I was issued a bottom bunk toward the back of the hall, a converted gym. Quickly settled, the next hour passed with my head in my hands sitting on the edge of the mattress, fighting the commotion of forty hungry, tired, filthy, less-than-civil adult males settling their asses in for the night. I stuffed my fingers in my ears, tucked my head between my knees, and fought the pandemonium until my stomach sounded the SOS. I dashed to the locker room—over, under, around, and through several people—to pray to the porcelain god; unfortunately, I had little to offer.

After praying to a point when my stomach lining itself was coming up, my knees ached more than my head. I climbed out of the stall and leaned against the wall of broken tiles near the sinks. I was beat. Through a thick cloud of caustic urinal cakes and lingering disinfectant from mops in the corner, a voice emerged. At first, by instinct, it registered as one of the Vigilantes, but listening further, the voice actually came from a stall at the other end of the room.

"I be safe in here. They never catch me," the voice said.

My back slid down the wall until my ear was on the floor and my eyes struggled to find the source.

"No, I ain't doin' what you say."

The voice mumbled something to somebody, but I saw only two feet in a pair of green and red bowling shoes. When I heard the crash of glass, the voice stopped. On the floor, by the shoes, lay fragments of an empty pint liquor bottle. The stall door opened.

A bag-of-bones black man emerged. His hair was an Einstein bush of misshaped kinky gray. His chin and cheeks were frosted over with a salt-and-pepper stubble of several days. When he saw me, he stepped back inside the stall.

"You ain't taking me nowhere, no how," his voice echoed from behind the stall door. He grunted as his fingers gingerly gathered pieces of the bottle.

I said nothing.

"I said you ain't taking me nowhere, no how," the man repeated, followed by a wet, guttural cough.

"I don't intend to take you nowhere, no how," I said, breaking hours of my own silence, mimicking his voice.

He stepped back out of the stall, his steps aiming toward a wheelchair I hadn't noticed across the floor. He walked with an uncoordinated wobble, keeping a wide base atop slightly bowed legs. His feet slid along the uneven linoleum surface until one of his shoes caught on an upturned patch in the floor, and he face-planted just short of the chair. I started to crawl in his direction.

"Get away from me. Don't touch my ass," he shouted and curled up. "Leave me alone. I'll cut your white-ass throat. Stay away from me. I have powers you ain't never seen before. Get away. I got a knife." I stopped moving and watched him drag himself to the wheelchair. With a sunrise of his butt crack showing, he hoisted himself off the floor. I was close enough to help him jockey into his seat, but he nudged me away. Only then did I notice he was missing his right hand.

Over-stuffed plastic bags draped along handles that bent downward at a forty-five-degree angle on the back of the chair. I slipped in behind it to push; besides, I needed the support.

"What the hell you doing? Where are you taking me? Let go of me," he hollered. "Let go of me." He frantically twisted his shoulders side-to-side, lost inside his oversized Georgia Bulldogs sweatshirt.

"Relax, ya old coot. I'm taking you out of this shit hole. Let me push you over to the chow line and—"

"No. No. They'll put poison in my food. No. Push me back there." He waved his arm wildly.

"Back where?" I said.

"Back there. Back by them chairs," he said with a brittle voice.

His screaming added to a headache that consumed me. There wasn't a square millimeter of my humanity that wasn't howling. The best pain management was to let my head dangle with one eye shut and the other only half open, pushing this wacko, old fart slowly to the far end of the gym floor. A chunk of rubber missing in one of the front wheels caused the wheelchair to limp. The closer we got to the back, the more the place smelled like an armpit. He motioned with the stub of his arm to go behind a cart of folding chairs where he had a single bed.

"Where'd you come from? Who are you?" the man asked softly. His voice still had a bit of a slur left over from the bottle. He twisted to look back at me. In the dim light the wrinkles along his forehead looked deep enough to grow corn. He had bags of elephant skin below his drooping upper eyelids and pores in his nose which reminded me of swiss cheese.

I moaned as I pressed my palms against my temples, waiting for my eyeballs to squirt onto this guy's lap. "Name's Chili. What's yours?" I pressed harder against my head. My stomach grumbled in response.

"Shh. Not so loud," he said with a spray of spittle. "They'll hear ya. What's your problem?"

Against another painful flare-up in my head and behind another moan, I said, "Bad day's all." I was hoping food would solve at least one of my problems. "Look, I gotta go grab some supper while it's hot. You coming?" I winced.

"Ain't no way. I told ya, they put poison in my food, keep me from talking."

"Sure. Okay," I mumbled, too fried to understand whatever he meant. "I'll bring some chow back with me. They won't know it's for you. I can taste if for you, first, then if I don't die—"

"Might not kill you for an hour or a day, but you be dead. Ain't doing that." He reached around into one of the plastic bags and pulled out a can of sardines and a can of fruit cocktail. "I got food. I'm good." He pulled a tab on the sardine can and set it on the bed. I took that as my cue to leave.

Supper took a while, purposely waiting for the food to kill me. Miraculously, that never happened. In fact, quite the opposite; the food dissolved my headache. After eating, I looked to the back of the hall and saw the old man slumped over in his wheelchair. On the far side of the room, a boxy black-and-white TV blasted out actors in a back-and-forth mudslinging courtroom drama as I weaved through the obstacle course of guests sorting through their personal items. As I approached the old man from behind, he rocked uneasily in his seat and gestured with his arms. I heard him calmly say, "Judge, I told you before and I'll says it again, I ain't done nothing wrong. Let me go. I don't deserve no prison." Then his tone changed along with his message. "It's none of your damn business. If I want to sleep here I will. I have a knife. I can defend myself. Tomorrow I'll go see my wife. She'll tell ya."

My approach from outside his peripheral vision allowed me to sneak up unannounced. When I flopped onto his bed, his eyes nearly popped out. He grabbed his chest and coughed, one of those wheezing, crackling sounds from deep in a phlegm-filled throat.

"Here," I said, before he could catch his breath, "have a cupcake. Taste-tested. Safe to eat, guaranteed."

He turned away, still hacking. When the coughing stopped, he mumbled something inaudible. He waited, nodded his head as if to agree to something he had heard— the TV maybe—then he turned and looked over my right shoulder toward someone or something. He mouthed another response, another mumble that made no sense, before he brought the conversation back to me.

"We can't talk with them around. Come on," he said. His feet quickly flipped up the footrests on the chair. I looked around. Using the tips of his shoes, he pulled the chair toward a door in the shadows marked "Boiler Room." He pulled up alongside the door and butted it open with his shoulder. "In here," he said, looking back to make sure nobody had followed us.

A single, dim, bare bulb outlined a beast of a boiler that moaned the slow, deep groan of a turn-of-the-century ocean liner. The air was thick with a vaporized oily sheen that coated the floor. The old man tip-toed his wheelchair to a corner away from the equipment. He swiveled in his seat, and from one of the many plastic bags tied to his chair, he pulled out a bulging scrapbook, filled with loose newspaper clippings and laced together with a shoestring.

"What are you doing? Why'd we have to come in here?" I asked.

He spent a few more minutes thumbing through the contents of his book as he began to talk. "I need to show you this. This here."

The book had no theme or obvious purpose. It was a scrapbook in its truest sense. Random bits of paper. "Who are you? What's your name?" I said as I grabbed a beat-up metal bucket, flipped it upside down, and took a seat near the foot of his wheelchair.

"Name? Names? Names are funny things, ain't they. Yours is Chili. Huh, Chili. What kind of name is that?" Before I could answer, he continued, "Lenny. Full name is Leonard Grant. Most people call me General. You know, after the Yankee in the war. What kind of name's Chili?"

Between the slur he carried from the bottle he had broken earlier and his fast-talking delivery, I could hardly understand him. His eyes shifted side-to-side along with a nervous tic, an up-and-down head-bob.

"Your real name? What's your real name?"

"Chili," I repeated.

"No. No. You got a real name? A proper name, like John Wayne or something?"

"Bob. Bob White," I said to play along with his questioning.

"Oh, that's outstanding. Outstanding." He looked back toward the book in his lap and stared hard at the image on the top page. "Okay, Ralph. That's outstanding."

Where had he come up with Ralph?

"Ya know, cleanliness is close to godliness, Ralph. Ya know?" He reached into another bag looped over the push handles of his chair, pulled out a grungy rag, and wiped the tops of his shoes. "You should really do a better job of cleaning yourself up." He looked around. "Isn't there a shower in this place? You should wash your clothes in the shower. Let me check." He turned away and said, "Hey, Tommy, is the shower working back there yet?" I waited for a response, but none came. There was nobody else in the room.

"Okay, okay," he said shooing flies away from his head. He busied himself flipping through the pages in the scrapbook. Several contained scraps of lined paper and napkins with sloppy printed letters and numbers mixed with articles torn from newspapers. "This is very important stuff here, see. Been collecting this." His brown eyes, one covered with a murky cloud across the lens, opened wider than a kid's on Christmas. He wet his lips with his tongue several times before he whispered, "I've developed a plan for a teleportation machine, ya see. You know what that is? You understand teleportation?"

My nod appeased him. He kept rolling, talking faster, slurring more.

"I got my notes and all this, right here." He looked at the page. "No, no. Not this book." He reached into his bag and pulled out a different scrapbook, scanned it, then pulled out a third book, stacked on his lap. "Ya see these here? These are clues. Pictures and numbers, right? Combinations of those pictures and with certain numbers ... like this one." He flipped page after page in his book, then went back to some pages he had skipped in his excitement. He pulled out a newspaper clipping. It had a photo of a sailboat, a racing boat. "See, see this boat? And see this number on the sail here." He turned the paper with the stub of his arm so I could read it. "You take that number there and multiply each number by the next number and get a number, then you subtract each of those individual numbers from that larger number and that gives you a new number. That number then is key, you see—key to the scientific equation for teleportation."

Words were flying out of his mouth, few of them formed into sentences but all laced with a degree of slur. While he talked, he rummaged through the stack of loose papers, looking for something. The arm with no hand helped align papers while the good hand madly shuffled from within the stack. "Then you have this one here. This page." He pushed out a page from the classified section of a newspaper. "It looks like a bunch of numbers for all these guys selling these houses. I use these to calculate more of the equation. It's all here." He smiled with his noticeable shortage of teeth. "You just gotta find it. See ... these are all clues. I look at these pages and the clues pop out. I have it all drawn out on a wall in the library."

He rolled a little closer to me. With his sardine breath he asked, "You ever been to the moon?"

Something inside me wanted to say yes, but I let him continue his story.

"I have. I was an astronaut. Travelled 35,000 miles an hour to get there. Landed, hopped out, shoveled some moondust, kicked my tires, hopped back in my spaceship, and headed home." With his good arm, he spun his wheelchair to face away and whispered, "Told you before …" then mumbled something else. When he turned back toward me, he confessed, "NASA and the CIA want to kill me. Afraid I'll tell everybody what I saw up there."

"Who are you talking to?" I asked.

"Galileo. Sometimes da Vinci. Least that's what they say their names are. A couple others." I shook my head. "They been real nice to me. Tell me I'm doing a great job, ya know. They help with my calculations, ya see."

Again, he reached for a different bag. He untied it with one hand and dumped its contents on the floor by his feet. Canned goods, clothes, an X-Men comic book, and a few small items dropped out. He fumbled around the pile. He held up what appeared to be a standard beeper carried by every appliance repairman in the country. "With this, I have superpowers. I ain't telling what all I can do with this baby," he said. Again, his eyes continued to shift left and right as he started to grin.

Before I had any chance to correct him with sad news, the General turned away and started another conversation. He babbled, easily, for over a minute. Nothing he said made sense; it was all jabber. He wasn't speaking English or any other recognizable language. It was gibberish. He turned back in my direction. His eyes shifted side-to-side and up and down; his lips moved, but nothing came out.

"What?" I said, leaning closer to hear better. He didn't seem to notice I was there. His lips kept moving but still no words. He finally looked over into my eyes. His lips quivered, trying to push out words stuck to his teeth.

Finally, words broke through his drool. "They ain't like you and me." His chin dropped to his chest. I thought the old guy had passed out. At the rate he'd been going, he was probably exhausted; I knew I was. I shook his shoulder. He didn't respond.

"Hey! General? You okay in there?" I asked. "How long have you been in this place?"

It took him a while to register the question.

"Never come in here 'cept when I has to," he said. He looked up and forced a smile. "I usually sleep with my boys in Box City down by the river, back in the bushes. Quiet there. No hassles." He let his head sag again while he talked. "But them ... them ones from the bathroom, they talked to me and said my boys was going to kill me tonight, so I come here." He paused. "I gotta place with a tarp and some wood. Helps keep my chair out of the weather."

"How long have you been living like this, in Box City, I mean?"

"Eight years or so."

"Why? How?" I asked. "You from around here?"

"Why you asking me all them damn questions?" he said. He pushed his chair back, and, one-handed, picked up things he'd dumped on the floor. I tried to help.

"Keep your hands off." He swatted me away and answered my question while he gathered, bent over. "Nah, I grew up in Alabama, I think it was. We was sharecroppers. I think there was some twins after me, but they died, some terrible sickness. My daddy dug them a grave out back the house, far back. Didn't have no headstone or nothing, just some rocks we stacked up and a small wooden cross."

While the General talked, he sorted through the scrapbooks again. This time his fingers traced down each line of print in the top book. He stopped at the numbers on one page then shifted to another and then back. He stopped, looked up at the ceiling for a brief second, lowered his gaze slowly, then stared just over my left shoulder, motionless.

"Daddy died," he said very slowly. "I went back to the farm to help Mama for a while, then I went into the city. Got married. Worked at the paper mill all night and drank all day to drown out the voices, the ones in my head. Couldn't keep them from talking. The more I drank, the more voices I heard. They'd tell me to yell at my wife and spank my girls, so I did. One day at work the voices told me to put my hand into a gear box, so I did and the machine ate my hand. After that I couldn't do no more work, so I got fired. I couldn't work, couldn't farm no more. The farm was gone. I couldn't pay my bills. Then my wife was gone, up and left."

Suddenly, the General's head swiveled back and forth, and then he twisted his body in the seat. His eyes started to ricochet. "Shh," he insisted. "The voices ... they're talking ... 'bout you." His earlier look of excitement turned to one of fear. "They're all around us," he whispered.

He scooted back deep in his chair. "There ... did you see that?" He pointed toward the boiler. "I saw him. It. The silhouette. He said I should kill you. Did you hear him?"

A quick look to the boiler. I saw a boiler, and only a boiler. "General, when did these voices start?"

"Shh. Don't talk." He slowly replaced the scrapbooks in the bag and moved his wheelchair closer to the boiler. He slowly turned his head to the left, then spun his entire body to the right. His movement flipped the wheelchair and pitched him hard against the boiler. He caught the door with the side of his head, barely missing his eye. I reached to grab his chair.

"Get away. Don't touch me," he yelled. "Leave me alone. All of you leave me alone."

No doubt, he was hallucinating. The first thing to do was to get the chair on its wheels and Lenny back in the seat. A stream of blood flowed out from under him. The side of his face was covered. He wiped at it with the stub end of his arm.

"I'll kill you. Stay away from me." Lenny pushed me away with his hand and slid closer to his chair. He swung his bloody arm in my direction to push me back, away from the chair. Ducking under his arm, holding the wheels while Lenny pushed, we managed to get the wheelchair upright but the blood hadn't stopped. Pulling Lenny back against the seatback, I slapped a rag over his face to wipe the blood. He brushed it away and screamed, "Help! Somebody help! He's trying to kill me. Help me. Somebody help!"

"Lenny, General, it's me. Chili. Keep it down."

"Don't touch me. I have a knife, I'll kill you. Stop. Get away." Made wild by his shock on top of voices and hallucinations, he wrestled to keep me away. He kept saying he had a knife as he fumbled with one of his bags until he pulled out a small Swiss army knife. Standing behind his chair, for my safety and his, I slapped the bloody rag over his face, into his mouth, and held it there. I pushed Lenny forward in his seat, his head on his knees. It dawned on me that if someone came in, the situation didn't look good for me. The thought of police drifted through my head.

"Listen," I said, pushing hard on his back and making it difficult for him to take a deep breath. "You're hurt. I'm taking you out front. Maybe someone can help you. We can see how bad the cut is. We need to stop the bleeding. Nobody's going to hurt you. Just relax. You'll be all right. Do you understand that?" His head moved in agreement, though he still pressed hard against the pressure of my hand. My final words as we approached the door were, "The voices, they're not going to do anything to you now. Keep quiet."

With Lenny still bent over, we opened the door and pushed out into the darkened gym. Only the emergency exit lights remained illuminated. Taking my hand off Lenny's back, he sat up and screamed, "He tried to kill me!" In no time, two staff members were next to us, an elderly matron and a palooka, probably the designated bouncer for the place.

"He tried to kill me, see." He pointed to his head, blood still oozing from the wound.

The woman bent down to check Lenny's head. "General, you got yourself a good one this time. I'll tell you what. Why don't you let Jeff here—you remember Jeff, right? Why don't we have Jeff take you over to the aid station and patch you up while I talk to this man, then I'll call the police. Okay?" This time, the mention of police was real.

Lenny sat there while the big guy, Jeff, pushed the General's wheelchair to the sign-in desk.

"You, sir, your name is Chili, right?" she asked. "I've heard things about you."

One more nail in my coffin.

She looked at me, sizing me up for a noose. "Care to tell me your side of the story? What happened?" She stood there, arms crossed in front of her chest, true schoolmarm-style.

My side of the story was short and sweet; my concern remained with her comment about calling the police.

When I finished, she said, "Yep. Kinda figured as much. Voices again?" I nodded. "The General hears them a lot. Did he explain anything about that? You know he was mugged, well, beat with a billy club back in 1965. He was part of that 'Bloody Sunday' incident in Alabama, the Pettus Bridge thing. I heard that story so many times from him. Lenny's been in and out of this place so many times, that's why he has a special spot back there, away from everybody else. He needs to get back to family. He needs family to take care of him now. He drinks too much. He's losing his mind. The voices, he always says the voices are talking to him. He needs help, more than we can give here. He won't listen to us."

"He mentioned daughters. Do you have their names as next of kin or anything?"

"We might, but I can't give you that."

"Just names? I'm not asking for anything. I'll find them." I flashed my big brown eyes at her, smiled sweetly, and she eventually agreed. We walked to the front and found the names in an old log. I also spotted the city listed: Atlanta.

Palooka Jeff put Lenny to bed. I went to work, writing.

Chapter 24

Sleep was a long time coming. What little brain I had left was fried after I finished the letter for Lenny. The less-than-symphonic snoring, the clanging boiler, the banging steam-heated pipes, not to mention the periodic outbursts of "Shit!" every time a body ran into something on the way to the head, all caused me to toss and turn. Emotions bucked logic. I decided to deliver each of Lenny's daughters a letter. The old man needed help. Only they could provide it. The letters had to evoke newfound loving concern for a father who'd never fathered now with a change of heart. And maybe, just maybe I could personally convince them how he had changed and how much he needed their help.

At some point, after the night shift volunteer caught the guy raiding the fridge, the rubbish in my brain decomposed, allowing me to doze off. It's well known that there are four stages of sleep, five if you count REM—rapid eye movement. These are periods where dreams tend to play out. Stages progress in a usual sequence, whimsical flashes of jumping into piles of leaves as a kid or tasting blueberries off a bush, chewy soft pretzels at the fair and squirts of chocolate syrup directly into my mouth.

None of that visited me that night.

A fiery REM took me to the deepest and blackest spot in the universe. And, within that space, to a shaft filled with fireworks. The reds, ambers, and greens exploded but never

no SHELTER for GUILT

disappeared; they multiplied. Lights formed words that pulsed and faded quickly, too quickly for my mind's eye to read. I was falling deeper down the shaft. Sounds popped in my ears, softly at first but growing louder as I slipped deeper. Beeps and whoops and buzzes, in no sequence, no set volume or duration, no detectable pattern. It was noise, not the friendly white noise many use to lull themselves to sleep. This was disturbing alarm clock noise, or worse, because it didn't wake me.

In the dream, everything was vividly real, except I was paralyzed—my arms, my legs, even my voice. Words formed in my head but refused to leak out. Panic choked my breathing. I was tumbling, so a voice yelled, *Roll left, roll left.* My body refused. Lights flashed brighter and faster and blurred. My skin began to burn. I was on fire. The voice piped up again, yelling *Power! Power!* Still paralyzed, I couldn't breathe. I needed air. I struggled for a single breath. I willed my brain to move my legs to kick, to run, to jerk myself awake, but nothing happened. The tunnel grew hotter. Lights grew brighter. Then, a flash, a colossal fireball. Everything was white. The loud noises were gone.

A voice echoed, this time a different one.

"Morning, gents. Rise and shine. This your happy sunrise wake-up call."

The white light was nothing more than the full-strength overheads in the gym. The voice was simply that of a morning-shift volunteer barking into a bullhorn. "Wrap up your bedding and place it at the foot of your bunk. Breakfast is hot and ready when you are. Line closes at 6:30. You snooze, you lose. Up and at 'em, guys."

My bedsheets were soaked, sweat likely, urine possibly, though they had no noticeable color. Nightmares had become a regular occurrence over the three years, but not quite like that one. Bodies around me grunted and grumbled as they rolled up their linens. A guy fell on my bed as he staggered by. "Sorry, mate," he said, bouncing up quickly and already gone before I could lift my foot to give him a swift kick.

At breakfast, Lenny was nowhere in sight. A check of his hidden area behind the rack of chairs came up empty. His bedding was dutifully placed as directed. I checked the boiler room where we had met the evening before, but there was no sign of Lenny or his wheelchair. Strange, I thought, for him to be up early and back in the cold, especially knowing he wanted to avoid the guys in his camp by the river. Given his condition, he might have headed anywhere.

An old oak table in the local library proved a worthwhile and warm daytime spot that day. The workspace was one of several in cubicles bolted against the wall where people could research, read, and relax. My primary objective was to search through the Atlanta phone book to find potential addresses for Lenny's daughters. With only their names, there wasn't much to guide me, but their last names were somewhat unique. There were over a dozen listings with the last name of St. James, but luckily only one with the first name Cicely. With the second daughter, Teresa, there was a lone entry under the name of Jefferstone in Buckhead. I went with that.

At some point between reading *Sports Illustrated* cover-to-cover, and a dated issue of *The New York Times* Sunday edition with little interest, I made two copies of the General's letter. Without his input, I wanted to be more direct and fatherly without making the letter sound phony. I had to be the voice of Lenny's heart, expressed in a way they would read as "Dad" and not some unconnected, unaffected schmuck ghostwriter.

The rewrite of the rewrite took much longer than I expected. The delay caused me to rethink my decision to deliver the letters. My rewrite was much stronger, enough to touch their hearts and move them to action. Given the cold, gusty winds and springtime rains that had intensified over the course of the day, the project had dragged on out of convenience as much as anything. In the end I managed to make it to the main post office before it closed. As I walked, I lingered to enjoy the sweet scent of the winter's rain. Too late to stand in line for a bunk at the shelter. Without the shelter comforts, given the conditions outside, the bus station became my best alternative. The next bus out was headed to Jacksonville.

Delayed by weather, we boarded the bus at half past eight. I hunkered down in a window seat toward the middle. To dissuade others from joining me, my backpack sat in the adjoining seat. A burly guy, probably pushing three hundred pounds, tilted the bus a little as he hoisted himself aboard. He squeezed down the aisle to the third row before he shoehorned himself in to straddle two seats. My luck ran out when the last person on board, a well-dressed woman probably in her fifties, quietly asked, "May I join you?"

I don't remember her name. I do remember that she was headed to Jacksonville and then up to Kings Bay, Georgia to visit her son who was scheduled for an extended deployment on a submarine. She was a proud and patriotic mother; she wouldn't stop talking about the kid. I offered an occasional nod, but couldn't get a word in if I'd wanted, which I didn't. In truth, the last thing I wanted was to talk to this woman, or anyone for that matter. I remained semi-comatose, eyes cast out the window, marginally rude.

Haunted by the nightmare of recent days, the miles of unlit country roads bored me in a good way and left me, gratefully, unable to sleep. We had been on the road for an hour and a half and she had been talking for just as long when, through the windshield, I spotted three armadillos heading across the road in the beam of the headlights in front of the bus. The driver swerved slightly left but the thump, thump, thump marked his contribution to Georgia roadkill.

Riding in a blissful nirvana, the thumps gave me pause to consider my deeper existence and, moreover, the existence of my friend, his wife, and, to a degree, the existence of the God the priest had described. The circumstances were an opening for me to profess my understanding of life and the hereafter. I wiped my hand across my face, turned to my seatmate, and assumed a change in conversation.

"Did you feel that?" I said, interrupting what had been a long-winded story about why her son had chosen the Navy over the Army. "That was death." She flinched at the word and drew her chin in tight enough for three wrinkles to bulge against her neck. "Or was it?" I continued in a low, private voice. It was my turn to ramble.

"See, death never really occurs. According to quantum mechanics, our body energy—all twenty watts of brain power—just moves on to one of an infinite number of universes because energy never dies. No. It just goes to a different place. That energy might actually enkindle another human form, a body." I leaned back against the window again. I held my hands out, palms down, and wiggled my fingers, then leaned toward her with a hideous, cuckoo's nest grin.

"But sometimes ... that energy might become the life source, the spirit, for a different animal ... or some bug ... or ... a plant ... or ...you have any pets? A dog, a cat?"

"A dog," she offered, hesitantly.

"Say when your dog dies. I hope it doesn't, but let's say it does. It might come back into your soul to help you experience life from a different perspective, one which your human body's third eye cannot see. That's shared energy. And, those thumps from a minute ago, the thuds under the bus ... those were armadillos I saw crossing the road. Now they're pancaked roadkill, but their energy ... who knows ... those armadillos might have been Cary Grant or Madam Curie or Cleopatra or Babe Ruth at some point, and maybe, instantaneously, now they are a part of me ... or you." Her face soured and turned toward the aisle.

"No, seriously. Ever wonder where your energy came from? Ever wonder who you were or what you were in the past?" She was befuddled, speechless. She wriggled away. I leaned closer and tapped her on the shoulder. I slowed my speech and punctuated every word separately. "Voila, now you know ... you are as old as the universe. As old as the Earth. Ha! So, when people ask your age—I know, you never ask a lady her age—but if or when they do, you can say, with all honesty, that you are older than dirt. Well, as old as dirt." I laughed.

She turned to face me. "Young man!" she huffed. People in the bus looked our way. She didn't say another word for the remainder of the ride.

With stops along the way, the bus docked in Jacksonville shortly after midnight. My seatmate was first into the aisle and out the door. I made the best of the bus station wrought-iron seating—away from the ticket counter, video games, and vending machines—and slept for hours slumped forward like a windsock longing for a breeze. When I awoke, every joint from my neck to my waist begged for mercy. I fed two quarters and a nickel to the vending machine and it served up breakfast: a Snickers for the road. But what I needed most was coffee.

With the skyline as my guide, the hunt for a coffee shop began in earnest. A sign in front of a bank said the temperature was forty-three degrees, but the breeze and humidity made it feel more like thirty-four at 5:30 in the morning. It didn't take long to find the first coffee shop; it was closed. I continued on in hopes of finding an all-night diner or a shop that catered to the early-bird crowds of reporters, firefighters, taxi drivers, and police, though I wasn't looking to explain my existence to any cop, regardless of the time of day. After reconnoitering three coffee shops—all closed—I took up residence on a bus stop bench near the third shop and waited. When it opened at six, I was second in line. The first sip of mud brought ecstasy.

With the rising sun, traffic along the street increased. I left my tall stool in the coffee shop behind and immersed myself in the crowds hustling to work, myself moseying along with no objective whatsoever. My pace, reinforced by my appearance, garnered the occasional stare. Or perhaps it was my spontaneous recitation of lines from *Hamlet* that drew the interest—no, not interest, probably curiosity. I didn't need the crowd.

My objective of the day was, once again, to be rid of people, the interactions of personalities. I aimed to bury myself in a library, at a reading desk tucked in an alcove filled with the scent of mildew and the flaking yellow pages of the stacks. Inside, I stared at Cervantes for an hour, deep into his quest for Dulcinea to the dismay of the duchess's handmaid, who pined for Quixote.

From time to time, when passages lagged, I returned to my impossible task of finding Mary Kay Keller. I thought maybe the post office would have a forwarding address. That would help. And I had often given thought to contacting the base. Ben Keller had been a Marine. I could navigate through their bureaucracy to find something about his wife, where she was. But I wasn't willing to expose myself to a government agency who might somehow expose me. I thought about the girl in Charlotte. Something she'd said dredged up another lead.

There was a girl, the maid of honor at Mary Kay's wedding. I wooed her on and off for a number of months after we met. I think I was too much for her, or she was not enough for me. Either way, our relationship never went anywhere. But I remembered her name and the fact that she lived in Mobile. I was lucky with the reference desk copy of a Mobile phone directory. I convinced myself to call her.

There was a pay phone in the lobby of the library. I stood and stared at the telephone push-button pad as if it were a combination lock for a nuclear device. Woozy after the rush of the Snickers had passed, and after two discontinued attempts, I keyed in all ten digits and listened for the ringer.

"Hello," a voice said, slathered with a Southern drawl straight off the plantation.

"Is this Melanie Winters?" I said, disguising my voice with my own version of a Mississippi accent. When she acknowledged that I had the right person, I stumbled through a spiel I had rehearsed on and off throughout the afternoon. Posing as a former high school beau of Mary Kay's who had recently heard of the tragic loss of her husband, I called to ask if she had any contact information for her.

"Why ... now, how did you get my name?" she replied.

"I attended Mary Kay's wedding. You probably don't remember me, but I had an old newspaper announcement with your name in it."

Melanie was impressed I had bothered to keep the announcement. Hearing her voice, I recalled both of us, drunk after the wedding reception, Melanie dancing around in her striped panties at some fleabag motel where we shacked up for the night. She went on and on about the wedding and her life for the past three years, and her dog, and her new job, and how she just couldn't stand the movie *Fatal Attraction*, talking non-stop until I interrupted.

"Say, do you have contact information for Mary Kay? Phone number? An address, perhaps? I'd like to send my belated condolences."

She advised me that Mary Kay might have remarried. The last contact information she had was an address in Wilmington, North Carolina. That was all I needed.

The bus station was a short walk from the library. With two ticket windows open, the short line moved quickly. When I asked for a ticket to Wilmington, the agent informed me he had nothing direct. Best he could do was to route me through Warner-Robbins, Georgia. I bought the ticket and waited an hour or so for the bus to depart, ample time to reconstruct my plan, until the voices spoke up. Over the course of the next three hours, the Vigilantes posited a scenario of doom. They convinced me that the authorities had connected dots between the incident and arrest in Macon to the incident that had me on the run. And, somehow, they would be waiting for me in Wilmington. Their advice: do not stay in Wilmington, do not talk to Mary Kay, do not be on the streets. *Hide.*

I hopped off in Warner-Robbins and started thumbing, trying to shake the cops. For fourteen days I traveled throughout the South, landing in four cities, never spending the night in a shelter; I nearly froze to death. A miserable existence, curled up in abandoned houses, boarded up buildings, run-down warehouses, train cars, under the bucket of a bulldozer, one night in the gondola of a Ferris wheel at a county park. Other than truckers who offered rides, I didn't talk to a soul. I scrounged for food, pilfered from stands and convenience stores, always leaving money on the shelf or counter but never going through the checkout lane. I sat alone. I wanted to be alone.

Deep thoughts. Thoughts of fear and love. Past and present. How I felt the first time I walked in total darkness. Walking off the back porch as a kid in the middle of the night to go to the shed. A path I'd taken hundreds of times, but as the first in total darkness, I had walked with my arms outstretched, petrified with a fear that lingered. I feared the things I screwed up in my life, how screwed up I was. How I never applied myself in school as a kid. How boxing was my only release. How I hated my father for what he did, but loved him for who he was. How I missed my mother who had taught me to read and write and the love of poems. How Ben Keller and I would go carousing and chasing women together in college. How he was dead and I wasn't. How my mistakes got me here. How I wanted it all to end. I wanted to be in a dark place, all day, every day. I talked only to myself and the unrelenting voices who kept me there. I thought about the first time I saw a ghost.

CARL E. LINKE

During those weeks, those days in isolation, poetry was my temporary release.

no SHELTER for GUILT

Chapter 25

Rebuff your radiance
Greened of tides and times the golden door
that massed blacks, browns, the yellows, the poor
Back ever turned to the beckoned, ever calling
Sealed lips 'neath torch-lit seas and shadowed shores
Your honor less armored less honored.

Dimmed the glare, the flame masked glow
Little warmth does it throw in its
compromise of equality against opportunity
Haves have and nots not nor
welcome framed in time past
offers of little more.

We, the People, scourged by promises deprived.
Plagued in circumstance.
Homelessness the condition,
Heartlessness the contagion, the plague, brotherhood
whittled away to Nimrods.
The bell of Liberty knells

Deafened by our Babel
a din in Our land full of talk of us,
not to us, not for us
Of dreams paraded in rejection

Carl E. Linke

dawn after dawn the silent sentinel.
The reaper's grim welcome.

The voice has stopped
I am not waiting.
What so proudly we hailed, was a hand up,
not a handout
Those dead, killed, to be killed
Dying amid amber fields of grain, sea to sea
My soul yearns.

Bombs bursting in air, the glare
Oh where, oh where … I dare
my forsaken heart to cry out
my denial. House-less we are, no
shelter for guilt, no peace.
Tranquility lost.

Perched buzzards, that lurk
to rip of silenced life.
The wake more deadly than the dead
bare head shine, virtues vanished
Green with prosperity or envy or jealousy or glut
of the harbor and We revere the cry.

The face of copper that cried with the siren's call
Black on white cars, red bulbs on top.
the shadow of death walks beside me.
Wisps of voices in my ear,
Voices that tell me it's time for us to fear.

Time for us to fear, time for us, time.

Chapter 26

Time thickened. It was time to face Mary Kay Keller. By the time the bus rolled to a stop in Wilmington, I was on my feet and at the door. The voices had stoked my fire, but I was out to do everything I could to defy them. I found a display with a city map and located the street Melanie Winters had given me over the phone weeks earlier. Under a checkerboard of white and gray clouds, I gave a cabby the address and wasted no time feeding him line after line of fast-pitch bullshit. The guy drove slower than a funeral march. I pounded on the back of his seat.

"Pull the fuck over."

Despite our slow rate of travel, when the fool slammed on the brakes, he nearly sent me through the windshield. I jumped out and grabbed his door handle. "Get out. I'll drive. You navigate, you moron."

The driver, a mousy looking guy wearing a t-shirt that read "Life's a Beach," spazzed out. He had no idea what to do. I kept pulling on his door handle and he kept pulling it closed then locked it. He tried to drive off with me hanging on the door and his mirror. I kicked the side of the door then jumped back into the rear seat. "You drive then. Let's go, doc. I don't have all fucking day." He turned his head to look at me. I kicked the back of his seat. He snapped his head back to the road and peeled off with no further questions.

From that point, the driver was focused. I bombarded him with a non-stop, fifteen-minute dissertation on the art of high yo-yos, hawk circles, loose deuce, and how to get into the spaghetti. When we arrived, he nosed the car in, bounced off the curb, and slammed to a stop. I anticipated that my visit wouldn't take long, so I instructed the moron to keep the meter running; I'd be right back. I was about half-way up the driveway when the asshole jetted off, down the street, without being paid. I offered the deserved middle-finger salute and jogged the short distance to the front door.

The house was cookie-cutter, same as all the others on the street. Two-story, wooden frame with a small porch across the front. Two hanging plants and a set of copper-pipe wind chimes hung from the eaves. Taking two steps at a time, I landed on the porch, rang the doorbell, and waited. I adjusted my ball cap while, in my head, I walked through what had to happen next. The door didn't open. There was a brass door knocker in the center of a wreath decorated with flowers. I lifted the striker and banged it three times, hard. Out of the corner of my eye I noticed the curtain in the window just to the right of the door move, then close slightly.

"Mary Kay. It's Chili. I need to talk to you." Nothing happened. I knocked a second time. Still nothing. I slipped to my right to peek through the window, though the curtain concealed most of the interior. The other window on the porch had a shade drawn. I walked around the side to the back and stopped. The only sound I heard came from traffic on the expressway, blocks over. I climbed the steps to the back porch and banged on the door. "Mary Kay. It's me. Let me in." Again, no response, though I knew she had to be there; I saw that curtain move. "I know you're in there.

Let me in. This will only take a minute." I waited for footsteps which never came. I rattled the door. It was locked.

Determined, I ran to a small flower garden along the back fence and snatched a goofy, stone gnome figurine. I went back to the porch and smashed the small pane of glass, stretched my arm through the open space and flipped the butterfly lock on the door. Immediately, I noticed drops of my own blood on the floor. Once inside I walked slowly while calling, "Mary Kay. It's me, Chili." I searched the kitchen. One door was a pantry; another opened to stairs leading to the basement. I flicked on the light and stepped down. The basement was nothing more than a storage bin filled with vintage junk, the stuff that yard sales and flea markets were made of. No sign of Mary Kay.

Something upstairs crashed onto the floor. I ran up the steps and into the living room where I saw a fat gray cat—had to be twenty pounds at least—teetering on the back of a sofa near the window with the partially closed curtain. I dashed up the steps to the second floor. Three small bedrooms, one bath with a leaky sink and old plumbing, nothing more. Only one bedroom appeared occupied since the others had no bedding. One bedroom had clothes across a cushioned chair. The patterns on the material were subdued. I held up a dress. The style was old, very old, maybe sixties old, and exceptionally large. Then I noticed the picture frames on a dresser.

The largest photo was of a gray-haired woman. Interestingly, probably in her fifties or older, the woman was wearing the dress I had held up. She had a round face, brown eyes, wide nose, and one ear that stuck out. The same woman appeared in other smaller snapshots. In one she wore a sombrero standing behind a birthday cake with two candles, one shaped like a five, the other a zero. It appeared to be the same woman as the one in the large frame, only at a younger age—and larger—wedged behind the wheel of a small sports car, wearing a grin from ear to ear. The convincing evidence was a stack of bills all addressed to Rebecca Long. Phone, newspaper, and electric bills. All addressed to the same woman. I tossed the entire stack in the air and pounded hard on the dresser. The force of my fist caused the framed photos to flop over. I grabbed one frame and flung it at the wall. I stopped before I did the same to the other frames. "Damn it. Damn it. Damn it. Shit, Melanie. Damn it."

The Vigilantes found this all too comical. I massaged my forehead as I stepped down the stairs. In the kitchen I opened my backpack and ripped a blank sheet out of a journal. I left a simple note for Rebecca Long or whoever owned the house. "Sorry for the broken window and frame. It was all a big mistake." The cat, with its belly scraping the floor, slunk into the kitchen, gave me a casual glance, and continued on to a pad of carpeting in the corner. To cover the damages, I placed several bills under a pepper shaker on top of my note and exited the same way I had entered.

With no cab I began to walk. I had been on the move less than thirty minutes when a car drove up, tires scraping the curb, and slowly poked alongside a skinny man on the sidewalk a distance in front of me. The driver, a female, with one hand on the steering wheel, kept leaning toward the man, possibly talking to the guy. Every time she leaned the car would ride up the curb before she jerked it back into the roadway, still at a snail's pace. Within a block, the car stopped and a rather large woman dropped out from behind the wheel. Dressed in an oversized T-shirt that stopped just above her knees and allowed for a few inches of baggy, rolled-up dungarees to show, she made her way to the sidewalk with the alacrity of a walrus. Her pigtails, tied off with pink ribbons, slapped against her face when she grabbed the skinny little man by the arm and dragged him toward the curb.

"Whoa, whoa, whoa. Hold on there, miss," I yelled as I stepped it up to approach the couple. "What's going on here? Is there something—"

"Just butt the hell out, buster. This ain't none of your business," she said. She twisted the guy's arm up behind his back and dragged him closer to the car.

"Let me go, Tina! For Chrissake, let me go, damnit," the guy cried. "Get your goddamn hands off me."

"Listen you jackass, you're comin' with me and that's the—"

"Wait! Hold on," I said. "Let the guy go." I reached in and grabbed her hand to keep her from ripping the poor dude's arm off.

The woman, easily twice my size, karate-chopped my arm. "I said butt out. We don't need no help. Just back off, baby."

I stepped back into the fracas. With my hand on her arm she hollered, "He's my brother and I don't need no help." I dropped my grip.

"Tina, I ain't going with you. I told you that before," the man yelled. By this point she had dragged him all the way to the car, then held him with one hand while she opened the passenger door with the other. He was a total dead-weight and offered no assistance—or resistance—to her effort. She reached down and lifted him like a baby, threw him in the backseat, and slammed the door. Then she walked up to me, her belly rubbing against my belt buckle.

"For your information, this is my brother. I go through this just about every week, baby," she said huffing after her scuffle with the guy. She leaned her head from one shoulder to the other, then put her nose up to the tip of mine. "See, Jerry here is mentally deranged. He ain't got no sense. He keeps running away. I take care of him at my place, but when he gets a wild hair up his butt, he up and walks out. I find him here every time. Says he has friends here and would rather live out there in the woods than under a roof with me. Well, I know that ain't true. And I sure as hell know it ain't the best thing for him."

A step backward settled my urge to coldcock her. There was no guarantee she was telling the truth. I tapped on the backseat window while she looked on.

"Hey. Hey! You know this woman?" The guy nodded. "She your sister like she says?" Again, he nodded.

She turned toward me with a sarcastic I-told-you-so smirk. She nudged me back with the palm of her outstretched hand, then turned to go back around the car. "Next time I suggest you just mind your own damn business, baby," she said before she closed the door and drove off with a pronounced list to the driver's side. So much for my Good Samaritan work of the day. A "strike two" effort.

Batting zero for the day, I acted on a previous lead. I connected with the telephone operator and asked her to ring the post office for my old stomping grounds. After the usual recorded messages on which number to press for a variety of reasons and departments, I talked to a clerk. She was most kind and very apologetic with her responses. First, she told me they would only have record for forwarding mail for one year, so she probably didn't have the forwarding address any longer. And, second, she was not permitted to disclose the forwarding address if she did. I sweet-talked her for a while with hopes that, since it had been more than a year, she could give me the outdated forwarding address; she declined. I pulled coins out of my pocket to dial the Marine base operator, but decided against it. The potential exposure seemed too great a risk.

With my arm cocked and ever-ready thumb extended, I walked, pissed about not finding Mary Kay in the house and running out of ideas. I thought: Maybe the voices were right. End this.

Chapter 27

Walking. The air readily defined my location. Neighborhoods bursting with aromas of stews and soups. Incense, near churches. The unmistakable smell of fast-food grease meant a shopping area was probably nearby. And when the wind shifted, in some places, the salty sea breeze helped draw me toward the water.

After slapping flat-footed for a few miles down the highway, a good ol' boy in a tractor-trailer rig pulled over to offer a lift. He was quick to tell me he was from a small town outside Gatlinburg, Tennessee. Not but four hundred people in town and that included him, though he was seldom there. He said he was headed to the port, but where I wanted to go was closer to the river. His truck wasn't allowed in those parts of town, so he gave me directions and dropped me at a busy intersection to hook another ride. Without any truck traffic, nobody was going to pick me up, not in my homeless state of mind or body.

After a stretch through a residential area, the sights shifted. Lawns and houses became parking lots and businesses, eventually outnumbered by overgrown supply yards and run-down warehouses. The saltier air explained the reddish-brown cancer of rust on abandoned structures where oil-slick floors offered temporary shelter for the likes of me and other homeless souls.

A plaque outside the building said that a circle of churches had founded the Interfaith Covenant Community decades earlier. They pooled funds from the pulpit and knocked on doors for donations to purchase an abandoned meat-packing plant that sat vacant for decades. The purchase and renovations were controversial because the place was rumored to be haunted. There is something to be said about pulpits that willingly fraternize with ghosts.

As is the case with most shelters, there were limited accommodations and an ever-increasing population of would-be guests. Consequently, at such places there is always a makeshift overflow area where those turned away from the shelter congregate and make camp. Some of these camps are well-established. Often times camps similar to the one I saw in Charlotte have permanent residents, those who elect not to spend time in the shelter and are unable or unwilling to live anywhere else. Wilmington was notorious for "Independence Town," an ad hoc homeless community which thrived in woods equidistant from the shelter, the railroad tracks, and the Cape Fear River.

A path through a thicket of scrubby trees marked the trail to the tent city. Fifty yards of fast-food cups, cans, and other trash littered the entrance. The first sign of life was a trash heap that reached well above my head. Next was a jury-rigged dwelling. Pallets tied together with twine formed a squarish footprint, covered with an overlapping quilt of ripped tarps that added protection to whatever or whomever existed beneath them.

I approached from the side. "Knock, knock. Anybody home?" No response. I moved on.

The vegetation thickened through an arbor of vines and spindly trees, a chute of green that led into an opening with a complex of tents, lean-tos made from scraps of wood, and layered cardboard structures. The place was a beehive of activity buzzing with worker-bee guests and residents who looked at me as I passed, then went on with their chores—lighting small fires, cooking on small camper stoves, sweeping their areas with branches or old, bristle-thin brooms. Assorted rags, probably considered as daily attire, hung wet and dripping from trees. All the bodies were male. What once might have been a bastion of virility now appeared as a weak study in Maslow's hierarchy. A few nods, the flash of the finger-V peace sign here and there, a simple "Hey" or a "Yo" or a "Morning." I didn't connect with most, only one.

A shirtless, shoeless, bony guy in a deep squat was striking a survival flint with a metal something or other, trying to light a wad of dried grass. His hand hacked furiously at the flint until the piece of steel flew out of his palm and landed by my foot. As I reached to pick it up, he looked my way.

He was an Asian kid, probably early twenties, much younger than me or anybody else I'd seen in the camp. His jet-black hair, a pouf on top of his head, hung straight otherwise, over his ears and covering his eyes. The kid looked like he had just popped out of a chimney; he was filthy. He had a nasty wart the size of a dime above his right eye, a turned-up nose, and a hairy lip, too sparse to consider it a moustache. Long sideburns that faded into nothing of a beard.

Staring at me, his face was a picture of fright. He jerked his head and eyes from side to side, surprised to see me and anybody else who might appear out of the bushes. I shifted my backpack to my other shoulder then walked over to return his hunk of metal. He snatched it out of my hand then walked backwards, still scoping out the area around us.

He retreated into a hovel of large, clear trash bags filled with cans. Bags stacked on top of bags rose eight feet or more in a circle that formed a cave of no more than six feet across. The space had no cover over it.

"It's okay," I said. "Relax. You need help starting the fire?" I pulled a pack of matches from my pocket. "I can help. Really." I struck a match. The kid rushed and tried to push me away, but my size allowed me to touch the flame against the tinder grasses. Fire quickly climbed up the teepee of twigs.

The kid, slowed by a limp, gathered branches and added them to the fire without a word, careful not to make eye contact. He squatted, his butt no more than two inches off the dirt and crisscrossed branches around the crumbling ash.

"You live here, there?" I pointed. He only nodded. "How long have you been collecting all those cans?" He had to have thousands bundled in plastic.

He didn't respond.

"What do you do when it rains?" He remained silent. "Do you go to the shelter?" I asked.

"They find me." He stuck his hand into the fire to reposition it, then yanked his hand out and rubbed it in the dirt. "Why you ask me? You Uncle Sam man? CIA? You capture me?"

I returned his puzzled look.

"You not take this Vietnamese boat boy. I stay stateside. You not send me back Vietnam. Not go back there. I dishonor family."

Those weren't the answers or comments I'd expected, but they explained what came next. He froze. His head rotated back and forth. He began a slow retreat toward his open compound like he expected others to jump out and overpower him. As he pulled back, he mumbled to himself in a language I assumed was Vietnamese; it definitely wasn't English. When he entered his circle of cans, he moved to the side and out of view. He then started screaming, then yelling, pausing between shouts as if he were waiting for someone else in a conversation to respond to his outburst. I listened for a bit to nurse his fire before I moved on. The only thing I understood in a shout was "CIA." I felt the same fear running from the cops.

Farther down the path, more makeshift shelters popped up in the trees before the path broke into another clearing. Two rusted car bodies and a shell of a minivan with rust-stained peace symbols and flowers painted on the side added ornamental art to the spread of tall grasses. Sprawling warehouse buildings with fenced-in equipment yards bordered the field on either side. One had eight- and twelve-wheel container chassis, old and new. Another had an assortment of telephone poles, transformers, and high-voltage power equipment. Beyond those, other yards were stacked with containers, red, rusted, and ready for use. I remembered the trucker who gave me the ride saying that the shelter was on the same street as the power supply yard. When the path split in several directions, I followed the trail closest to the yards.

In the distance, a guy with a shopping cart turned in from the road onto the path, heading toward me. He had walked a short distance up the path before another guy followed in behind him. I was probably a hundred yards away when I saw the second guy jump the man with the cart. He shoved him around, then body-slammed him to the ground. When the victim attempted to get up, the attacker kicked him hard in the head. It was obviously not another case of sibling care. I held the strap of my backpack and hustled down the path. The guy on the ground, an older man, was likely headed to the tent city. The attacker was young, a teen. I grabbed the kid, swung him around, and pulled him off his older victim.

"What the hell you doing, kid?" I yelled.

"Get the fuck out of here, man," he said as he pushed me in the chest. The kid was a little bigger than me. Totally impressed with himself and overestimating what he had gotten himself into, he took a swing at me. That was all I needed: a provoked assault. I laid him out. With one punch, I put the kid on his ass.

"Hey, man! Why'd you do that?" he shouted. He stood and took a short step toward me. I stepped closer. He snarled and shoved me with his hands again. I staggered and cocked my arm to lay the kid out once again. When I did, someone, or a couple someones, grabbed my arms from behind. While my arms were locked, three other teens came into view and pummeled my head, chest, mid-section, and groin. With all the attention on me, the older man ran off, leaving his cart behind. The odds were six to one in their favor. I remember hitting the ground, and I remember the first few kicks. The first to my groin, the second to my stomach, and the third to my head.

The next memory came sometime later. I awoke in a cocoon of white, blinded by bright lights and tethered to a NASA-style bank of monitors that beeped with every bodily function imaginable. I was alive, or so it appeared, and staring at the ceiling of some unidentified medical facility with the look of a hospital emergency room or trauma center. It was a haunting flashback of a previous awakening years earlier. I ached, everywhere. I tilted my head forward and confirmed I still had hands, arms, legs, and feet, the essential body parts. And, despite the fact that I could see and hear, I was not certain I had a head, except for the pain above my shoulders.

"Well ... welcome," a voice declared from the far end of the bed, the blurry end. A black man in a white smock came into focus as he approached my pillow. He pulled a clipboard from the metal rail on the side and studied it. "I'm Doctor Jordan. How are you feeling, Mr. George?" he said as his long fingers flipped through several sheets.

"What?"

"I asked how you feel? You've been through a lot apparently."

"It's Bob. Not George. Name's Bob, er, Robert, Robert White, and let's say I've felt better." I didn't have the energy to argue with this guy.

He rechecked the paperwork. "They have you listed as Mr. Fletcher George. You were unidentified when they brought you in. The ER attendant found your military ID card in your backpack according to the notes here."

In my fog, what he said took a few seconds to register, and a few more to elicit a response. "Nah. Nah." I dropped my head back on the pillow and tried to explain with my eyes closed. "A trinket I found." My throat was so dry I could barely talk; my head hurt so bad I didn't want to. Words, even short ones, pricked the pain. "Little secret, between us girls, eh, doc?" I opened my eyes long enough to give him a wink, a simple movement that made my head throb. "ID cards come in handy on the street." He lowered the clipboard and made eye contact; mine were only half open. "Use it when convenient." I dropped my head back onto the pillow and took a series of shallow breaths. "Name's Bob. Friends call me Chili." His face was less than reassuring. He looked at me, turned his head toward the wall, lifted the clipboard, and scribbled an entry. I closed my eyes.

"Says here you were jumped by six teenagers in a field. A guy in a car saw it and stopped. When he approached the kids, they ran off. Looks like you did okay for yourself, given those odds."

"Don't recall. Didn't die ... yet." I remained still.

"Well, we all die sometime, but you're not going to die anytime soon, least not from this brawl." The doctor took a closer look at the results on one chart. "Nothing punctured. Nothing broken. You have some significant edema, but that will go away. The pain meds will help for a few days, at least."

"Love your bedside manner, doc," I said, rolling my head to the side. He was right; the meds were helping, marginally, but I had a different feeling. "When do I get out of your little house of horrors here?"

He popped up from his paperwork and gave me a dirty look. "Let me take a look and we'll see." He pushed a button on the side of the bed to raise me to a sitting position. "Okay, can you lift your left arm? Hold it straight out. Point at that picture there on the wall."

Despite the pain, I didn't want any part of his doctoring. I didn't need the scrutiny of the who or what or where I was from; the Vigilantes were already plotting the Great Escape. I groaned softly. "Tell you what. How about if I take a raincheck on all your medical magic and ..." I dragged my leg out from under the sheets, aiming for the floor.

"Hold up, Mr. White. Just do as I ask, please. Okay? Nothing more." He put his hand lightly against my sternum and held me back, then gently guided my leg back under the sheet. I disguised my wince with a bogus, pain-filled smile.

"Doc, need to walk out of this joint right now …" I shared another groan, "gotta find the dudes who gave me the free ticket to your little sideshow here." I turned my head slightly to find a clock. "And you want me to raise my arms?" I flapped both arms like a bird; the pain was horrendous, and I doubted that my fake smile was convincing.

Unimpressed, my medicine man hung a subtle grin, grabbed one of my arms, and held it down. I cringed. What was a little pain? I flapped faster with my free arm. He dropped his clipboard on the bed and, with his free hand, reached for something I couldn't see near my ear. Seconds later, two nurses in white dashed through the door and grabbed my flapping arm. The three of them plastered me to the bed.

"Mr. George, please … just do as I ask."

The craziness crackled all around me. I laughed an insufferable, groggy laugh. The voices were at work. Words, mixed up in my head, started to fly. "Seriously, doc, you better get your hearing checked." My eyes barely recognized the doctor. "The name's White, as in Snow! Or, if you want to get personal, big fella, it's Chili to you." He was not amused.

"I'm telling you, there is nothing wrong with me." I grunted then cleared my throat. "I mean I could fly out of here in a heartbeat," I said with my eyes closed. "I'm a flyer, you know. Bingo. Bango. Bongo. I lift these arms and off I go into the wild-blue yonder," I said, adding a little melodic, "Fly like an eagle. Up, up and away." I tugged to free my arms. "And nothing could catch me. I'm fast as anything. Faster than a speeding bullet. More powerful than a locomotive. Superman in the sky. That's me. I just let 'er rip whenever I want—"

"Mr. White, just relax and do as I ask, please."

"Sure, doc. What was the name again? Right, Jordan. Got it." The room was spinning. Every fraction of my body ached, but my jaws kept flapping. "Okay, Doctor Jordan. Say ... you related to Michael? You play ball? I mean that guy is the greatest ever. He's a wizard on the court. Unstoppable. He can shoot. Man can he shoot. And jump? Holy cow! He's probably better than Ali but in a different sport, I guess there are—"

"Just relax. Maybe we should check your hearing, too," the doc said, his brow furrowed. "Just lay there, peacefully. Quietly. I need to test—"

"No need to test, doc. I'm fine."

"Okay then, humor me, Mr. White. Just be quiet for two minutes and let me see how well you respond to stimuli. Raise your arm like I asked, please."

I followed the doctor's orders and entertained the nurses with my gibberish. I lifted my left arm; it weighed a ton. He held my left hand and rolled my arm from side to side, then lifted it up overhead. "Any pain or pulling when I do this?"

"Pain? Oh, hell yeah, doc. It's killing me. It's killing me." I winked, another false response.

He was still not amused. "And do you feel any pulling, no?"

"Pulling? No."

"The pain is probably from bruises. If the pain doesn't slice through you, then there's nothing to worry about."

"What? Me, worry? Doc, I don't worry. I get even."

"Let's try the other arm," he said.

He gently placed my left arm flat by my side, then lifted my right arm overhead. When he raised it, he took a longer look, chuckled, and placed it back on the bedsheet. He dropped the bed back down to flat and asked me to roll onto my right side. He pulled the sheets back, then had me move my leg in different directions, twisting and turning it as I moved. He then had me roll onto my other side and repeated the same procedures on the other leg.

"Okay, you can roll onto your back and cover up."

Easy for him to say. He jotted something on the clipboard sheet. While he was writing he said, "Interesting birthmark you have there on your right arm, by your tattoo. Looks like a horse fly, legs and all."

"Never paid much attention to it," I lied. "Don't make it a practice to stand around in front of a mirror admiring myself." Despite all the manipulation, as long as I was stationary, the pain wasn't bad.

"Weird. That birthmark. I saw a mark same as yours once, years ago. Playing rugby, University of Maryland. The guy's arm about yanked my head off," Dr. Jordan said, writing more in my chart. "Put me in a neck collar for weeks. Don't remember a tattoo though. You play rugby? If that was you, it's payback time," he said, measuring a grin.

"Hold on, doc. No clue what you're talking about," I lied. "Played some football and did some boxing as a kid, but—"

"My turn to mess with you." He slapped the clipboard against his thigh. "Let me get this paperwork to the admin folks. They should be able to process this and we'll have you out of here in an hour or so. Until then, just lie there and count your blessings. No hopping around or flapping your arms. No flying around the room. Let my nurses get some rest." He nodded to dismiss the two ladies in white. I swear one of them gave me a wink as she left. "You're lucky there were no internal injuries. Head looks okay and your bruises will be not-so-fond memories for only a few days. Good luck to you." He patted my leg under the sheet and walked off.

    Doc Jordan had screwed up the paperwork. In short order, a nurse and orderly moved me from the emergency room triage area to a private inpatient room. My protesting did nothing to change it. Doctor's orders, they said. The next morning, I overheard my name mentioned in a strange and somewhat disturbing conversation outside my room between a nurse and a police officer who had showed up. The crux of the discussion seemed to be more than investigating my altercation with the teenage assassins that mugged me. Regardless of the topic, I didn't need to become a familiar name associated with a face.

    Per Newton's third law of motion, every action on my part had an equal and opposite painful reaction. Every move resulted in pain, excruciating pain, but finding my backpack and escaping the hospital became paramount. I stuffed my pack under my open-back hospital gown, slipped into the wheelchair in my room, and wheeled myself into the hall. With a nod, the nurse gave me approval to visit the hospital library. At a restroom at the end of the hall, I rolled in, changed into street clothes, hobbled down the stairs, and loped straight out the front door with a fond sayonara.

    Given my comatose state upon arrival at the hospital, I was completely disoriented. I stopped in a convenience store not far from the hospital to get directions to the Interfaith Covenant Community shelter. They were clueless. Despite a raging headache and body pain that wouldn't quit, I remembered the shelter was near the Cape Fear River. They pointed me in that direction.

    As the sun drifted below the trees, darkness slipped in. Angry pain in my legs and hips shortened my stride. At this hour, the shelter doors were probably locked for the night, which meant I was destined to sleep under the stars. As I saw it, it was still a safer alternative than the hospital with the police nosing around, asking questions about me.

Unable to find the tent city—more accurately, unwilling to return to the scene of the crime—I came upon a small wooded park with a secluded shelter, a single picnic table, and a fire pit. I stumbled about gathering kindling and some firewood in the event my overnight with Mother Nature became too much for my aching bones. After three days and two nights in the comfy hospital—measuring vital signs every four hours—I wanted to sleep. I sat on the hearth above the empty firewood box and snacked on the packet of cookies I'd saved from my evening meal. As I nibbled, I dozed off until I heard a voice.

Chili. Hey, Chili.

I snapped out of my fog. I looked around. Nothing.

Outside the luxury of nights in a shelter, days were meant for sleeping, and nights were usually spent moving to stay warm. Tonight would be an exception. I ached. The walk had from the hospital had taken every bit of my energy. I needed to rest. Building a fire was an option, but that meant I would need to stay awake. Sleep was more precious. Every muscle in my body screamed as I dragged the picnic table closer to the brick fireplace. Exhausted, I collapsed on the top of the table and, ever so gently, began to rock myself toward sleep, drifting into an unfamiliar dream.

I was in a backyard, or maybe at a playground, with swings and a see-saw. There were no kids around except one small, very small boy just learning to run. He plopped face-down across the seat of a swing, up on his toes, rocking back and forth. His mother walked up and pushed him gently. He laughed and dragged his feet as the swing arced higher, eventually too high for his tiny legs to touch the ground.

no SHELTER for GUILT

The boy laughed while the young mother pushed the slack chains. I thought of myself with my mother, the fun we had shared when I was a kid, then I appeared, grown up, wearing a smile, and watching the two by the swing. The boy in the dream suddenly caught the ground with his foot and skidded to a stop. He hopped off the swing and started his awkward run toward me with his arms wide, wearing a giant smile on his face, yelling, "Chili, Chili." As he came closer, his smile faded, his yelling softened, and his run petered out to a clumsy walk that took him past me to another figure, another man in the dream. I turned to follow the boy and saw Ben Keller.

A blast of chilly air awakened me as it escorted a veil of fog across the park. In the cloud, I recalled another place, another time, earlier voices, and pain. I relived all of it until the sun announced the day.

Chapter 28

"Hey, Mack, how about a ticket on the next bus out of town?" I said, wincing with every syllable, "and make it snappy, ya see?" I added in my distressed Humphrey Bogart voice, forcing a pained smile. Despite the difficult night in the park, the fact that the police were asking questions about me back in the hospital had hinted that it was best to get my aching body out of town.

The agent at the ticket counter in Wilmington sized me up and remembered me from a few days earlier. "You get run over by a bus or something?" He bent closer to the cage on his ticket window and gawked, cross-eyed, at the shiner that highlighted my swollen face.

"Got jumped by a posse of your town's finest citizens, ya see. Put half of them in ambulances, ya see, and the other six un-assed the area before I could chime their bells." I covered my blackened eye with one hand, gripped the bars on the agent's cage window with the other, then rattled it hard enough to pop loose a screw on the top.

"A dozen, huh?" he said while he checked his schedule and printed a ticket to Florence, South Carolina.

"Maybe more. I was busier than a one-armed paper hanger on a pogo stick. It was a Keystone Kops comedy. I'd head-butt one guy and toss him into another, who would knock down a third, then I'd haul off and smash a few chins, pop a few guts with some kicks, and stack them up on the ground. You ever smack a guy so hard it tore the skin off his face, not a cut but just ripped the skin right off?" I inhaled but stopped when I heard my ribs scream. "Yeah, the more of them that came at me, the faster I moved. A real Kung Fu fighter. I grabbed one guy. Hung him on a branch. I laughed my ass off." I paused for a short breath and continued. "That's when a couple guys grabbed me from behind. I did a double-drop takedown …" I stepped back and jerked through a painfully slow-motion demo at the window. "… then dropped to my knees, did a front roll and shoveled dirt with their faces. It was a beautiful thing," I said with a wrinkled smile to mask the pain.

The guy behind me in line, a middle-aged chubby sort, took the opening to step closer to the ticket window. I curled my lip, took a step toward the guy, and gave him a cautionary look that had the veins in my neck and forehead twitching. "Have you not heard a word I said?" I asked, not expecting a verbal response. He stepped back.

I looked down and rubbed my swollen fist with the other swollen hand. "Bruised my damn knuckles. One by one they beat feet and ran. When the action died out, I sat on a bench across the street to catch my breath. Watched an ambulance clean up the battlefield, pick up the wounded. Somebody must have called 911. 'Cleanup on aisle six!' No idea how they knew they would find those dudes there, on the ground."

The ticket agent raised his chin and took another hard look at my eye, seemingly unsure whether to laugh, choke, fly the red "bullshit" flag, or wave me aside to take care of the people stacked up behind me.

"Here you go," the agent said as he shoved the slip under the bars on the window. I hesitated only long enough for him to look over my shoulder and say, "Next."

My conversation didn't end at the window. In the lobby, I limped corner to corner, back and forth, staring at the sunlight through the glass front. The Vigilantes drove me deeper inside my head with their persistent badgering. Id stop to argue and shout or poke a finger in the chest of an imaginary person. Other travelers scratched their heads at my outbursts. At one point, I swear I watched the clock on the wall melt, plastic dripping onto the floor below. A poster in the corner caught my eye when the colors actually unglued themselves, one color at a time, until they were all floating like snowflakes in a chilly draft.

"Hey, you see that?" I shouted, looking into the center of the sleepy, waiting area. Most people looked away or pretended not to hear me. "You? Those colors? See them floating? You see that?" Those close to me moved away when I approached them. I could feel their stares prick my skin. I stood there in this kaleidoscope of color that nobody else seemed to notice. The colors and splotches formed weird lava lamp blobs for seconds at a time.

"Now boarding. Travelers holding tickets for Florence, South Carolina are called to move to the bus for boarding. Bus departs in fifteen minutes," the announcer said over a too-loud speaker before he dropped the microphone, or so the rumbling sound over the PA suggested. The announcement sopped up the color and pasted it back onto the poster. My fellow travelers offered me a wide berth as we approached the door to board the bus. That ride and the following six days I spent on busses travelling between Florence, Fayetteville, and Columbia in my continued effort to lose the cops. At the end of the week, I had been first to board. on a morning ride to Charlotte.

I chose a seat in the back and waited for others to join. The driver popped in the door to assist a blue-haired woman in a lightweight lavender raincoat when she stumbled over her cane climbing into the bus. He held her elbow as she sat down. She smiled and thanked him, spread three plastic carry-on bags across the space next to her, then pulled out a number of items. By the time the driver closed the doors and pulled away from the curb, we were the only two passengers aboard, very unusual.

Days on the interstate were boring. From time to time, a chatty person seated next to me occupied my time, or another might distract me with headphones playing godawful music loud enough for me to hear and to render them legally deaf. Ideally, the rocking motion of the climate-controlled bus usually lulled me to sleep. This ride was different.

There were no distractions, yet my attempts at sleep never kicked in. It was as if the suspension system on the bus was hooked to my eyelids. Catnaps on smooth road interspersed with potholes—which the driver seemed to like—rattled me awake.

Eyes at half-mast, the countryside whisked by mile after boring mile. Over time, my stare became more distant, unfocused. Shapes disappeared. Colors melted to smears. My eyes shifted farther and farther up the road. Mile markers flicked by, barely visible, a normal phenomenon which became more phenomenal.

Impossible. A check of my watch calculated that we passed each new mile marker in under ten seconds. In my drowsy state, that math meant we were traveling somewhere in the neighborhood of three hundred and sixty miles per hour! On the ground, in a stinking bus. I took another look and double-checked my math. By that point, the signs had no numbers. The signs themselves were merely skewed shapes. I looked toward the front of the bus. The old lady was quietly concentrating on something in her lap. The driver, eyes fixed on the road, tapped the oversized steering wheel, beating out the rhythm of something. I turned back to the window. In the reflection, the skin on my face was peeling back, as if I were standing in a wind tunnel. I squinted. It was starting again.

Road signs rocketed by. I shot a look as far as I could see up the road, and my focus point passed my window before I could quickly count to ten. This wasn't right. Something was wrong. I closed my eyes and leaned back in my seat. My stomach lurched. *Relax. Get a grip.* I looked out. The fields and pastures streaked by. Even with my eyes closed things remained a green blur. My body floated; I was weightless. My heart raced. The greens wilted, melted, and bubbled to a deep, deep blue. From a distance, green lines flashed, then a yellow line. Then, white lights bubbled up from the bridge of my nose to form the letter T that suddenly burst. Blackness returned.

My eyes burst, opened wide. The blackness was gone. I blinked a few times in the sunlight and saw a red barn surrounded by black and white cows. Trees stood solemn along the roadside. Leaves, in Spring green, swayed gently with each car's passing. A yellow line still marked the center of the pavement. My heart settled and allowed my breath to do the same. With everything appearing normal again, I rolled my eyes, laughed, and drifted into song. "The wheels on the bus go round and round, round and round, round and round," I sang softly to myself.

The bus arrived early in Charlotte. With my earlier visit to Charlotte, I knew the location of the Little Room in the Inn shelter, though I'd never spent a night. Thankfully, it was mid-morning, which allowed me the better part of the day to get to the far side of town. Between travels and lack of facilities I hadn't showered in nearly a week, but my first order of business for the day was flying my sign, panhandling.

Finding a spot with direct sunlight in a high-traffic area—one that didn't already have a regular occupant—was not always easy. This day was an exception. I pulled a book of verse from my rucksack and performed soliloquies: *Hamlet* and *Lear*, *Othello* and *Julius Caesar*; odes by Keats, Shelley, and Tate; poems of Sandberg, Frost, and Whitman. All done with the pomp and pageantry, diction and eloquence fitting of each piece. As passersby approached, I took pleasure in walking shoulder-to-shoulder for short distances, or confronting individuals face-to-face by walking backwards, reciting each award-winning performance as the Minstrel of Market Street.

As the noon hour approached, foot traffic increased, which brought an appreciated increase in coins in my cap. For the most part, people were accepting of my presence. A few stopped to listen to my verse; most simply passed by. On occasion I would hear a grumble, even an infrequent "Piss off. Get a job!"

Only once did the comments spark me to respond. A young dude, dressed to the nines in yuppie business attire, passed with a girl, obviously one he was trying to impress.

"How's hitting the drugs and dropping out of high school looking to you now, fella?" he said with a chuckle.

I replied simply, "Go fuck yourself, boy." That stopped the jerk in his tracks. He left his girlfriend standing wide-eyed on the sidewalk and sauntered back to me.

"Hey, listen you bum. I don't need to take any of your shit. Not in public and definitely not in front of my lady friend."

I stared at the guy, unwilling to give him any more recognition. He smirked.

"This isn't some dirt-ball beggar's bazaar where you can roll out a blanket on the concrete and disturb every person that walks by." As he talked, others who were passing turned to listen to his insults.

"I reiterate, fuck off."

"Get your filthy ass out of here, man." He kicked my cap, sending the coins rolling across the sidewalk and off the curb into the street. My anger hissed like steam from a pressure cooker.

I hopped up, and before he could step back, I grabbed the short end of his tie. With my other hand I slid the knot tight against his throat, tight enough to choke the guy. I scowled and said, "Listen, pretty boy. When, or if, I let you go, you just walk your pimply puss right on down the street and call it a day. Otherwise, somebody's going to have to carry you out of here and I don't think you want that pretty little lady friend of yours to see you licking concrete, now do you?"

When he grabbed my wrists, I cinched the knot tighter and jammed my knuckles into his Adam's apple. He gasped for air. I pressed the knot deeper into his throat and pushed up on his chin, which brought him to his toes. A crowd formed. Two of the onlookers converged on me from opposite sides. When they did, I dropped my grip and took a step back, waiting for the punk or others to lunge toward me. Nothing happened. My little cherub friend adjusted his suit, reached up and straightened his tie with a look back toward his nooner date. He cleared his throat, turned, and walked off, followed reluctantly by the gathered bystanders.

With that, I had violated the golden rule of the homeless: thou shalt not disturb the peace lest a yahoo,

no SHELTER for GUILT

street-walking lunch crowd sends the cops out to nab you as a public nuisance. Recalling my night in the slammer in Macon, I retrieved the coins from the street, disregarding the squawk of horns from passing cars.

Roused by the brief schoolyard tussle, the voices in my head rallied. I packed up and talked as I walked.

"I should have ripped that fool's head off."

He's like all the rest.

"Sees me, sees us, on the street and thinks because he has a fancy suit, he can tell us what to do."

Tried to shame you with his shitty comments.

"Drugs? Ha. School? Ha. I have more brains in my little toe than that asshole has in his entire body."

A car horn blasted me out of my conversation and left me standing in the middle of a crosswalk. I flipped him off and continued walking and talking and flailing my arms while the voices convinced me of my new identity. I looked in a puddle from a leaky hydrant. My reflection appeared wearing a crown ... of thorns. I did a double take, then stared back at myself with a smirk.

At the next intersection, another panhandler claimed squatter's rights. He flashed a flimsy sign printed on a brown grocery bag. It read, "No job. No home. No family." I stopped. I didn't say anything. Without a word, I reached into the ankle money belt hidden under my sock and pulled out sixty bucks. I handed it to the guy.

"It's neither loaves nor fishes, but just out feeding my flock," I said, thinking about the ungrateful bastard who had shown no empathy for me moments earlier. With my right hand I made an air-cross over the guy on the sidewalk, placed my hand on his head, and said, with a wink and assuring nod, "God will save you. God will save us all. My father is a mighty God. Yes, He is!" I removed my hand and motioned like I was going to hug the guy, and then I said, "And I am His only begotten son. Can you believe it, brother? You just met Jesus Christ himself. Thank your lucky stars, bubba. I'll see you in paradise." He reared back, grabbed the cash, grabbed his sign, and headed away from me as fast as he could walk. "Hey, my son? Is there any room at the Inn? I need a place to sleep," I yelled. He turned back and waved his arm this way and that, saying something which I didn't understand.

It was close to four in the afternoon by the time I made it to the Little Room in the Inn, thanks to a wrong turn and a city worker behind a jackhammer who had helped get me reoriented.

The line was over a block long. I used the time to preach my old man's gospels and the word of God the Father to the crowd, with an added touch of humor. And, of course, I let them all know I was their Lord and Savior, the One, the only. Short of water to walk on, I hopped out in the street, jumping in front of cars with my arms outstretched, a rerun of my crucifixion. Tires screeched. Bumpers stopped less than six inches from my knees. The crowd went wild. Horns blared. Drivers acknowledged my miracle with accustomed pleasantries. Guys in the line laughed. "You crazy, man," someone hollered, the compliment returned with a raised-hand blessing.

The shelter staff smothered the typical chaos. In a cavernous room filled with flatulence and funky body odors, cussing and an occasional shoving match, timid staff members quickly jumped into action, nonetheless, my performance continued. A few more recitations from the Bible, a little self-promotion, Sermon on the Mount albeit nothing more than a cot. "Believe in me and you will not perish." And, "I am your shepherd. Thou shalt not want,"

no SHELTER for GUILT

and, "Blessed are you, you poor, meek, hungry souls." I closed with a rousing, "So do not fear for I am with you." When my actions failed to get a response, I channeled my message differently.

I stood on my cot, legs spread across the frame, raised my hands high above my head, and yelled, "It is I, Jesus H. Christ. I have come to turn your water into wine." My announcement brought cheers and comments like "Make mine Mad Dog 20/20!"

Standing there, pious as the pope, my arms still outstretched, in the back, near the far wall, I noticed a face that looked familiar, one from somewhere I'd been.

"Sir, please get down. This is not a religious gathering. If you must, pray quietly, to yourself." The staff volunteer was so polite, I couldn't argue.

I hopped off my cot and zig-zagged to where I saw the familiar face.

Still in Jesus mode, I gave him a slap to his knee. "Hey, bud, don't I know you?" I said, standing all akimbo, chest popped out.

"If it ain't old Chili-dog himself." He stood and whipped a bear hug on me. "Fancy meeting you here. You 'member me? Jimmy. Jimmy Pickett?"

"I thought I'd seen you before. Wait. When I saw you, it wasn't here, was it?"

"Nah, last time we seen each other was on a bus down in Alabama," he said sitting down.

"That's right. You were headed to Birmingham—"

"Gadsden."

"Right, going to hook up with a friend. Do body shop work. So, what happened to all of that?" I asked, putting my foot on the edge of the cot and leaning forward on my knee, closer, better to hear over the noise in the room.

"Me and him got into a pissin' contest few weeks into it. He told me to get lost. Been thumbing around since."

"Why didn't you head back home? Where was that?"

"Turkey Knob, West Virginia." He laughed. "I can't go back to West Virginia. Ain't got no job. I'm so poor, I can't even pay attention. Besides, too many people there still gunning for me." He reached under his cot for a plastic bag and pulled out a pouch of Red Man tobacco. He mashed the pack a few times, then pulled out a two-finger wad of tobacco and shoved it in his cheek. After a couple of drools into a cup he had under the cot, he spit a flake of tobacco off his lip.

I sat down next to him, leaning with my elbows on my knees. So many guys had said the same thing. They couldn't go home. Reasons varied, but the issue was more than money or people. It was their personal fear of failing. I was convinced. Men need to "man up" and strike the personal fortitude to make things right. Jimmy was no exception. I thought for a minute before I spoke. "You willing to try again?" I paused before I added, "I'll take you back home. Come on, man." I hopped up and turned to face him. I wasn't Jesus anymore; I was simply the Good Samaritan.

"Nah, man. I told you, I can't go back there." Sadness found a place on his face.

"Come on. Let's go get tickets. We'll go to West Virginia, back home, together. Back where you belong. Off the damn street. Come on. We can go now. Come on. Let's go get tickets and blow this joint."

Pickett shook his head, still looking toward the floor, fumbling with the tobacco pouch.

"You need to end this shitty life sooner or later. Now's as good a time as any. Your folks want you back? Sure they do," I said, bumping him with my shoulder.

no SHELTER for GUILT

Pickett looked away. He sniffled a couple times, then turned back toward me. His face was mapped with confusion—joy flooded by fear. "Man. I don't know, man." He looked at his feet, then sat up. "Okay. Okay. If you want to do this, if you go, I'll go with you. Not tonight. Doors are locked. Tomorrow," he said, looking straight into my eyes, a nervous stare from deep down.

We sat together for dinner then went our separate ways, back to the well-used cots. Hard telling how many sweaty bodies had slept there or used them for other pleasures. The line for the showers was too long to bother.

After my time with Jimmy Pickett, the voices seemed extra quiet for a change. No longer fighting racing thoughts, I lay on my back and thought about going home. Didn't really have one myself, but to get Jimmy home felt good, felt right. For me, just another bus ride, this time with an old "friend." Hadn't really done anything with a friend, since Ben Keller. That thought stuck with me until lights-out.

The next morning, I took my sweet time knowing the day ahead entailed a trip to the bus station and a long ride. I gathered my things and headed back to hook up with Jimmy for chow. He wasn't there. I asked around; nobody had seen him. I checked the staff member manning the front desk. They checked the log. Jimmy Pickett had checked out of the shelter as soon as the doors opened. He was gone.

With my nose buried deep in a Styrofoam cup of morning java, the Vigilantes rejoined me, a little breakfast coffee talk.

Loser. You lost another one.

"No."

Nobody wants you. Can't find that wife. Loser.

"Nothing's easy."

You're right. That's what you got, nothing.

"I'm not done."

Yes you are. It's over. Nothing but dead ends.

"I'll find her."

Nothing, ha, 'cept the noose the law has around your neck. It's real.

What was real was the fact that I was beginning to believe them. A dark corner at the back of the hall provided needed solitude where thoughts of suicide began a little war chant, a solution, the escape, that is until morning volunteer found me crunched over in a folding chair.

"Time to go, partner. Shelter's closed. We reopen at 4:30, but you can't stay here during the day."

I wanted to argue, but I couldn't. I wanted to beg, but I wouldn't. I was the last one to leave, and the voices came with me. For four hours of heading nowhere, they hammered me with their case for suicide. I was so tired of fighting. Their monotonous chatter made it impossible to hear myself think; my walk became a zombie shuffle. At wit's end, I sought refuge the only way I knew how: in a bar, in a bottle. Several bottles.

Country and western tunes that crackled over house speakers enlivened the place with a carnival atmosphere, a sharp contrast to my mood. It was half-past eleven in the morning when the bartender slid that first beer toward me. It was the old family secret recipe for soothing a bad mood, but never seemed enough to drown the voices. For the next three hours the bartender was willing to listen to me mumble, drinking alone, nonstop. There was a time in my life when I drank beer by the bathtub and never failed to walk steady as a rock down the centerline, much to the dismay of the cop who challenged me. However, when that bathtub-plus-one beer hit, the horse was out of the barn.

When I staggered out of this place, the stall was empty. I left the Vigilantes inside the bar to celebrate on their own. I was sloshed. The come-on from the deep-fat-fryers at a flea market across the street beckoned. In a span of five minutes, two greasy corn dogs and a large cup of cheesy fries joined my three hours of suds; and an unfortunate intestinal chemistry ensued. As I wandered table to table, admiring the full array of un-appraised and, for the most part, unwanted priceless antiques, while the battle raged in my stomach, I spotted the girl from the cult, Trixie.

Chapter 29

She was sitting behind a cockeyed wooden table, tucked between period-piece furniture and comic book collections. I wasn't in any shape for talking but I had to tell Trixie about my Christmas visit with her grandparents. She had to know they would welcome her back. She needed to hear about her daughter.

Two people in front of me blocked the table while I watched Trixie sort flowers in cans. Though blurry, the few I recognized—daffodils, tulips, and peonies—were fresh and beautiful; I couldn't say the same for Trixie. I remembered her fresh-flower fragrance as she had passed me wrapped in that towel, coming out of the shower months before. Now, dressed in her mismatched, dirty clothes with hair twisted into six braids wrapped with ribbon, it appeared her life on the street hadn't changed.

"Knock, knock," I said, rapping on the tabletop with my knuckles. She flinched, looking up from her work. "Remember me?" I said, weaving in front of her, my palms on the table for support.

"Uh ..."

"The guy from the motel room that night," I whispered to coax her memory a bit. My stomach shifted. A violent hiccup lifted my shoulders with a shrug.

"Uh ... sorry, been in a number of motel rooms, different guys," she said, obviously less than enthused with my question. She shifted her eyes back to the table, her fingers busily working with the flowers. "And you would be …"

"Chili. Last fall. Little scrap in the woods." Hiccup. "We high-tailed out of the camp and spent the night in a motel."

She cocked her head slightly. "Oh … right," she said to the side and squinted. "You're the guy, the guy who didn't want anything …" She flashed an affiliative smile. "… just wanted to help. Sure, I remember now." She stood there momentarily before going back to sorting flowers.

"And I wrote that letter to your grandparents." Another hiccup. I leaned harder on the table, my knees undecided.

Her hands stopped sorting, but she kept her eyes on the table.

"I saw your daughter."

She placed the bouquet of flowers she was making on the table and looked up. Her jaw dropped, stretching her gaunt face. Slowly, her eyebrows lifted and her eyes widened. "You did?" She covered her mouth with her hands.

"She's a beautiful, happy, polite little girl." At this point my stomach made it difficult to share the happy news. I swallowed deeply, choked by a qualified smile across my pallid face. "She's cute, looks healthy and happy, certainly was enjoying the holidays. I saw her on Christmas Day."

Her face brightened with a forced smile that grew along with tears that welled in the corners of her eyes. Walking around the table, she wiped her hands on her dirty jeans. Her head dipped as she ran both hands through her hair then covered her face and the tears that followed.

"I met your grandparents, too. Fine people, obviously doing a great job. They invited me to share dinner with them." My words were slurred and the thought of food got the best of my stomach.

While Trixie stood crying in front of me, I doubled over with my arms wrapped around my midsection. My knees buckled as I turned, staggered to the side of the booth and upchucked a frothy mix of corndogs, fries, and beer. Fortunately, nobody had been walking past.

Trixie, still crying, supported my elbow and led me behind the stall of tables. She pulled her chair around and had me sit, bent over, ready for another surge of nausea. The pain was sobering.

"Are you okay?" she asked timidly, her arms folded across her stomach in empathetic pain. Her tears had stopped.

I waved her back, spewing a second time before the chair wobbled, collapsed, and pitched me into the mess. Trixie scrambled to get me back on the chair, then stopped as I lay wallowing in distress.

"I need a toilet," I moaned, fearfully.

"Are you going to be all right? Do you need a doctor? Want to go to the emergency room?" she said, bending to look at my face, her arms still wrapped around her stomach. "Where are you staying?" she asked. "The shelter? Little Room in the Inn?"

Keeping eyes mostly closed to avoid light or anything else that might slip in, my head rocked, no. "Any motel close?" Eking out the question without a reflux response wasn't easy. I uncurled and dragged myself onto the chair. My head dangled, helplessly, repulsed by the smell. Everything was spinning, out of sync with my stomach.

Trixie panicked. She rubbed her forehead with her hand as she paced a short path in front of me; then she confessed she didn't know of any motels nearby.

"Sit there. Wait while I ask around." Moments later, she was back. "My friend Tiffany has a truck," Trixie said when she rushed back, then quickly took a step backward. "She says there's a motel, not far. She can drop us off there." Trixie turned away for a deep breath of fresher air. "Tiffany is breaking down her stall. She said she will pull her truck over behind us." When the truck rolled up, I moaned, helplessly, as they loaded me in the bed of the truck.

The girls went inside the motel office to get a room. Not long after, Trixie came running back to the truck. "We need to pay up-front for the room."

Slowly I motioned for her to reach up my pant leg to the ankle belt under my sock. She pulled out a wad of bills, whatever I had. I didn't know and, at this point, I didn't care. After paying, the two of them popped back into the truck and drove around the end of the motel to the back row. They hoisted my arms over their shoulders and dragged me into the room. I offered no help.

With me soiled inside and out, front and back, Tiffany helped Trixie lay me in the tub before she left. Trixie pulled the curtain and turned on the shower. The initial ice-cold spray was a shocker that slowly warmed to a godsent summer rain which soothed my aching stomach but offered little relief from the thunder that clapped in my head. As I sat, motionless, there was a comforting hypnotic effect of the brown water as it swirled down the drain. Everything around me was melting. I could feel myself melting into the porcelain of the tub and down through the floor and then to nowhere.

No telling how long I was there half an hour, maybe longer. I vaguely recall Trixie sticking her nose in twice to check on me and to ask if I felt better. Each time I simply moaned.

Motel hot water can spring endless. It was comforting but less than magical. It rinsed the muck from my clothes, warmed my painful chills, and provided a steady white noise to distract me from the pangs in my stomach, but the war in my head continued. Over time, my skin shriveled. I scooched around and wrestled my clothes off without sacrificing my sitting position. Less movement falsely reassured no relapse. Leaving the wet clothes in the tub, I turned off the water and attempted to stand. Both my stomach and sphincter puckered, which left me jack-knifed over my wrinkled toes. The sink offered support until the spasms passed. I pulled a towel from the rack, wrapped it around me, and dragged myself into the outer room.

Trixie, propped against a wall of pillows, turned away from the show on TV. She had changed out of the shirt she had been wearing when she carried me in. She wore an oversized tank top which hung low and loose over her body. "Any better?"

"I'm clean, empty, and feel like a million bucks …" I paused. "… just ran over my ass," I replied with a grimace atop my humor. Still in a daze, I sat on the bed next to Trixie, uncertain whether the best position was standing, sitting, or lying flat on the mattress. The look on her face gave me reason to believe that I looked as bad I felt.

"That was awful. Any idea what's wrong? Did you eat today? Recently? Anything?" she asked with a sickening frown.

"Not much." I was slow to respond, trying to recall where I'd been, what or when I'd eaten. "A couple delectable corn dogs at the flea market …" Trixie cocked her head and furrowed her brow; I continued, "On top of a boatload of beer."

She shook her head. "Oh, bad choice." She cringed. "Had to be the dogs."

I eased myself flat on the bed, rolled toward her, and re-tucked my towel. She didn't hesitate to expand the conversation. "So, you said, you think I can go home?" She gnawed on her bottom lip, waiting for my reply.

The buzz in my head warned me not to talk. I disobeyed. "Yeah. Your grandparents would like you back." I swallowed and added, "And I know your daughter needs you." I paused for her response. She sat there. I could almost hear the wheels spinning in her head. "Are you ready?" My stomach lurched; I swallowed. "Back to a normal life? Not the normal you had before you left." I took another deep swallow. "But better, a normal life as an adult, as a parent, a responsible parent?. Are you ready to be a single mom?"

It quickly became obvious that I wasn't ready for conversation; my stomach tightened in an unwelcomed knot. Rolling back to the edge of the bed, I staggered back to the bathroom, doubled over, losing my towel somewhere along the way.

My reflection in the bottom of the toilet bowl didn't capture even an inkling of my misery. I remained on my knees, hugging and hoping. When I returned, I recovered my towel and rewrapped my waist. Trixie was poised upright in the middle of the bed, eyes locked on a distant source with evidence of tears on her cheeks. I leaned back against the headboard, with long, slow breaths, and waited.

"I'm ready," she said. "I need to. I have to." Wiping her tears, she turned toward me. "I can do it. Yeah, I want to go back." She nodded, still looking at me. She sighed. "You okay?"

"Like I said ... like a million bucks," I replied with a pained chuckle. "Otherwise ... better."

We sat there a good while, in silence, each in our own little world. She asked if I was hungry. I huffed and slowly shook my head no. I asked her the same, but got no reply. Able to relax, finally, my exhausted body dozed. At some point, Trixie must have flicked off the lights and TV and dozed as well.

Nausea and pain covered me through the night with chills and sweats that soaked the bed.

The empty space between the closed curtains grew bright before Trixie awoke. She rose quietly, still in her tank top, and spent a few minutes in the bathroom. When she returned, she was wearing street clothes and whispered, "Are you awake, Chili?"

"Have been most of the night," I said in a low tone.

"Feeling any better?"

"Only if I don't move," I groaned. "Guess I can't lie here forever."

"I reserved the room for two nights. I wasn't sure how bad you were. Stay here and rest," she said as she gathered her things. She looked my way, smiled, and walked out the door.

"Hey, where're you ..." She was gone.

By late morning, the cramps in my stomach gave way to pangs of hunger. By noon I was able to relocate, permanently, to the bed where I continued to deal with the headache from hell. Late in the day I heard a faint knock on the door.

"I hope you don't mind," Trixie said, cracking the door enough to show her face. "I kept the key when I left. I didn't expect you would be going anywhere," she added as she quickly entered, closing the door, leaving sunlight outside.

"You guessed correctly. I've been here all day admiring the plumbing for the most part. Thanks for hanging up my clothes in the bathroom."

"I tried to wash them a little before wringing them out. Hope they're okay. I also brought a few things to eat if you're hungry, some of the money from the room," she explained. "Here's the rest." She handed me a wad of bills, then reached into her backpack and pulled out some pudding and bananas. Soft foods, ready to eat, which I did.

Within the blue light cast by the TV in the background, we spent the evening talking, catching up. Her life on the streets. How she existed. What turns her life had made, the tricks she pulled. I explained my manic episodes but spared her the weeks of depression; she needed no more talk of misery or thoughts of suicide. Most of the talk focused on my visit with her grandparents. Trixie had dozens of questions about her daughter—how big was she, what color was her hair, what did she sound like, what did she like to do, what was she most excited about, did she miss her mama? As we talked, her smile grew broader and brighter.

Rested, relaxed, and reassured, Trixie took advantage of the motel room's private bath. After she showered, she walked out of the bathroom naked and slid under the covers next to me.

"I can never thank you enough," she said, placing her head against my shoulder, her hand stroking my chest. "You've been kind to me. You've given me hope for my life. You've given me a reason to live," she said.

Lying in bed next to Trixie was unsettling, especially coming off my thirty-hour near-death experience. I offered a polite smile. The rose-scented shampoo and the spring freshness of bath soap gently washed away my surface anxieties. Relaxed and desirous—I was a man with a woman in bed—a different kind of shiver crept through my body.

"Weren't you looking for ... some woman?" she asked.

Her question whisked me back to reality. "What?"

"Did you find her?" she asked.

"Who?"

"I don't know. Didn't you kill some guy?" She rolled away. "Weren't you trying to find his wife?"

I hesitated. I'd forgotten; she hadn't. The last time we were together, Trixie had convinced me that my issues, my guilt, and the voices would all go away if I found Ben Keller's wife.

"Oh ... yeah. Sure. No, I haven't found her."

"Have you tried? It won't just happen, ya know. She won't just ... appear. She might be hiding from you. Ever think of that?"

"Hiding from me? Huh? Well, yeah, I've tried. I thought I was close a few times. Dead-ends. Still looking. I have other leads," I said, hoping to avoid the discussion.

"You've got to do it. You've got to. You need to think about yourself, for a change." She snuggled closer.

Thinking about myself was the problem. I spent too much time thinking about myself already. Who I was and why I was. Why I was still alive; I should have been dead. The Vigilantes approved of that truth. I thought about myself and the moment. The discussions ended.

We lay there, touching, unmoving for a time. Instincts, tempered by caution, guided our motions, both slow and sensitive. She rolled on top of me. We kissed, short at first. Fueled by the seduction, the kisses grew passionately longer. A certain, anticipated heat simmered. Hands wandered. We touched each other—slowly—everywhere. We inched closer, and for hours through the night, we satisfied mutual desires.

I awoke early, Trixie against my chest, our legs stuck together like teenagers in the backseat at a drive-in theater. The night's activities had cured my headache, settled my stomach, and left me more rested than I had been in days, though the relationship heaped a heavy guilt onto my soul. I slipped out from under her and took a shower. By the time I dressed, Trixie was awake, only her head showing above the covers.

"Mind if I take a shower?" she said with a come-on wink.

"No, not at all. Be my guest. The water's fine," I replied with a nod and a satisfied smile.

She rose from the bed, naked, and brushed past me and into the bathroom. Once I heard the shower, I sat on the bed and used the nightstand to write a note.

> *Trixie, this money is for you. It's all I have but should be enough for a bus ticket to Atlanta and cab fare to get you to your grandparents' house. Enjoy watching your daughter grow into the person you had envisioned for yourself. Give her what is most important—love. I wish you the best in your new life. Chili. P.S. Thank you for taking care of me in my hours of need.*

The voices were hard at work. I needed peace. I needed to think. I needed to run. As I waited, I thought about where the running was taking me, where the search was leading me. There were no answers, except the one the Vigilantes offered, repeatedly.

Chapter 30

It wasn't only the night in bed with Trixie. It wasn't only what she'd said. It was the realization that there was no out for me. Seven days in hiding followed, subjugated by voices. My head was a hot air balloon, drifting beyond the clouds; I held on to it, literally, constantly. It was the illness.

When I slept, if I slept, I dreamed of walls squeezing closer, closing in on me. At night, too weak to stand, I crawled. Crying was a constant, but for no particular reason. I avoided everybody and everything. Hour after hour, memories dragged my spirits deeper in a death spiral.

Life was a perpetual hangover without alcohol. Brain fog muffled my senses in the shadow of paranoia. Words became complex concepts, too convoluted to speak. No voice to speak them. No ears to hear them.

My conscience mocked me, betrayed me, convinced me to do things I didn't want to do. Decisions—big or small—became fuel for self-blame, more guilt. What did it all matter? Life didn't matter. My existence didn't matter. My life, a charade—hopeless, worthless, too complicated.

I longed for a how-to manual for suicide. There was no future to my existence. Dying would release me. No turmoil. No running. No voices.

I needed to raise the quiet noise of sorrow, saying, "I'm sorry."

Chapter 31

Life was the inside of an abandoned boxcar on a railroad siding, overwhelmed by the simplest of things. Tying my shoes. Walking. Lighting my candle. Mid-week, while trying, unsuccessfully, to open a can of tuna, I recalled that months earlier the bridesmaid had mentioned a librarian who had also attended the Kellers' wedding. Was there a name? A number? An address? The thought passed.

Days later, a ray of sunlight through a hole in the roof of the boxcar reflected off a zipper on my backpack. Fascinated, I dumped the backpack's contents. I sat in the sunbeam and marveled at how the zipper slowly pulled the teeth together, linked them into one strip and pulled them apart. After the magic of the zipper faded, collecting items to put back in the pack, I found the librarian's name and address on a balled-up piece of paper with a poem I had written. I stuck it in my shirt pocket and checked it every day, powerless to do anything more.

By week's end, my head cleared and strength returned, I came out of hiding and took a bus to Lynchburg. There, sunlight restored my ability to talk. I dialed information from a pay phone to request the phone number for the librarian. The operator told me the number was unlisted. I had delayed my search for far too long. Renewed by the find, I decided that if I couldn't talk to her, I would pay her a visit.

Carl E. Linke

The Loaves and Fishes Ministry in Lynchburg offered a homeless trifecta experience: a short line out front, extra food at dinner, showers that were plentiful and warm—truly a special comfort after my isolation in a boxcar in Charlotte. For the first time in a week, I showered, washed some clothes, and pulled a used razor from the trash to shave off the scruffy growth on my face.

The comforts came with a cost. A dream or something deeper still—something more nightmarish—brought voices, more than the Vigilantes, and another omen.

I lay there under the dim light from an exit sign, eavesdropping on the conversation of the volunteers at the front desk. Outside, the sounds of eighteen-wheelers downshifting, snarling dogs in a distant fight, and the far-off whine of a police siren were the last recalls before drifting off, then a tone—nee-ner, nee-ner, up and down, nee-ner—that ebbed to a hiss. Then I heard the first voice:

You're going to die.

The hiss returned.

The voice: *I'll kill you.*

A different voice: *Slightly ball, slightly right.*

A third voice: *287*

An immediate, elastic *whooooop-whooooop* tone.

Again, the hiss.

A voice: *Slightly above.*

Another *whooooop-whooooop.*

And, again, a voice: *Slightly below.*

A different voice: *Don't do this, Chili. Back off.*

A hiss.

Then the voice: *Pull up. Pull up.*

Whooooop-whooooop.

Hiss coming from a distant flashing amber light.

A voice: *Bingo! Bingo!*

no SHELTER for GUILT

The original voice: *Don't wimp out. Do it and do it fast.* Then, I was running. Running toward the lights. Green lights split by yellow. Sounds accompanied by a red light, pulsing slowly.

A voice: *'Thus conscience does make cowards of us all ...* ' I stopped running. Again, flames, no heat. I was cool, wet, spent.

I jerked up at the sound of another siren. It was real, closer. It was the shelter wake-up alarm, in stereo, from speakers mounted in the corners of the hall. I rose, ate breakfast alone, piecing together the images of the nightmare I had seen so many times before. After eating, despite the killer headache, I called for a cab which took me to the librarian's house. Comfortable and somewhat presentable, I knocked on the door, to no answer.

It was relatively early on a Wednesday. At this time of day, she could be most anywhere— out running errands or possibly at work, maybe out of town? I decided to wait it out, desperate to contact her. I released the cab and walked. Periodically I wandered back to check the house. No response. The more I walked, the more I recalled my previous house visits, my failures, my wasted time; this one could be the same. Overwhelmed, I doubted my intentions. I walked back toward the main thoroughfare, looking for a phone, for a cab but instead, I reversed course and returned to the house to knock one last time.

The woman who answered the door was extremely nice, a little older but very attractive. I fed her my old line about being a former beau wanting to express my sympathies for Mary Kay's loss. The librarian didn't question my story or my intentions. She acknowledged being a friend of Mary Kay and confirmed that she had attended the wedding, but she had not seen or heard from Mary Kay since then, other than a thank-you note for a wedding gift she'd left. She had no contact information whatsoever. When I pressured her about mutual friends with Mary Kay, she became annoyed and assured me that, since she was several years older than Mary Kay, she did not run in the same circles. She only knew her because Mary Kay had helped out at the library while in college. I tried to argue but it aggravated her more.

"Surely there is someone, anyone you know who can tell me where Mary Kay is?" I pleaded, desperate to learn something, a lead, anything.

"I'm sorry, Mr. White. I've told you. I don't know anyone who might know. Now, if you'll excuse me ..." She closed the door. I bit my tongue, thanked her through the door, and walked away.

I can't go back to that shelter, not after the nightmare of last night, I thought. I needed to regroup, to rethink my plan. The search. I had an eerie, sick feeling in my gut. Somebody was following me. As clouds gathered, bringing rain, I stepped inside a post office for temporary shelter. Wandering around inside with an eye on the weather, I saw a bulletin board above the scale and copy machine. Posted in the middle was a binder clipboard with "wanted" posters. I stared at it. I began to thumb through the sheets, but stopped. I wanted to know if I ... Though the rain was heavier, I left. The weather mattered little. What concerned me was the sudden urge to forget about finding leads and run. I thumbed a ride to the bus station, and hopped the next bus to depart, a short ride to Charleston, West Virginia.

The Greyhound was not quite full when I boarded. I took a seat close to the back. I purposefully plastered an evil look on my face to ward off would-be neighbors. By all measures, a good tactic; nobody sat next to me or on either bench, front or back. The rain, at times a mere mist, at others a downpour, slowed the bus and further dampened my spirits. Despite the dreariness of the day, I fought to stay awake, fearing that a snooze would resurrect the nightmare I rushed to leave behind.

I understood the significance of the recurring dream, the events and their meaning. Each bore a subliminal message, a deep wound that shamed me. The shame had become me, one who did not deserve to live. Shame for my arrogance. Shame for my lies. Shame for my charade. Shame for my silence.

At one point along the route we entered a tunnel where bright white lights along the walls whizzed past in strobe-like fashion. Flash after flash. Each made a sound, a thwack, like a bullwhip. The sights and sounds, compounded by the fragile state of my senses, summoned the voices. As I watched, the lights changed from bright white to flashing green to solid red. *Stare at the lights.* The voices grew louder. Echoing. Closing in. I wasn't sleeping. It wasn't a nightmare. I closed my eyes. The voices continued. *You're going to die. When you come out of this tunnel, he's driving this bus off the side of this mountain. We told you to kill yourself. Now you will die.*

"He's going to kill me. He's going to kill all of us!" I screamed. Startled, the other passengers turned. Thirty-two sets of eyeballs all on me. "He's going to drive the bus off a cliff!" I warned as I scrambled to clear the edge of my seat and up the aisle. A male passenger twice my size, two rows up, slid into the aisle. While I tried to claw my way over the guy's shoulders, two other guys, more my size, pinned me against an empty seat. People panicked. I pushed the two smaller guys aside with my legs, but then the mountain man slid in and pinned me down in the aisle.

"Get off, asshole," I said. "Let me go. He's going to kill us!"

"Shut up, man. What's your problem?"

"The voices. They said the driver's going to kill us." I nudged my chin around the huge dude to fight for air, to wrestle myself free. The two smaller guys now had my legs.

"You're nuts, man," the guy on top of me said.

"Bad dream, bud," one of my smaller captors said.

"Relax. Just relax. Count to ten or something. Chill out. Ain't nobody going to do nothing. Just relax."

"I'm telling you ... he's going to—"

About that time the bus came out of the tunnel, back into daylight, and immediately swerved to the right. We slid on the wet pavement, out of control. The bus began to tip to the side. Passengers screamed. The movement rocked the small guys off balance, but they quickly reengaged; the big guy barely leaned.

"Sorry about that, folks," the bus driver said over his PA system, bringing the bus back upright and straight. "Didn't mean to scare you. Lost a little concentration with all the commotion back there. Some NASCAR wanna-be in front decided to cut across our lane. Had to swerve to miss the fool." The driver steered back between the lines. On this side of the tunnel, as the rain splattered hard against the window, I noticed the two smaller captors were ashen and trembling. Both were younger guys, clean shaven. One sported long locks of golden blond curls. The other a shaggy-dog look of straight brown hair.

"You're going to be all right, bud. Just lie there nice and calm and all. Just relax," curly-top told me with a bit of a quiver in his voice.

And I did. I closed my eyes and listened to the rain, the wiper blades slapping time. The sway of the bus comforted me. A lullaby. My breathing slowed. The voices were gone. I felt better.

no SHELTER for GUILT

"Guys, I think I'm okay now. Sorry," I said, apologizing to the strong-arms around me. "Not sure what to tell you." The best I could come up with was, "I have these dreams sometimes."

"You sure you're all right?" shaggy said.

"Yeah. I'm okay. Let me up. Please," I said.

The two guys on my legs exchanged a glance and simultaneously looked toward the big guy. He nodded. They all released me and worked their way back into their seats. I did the same.

When we arrived at the bus terminal in Charleston, while I waited for the others to offload, out of the corner of my eye I noticed the bus driver talking to a blue-suit policeman taking notes on a pad just outside the door. I didn't like the scene. My shoulders tightened and my stomach knotted up. When another officer and an EMS medic strolled up behind them, my feelings went from a minus ten to a minus fifty. I hesitated, lagging well behind the others. I was the last one off.

"Say there, sir. May we talk to you for a minute? Just take a minute," the officer with the pad said as I stepped to the ground. The others formed an arc around the officer and me.

I had avoided any confrontation with law enforcement since my overnight in Macon. I sighed and flashed him my best go-fly-a-kite look. I caught his eyes then checked the others, then looked back to the speaker.

"Sure. What may I do for you?" I took up a wide stance and leaned back slightly, placing my hands in my pockets to hide my jitters.

"Mister Sampson here, the driver, reported an incident on the bus," he said. "Said you were yelling and screaming crazy things, kinda jeopardized the other passengers and endangered their safety."

"I am so sorry," I replied, short and sweet.

"May I see some form of identification?" he asked, placing his hands on the belt riding cock-eyed on his slim hips.

These were words I feared from anyone, but especially from a cop. I didn't need this.

"It must have been something I ate," I said quickly. "Seriously, it was nothing. Bad dream, maybe. Popped up too fast, still half asleep. Meant no harm," I told him, deliberately ignoring his request.

He looked at me.

I looked at him.

"ID?"

"Honestly, officer, see sometimes things set me off out of the blue, like flashing lights and all. Somehow, they make me go loco, you know, kinda cuckoo, sorta. Sometimes I hear voices and such. They say dumb things and I scream back at them, at the voices I mean. It's nothing. Really."

He eyeballed me, head to toe, side to side, then took a step backward. He looked to the medic who tipped his head to the side slightly.

"Mister Sampson, you okay with that?" the cop asked the bus driver.

"Well, it's all water under the bridge, now. I can tell you it wasn't a laughing matter back up the road. It's okay now, I guess."

The cop took another short note, closed his pad, and looked up. "Okay." He paused, his face scrunched in a look of uncertainty. "Sorry to trouble you," the officer said. "You take care of yourself," he said, placing his pad in his pocket.

no SHELTER for GUILT

"You may want to see a doctor about that stuff. Sounds serious. And, watch what you eat."

I smirked. "One of my allergies. Break out in hives when I get around doctors," I said as I slipped the strap of my rucksack over my shoulder and walked off. A secure ten feet away, I took a deep breath, closed my eyes briefly, and continued on.

The near-miss got to me. The best therapy for near-miss law intervention recovery was to walk and keep walking. Unfortunately, the voices walked with me and dumped me back into my abandon state of mind. *Kill yourself, or we will, or the cops will.* They shamed me for my spineless excuses to the cop at the bus depot. I talked back at the voices, yelled. They responded with their mocking, sarcastic titter. Impulsively, I groaned and whacked my head with the palm of my hand. Others on the sidewalk stopped and stepped aside as I passed. Overwhelmed by the Vigilante chatter, I ducked into an alley where I tucked myself into a ball behind a dumpster. I sat there for hours, gently rocking, unnoticed, listening as the voices swallowed me with one repeated message: *You are worthless. Kill yourself.* That thought, their repeated message choked me like a fishbone in my throat.

Nauseated by the voices, I vomited twice. Along with the stench, the torment drove me out of hiding. I walked. I wandered, aimlessly. Nothing silenced the voices. I followed the river to a point where I saw a railroad bridge cross over it. I climbed the steep bank and walked the tracks to the middle of the bridge.

Go on! Jump, you worthless chickenshit.

The water was probably seventy feet below, swiftly moving with runoff from the recent rains. I crossed over the rails and stood on the edge of the truss, holding on to the middle vertical post.

Jump. Just do it, bitch.

Voices. Convincing voices.

I would be welcomed by the river. A new start. A new spirit. "Energy doesn't die" had been my own words to the woman on the bus; it just moves on to another form. A new body, in a new time, a different world possibly.

I loosened my grip. Flakes of rust shot up in front of my face moved by the updraft from the water below. I listened to the sounds around me. An eerie stillness, a white noise from the beckoning downstream turbulence of the waters. With a white-knuckled grip, my pulse pounding deep in my chest, I took a last look. On either side of the tracks beyond the bridge, dilapidated factories and warehouses—in their end-of-life forms—lined the rails, roofs caved in, walls covered in vines.

A fish jumped out of the water directly beneath my feet. A sign. In the ripple I saw him. A smiling little boy, running awkwardly to a young woman with open arms. She knelt down and hugged him as he leaned forward for a kiss.

The bridge shook. Diagonal struts twisted. Bolts and rivets rattled. Loose rails bounced on crumbling wooden ties. First the horn, then the light, then the train as it rounded the trees back toward the spot where I had entered the bridge. I was caught.

Jump, chickenshit. Jump.

Chapter 32

My body replayed the seconds of panic in slow motion. I recalled running. I recalled diving. I recalled hitting. I recalled rolling. I recalled grabbing at the tall grasses on the embankment at the far side of the bridge as I rolled away from the tracks. I stopped. I lay there, stunned and numb, while the train rumbled past above me. Clouds drifted by in a red haze, colored by blood that trickled into my eye. A palette of crimson dabbed with purple blobs, tinted with the yellow-green mucous that appeared on my sleeve when I rubbed it across my face. Trickles of blood tasted warm and sweet. Patting my face with my hand, my only injuries were an apparent gash across my forehead and a bloody nose. The cool grass slowly quieted the tingling in my limbs and restored the rhythm to my heart. Most notably, the voices were gone.

Drained, I didn't bother to look for a shelter. I walked along the river, unwilling to move toward civilization. Warehouses and loading docks along the floodplain were covered with the trash of industrial sprawl. Miles down, I spied a Little League baseball field with cinderblock dugouts. I found it a much-appreciated refuge, a place with a bench for me to lay down. But, when the winds shifted, it became apparent that the city sanitation department parked its trucks beyond the outfield fence in a lot across the road. I moved on.

Farther down, beyond the manufacturing district, I came across a Baptist church, a complex of two buildings, the main church and a community center. Between them, a courtyard with a bench. I retrieved a lengthy piece of silt-barrier plastic from a ditch opposite the church. Wrapped over the back and under the bench, the plastic made the bench a jury-rigged cocoon. With my rucksack under my head, I curled up in a fetal position, out of the wind and spits of rain that followed. More exhausted than I'd been in weeks, it took quite a while to find sleep. It wasn't the discomfort of the bench or the wind that kept me awake; it was the fear of the previous night—the nightmare and the voices. It was still dark when someone peeled back the plastic over my head.

"Hey! Hey! What are you doing?" said a froggy voice in the dim shadows, the twilight before sunrise. The question came from a tall man in jeans, a plaid shirt, and an open camouflage hunting jacket with tattered orange shoulders. The guy had to be at least sixty-something, obviously a man of the woods, with more whiskers than flesh showing on his face. I rubbed the remnants of sleep from my eyes.

"What's it look like? Sleeping," I said, not bothering to jump up or come out of my cocoon.

"This ain't no place to be sleeping. How'd you get here?"

"I don't know." Tempted to tell him that I just flew in, I settled on, "I just walked in and made myself at home."

"You eat?"

"What?"

"I said, did you eat?" he asked, taking a step back. "Have you had anything to eat?"

"Not lately."

"Come with me." He started to walk away. "Name's Jake. I work inside the church. I'm the cook, I'll fix you up," he said. "Come on." He put his hands back in his pockets and continued around the side of the building. He turned back and waved for me to follow. "Hurry up. I ain't got all day." I unwrapped the bench and left the black material next to a trash can on the way to the back door.

Jake cobbled together a breakfast fit for a king—actually, enough for an entire court. The Baptist church provided food for the local shelters. Jake came in every morning, every day of the year, to cook breakfast. He would load it into Korean War surplus mermite cans and deliver the food to seven different church shelters without in-house kitchen services. He invited me to make the day's delivery rounds with him, which I did. When we returned, I helped Jake clean up the kitchen and the cans. When we finished, Jake started all over again; he made the evening meal as well.

During his evening rounds, Jake dropped me at Friendship Place, the main shelter in Charleston. Although we arrived after the doors closed and others had been turned away, saintly Jake pulled strings and got me in.

The space was huge, a former steel mill. The perimeter of the expansive structure was a tenuous skeleton of metal decks and posts of toothpick scaffolding around dinosaur-sized furnaces. The space was connected by overhead cranes on rails. Bucket ladles the size of a dump trucks hung catawampus from failing ceiling I-beams. The outer walls bore the scars of molten metal and open-hearth processing. The floors—all bare, pitted, and burnt concrete—had been sanded and buffed to a gray finish, the luster of a pond surface on a windless, cloudy day. Graffiti filled the voids on walls not covered with soot.

In the middle of it all, a clear space provided ample room to house hundreds of cots, though only half of the space was used. My cot, assigned by a roly-poly jester of a guy, was at the end of the row just short of the restroom door, not ideal by any stretch but indoors, dry, and out of the wind.

After dinner, I meandered among the cots, chatting with others, though my real interest was strangely drawn to the old blast furnaces beyond the rope barriers with "Danger—Keep Out" signs. As a kid I visited a steel mill like this, a mill where my dad worked. I imagined my father standing not more than an arm's length from fire-breathing ladles, in a shower of sparks, as molten iron poured into blast furnaces, brighter and hotter than the surface of the sun. The lost memories of the acrid stench of burning coal and the explosive steam that scorched my face as it exploded from cooling baths. Or the rumble of giant cranes as they churned down the rails, beepers blaring to warn people of the movement overhead.

Curious, I scaled the scaffolding and climbed into one of the furnace buckets layered with ash, pushing myself through a blanket of dust and spider webs. Inside a splash of fluorescent light above the dining area, I fiddled with dials and wheels, chains and gears, and imagined the hands that did the fiddling were my father's hands, doing what he did best and enjoyed most. Then, I sat there, and listened. Guys playing poker, telling lies and bartering for cigarettes, pills, and other essentials of life on the street. Beneath it all, I felt the dull existence of men the world had rejected. Men like my dad, who lost sight of reality inside a bottle and elsewhere. I recalled the day when it all happened. I brushed the memory aside and filled it with my memories of Ben Keller, which led me back to my search for Mary Kay.

no SHELTER for GUILT

A metal-on-metal clunk from below dissolved my train of thought. Startled, my foot hit a pile of ash at the edge of the furnace. A cloud of dust showered a guy bent over a shovel that he'd apparently knocked down below me. He did a double-take as he wiped his eyes and looked up, his mouth wide open. It was the weathered face of an older man.

His head, neck, shoulders, and hips all made the move together as if his entire body had fused into one aching, inflexible rod as he picked up a good-sized shovel. "What the hell?"

"Sorry about that. I heard the shovel fall and wondered how big the rats were around here," I said.

"No rats down here, son. Be careful up there. That dust don't come off easy, ya know."

"Yeah, I know. My old man worked in one of these places when I was a kid." I grabbed the metal framework on the side of the furnace and worked my way back to the floor.

"Yeah? Your old man worked here, ya say?"

"No. He worked in a mill, but not here. In Ohio."

"Where?"

"Down south, by the Ohio River. Placed called New Boston."

The old man jerked back. "What's your old man's name?"

"Ted George."

"Well, God bless America. I used to work with your old man," he said. "Name's Harold Fellows." He extended his hand and we shook. His skin was dry and leathery, reptile-like and disfigured by arthritis, but his grip was probably as strong as when he wore a younger man's clothes. "What's your name?"

"Bob," I replied. "Some folks call me Chili. Out here, not sure who or what to believe."

He wandered a few steps away and sat on the lid of a wooden crate that had the ends of large, rusted chains sticking out. As he sat, he coughed and pounded his chest with his fist.

"Damn this stuff. These mills ain't good for your health." I nodded. "What brings you here, Bob?" He coughed again, a wet cough.

"I was just about to ask you the same question," I said to avoid any further discussion of my background, at least for now.

"My Lord and Savior, Jesus Christ, put me here," he said.

I cringed and held my tongue.

"No, I went through a bad spell and the Lord, he gave me a new life," he added.

"Why? What? He didn't give you a good life before? What happened to your other life?" Simple questions for a man who obviously had more to say while I had much to hide.

"Satan stole my life from me. Praise God I didn't follow him to the end." He bowed his head and grabbed at his chest before he started coughing again. After his hacking, he turned his head and lofted a wad of spit, end over end, several feet away. When he placed his hands back on the lid of the crate, blood seeped from his dry knuckles. "I dropped out of school to become a Marine. Once a Marine, always a Marine, they say. I did my time in Korea, in the war." He coughed again, leaning back to allow for more air. "Got all shot up at Punchbowl. Ever heard of it?"

I shook my head.

"Nah, don't suppose so. Nobody did. Over three hundred of us got wounded. Took us almost three weeks to take that ridge. Came back and met my daughter for the first time. Probably the bright spot in my life. Started at the mill as soon as I got back and took a bad case of combat fatigue with me. All the noise and heat and pressure would set me off, doing crazy things. They never fired me or nothing 'cause they knew it was the war coming out of me. When the plant closed a couple years back, I couldn't find a job, what with no high school diploma and all that war stuff. Your old man do okay after the plant folded?"

"He died."

"Sorry. But you know, the good Lord giveth and the good Lord taketh away." He shifted on the wooden crate while a grimace crossed his face.

I took a seat on a pile of scrap metal across from him. Harold paused. "What was we talking about?"

I waited before I answered. "You were telling me about your job."

"A job? Don't have no job" He hesitated again.

"A job in the mill."

He leaned forward, placed his head in his hands, and massaged his forehead. "I drank a lot. Got taken by a guy. Guy knock on my door one day. Said he was from the VA and he'd help me get a job. Filled out some papers with all my information so he could send money to my bank and all. Next thing I knowed he had cleaned me out, every last cent. My wife said she'd had enough and left me. So, I came here. Not exactly here, but around."

"Can't you make it up to her?"

"Don't know how. Don't know where she is."

"What about your daughter?"

"I know where she is, but I can't go asking her for nothing. I've been a lousy father. I mean all that drinking and flying off the handle at home with all that war stuff, that combat fatigue stuff. I ain't never showed her how much I love her." The old man's eyes were filled, but he kept blinking fast so no tears fell. He stood up long enough to pull a small bottle of Listerine from his pocket. He sat down and drank half of it then ended with a huff. "Ugh, that burns."

The coughing started again. He responded the same way, pounding his chest. I'd seen many guys slug down Listerine for the cheap alcohol-hit, but could never understand how anyone could do it.

Harold's suffering reminded me of my father, his pain and helplessness. I felt sorry for this old guy. I felt sorry for myself for not doing the same with my dad. Patching things up. Making amends. Telling him what he really meant to me.

"Harold, you should be with your family, with your daughter," I said above his coughing. "You said you know where she is?"

He continued to cough, but nodded his agreement.

"What if I write to her, send her a letter? Maybe I can smooth things over, explain how you feel, in the letter. I can ask her if she's willing to help, to meet you, to help you, somewhere, somehow, anything." His coughing spell ended but he was too short of breath to talk, so he nodded.

"How about we go back to my bunk? I'll grab a pad and pencil and we can work on a letter. I can show it to you in the morning. What do you say?"

Though my cot was close, by the time we got there, Harold was out of breath, and when I started to ask about his thoughts for the letter, he didn't recall anything about me writing any letter. He mentioned a number of female names before he settled on one that he was sure was his daughter's. Fortunately, at his cot, he emptied a torn and faded olive-drab duffle bag where I found an envelope addressed to Harold and his wife. He said it was from a Christmas card his daughter had sent just before his wife left him.

I left Harold, went back to my cot, and wrote. At lights-out I was still deep in thought, composing, so I finished the letter on the commode in the men's room—the only semi-lit area in the shelter. It was sometime after midnight when I finished and stumbled my way back to bed. Something about this letter—or maybe it was Harold—had me tossing and turning on my cot, in and out of sleep until a commotion roused me.

A trio of medics, a firefighter, and a policeman hovered outside the door to the restroom, down the aisle from my cot. I watched from a distance, not anxious to rub elbows with the law for a second time in as many days. Within minutes, a pair of medics raced by with a gurney. Minutes later, they were back out again, this time with a body aboard. As one of the shelter's night staff walked by, I asked what was going on. He said an old man had a heart attack or something, a guy named Harold.

I paced outside the restroom for the rest of the night. When I heard some banging in the dining area, I found Jake.

"Can you take me to the hospital?" I asked, then explained why.

"God bless. Sure," he said. "Help me with these mermite cans and we'll head out."

If Harold knew how much I lied to convince the hospital staff I was his son, his Lord and Savior surely would have personally condemned me to everlasting fire. By the time I arrived, they had moved him from the emergency room to a bed in the cardiac intensive care unit. The nurses spared me the medical mumbo-jumbo and told me Harold had suffered a heart attack. He was stable, but would undergo more thorough testing later in the day.

Harold was asleep when I entered. He was the only patient in the unit at the time. Nothing about what I saw in the room echoed the confidence the nurse had projected during her explanation. The oxygen mask over his nose and mouth, the hydra of tubes connected to his body, and the cabinet of beeping panels and spiking monitors—it all overwhelmed me, although I had been a part of such a scene years prior.

When Harold awoke, he was not fully alert. It could have been the meds, the lack of oxygen, pain, exhaustion, or all of them combined. Given his state of mind and responses during our conversations the evening before, I didn't know exactly what to expect.

"Harold. Hi. Remember me? It's Bob. Chili. Remember? The guy in the furnace? You worked with my dad." He blinked his eyes in recognition, but didn't speak or, maybe, couldn't.

"You gave us quite a scare back there, pardner."

He rolled both eyelids in acknowledgment.

"I wrote that letter we discussed. I want to get it to your daughter for you. I wanted you to hear it before I sent it off." He blinked, though I wasn't quite sure he remembered. I began to read.

Chapter 33

I started with the address, in hopes it would help Harold recall the letter we'd discussed.

Mrs. Katie Gentry
532 Meads Road
Norfolk, VA 23505

February 12, 1988

Dearest daughter,

    A friend saw me crying today and asked if I needed help. I said I needed to send a letter to my daughter. There were things I had to tell you. He helped me put my feelings onto paper.
    With all my heart and soul, I am sorry. I'll understand if you can't forgive me, because I can't even forgive myself, though I beg you to let my heart speak.
    I was a rotten father. I didn't try hard enough. I take all the blame. My selfishness and stupidity got in my way. When I should have been protecting you from thunder, I was lost in the storm, unable to

recognize my role. When I should have been sowing seeds for a loving family, I was threshing us apart. I didn't know who I was and I was lost trying to find me, but I know I was the problem. Despite my shortcomings, in my heart, I want you to know, I've never stopped loving you. Never.

I dream of fathering you as I should have fathered. The scars of my past cannot be healed if I ignore them. Forgiving, by nature, begins with the heart, and from my heart I ask that you forgive me. Hopefully, one day you will, and if I'm alive, I hope we can reconnect in a relationship based on mutual love.

You will always be the most beautiful part of my life. Thank you for being my daughter.

Dad

Chapter 34

"Why?" Harold's voice, muffled by his oxygen mask, was faint, whispery. The mask covered most of his face; only his eyes expressed his emotion.

"Why what?"

"Why ... are ... you ... doing ... this?" Between each word he wheezed, his eyelids drifting upward to reveal mostly the whites of eyeballs rolled back.

"Like you said, once a Marine, always a Marine," I replied. "I'm a Marine."

Harold's chest rose slowly, filling with the oxygen mix from his mask. With one extended breath, he said, "A Marine? Nam?" Raising his brows, he opened his eyes and looked deep into my mine, deeper inside my head. As he dragged his arm to the top of his covers, the IV tube snagged on the sheet.

I shook my head. "No, a Marine pilot. Flew F-18s. I was one of those *Top Gun* guys. You know, those movie guys." Thinking about it caused my heart to race, sending a satisfying warmth through my body. I hadn't spoken those words for years. I had filled my life with lies. The truth felt good. "I was the 'best of the best.' Guarantee, I could outfly anybody, anytime, anywhere. I could out fly any of my instructors. That's why they called me Chili. That was my callsign, because I could be hot as fire or cold as ice when I needed to be, no matter what." I pulled a chair close to the bed. The nurses were busy with other things, not concerned in the least, although the beeps grew louder and the bleeps peaked higher on the monitors surrounding Harold's bed.

"Why?" Harold said once more.

"I just told you why."

His eyes were closed. "Why ... aren't ... you ... flying?"

I hesitated, stone-faced, as I searched for a response while the sound of life-giving air hissed in and out of his mask. I could not escape his sad eyes. It was as if I were looking back in time, past his wrinkled, scarred face, to somewhere deep within his soul. What I saw was a Marine at rigid attention, saluting sharper than the edge of a ceremonial saber. I knew, despite how we met or where we met and why we met, that what I saw was a Marine who shared the Corps values of Honor, Courage, and Commitment. I had to be straight with him.

"Because I killed a guy."

Above his mask, Harold's eyes looked on in disbelief. I returned his look, hesitantly. I saw courage—his courage—while mine slipped away; my body was weak. My eyes drifted toward my hands. Embarrassed or maybe ashamed, my fingers nervously tapped, tip to tip. I'd never been with an old Marine, one who had lived through combat in Korea. I tucked my trembling hands under my armpits and sensed his stare as my words began to flow.

"We'd been in the air about seven hours, hit the tanker along the way, and planned for a standard recovery in daylight. By the time we got there, weather socked-in the area. I mean, there was no seeing nothing, the perfect black. My flying buddy Ben Keller was there at the other end of the cockpit. He reminded me, 'It's always sunny above the clouds.' His go-to encouragement, no matter what."

no SHELTER for GUILT

The noise in the room was more settled now; the beeps from monitors sounded further apart. Harold might have dozed, off and on, while I rambled.

"I was the slob, always a little wacko in the head, too much boxing or rugby or partying. We were the quintessential odd couple. Finishing each other's sentences. Anticipating each other's thoughts kinda like husbands and wives, though I didn't have a wife. Ben did. Mary Kay. Sweet gal he met during basic flight in Meridian, Mississippi. They had a toddler, Adam, who was learning to talk. Mary Kay swore that the first word Adam learned to say was Chili."

A slight wrinkle appeared at the corner of Harold's eye as he blinked.

"We were nabbed for a special evaluation. The Wizards of Wonder in the Pentagon put us together in a two-seater D-model F-18 to launch off a carrier. And there we were, best friends turned special mission test pilots."

Harold's eyes opened a crack every so often, but remained closed a good bit. His chest rising and falling was the only movement in the bed. I looked down and continued. "At ten miles from the ship, the radar altimeter warbled. We leveled our descent at 1,200 feet and sat there awaiting further instructions from carrier air traffic control. We were the only plane in the air, fortunately, so there was no waiting for the yahoos ahead of us."

A series of beeps caught my attention. Harold was awake. His wide eyes told me he was still listening.

"When the TACAN registered eight miles from the ship, we started the landing checklist. Landing gear down? Check. Flaps down? Check. Hook down? Check. We were six miles out and no sight of the ship or anything. At three miles out, systems kicked in to get us on the proper glideslope. We were descending at 700 feet a minute, which gave us a little less than two minutes to park that baby on the deck. That started the longest two minutes of my life."

The bedding moved as Harold rolled his shoulder and one of his feet toward my side. I held off, anticipating a question or comment. He settled and nodded for me to continue.

"Then the tower sent word. '287, on course, on glide path, three quarters of a mile. Call the ball.'

"Clear as a bell I remember the response. '287, Hornet, ball, four point five.' Aviator talk that we acknowledged their question, and we had forty-five hundred pounds of fuel left. In case we had to scratch the landing.

"Tower radioed, 'Roger, slightly high, slightly right, course correcting, 42 knots, deck is all over the place, slightly low.'"

As I worked through my story my palms began to sweat. My voice nervously pushed out the words as I shifted in my seat. "Gusts from the left continued to push us off center. The correction was to oversteer with more rudder and added power. The carrier's deck bobbed all over. With the wave action, when the stern popped, the lights on the deck looked like a pole. Then, seconds later the boat dipped, and there was no deck visible at all. We were on instruments. Had to land. No choice. Twenty seconds out." I rubbed my hands on my knees, still refusing to blink.

Maybe it was something I said or did that caused Harold to stir. He coughed before he slid his mask to the side. His coughs were dry, hoarse, guttural sounds followed by desperate gasps. A nurse rushed up, full-stride past me, saying, "Go, outside the double doors, please."

I hurried through the doorway. A swarm of starched white smocks rushed by into the room. I turned to follow them, but was politely nudged back into the hall. The doors

no SHELTER for GUILT

closed. I could hear Harold's cadence of despair through the monitors. The more the voices inside the room shouted, the faster the machines echoed. My ear was against the door when the beeps flattened to a steady, single tone. I pulled back. Moments later, one of the white smocks walked out of the room with a downturned look on her face to confirm what I had painfully suspected. Fate had called time for Harold.

Our relationship, measured by brief hours, had opened me. It could have been the Marine connection, or possibly his link to my father. It may have been spirits of the street. Maybe it was just me being there for him.

Outside Harold's room the space was a blizzard of white, floor to ceiling, except the blue molded plastic chair that provided me with a contemplative resting place while I processed so many things. The paging system called doctors to phones; people hustled every which way. Nurses popped in and out of rooms. Routine, I guessed. And I suspected they were unconcerned about the Marine, the veteran, the soul who had breathed his last. I sat, silent. At some point—no idea how long I sat there—a concerned nurse asked how I was doing. "There is nothing more you can do here," she offered, then walked with me to the hospital exit.

Just shy of the revolving door leading to the street, I told the nurse I would be fine, thanked her, and suggested that she head back to her duties. When she left, rather than leave the building, I backtracked to the middle of the hall and entered a room marked, "Chapel."

The space was a windowless room that smelled of flowers and chlorine bleach. Four rows of straight-back hardwood chairs, three across on either side of a center aisle, led to a lectern beneath a dim, brushed-metal cylindrical pendant light. A six-foot panel, illuminated with a stained-glass cross, rested on a carpeted platform one step up from the tiled floor. The chairs were cold with the exception of one in the front row, occupied by a young woman. When she heard the door open, she turned, stood quickly, genuflected on her right knee, and walked by me with her eyes cast toward the floor. Unlike her, I took a seat in the back, on the side. I looked around to be sure I was alone.

"Harold, if you're still around here, I need to finish my story, the last twenty seconds. It's taken far too long to tell. During those final seconds of the approach, voices, all talking at once, ran through my brain bucket, but I remember saying over the intercom, 'Don't do this, Chili. It's not right. Don't do this. Back off.' The response was quick, direct, no questions asked. 'I got this, Gas Man. Going down!'"

"The squelch in my ears stopped when the *whooooop-whooooop* alarms sounded off, accompanied by the recorded voice of Bitchin' Betty. '*Pull up.*' *Whooooop-whooooop.* '*Pull up.*' Then, a different male voice, calm, cool and collected. 'Little power. Get the nose up.'"

"'Little throttle, nose up.' My head filled with a static hiss, the kind from a radio off frequency just a hair. 'More power. Still low. More power.' Same male voice, this time more concerned. Then, more hiss from the radio squelch."

"'Power up. Back on glideslope.' The voice calmed again. 'Easy with it. Nice and easy now.'"

"Sweat dripped into my eyes. The winds were a lot worse, without a doubt worse than in anything I'd ever flown in. I kept telling myself: *We can do this! We can do this! Slight corrections. Easy on the stick. Tap it. Gently. Little left, slip left. Tap right, slip right.*'"

"A male voice said, 'Slow down. You're too high. Watch your speed.'"

I paused and looked around the chapel. Nervously, I massaged my forehead as my memory foreshadowed what came next. "Harold? You still there, Harold? Listen up, Marine! Listen up!" I commanded in the voice of an old drill instructor, hoping to calm my nerves. I waited for a response. Nothing. The only sound came from a squeaky fan in the airduct overhead and the constant paging for doctors over the speakers in the hall. With my elbows on my knees, I hung my head.

"'Tweak the throttle, a whisker.' The w*hooooop-whooooop* went off again. You know the sound I'm talking about? Like a kid blowing a sliding whistle? Then the cockpit lit up. The 'Master Caution' warning light came on. At the same time, the 'Left Bleed' warning light lit up and Bitchin' Betty started yelling, '*Bleed air, left, bleed air, left.*' I was cross-eyed, looking at flashing amber lights when the red light popped up. FIRE."

"Before we could radio the ship, a panicked voice hollered, 'You're too low. Power! Power! More throttle. Easy with it. Easy with it.'"

"That was the last command. The twenty seconds was up."

"I knew the maneuver. I had been through this beaucoup times, but never under a FIRE warning light. *Pull the stick. Push to max throttle.* The difference this time—the stern of the carrier came up as we came down."

"We hit, hard. The rough seas tossed the carrier and slid us to starboard, nosing the plane toward the stacks of the tower island. With metal-on-metal sparks flying everywhere, crew members looked like jumping-beans, scrambling for safety. The front landing gear snapped off against a generator trailer. When the nose of the Hornet slammed into the island below the bridge, the engines were still under full power. The plane exploded under my seat. The tail section careened sideways, making an accordion out of my left wing. In under three seconds, we'd become a $29 million fireball."

Air from the duct above stopped. Speakers in the hall went silent. My eyes were closed. I heard myself breathing, exhaling hard through my nose. "Harold ..." I coughed to clear my throat. "There was the burst, the flames, the heat, the sirens. I vaguely remember getting pulled from the wreck." I choked through my next words. "I never saw my friend again."

I looked up. The cross glowed with an eerie light. "Ben's funeral took place before I was released from the hospital. He was my best friend." Salty tears found the corners of my mouth. "And I never got to say goodbye. I was in the hospital for over a month with burns and internal injuries. My head's never been the same. The Navy docs did their best to return me to flying status, nothing worked. The trauma is still there. Not the flying part. I would still love to fly. Even with the crash."

"But my fear, now my biggest fear, is facing Mary Kay Keller," I choked on each of her names, "to tell her how sorry I am. How terribly sorry I am that I killed Ben. I ... I k-k-killed my b-b-best friend. I killed her husband." I stopped there, waiting, hoping, to magically hear Harold's voice. The silence continued. "Sorry, Harold. Sorry. Just another Marine's story."

I sat with my hands clasped between my knees. The scent of flowers perfumed the air around me. I lifted my head and spied a potted gardenia peeking from behind the lectern at the base of the glass panel on the platform; its simple beauty choked my spirit. I looked up at the cross.

"So why, oh great and wondrous God, all great and powerful—why Harold? Why now?" I sneered. Every bit of me questioned why. My head cocked to one side; I stared unfocused at that cross. "I would have given anything to put my heart in Harold's body. One of us deserved to live, and it wasn't me. You took Harold. Why?"

A family of four came through the chapel door. Two small children raced to the front, pushing and shoving to claim the seat closest to the platform. When the parents noticed me, they did their best to hush the young laughter. The kids joined their parents and knelt before the cross. I took that as my cue to leave.

A banner on the lobby wall behind the admissions desk read, "Happy Valentine's Day." Knowing Marines never leave a Marine behind, I was not going to leave Harold behind. I had to let his daughter know. I had to hand-carry Harold's letter to her. She had to know he loved her.

The ticket agent at the bus station was little help. Preoccupied by the old man's death, postponing my search for Mary Kay was the least I could do for Harold. When I asked for a ticket to Norfolk, the city where Harold's daughter lived, the agent went around and around about routing me through D.C. or Raleigh. I nearly went through the glass of the ticket window. Smidley was his name. When he talked, before each sentence or phrase, he would sniffle and squint. With his short questions, the habit made him look like a rabbit twitching its nose. I rested my forehead on the counter in front of the window, half-afraid I would laugh before I'd rip down the glass between us and strangle the moron.

"Are you all right, sir?" Smidley asked with a sniffle and a squint.

I lifted my head. "Pardon me, sir, but who ties your shoes?" I asked, slowly and politely; the sarcasm went unnoticed. Then, raising my voice with each word, I added, "To answer your question ... I will be just fine if you would be so kind as to give me a goddamn ticket to Norfolk, Virginia. I don't care if the bus goes through Saskatchewan, just get me there, pronto, will you ... please?" He pressed a few keys on the terminal and handed me the ticket. With a smile, I softly said thank you.

Chapter 35

My guess is a crow never flies direct from Charleston to Norfolk, and Greyhound doesn't either. I didn't expect to make it to Norfolk the next day, Valentine's Day, given my late start and no thanks to my friend Smidley. But routing me through D.C. was a time-travel nightmare; it cost a day to get through issues with missing bus drivers and maintenance problems. I caught a few winks here and there on the bus. During a delay, I stretched out on the original wooden benches in the old D.C. bus terminal. To pass some time, using the edge of a pull-tab from a soft drink can, I carved my initials next to a Kilroy face someone else had artfully created.

Out of D.C., we headed south on a pinball route in and out of every military city along the interstate. The circuitous route from various points A to unannounced points B allowed time to revise my initial letter for Harold. In light of his death, I arbitrarily amended my writing to insert more emotion into Harold's words, deeper apologies and heartfelt longings to make things right with his daughter. He would have approved.

I arrived in Norfolk on Monday, mid-afternoon. First order of business was to make myself presentable. I probably should have showered, but I didn't want to delay the letter any more than Greyhound already had. I bought a disposable razor at a convenience store, stepped into the restroom and worked on shaving off five days of growth.

Big mistake. I went back out, bought three more cheap razors, and, this time with the aid of some shaving cream, gave it another go. Aside from a few nicks that left me looking like someone had walked across my face in golf shoes, my face was presentable, marginally. Before stepping out, I used a paper towel to wipe off the scum covering my teeth that felt like 150-grit sandpaper.

A while later, after standing around looking at magazines, it appeared nobody needed to use the restroom. I went back in, locked the door, and washed my hair with the remaining shaving cream. It lathered up nicely, a Bichon Frise look, but rinsing under a faucet in a sink was not easy. After I had used the entire dispenser of paper towels to dry my head, a guy slid a note under the door that read: *I know you are getting a blowjob in there. If you don't hurry up, I'm telling the cashier.* Stepping out of the restroom, I strutted past the impatient customer leaning against the wall, legs crossed, clutching his crotch. Outside, in the thick coastal air, my eau de toilette á la Gillette didn't last long.

After I peeled off the wad of gum in the coin slot of the pay phone on the side of the convenience store, I called a cab. The envelope where I had written Harold's daughter's address was all the cab driver needed to get me to Katie Gentry's house.

As luck would have it, the cabby was a chatty, older man from the Philippines who provided a needed distraction. The fourteen-minute ride allowed for a summarized, I assume, version of his life story, which, oddly enough, included details of his vasectomy at age thirty-seven. I caught dribs and drabs of his narration, electing to concentrate on how I would introduce myself to Katie, unsure of how she might receive me or the sad news.

Once the driver pulled off the main boulevard and into the residential neighborhoods, my stomach gurgled. Calming breaths eased my anxiety, as I rubbed my sweaty palms along my pant legs. I stuttered a bit when I reminded the driver the meter was still running; he apologized and cranked the flag to the waiting time position. My fingers fumbled with the Velcro strap on my ankle wallet. I dropped the bills on the floor, twice, before I could count out the fare.

As I reached across the back of the driver's seat to pay him, I hesitated. Unsure how long this visit might take, I pulled back my hand. *Hand her the letter. Explain Harold's death. Hop back in the cab. And on my way.* It seemed too cold. Chances were that she would not even want to talk about her father. I mean, according to Harold, he had never really expressed any interest in his daughter. Regardless, I owed it to Harold to spend some time with her and relay his final hours, so she could learn how he had lived and how he had suffered, and, most importantly, to convey how sorry he was to have failed as a father. I paid the cabby and got out. I moved slowly with my backpack over one shoulder, my legs as weak as loosely wound springs.

The driveway sloped uphill to the front of the colonial-style house. Traditional brick, one of several along the street. A peaked pediment, supported by fluted columns around sidelights—all in white—that was designed to welcome visitors, appeared as a barricade to me. Grasping the handrail, I climbed the three steps to the porch and rang the bell.

The chimes ding-donged inside as I surveyed my body one last time. I dangled my arms to shake out tension, then rubbed my palms on the sleeves of my field jacket. After a short wait, the door appeared to open automatically. There was no one on the inside, or so it seemed, until I looked down and saw a young boy with blond hair wearing a Teenage Mutant Ninja Turtle T-shirt staring up at me. I bent lower to say hi, but before the words came out, he turned away and yelled, "Mommy, there's a man at the door." Then, a little softer as he walked off, I heard him add, "He smells funny."

A woman poked her head around the door. She was blonde and attractive by every measure. With that first glimpse of her, my wobbly legs grew weaker, my eyes opened wider, my tongue thickened. Having met Harold, I would never have guessed this was his daughter. I gulped.

"Hello," she said, clinging to a subtle Southern drawl as she rounded the door and looked at me. Her eyes were the most magnificent blue I'd ever seen. And I had seen them before.

"Katie? Are you ... Katie Gentry?" I said, doubting my own words. I could hear my heart pounding, stuck in my throat.

She nodded her head in agreement, but didn't speak. She hesitated and stared, then cocked her head to one side as her eyes widened to match mine. Her jaw fell slack before she covered her mouth with both hands. We stood there in silence, quizzically staring at each other.

"Fletch?" she said, timidly. "Really? Is that you?"

When she said my name, it sounded stiff, like starch. I nodded and, with a smile, forced the lump down my throat. "Mary Kay. What ... I ..." My brain-to-tongue function was still unable to form words. *"Katie?"*

"Fletch!" She stepped through the door and hugged me. The person I had feared every day while I walked the streets was now holding me tight. Stunned and dazed, too shocked to move my arms to hold her. My knees quivered. My stomach roiled. My trembling hands raised slowly to press ever so lightly against her back.

"Fletch," she sobbed, her head against my chest. "Oh, Fletch." She clung to me, tighter still, and wept. After a time, she looked up at me. "Fletch, oh, Fletch." She placed her head against me and wept more. I continued to hold her gently, still fearful of words and unable to speak. I allowed her to do what she felt she had to do; I knew what I had to do, and I had to do it soon.

With her head still against my chest, I nuzzled into the blonde hair on top of her head and whispered, "Mary Kay, I am sorry." Five words. My entire vocabulary for this tragedy was all of five words, all I could manage. Five words I had wanted to say for three years. A new and bigger lump in my throat choked each syllable, adding, "I'm so sorry." Then, I cried, weak kneed and limp. Tears like I had never allowed before. Cleansing for a sin. I had killed my best friend. I had killed Mary Kay's husband. For years I carried the guilt, not only for his death, but also for the fact that I never had the courage to tell his widow how sorry I was. Finally. Finally, I could share my loss with her. We embraced and cried, one supporting the other.

A male voice from inside called out, "Hon? Katie? Is everything all right?"

She sniffled and pushed back but held my hands in hers. "Yes, dear. Just an old friend." She squeezed hard and looked up. "A dear friend I haven't seen, in years, has surprised me is all."

"Fletch, come in, please. Come in." I wiped the tears with my sleeve as I stepped through the doorway.

The hours of that day were a reunion filled with teary sadness parsed with equally teary laughter. It started with the letter from Harold. I explained its origin and my short-lived introduction to Harold. She read and re-read his letter. There were moments when she stopped reading and glanced at me with flooded eyes, tears streaming down her cheeks. When she finished, she stared at the letter in her hands on her lap, then she looked up, tears still falling. She smiled and said, "Thank you." I flicked the tears from my face, nodded, and returned her smile. She begged to hear what I knew about Harold and wanted to reminisce with stories of Ben.

I'm sure my B.O. was less than inviting, but somehow she managed to overlook that. After Ben's death, Mary Kay returned to using the nickname she grew up with, Katie. She introduced me to her new husband, Kyle. He was a Marine Warrant Officer, a maintenance engineer working at the Naval Air Station in Norfolk. She met him back in Meridian, Mississippi visiting an old friend. She reintroduced me to little Adam, Ben's son, now a five-year-old preschooler. When she told Adam who I was, he made my day when he asked to hear stories about his dad.

Hours later, I asked to use the phone to call for a cab back to the shelter. Mary Kay would hear nothing of it and insisted I spend the night. Having settled my conscience, I accepted her generosity, floating on air. While Mary Kay read stories to Adam and tucked him in bed, Kyle and I swapped tales about the flight line and the F-18, only lightly touching on the crash. Kyle's dream, unattainable due to a vision problem, had always been to become a pilot. He drooled over my stories and appreciated my answers to his questions. When Mary Kay returned, the three of us talked until well past midnight.

As I lay in bed, the seismic impact of the day rolled over me. I tossed and turned, unable to sleep, my energy level on the rise. I sensed what was to follow. Every attempt to sleep brought flashes, back-and-forth images in my head. Thoughts stampeded, ear to ear. Fibers in my leg muscles twitched so much that I had to get out of bed. I paced back and forth in my room. I shook. I pulled at my hair. I did push-ups. I wrote in my notebook. I unpacked and repacked my backpack, over and over, each time folding and unfolding, unwrapping and rewrapping every item. I needed to do something more. I had to build, borrow, or buy something. I had to get out.

I snuck downstairs to the kitchen wearing only my grungy boxers. I pulled out pans from cupboards, then raided the refrigerator for eggs and bacon. I scavenged filters for the coffee maker and cranked that puppy up. I pulled a stack of bread from a bag on the counter and plopped slices in the toaster. In my search for filters I had found a liquor locker, a closet where Kyle stored ample supplies of beer, liquor, and wine. I eyeballed the stash and read through the labels before I decided on a fine Asti Spumante, not chilled but nothing a few cubes of ice couldn't cure. Though I had sworn off drinking after my second night with Trixie, I needed, maybe deserved, to celebrate. I popped the cork and enjoyed a four-finger glass over ice while I fried bacon. I poured a second glass, a taller glass, while I fried a half-dozen eggs. I was in the midst of rummaging through cabinets for hot sauce when Mary Kay appeared in the doorway, wrapped in a terrycloth bathrobe.

"Fletch?"

"Hey there. Thought I would surprise you with breakfast. Great stuff here. Oh, and the champagne ..." I kissed my fingertips. "Magnifique."

"Fletch, its three-thirty in the morning."

"Oh, that's okay." I finished off my tall glass of Spumante. "I don't mind the work. In fact, it feels good. It feels great! You know, up before the sun. Get the ol' day started. They say Marines do more work before sunrise than most people do all day long. It's great."

Her face clouded over.

"I can make more eggs," I said. "How do you like them? Sunny-side up? Over easy? Scrambled? That's my specialty. Omelet, poached? Ha, choices. Or if you prefer, I could whip up a coffee cake instead. Got any Bisquick?"

I opened cabinets, looking first then slamming doors shut while I talked. "Apple strudel? Can do easy. A specialty there, too. No problem. Oh yeah, and I make a mean crêpe, aussi. You should try it." I teased her, grabbing my glass and a wooden spoon. "But," I said, raising a finger, "if you have a waffle iron I could—"

"Fletch ... dear, it's—"

"No, no. No problem. No problem at all, Mary Kay. No problem at all. I'll just do this and ..." I looked toward the porch where I saw a mop. "I can mop the floor while things are baking. Oh, and the pantry? I'll square that away. Make things easier and more accessible."

"Fletch, please. Go back to bed, dear," she said, standing with her arms crossed, her face wearing down into a drowsy, concerned frown.

"Shit no. I'm not going to bed. I said I could cook and damnit, I'm going to cook. I'll show you," I yelled.

Kyle came into the room seconds later.

"What the hell you want, big guy?" I said. "I got this. Just buzz off, I can cook. I'm a damn good cook." I grabbed a saucepan from beneath the counter and slapped it on the burner. The flame went halfway up the side of the empty pan. I took two eggs, cracked them, and dumped them into the saucepan. I took the wooden spoon and stirred furiously, sloshing egg out of the pan. Kyle stepped toward me and I raised the egg-coated spoon above my head. "Don't take another step, Kilroy, or I'll turn this spoon into an Olympic torch."

He stepped back and whispered something into Mary Kay's ear. When she backed out of the room, I grabbed the toast from the toaster and flung it, frisbee-style, at Kyle. By then the eggs in the saucepan had cooked and burned. Smoke started to rise. I used the wooden spoon to scrape them from the bottom of the pan and into the sink. Each time Kyle made a move toward me, I placed the spoon into the flame on the stove.

It could not have been five minutes after she had left the room when two blue-suited Norfolk policemen showed up in the doorway. Mary Kay tucked in behind them as they approached me. I headed for the back door where I ran into the chest of a much bigger man-in-blue. He blocked the door while the other two cops grabbed me. That was the end of my night and the beginning of a new day for me.

Chapter 36

Hospitals are full of germs. Mostly the microscopic kind, but often they are the two-legged type. I spent six months walking among many of that type. They bop around in their white coats and smocks with pocket protectors carrying clipboards and charts. I believe it's never good to be someplace where people in white need to put their name on their pockets. Never could decide if it was because they wanted to broadcast who they were, or if they couldn't remember their names. I made a point of always mispronouncing the names or randomly coming up with completely different names for them. I'm sure that little game contributed to my extended stay, a six-month encampment filled with med cocktails and the very best superfecta therapy regimen with special achievement awards or what they called electroconvulsive treatments. The name speaks for itself.

I quickly became the poster boy for the place, a testament to modern methods. I sat through sessions of behavioral therapy for so long, my butt developed calluses. As I mastered those, I graduated into cognitive therapy mixed with interpersonal therapy. I was the star in our group. Members came and went, but I stood my ground and stayed, week after week. I was a moderating actor for so many people, though the feedback from the staff earmarked me as "failing to conform." Because of that, occasionally I was required to attend social rhythm sessions. What a bore—as if I needed to be more sociable.

Mary Kay visited often at first, but I didn't see much of her after the first two months. One Tuesday I received a note from the staff nurse that said Mary Kay wanted to visit on Thursday. When I read the note, I couldn't help but smile. Finally, someone wearing something other than white and without a name on her shirt. In the beginning we always met in the community social room; that day was no different.

The day of her visit, things didn't start off well. My eggs over-easy were hard, grits were cold, and the coffee was bitter, almost chewable. Looking out the window—my time outside the building was restricted—trees drooped and steam rose from the asphalt lot after a brief morning shower. Dark, dark greens of summer had long since replaced the color of spring.

Mary Kay entered, accompanied by Doctor Emerson, was my primary doctor, one of the cadre of docs I saw weekly, regardless of the therapy. They looked my way, but remained by the door for a brief but serious discussion. Mary Kay did most of the talking. The doctor nodded as if to approve of what she said. He handed her an envelope, then placed his hands on the sides of her shoulders for one last comment. She nodded before the two of them turned and walked toward me. I met them in the middle of the room. Doctor Emerson shook my hand but didn't offer any words, just turned and walked off. I smiled and guided Mary Kay back to my table in the corner near the window.

Though this was a community meeting room, I practically owned that table. I sat there to play chess against invited challengers, but more often, I wrote poetry in my notebooks, then used the pages to make paper airplanes which I'd wing across the room. The other resident guests knew better than to use that table. When they did, I tended to be somewhat possessive and confrontational. Those were my rules.

"Looks like a scorcher out there, like even the trees are melting, Glad they locked me inside for a change," I said with a chuckle.

"Talk about hotter than Hades. If this morning is any indication of what is coming this afternoon, I'm headed for the beach. I can't take much more of this," she said. She draped her purse over the back of the chair and took a seat far from the table. When she looked up, she wore a worried smile, far beyond her weather forecast.

"You should have picked a better day."

"Sometimes you gotta do what you gotta do," she said, trying to brighten her face.

I shrugged my shoulders. "Well, it's not like you had to visit today. I mean—"

"Oh, I could have waited but I just felt the need to see you. It's been a while."

I nodded.

She reached across the table and held my fingers in her cool, sweaty hands. Was she nervous? To see me?

"I spoke to the doctor."

"Yeah, I saw."

"He says you've made big improvements since the last time I saw you. He says you've responded well to most of their work."

"Yeah. I'm the new poster boy for this place." I smirked. "I'm sure you'll see my face everywhere around here. Maybe on TV. Who knows?"

She laughed and held her smile. Her stare never left my eyes. She rubbed my hands, patted them gently. "How do

no SHELTER for GUILT

you feel, Fletch? I mean, how have things been for you here?"

"Other than being sick of this place, I feel fine. Three hots and a cot. Plus, I get individual treatments, group treatments, and—as a bonus—private shock therapy. I mean, what more could a guy ask for? A top-of-the-line spa."

She winced, sighed, and pulled her hands back. I looked away, thinking maybe I had said something wrong. She reached for her purse and pulled out a document-size manila envelope; it looked very similar to the one the doctor had given her when she arrived. She slid it across the table and under my hands. I turned back to face her.

"Open it. Take a look," she said. Her expression was bothersome. I averted my eyes to concentrate on the envelope. It wasn't sealed, merely clipped in back. As I opened it, I snuck another look toward her. Her eyes were on the table, not me.

Inside was a sheet on official hospital letterhead. The text was short. The letter outlined my official release from the hospital, set for the day after next. I took a long breath and closed my eyes.

"Fletch, how do you feel ... now?" she asked again.

"It's ... uh ... hard to say, actually. Stunned, I guess. I wasn't expecting ... I mean ... it's been a while ..." I answered. Few other words came to mind.

Mary Kay sat there, watching. Emotionless. No more smile. No frown. No tears of joy or relief. Motionless. "I'm so happy for you. So very, very happy for you. You've been through a lot and you've handled it so well. I'm so proud, so happy."

Her face belied her comments, though.

"Fletch, there is something I need to tell you, something I need to share."

"Sure."

"I've worked with the doctors throughout your stay here. I'm sorry I never shared that with you, but the doctors and I felt that it was best to allow them to work with you, to walk you through their treatment plan, to condition you, slowly. They wanted to work with you, your grief, your PTSD, your bipolar issues."

I nodded.

"They kept me abreast of your progress during those weeks and months I never visited. In fact, they asked that I not visit, not make contact, to stay away and let their treatments establish themselves in your mind and personality. For you to feel more comfortable with yourself, in your condition, that is. And you did a great job, according to them."

As she talked, her delivery slowed. She rubbed her hands, occasionally touching her forehead. I leaned in, placed my elbows on the table, cradled my chin in my palms, and listened with interest.

"Fletch, I have something to tell you that might hurt." She leaned closer. "The doctors feel you're at a point in your recovery that you should be able to handle what I'm about to tell you."

I couldn't imagine what she was driving at. She had just given me my release papers. Sounded like the doctors were okay with things the way they were. Was she supposed to add some sort of conditional release requirements? You can go "but" or you can go "if" or "when." Her hands were flat on the table, but shaking. I didn't want to upset her any more than she appeared to be, so I leaned back and folded my hands I nodded.

She closed her eyes and inhaled deeply. Her body remained rigid in her seat. She bit her bottom lip, then wetted both lips with her tongue. When she reopened her eyes, I could see the tears. She cringed and shook her head ever so slightly.

"Fletch ..." She paused and tilted her head back. Looking at the ceiling, she sighed, and she looked down again. "Please allow me to finish before you say anything. Please." She sniffled and took a deep breath. "And please don't ask any questions until I'm done."

I felt my eyebrows poking into my skull. My eyes were half closed as I nodded.

"Fletch, you weren't responsible for the crash. You weren't flying the plane. Ben was. My husband Ben." She stared, gripped by a ghost of a haunting memory. "Fletch, dear, you're not a pilot. I know ... you've always wanted to be a pilot, but ..." she broke down, bowed her head, and cleared her throat, then looked up again, the same distraught stare defining her face. "You were in the backseat, Fletch. Your real callsign is Gas Man. Always has been. Chili was Ben's callsign."

Again, she bowed her head. A tear dropped to the table. I remained silent. She cried for a minute or so while I watched.

"You thought so much of Ben. You wanted so much to be a pilot, like Ben. With the crash and all that followed, the anxiety, the guilt, the trauma, you ... you ..." She slowed her delivery and stumbled on, "you thought you were Ben. Well you thought you were the pilot. You thought you were Chili. But you're not. You're Fletch. Fletcher George. Always have been Fletch. Always have been the Gas Man."

"May I—"

"Let me finish, please." She reached across the table to hold my hands. I could feel her nervousness. "I've been afraid to tell you. Ever since the accident, the shock of it all and the mourning ... I had to leave Norfolk. I went back to Mississippi. You were still unconscious. They put you in a coma for the burns to heal. I couldn't say goodbye and a note wasn't enough. I couldn't write my feelings." She stopped, pulled a tissue from her purse, and wiped her nose. "Then ... as time passed, I grew more and more afraid to call you. I was so sorry. Then, I lost you. The Marines lost you. Despite their efforts you would never check in. They knew you were receiving pay but had no idea how to contact you."

"May I say something?"

"In a minute, please ... please let me finish. This has been inside me for a long, long time."

I just stared at her, all my emotions suddenly locked in an emotional deep-freeze.

"When you came to my door, I was stunned. Scared. Scared like the whole event was happening, again. The chaplain coming to my door to tell me about Ben. I didn't know what to say or do. After that night, the night the police took you away, when they placed you in the hospital, I grew more scared. Well, maybe not scared but sorry, scared for you. Over the past months the doctors have explained your journey, your medical and mental issues. I felt terrible. When I told them the truth behind the crash, they realized it would take them time to get you to a point where you could understand, maybe accept the truth.

"I pleaded with them not to tell you. I begged them to let me be the one to say all of this. They agreed. And they agreed that, when you were ready, I could be the one to address the crash. Today was the day. Today is my day to

no SHELTER for GUILT

say I'm sorry. Fletch, I'm so sorry." She squeezed my hands, then wiped her tears.

Finally, she nodded for me, to answer. "I ... I don't ... I can't ... think. I ... I'm confused. I ... I have always wanted to fly. Ben was my best friend. I couldn't bear to see him gone. He ... he meant so much to ..." I stopped. "And I looked for you. I ... I ... I had to say I was sorry that I killed Ben. And ..."

She squeezed my hands tighter. I stopped there to reserve the sincerity in my voice. Words, any words, would have come out wrong. I could say more with my eyes, my face, my hands. She had done most of the talking. I allowed her to break the silence.

"Fletch, grief is the most difficult emotion we all have to overcome. We numb it, then avoid it. We never force or address or fight to end it." She paused. "I'm sorry."

A sliver of sunlight broke the overcast skies. I watched it climb the wall behind her. It cast a halo above her head, a slice of heaven onto her shoulders. I imagined what might have been.

EPILOGUE

It's been years since I sat in the backseat of a two-seater plane. Doubt I'll ever sit there again, given my illness. The episodes are gone but I would never be cleared to rejoin the friendly skies. I religiously take my lithium and a few other assorted remedies to squelch the voices that once vexed me. My life has changed a lot since those days.

Oh, I still mingle with the homeless guys, and now ladies, as well. I've partnered with a few other veterans to open a shelter of our own. It took a while to scrape up the money, to find the building, and sign up volunteers to work it. In the interim, I traveled, not for pleasure so much, but to revisit people.

I kept a log of my letters over the years. Two hundred and seventy-four in all, my opportunity to get beyond their beating hearts and touch their souls. I've been able to reconnect with a good number, using the names and addresses from their letters.

Emmett Pharren, the fella who trashed my letter before mailing it, I never could find. The address, back to the farm his father owned, the one to which he so desperately wanted to return, is no longer in the family. Folks on the farm now told me Emmett's father died, the farm went to auction, and Emmett was not in the bidding war that followed, unfortunately, because it is a beautiful property serving the local community.

no SHELTER for GUILT

Diago Saldana, "Sal", returned home and helped out his parents His family said he licked his habit of betting on the ponies and managed to find a solid job as a mechanic. Soon after he was settled, he was diagnosed with AIDS. Though he was in treatment for the disease, he died of AIDS a little over a year after I saw him. His family misses him dearly.

The General, Lenny Grant, is happily living near his daughters in the Atlanta area. Lenny works part-time for a small rug manufacturer. His hair is shorter, his chin is cleaner, his wrinkles are deeper, and his smile is ever-present. He no longer feels the government is out to lock him up. He still has a box of scrap paper, the ones he showed me in the boiler room that night, the ones with all the hidden messages. He still believes some of it and says he still talks to people in his head about what the codes mean, but he's not afraid of people trying to poison him or get rid of him for what he knows.

Jimmy Pickett, hmm. On a lark I traveled to Turkey Knob to see if he ever made it back. He had. Surprisingly, he married the little girl who had made life so miserable for him. (He told me it was a deal with her old man.) He works in an auto body shop using the skills he learned from his friend down in Alabama. Over a cup of coffee, he broke down and told me how much I meant to him. The fact that someone, a stranger basically, would listen and offer to help set him straight, was a life-changer for him. The hand up was exactly what he needed. Best part of the visit was when he apologized for not sticking around the morning after we talked when he promised we would go back to West Virginia together. I didn't need his apology, but his smile told me it made both of us feel better.

And Debra Trixton is a wonderful mother. Trixie settled in with her little girl and accepted life. She is engaged now, hoping he would soon be a father for little Lila. She is working during the days at a florist while Mimi and Papa, her grandparents, take care of her daughter.

There is comfort in those visits, a certain pleasurable satisfaction that made my days with the Vigilantes almost worth the pain. They're not druggies and drunks or dropouts like many people think. Most are victims of one event or another that left them on the street. Many have serious medical issues, far worse than mine. Beyond their appearance, they seek dignity and self-worth, expressing unexplainable gratitude and humility.

Of course, I talk to Mary Kay a good bit. She has a little girl now in addition to Adam. Regardless of what we discuss—who is venting or who is listening—we always spend time to talk about Ben. And she never fails to boost my spirits with Ben's old line, "It's always sunny above the clouds."

They are my family. We are all homeless. None of them remain invisible.

ACKNOWLEDGMENTS

Despite the explosive growth in automation and the surging development of artificial intelligence, this work partnered with neither technology. A long list of extraordinary, willing people offered their time and talent to help make this story possible. Their efforts came at various stages in the book's birthing.

To my wonderful wife, Penny, who has been by my side and behind me day after day, allowing me the pleasure of time to write, a willing ear to hear me grumble, the energy to prime me through the stagnation of writer's block and a smile to overcome the loneliness of writing alone.

To my trusted friends Phil Bardsley, Alex Dunlap and Barney Forsythe. Their moral support became beacons during the dark days and darker nights when writing slowed in a fog. With unrelenting honesty, they steered me forward, reading draft upon draft, providing comments to keep me on course. To them, I owe a debt I could never repay in a thousand lifetimes.

To others, a special group of early readers, who offered advice and support, par excellence: Cheryl Mansson, TZiPi Radonsky, Greg Saboeiro, Beth Baker and a few who wish to remain anonymous.

For technical assistance, guidance, background and frequent shots of reality I turned to experts. For their time and expertise, I owe many thanks to: Dr. Mary Hill, Rev. Dr. John Dortch, Brad Hipp, Graham Kerr, and "Chester" Waldron. Though, I must admit, at times I may have gone astray, neglecting your counsel. Please accept that my intent was merely an expression of literary license.

Editors often times have the dubious task of telling the writer things we'd rather not hear, like "your baby is ugly" kind of things. To my editors, Ron Seybold and Megan Nicole Swenson I have nothing but praise for their work. Their input made Chili's story better. Where there are faults, I obviously didn't listen nearly enough. I'll do better next time; I promise.

To my many friends who nudged me along in subtle ways, I love and appreciate each and every one of you: Katie and Ken "Oh Captain! My Captain!" Schneider, Jan and Phil Bardsley, Jane and Barney Forsythe, Janelle and Bob Proctor, Wendy Wilson, Mary Mack, and my friends "The P.O.E.T.S."

And, to my family, for their encouragement through critical comments couched in love: Carrie, Ryan, Casey and Jay.

The Author

Carl E. Linke is the author of three previous novels based in the south: *Haint Blue, Flagrant Three* and *The Secret of the Gullah Treasure*. He lives with his wife Penny on Lady's Island in the Lowcountry of South Carolina. They have two grown children.

Made in the USA
Columbia, SC
22 July 2024